PRAISE FOR

SEAL's Honor

"Megan Crane's mix of tortured ex–special ops heroes,
their dangerous missions, and the rugged Alaskan wilder-
ness is a sexy, breathtaking ride!"

—*New York Times* bestselling author Karen Rose

D1115937

SPECIAL OPS
Seduction

AN ALASKA FORCE NOVEL

MEGAN CRANE

JOVE
New York

A JOVE BOOK
Published by Berkley
An imprint of Penguin Random House LLC
penguinrandomhouse.com

Copyright © 2021 by Megan Crane
Excerpt from *Delta Force Defender* copyright © 2021 by Megan Crane
Penguin Random House supports copyright. Copyright fuels creativity, encourages
diverse voices, promotes free speech, and creates a vibrant culture. Thank you for buying
an authorized edition of this book and for complying with copyright laws by not
reproducing, scanning, or distributing any part of it in any form without permission.
You are supporting writers and allowing Penguin Random House to continue to
publish books for every reader.

A JOVE BOOK, BERKLEY, and the BERKLEY & B colophon
are registered trademarks of Penguin Random House LLC.

ISBN: 9781984805546

First Edition: January 2021

Printed in the United States of America
1   3   5   7   9   10   8   6   4   2

Cover image of couple by Claudio Marinesco
Cover design by Sarah Oberrender
Book design by Tiffany Estreicher

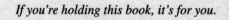

If you're holding this book, it's for you.

One

The sudden explosion wasn't the first clue that all was not as it should be in this supposedly abandoned saltpeter mining town in the Atacama Desert at high elevation west of the Chilean Andes, but it was the most emphatic.

And it almost knocked her over.

Bethan Wilcox—former Army Intelligence, psyops, technically an Army Ranger, and current member of Alaska Force—had already had the sinking feeling this particular op was heading south. That queasy little twist, down in her gut, that she'd learned to trust implicitly in a different desert long ago.

But inklings and gut feelings were one thing. A bone-rattling C-4 blast was another.

"Who knows we're here?" came a pissed-off growl over her comm unit. Even with her ears ringing, Bethan knew the speaker without him having to identify himself. Jonas Crow, who was a great many things—all of them complicated. But most important for her purposes at the moment, he was in charge of this operation. "Report."

"Holding steady," Bethan replied, easing out from the protection of the structure she'd been hunkered down behind. It was dilapidated at best and bore the evidence of misery and regime changes in its bullet holes and vandalization, but it had kept her safe.

She scanned the open, arid square ringed with empty, decrepit buildings, trying to see *who* had found them here so she could work on *how.* But there was nothing to see. Just the same old empty nitrate town that was rumored to have once been a dictator's favorite place to stash dissidents. It had taken them three days to climb the three thousand feet from sea level, moving only under the cover of night in almost complete radio silence as they picked their way through the distant gunfire of drug lord and Mafia-controlled territories to access the town.

Bethan could have sworn they hadn't been seen. Much less followed.

That likely meant the threat had been waiting for them here, not stalking them across the desert.

Bethan turned that over in her head as the rest of the team checked in. Rory Lockwood, former Green Beret. New Alaska Force hire August Vaz, former Army Nightstalker. And Griffin Cisneros, former marine sniper.

"Could be a coincidence," Griffin bit out in that cold voice of his. "There are land mines all over this area."

"Do you still have that line of sight, Bethan?" Jonas asked in that same low growl of his, though, as always, there was the way he said her name.

Bethan was a professional. She had just spent three days creeping through this bright, dry slice of elevated hell, keeping altitude sickness at bay by sheer force of will, always keenly aware that she was the only female member of Alaska Force. Meaning she always, always had more to prove.

But she was used to that. It meant she worked out harder and longer and with more intensity and determination, back in Alaska at headquarters and everywhere else. It meant she always had to be conscious that she couldn't be only herself, she had to represent all the women who fought so hard to win coveted combat assignments, in the military and out. It meant she could never, ever lose her cool, no matter the situation.

It certainly meant that she was not about to admit to herself or anyone else that there was something about Jonas that got to her.

The way it always had.

"I can see just fine," she replied matter-of-factly. "The question is, Was that blast for us personally, or was it a little perimeter gift for anyone dumb enough to come out here? Is it supposed to put us off our game?"

"Do you feel off your game?" Jonas asked.

Because of course he did.

He didn't actively disapprove of her. Not Jonas. The man barely spoke of his own accord off mission, so it wasn't as if he'd made any speeches about how he didn't want her here. Still, he got that across. It was the distance, even when he was standing in front of her. The total silence that greeted any remark of hers that didn't require an operational response.

"Negative," she replied.

Bethan had been highly trained in a variety of scenarios. She'd signed up for the army right out of high school, mostly to appall her high-ranking air force general father. But then, spite enlistment or not, she'd loved basic training. She'd loved it when she got into psyops, too, and for a time, she'd greatly enjoyed her work as an interpreter, translator, and interrogator, connected to highly classified missions all over the world. It was after one of those missions—the one where she'd met Jonas, though neither one of them ever spoke of it—that she'd decided she wanted to be able to do more. To *do something*, on a grand scale.

That had led her to becoming one of the very few women to ever make it through Army Ranger School.

But the army hadn't given her what she wanted, and now she was here. Using all her years of army training to stay calm in the face of provocation. Whether it was a building that shouldn't have blown up or Jonas freaking Crow.

"Proceed," Jonas ordered her.

"I have you covered," Griffin said, cold and precise.

Bethan's gut was working overtime, but courage wasn't the absence of fear. It was using it as fuel. She eased out of her protected position, squinting past the billowing smoke from what they'd had down as a meaningless outbuilding in this creepy, abandoned place. She could feel eyes on her, no doubt friend and foe alike, and wished she were in full combat gear—but that wasn't how they were playing this.

She quickly considered her options. The inhabited ruined building was directly across the square from where she was. The original plan had been for her to take the long way, skulking around the back of what was left of the row of houses where she'd been squatting. Then find a way in through a window that was almost certainly alarmed, if not actively guarded.

Bethan hadn't seen any guards yet. And it was always possible that someone was blowing stuff up on the outskirts of this crumbling ruin of a mining town for reasons that had nothing to do with why she was here. Anything was *possible*.

But the more likely scenario was that there were guards, and those guards knew Alaska Force was here. And that they'd expressed themselves with a little C-4 as a welcoming gift, so there was no point sneaking around anymore.

Bethan stood. Then she sauntered around the corner of the ruined house like she was out for a stroll somewhere civilized. She headed across the arid dirt square, in the kind of broad desert daylight that made her lungs hurt, to go knock on what passed for the front door opposite.

"I like it," Rory said with a quiet laugh from his position

around the far flank of the building she was approaching. "A frontal assault always confuses them."

"Shock and awe, baby," August agreed.

Jonas, naturally, was completely silent.

Bethan knocked. The sound echoed strangely out here, with the Andes towering in the distance and that profound, if deceptive, emptiness all around. She knew how American she was, because she wanted to see a tumbleweed roll by, or a creaking saloon door, or the beginning twangs of a Wild West theme. But there was nothing.

Bethan knocked again. Louder.

She could feel all the targets up and down her back as she stood there. As if the eyes on her were punching into the light everyday tactical gear she wore, and worse, directly into the back of her deliberately uncovered head.

Look how friendly and approachable I am, her clothes were meant to proclaim across the desert, to all the various bad guys lurking around. *No need to shoot.*

Every single alarm inside her body was screaming bloody murder and she wanted nothing more than to duck, cover, and hide. Instead, she stood tall. Because she knew the fact she wasn't visibly cowed was as much of a statement as a blast of C-4. A bigger one, maybe.

"I know you're in there," Bethan said through the makeshift door, leaning against the gutted wall beside it as if she felt nothing but casual, here in the middle of a creepy, abandoned desert village in a place even the few hardy locals avoided. "The trouble is, everyone knows you're in there. And sooner or later, they're going to come. All of them. And they won't knock at the door, as I think you know. They'll come right in—if they haven't already."

Languages had always come easily to her. This one, a specific dialect of a language very few of her own countrymen knew existed, much less could speak, had always been one of her favorites. *Tongue gymnastics*, she'd said, laughing with a friend, way back at Monterey's Defense Language Institute, where she'd first started learning the kinds of languages that made her invaluable in the field.

She waited as the pitiless sun beat down on her. She had that same sort of split focus she often did in situations like this. There was a part of her that was all here, right now. She was aware of everything, from the faint sounds of life from the other falling-down structures around the square, to the wind from the far-off mountains, to that skin-crawling sensation of being in the crosshairs of too many targets. And on the other hand, she found herself thinking of her home of a year and a half now. In faraway Alaska, where a March afternoon like this one would almost certainly be gray. And wet. It might even be snowing.

For a girl who'd spent a significant part of her life in sunny Santa Barbara while her father ordered people around on Vandenberg Air Force Base, the idea that she could long for a place like Alaska should have been funny.

Some days it was.

Today it felt like a much-needed moment of centering. Reminding herself that she had a job to do here and a home to go back to, which let her focus in more sharply.

"All I want to do is ask you a question," she said to the door. Conversationally. "What will the rest of them do, I wonder?"

Another eternity passed while the sun blazed down on her, lighting her up and giving every sniper in the village ample opportunity to take her out.

But no one did.

Far in the distance, she heard what sounded like a foot dragging. Faintly.

"There were three guards around the perimeter," Rory said into the comm unit a few beats later. "Neutralized."

Griffin's voice came like a knife. "Three seems like a low number."

Bethan knew their best sniper was up high on one of the buildings around this square, but she didn't bother looking for him. She knew she wouldn't be able to find him unless he wanted to be found.

"A little house-to-house turned up some more," August said quietly. "Bringing the total to an even eight, which is still low for an asset like this."

"I don't like this," Jonas said in that stern, considering way he had.

Bethan was sure he was about to recall her—order her to fall back and find a defensive position—but that was when the door cracked open.

She waited, aware that she looked relaxed when she was anything but. Her weapons were holstered, so she simply stood there with her arms loosely at her sides, looking as unobtrusive as any of them did in their tactical gear. Her cargo pants and a combat-ready shirt weren't as dramatic as army fatigues, but she doubted very much that the slender woman who stood there in the sliver between the board masquerading as a door and the questionable wall would confuse Bethan for anything but what she was.

For a moment the two women eyed each other. Bethan smiled. The woman did not.

"Hi, Iyara," Bethan said quietly. Warmly, as if she knew the woman personally instead of from photographs. "Do you want to tell me where your brother is?"

"How do you speak the language of my childhood?" Iyara Sowande asked softly in return. "How do you know a single word?"

"I'm only looking for your brother," Bethan repeated in the same steady tone. "I don't mean you any harm."

"What is harm?" Iyara asked bitterly. "You're too late for that."

The door was wrenched open wider then.

And suddenly there were guns in Bethan's face.

"What are you saying? What does she want?" a male voice was yelling in a completely different language from the one Bethan had just been speaking.

Hands grabbed her, roughly. She let them drag her inside, protesting ineffectually. Mostly so they would yell louder as they slammed the door behind her, trapping her in the boarded-up ruin of a row house. Then they shoved her roughly toward the ground.

Bethan went down on her knees and lifted her hands in the air, cowering a little while she did it. Because they expected her to cower. And likely wanted her to so they could feel big and bad. That made it an excellent opportunity for her to take a quick sweep of her surroundings.

"I don't know what you want!" she cried out, making herself sound shrill and scared. "I'm only here to deliver a message. Why does that take three guys? With rifles? What did I do?"

"Received," Jonas clipped out in her ear.

"Shut up," one of the men with a rifle aimed at her face snarled. He shoved the other woman down on the ground next to Bethan, and from the corner of her eye, Bethan could see that Iyara really was cowering. "Tell me what you said to each other or I'll start shooting."

"I have a message for my old friend," Bethan protested. "How could I know she wasn't here alone, the way I expected?"

The man before her bared his teeth at her. "What is this message?"

Bethan glanced at the woman beside her, then grinned widely and incongruously at the man towering over her. "Well. It's our high school reunion. I take my duties as a reunion chair very seriously, and insisted that someone come out this way to see if everybody's favorite prom queen could make the trip."

She heard someone on the comm unit laugh. The man in front of her, however, did not so much as crack a smile.

"Do you think I'm a fool?" he snarled at her. And then, less amusingly, the barrel of his rifle was there against her forehead. But that was a tactical mistake on his part. "You think I don't know exactly why you're here?"

"I already told you why I'm here," Bethan argued, and the barrel of the rifle dug deeper into her forehead. Hard enough she knew it would leave a mark.

"Understand that he will hurt you," Iyara murmured next to her, in the language the man did not understand. "Badly."

"Tell me what she's saying!" the man screamed at Bethan. "Tell me where her brother is!"

Bethan risked another glance at the woman kneeling beside her. Iyara was shrinking there where she knelt, but there was a certain set expression on her face.

Bethan understood in a flash that these men had gotten no information out of Iyara, sister to the scientist they were all after. And that the only reason they hadn't shot Bethan on sight was because she appeared to speak the same language that the woman did and they figured they'd use Bethan to get what they wanted.

Too bad for them that wasn't how this was going to go.

"Why can't you understand her?" she asked the man with the gun at her head, and cowered a little bit more, on the off chance he might think she really was scared. "Out of the three of you, not one of you knows how to communicate with her? Why would you come all this way, then?"

"In position," Jonas said into the comm unit.

"You have ten seconds," the man with the rifle to her head snarled at her. "Then I'll shoot your head off."

"Is that smart?" Bethan asked him. "You don't know what she told me. And it sounds like you can't ask her."

The barrel jammed into her forehead. Harder. "Then you both die, bitch."

Bethan blew out a breath.

"Ten," the man said. "Nine. Eight."

"On his three count," Jonas said.

Bethan had the stray thought that she liked his voice in her ear.

"Seven. Six, *puta*. Five."

Beside her, Iyara began to murmur what sounded like a prayer. Or a very long curse.

Bethan shrank, there on her knees, trying to make herself as small as possible. And in so doing, angled herself even closer to the long muzzle of the gun.

"Four," the man snarled.

"No, no, no," she cried, the way a victim might. "Please don't hurt me—"

"Three," he said.

And then a lot of things happened at once.

Jonas burst in through the front door like a reckoning.

She heard shouts and loud thuds at the same time, which told her that at least two other members of her team had come in through the windows.

But there was still that gun at her head, so she handled it.

Bethan grabbed the muzzle of the rifle and wrenched it to the side Iyara wasn't on, removing them both from the line of fire. He fired in the same instant, a deafening blast that she'd expected, but it still slammed into her like a wall of noise. The barrel was hot in her hand, but that was a lot better than a bullet in the face, so she kept going.

She controlled the weapon, yanking it so hard the man lost his balance and came down to the ground. Then she was rolling with him, over him, battering him in the face with his own weapon until he let go. She surged to her feet in a tidy little flip, taking the rifle with her. Then held it on him.

The way he was moaning and grabbing at one hand, she was pretty sure she'd broken at least one of his fingers.

"Stay down," she told him, calmly, her ears still ringing. "I want you on your belly with your hands laced behind your head and your ankles crossed. Do it now."

She flicked a glance at Iyara and found she'd scrambled back to press herself against the nearest wall. She was panting, her eyes wide, but she looked fine. Bethan kept her weapon trained on the man she'd taken down as she listened to Jonas and the others clear the house.

Had she really been thinking about *his voice in her ear*? *Get a hold of yourself, Wilcox*, she snapped at herself.

There was a brief electric sort of silence. And then outside, the sound of a body hitting the earth. Hard.

"Bomber down," Griffin said without inflection.

Then Jonas was beside her, tall and forbidding, his own weapon aimed at the man on the floor. His dark gaze moved to Bethan, then away. "Get her brother's location. I'm going to see if I can find out why we didn't know there was going to be a welcoming party."

"Yes, sir," Bethan replied.

Then froze, because she hadn't meant to say that. They weren't in the military anymore. And Jonas was in command of this op, but he certainly wasn't her commanding officer. The way he took his time sliding that dark, reproachful gaze of his back her way told her exactly what he thought of it.

She was a soldier. She did not flush. "Force of habit."

"Break that habit," he suggested.

Then without another word—or another searing glare— he headed back out into the blinding light of the desert.

Bethan ruthlessly shoved the entire interaction out of her head, because what was the point of treading that worn ground some more? Jonas was Jonas. Always and ever. She could sit here, seething and fuming over things that would never change, but they were still in the middle of this creepy, dangerous desert town. And just because they'd handled this particular group, it didn't mean there weren't more lurking around or heading for the same quarry.

Besides, she knew from experience that the little cabin she lived in now, stuck in the woods on the rocky, green, fog-shrouded hillside of a remote Alaskan island, was solitary enough that she could spend night and day brooding over the things Jonas did or didn't say to her. And had or hadn't said to her for years.

No need to do it now, when it could get them all killed.

But it was far easier to tell herself that she wouldn't brood about it than it was to stop doing it.

"Are you going to tell me where your brother is?" she asked Iyara, squatting down next to her and digging into the pack she carried so she could start addressing the woman's cuts and bruises.

But Iyara knocked her hand away. "Why should I tell you anything? Because you speak my grandmother's dialect? It's just another trick. At least they"—and she jerked her head at the men lying in various degrees of pain on the floor, moaning—"never disguised their real intentions."

"Here's the difference. I know what kind of scientist your brother is. I know what he's made." Bethan kept her gaze as steady as her voice. "I also know what's likely to happen to the world, and to him, if this invention falls into the wrong hands. I think you do, too, or you wouldn't have tried to hide in a place like this."

Iyara let out a bitter laugh. "You can't possibly think American hands are less dirty?"

"I can't tell you who has clean hands," Bethan said. "I like to think it's a sliding scale, but none of us come out fresh on the other end of it. I will tell you this. Our client is an individual whose concern here is not building himself a weapon but studying the effects of the science involved in controlled, nonmilitary environments."

"Why should I trust anything you say? Because you're a woman?" She shook her head. "I know better than that."

Bethan held her gaze. "I'm not asking you to be my friend, Iyara. I'm asking you to think about what future you want. A brutal death at the hands of men like these? Because you must know that's what's on offer if we leave you here. Or a chance at a real life?"

She saw something like hope move across Iyara's face, quickly blinked away, but Bethan knew she had her.

"How can I trust that?" Iyara asked, but Bethan heard the ache in her voice for the first time.

Bethan handed her the pack she carried, with the medical supplies. This time, Iyara took it.

"The world is a grim place. We both know that," she told her softly. "Don't trust it. Trust me. You can, Iyara. I promise."

Two

Jonas called in the cleanup crew on their way out of the decrepit old mining town, despite his serious doubts that anything would be there when they arrived. Not when this particular sector of the Atacama Desert was home to far too many desperate and dangerous individuals—not to mention whoever was behind the group that had met Alaska Force there with so much unexpected force.

Then it was a long four days to get back out of the high desert, made more precarious this time because they were transporting the scientist's sister. Iyara Sowande might have held her own against the men who'd held her in that run-down building, but that didn't mean a civilian recovering from a traumatic event was prepared to travel at the same pace as the team. But she did her best without complaint, and once they made it to their waiting jet in the port city of Antofagasta on the Chilean coast, it was a comparatively smooth and quick flight to Lisbon.

And once there, Iyara took them directly to a nondescript

flat outside of Lisbon proper, in an unremarkable suburb that wasn't notable in any way.

Jonas called into command back in Alaska. Oz, resident computer genius, listened to the mission rundown in silence, though Jonas could hear Oz tapping away on his keyboard.

"Should I let the client know the package is incoming?" Oz asked when Jonas was done with his report. "Or do you think there will be more roadblocks?"

Jonas took a quick scan of his team, the scientist and his sister, all crowded into the small apartment in a Portuguese city half a world away from the desert where they'd found Iyara. "We'll be wheels up inside an hour and on our way to Montreal. Make sure the client is ready."

"Roger that," Oz replied.

When the line was terminated and his duty done for the moment, Jonas stayed where he was in the farthest corner of the flat, not quite ready to rejoin his team.

Who was he kidding? It wasn't his team that he needed to keep his distance from. It was Bethan. Jonas had been working with Griffin for a while now. He'd always liked Rory. And August, one of the new crop of Alaska Force members, could more than handle himself. Jonas had spent his entire adult life in militaristic scenarios like this one, in and out of the service, and had always been good at teamwork.

Better than good.

He just wished that Bethan Wilcox wasn't quite so good at what she did.

If he'd had his way, she never would have been accepted into Alaska Force in the first place, but no one had asked him. And he hadn't had it in him to veto her selection, which he could have done. Not for her sake, but because he had no intention of telling anyone why it was she got to him.

Not even the only men alive he considered brothers and

friends, Isaac Gentry and Templeton Cross. Together they'd been in and out of too many fires to count. The three of them had started Alaska Force after the last mission they'd all been on had gone so spectacularly wrong.

But Bethan was his very own ghost. She'd been haunting him for years.

Jonas hadn't been prepared for the kind of damage she could do to him by actually being there, in the flesh.

He still wasn't.

As usual, Bethan was aware of it when he stared at her too long. She looked up from her position next to Iyara on the small couch, and he saw that deliberately blank look take over her face.

The same expression she always threw his way, and more power to her.

But he remembered too well. That was the problem.

He remembered her eyes wide and terrified. And worse, determined. He remembered her hands on him, checking him, coaxing him, then somehow, while he flickered in and out of nothingness, physically dragging him across rough ground.

He remembered those long hours of consciousness, too, and that was worse.

He remembered too much.

And he found it all as unforgivable as he always had.

She rose and crossed the room to him, which didn't help.

"Are we good?" she asked.

Not for the first time, Jonas wondered why no one else seemed to hear the challenge in her voice. As if she were forever daring him to say the things he really thought. About her or anything else.

Because she, better than anyone, knew that he wasn't the ghost he liked to pretend he was. She knew he bled. That he was flesh and bone, and both too fragile.

He didn't think that would ever sit well with him.

"Everything's fine," he said shortly.

Griffin stood over by the door, that cold gaze of his out the window beside it, watching. Waiting. Rory was directing Dr. Tayo Sowande, their scientist, to pack his things. August had point at the far end of the apartment, where there was potential access through another window.

Jonas didn't scowl at Bethan, because that was the same as broadcasting an emotion, and he'd stopped making mistakes like that when he was still a kid. But if he expected the blank look he trained on Bethan to get to her, he was disappointed.

He always was.

"Shouldn't you be tending to the sister?" he asked in a low voice.

"She's had enough tending," Bethan replied.

She irritated him by not standing before him, searching his face for answers, as if she wanted something from him. He would have known what to do with that. Instead, she treated him the way she always did now that she was in Alaska Force. Now that she'd distinguished herself by being one of the few women in history who'd made it through Army Ranger School. Now that she was, indisputably, a superhero in her own right. Something he would have celebrated, had it been anyone else.

But it was Bethan. And she stood next to him, shoulder to shoulder, the way she always did. As if their history bothered only him.

Insult to injury, as far as he was concerned.

"I can't help thinking that this was all a little too easy," she said.

That was what he should have been thinking about. The mission. Not a murky, tangled little knot of personal history that he had no intention of discussing, anyway. With anyone.

"I would agree."

One of her eyebrows lifted, but she only replied, in the same even voice she always used when speaking to him,

"The mining town was packed with C-4. They could have taken us at any time. Instead, they let me walk right into that house."

Jonas nodded. "The shed was a diversion."

"Yes, but not necessarily for us."

"None of it felt right," he agreed. And then, accidentally, he glanced over at her. She glanced back.

It was that same somersaulting sensation again. The one that made it hard to remember if it was then or now, when either way it was clear that they could communicate without words.

He didn't want to remember that, either.

That must have shown on his face, because she stiffened. Almost imperceptibly, but he saw it.

"My apologies," she said, with excessive politeness behind that smooth, blank mask. "I know you prefer to discuss your missions with the men you trust."

Emphasis on the word *men*.

Jonas didn't take the bait. There was no point to it. Because the truth was, he would rather she think he was a sexist idiot. He wished he were a garden-variety Neanderthal, because that would be easier. Also, he wouldn't care.

What he would give to not care.

Instead, he held her gaze until she dropped hers. A few moments later, Rory came out of the second room with the scientist and a suitcase, and Jonas happily ordered everyone to get moving.

And then he went out of his way to ignore his Bethan problem all the way back to Alaska.

They landed in Juneau on the same day they'd left Lisbon—give or take half the planet and some nine time zones. The team, in various states of sleep or agitation, depending on how each member handled their adrenaline, shuffled from the jet to the seaplane that would carry them back to Alaska Force headquarters, tucked away on the back of a little island that was hardly notable among the more than a thousand others off the coast of Southeast Alaska.

Jonas took a deep breath of the Alaskan air. Clean, cold. It was the end of March, with a temperature hovering somewhere in the midthirties. The sun was still up, though it was a gray, blustery day, which made a nice change from real winter, when the sun barely made itself known. Given that he'd grown up being dragged through the least hospitable parts of South Dakota, Wyoming, and the Alaskan interior, Jonas felt right at home in the relatively balmy Juneau version of March. And he'd lived through enough to take the feeling of home pretty seriously.

And maybe that was why he resented it so deeply when he looked to his side and there was Bethan.

The proverbial thorn.

She'd showered on the flight from Montreal, after they'd delivered the scientist and his sister to the safe house waiting for him near McGill University. Things Jonas did not need to notice included the fact she'd showered at all, when he had yet to note the freshness of, say, Griffin. The subtle scent of her shampoo, like coconuts. The way the brooding Alaskan light shifted over her face, making it impossible not to notice the faint spray of freckles across her nose and cheekbones that made her something perilously close to cute. A word he'd banished from his vocabulary a long time ago. And worst of all, those hints of red in her hair, which reminded him of things he refused to let himself remember.

Of all the ghosts that haunted him regularly, too many to name, Jonas never would have imagined that a woman he'd first known as an intelligence asset under his protection would be the worst. The most insidious. The one he never seemed to get any peace from, no matter what he did.

The one who'd lived.

"After you," Bethan said, with scrupulous courtesy that wasn't *quite* sarcastic, waving him in front of her to head up the stairs onto the seaplane.

A typical challenge. Jonas could have explained to her that it wasn't that she was a woman that made it hard for him to take the lead the way he would have if she were any other soldier. It was the fact that she was . . . her.

But he would rather she think the worst of him than know anything about that.

He went up the stairs, then suffered the further indignity of having her right next to him for the entire flight back. It was a short enough hop from Juneau to Fool's Cove. He knew that rationally, but it still felt to him like an eternity.

When the seaplane finally landed, skipping a few times across the cove, Jonas thought he might actually come out of his skin.

He knew no one could see it. He was far too well trained.

But he could feel it inside himself, that jumping, skittering feeling that brought him back to the worst time of his life. It was that quick and encompassing.

No way was he going back there.

It was one more reminder, not that he needed it, that there was no satisfactory remedy for the problem that was Bethan. He'd thought about quitting Alaska Force. He'd thought about requesting a deep-cover mission somewhere far, far away. He'd rejected both of those options for a variety of reasons, but right now, he would have taken either one. Anything to get away from this . . . torture.

He'd rather be in the hands of his enemies again than deal with this.

The rest of the team jumped out onto the dock and made their way up the long set of stairs toward the former fishing lodge that had been in Isaac Gentry's family for generations. Isaac, Templeton, and Jonas had transformed it into their main headquarters. It sprawled there, up above the waterline, its wooden boardwalks connecting the main lodge building to a number of freestanding cabins. Behind it, the island was a steep hill toward an almost-always-impassable mountain, with more cabins set down here and there, allowing Alaska Force team members more or less solitude, according to their level of general twitchiness.

Fool's Cove was remote. It had been likened to a fortress, and the description fit. The only way in was by water or air, unless the mountain pass was actually open and non-lethal, for a change. That meant they could always see any intruders coming.

Jonas's idea of paradise.

"Briefing in two hours," he called out, and got a variety of head tilts in reply.

Except for Bethan, of course. She actually stopped a few steps up, turned around, and met his gaze. And then nodded.

Jonas told himself that she was simply overzealously responding, the way she did sometimes, which made sense from a woman who'd had to fight to be more correct and more perfect than any man in the service ever had.

But to him, it always felt like she was throwing down.

Maybe you wish she would, something in him suggested. He ignored it.

"Do you have something you need to talk to me about?" he asked coolly as he came to the bottom of the stairs. He hated that blank look. Those cool, assessing, green psyops eyes of hers that, thanks to her years in Army Intelligence, saw too much.

That always had.

Her chin lifted a fraction. Just a fraction, but he saw it.

"No," she said quietly. "I don't."

And again, there was a moment, just a moment. The same rabbit hole. The same memories.

The same problem he didn't know how to fix, when it was his life's work to get out there and turn problems into solutions.

He hated it.

She did something with her mouth, maybe bit her tongue, and then she turned around again. Then ran up the long staircase a lot quicker than necessary.

Jonas took his time following.

And when he made it to the top, he took another moment to look around. To remind himself that he was not only glad to be alive, he was glad to be here. Right here in Fool's Cove, doing things that mattered. Better still, knowing that on this side of his murky, highly classified years in the service, he was on the right side. Always.

The only quagmires he faced these days were in his own head.

He'd met Isaac when they were both in what was called Delta Force by some. They'd found themselves on a mission together in a city dancing its way toward a crisis. And while they'd waited for the inevitable crisis to happen, they'd had all kinds of discussions. Nothing like a shared foxhole to inspire a lot of gallows humor. But the usual talk about nothing in particular had shifted into more personal territory, which was how they'd found out that they'd both spent time in Alaska. Isaac had grown up here. Not in the family lodge but in Grizzly Harbor, the fishing village on the other side of the island. He even had an uncle here, living off the grid in the woods.

Jonas's family hadn't been quite so settled, to put it mildly. They'd spent a winter in Ketchikan, then a much colder summer out toward Nome. Then a couple of years north of the Arctic Circle in Fort Yukon. All of which paled in comparison to the time he'd spent in the Alaskan interior, after that final, terrible mission. After the Washington, D.C., nonsense was finished and the threat of court-martials had flipped to employment offers and commendations, Jonas had needed to go sit with himself. Alone.

Alone except for his gun, that was.

He hadn't quite gotten there, despite more than a few

nights that skated pretty close to that permanent eject button. But Isaac and Templeton had come and found him, then knocked some sense into him. Or tried. They'd convinced him that Alaska Force wouldn't simply be an opportunity to keep doing the things they were trained to do. It would be more than that, Isaac had said. It would be an opportunity to heal. To be their own masters, for one thing.

And most important to Jonas, to make absolutely sure they never found themselves fighting on the wrong side.

All things considered, this iteration of Alaska was a lot better.

He had his own place in the dark forest on the hill. Unless Jonas was inside the lodge, actively involved in mission prep or monitoring, he could simply melt off into the woods. Sit in his own cabin, where he had a generator and access to electricity, though he rarely used it.

He knew the rest of the Alaska Force team liked to call him hard-core. He wasn't. He'd been in a battle for survival for the whole of his life. Now he was safe, physically. But that only gave the ghosts inside him more opportunity to make their move—and if he yielded to any softness, he knew that was when they'd win.

Jonas couldn't let that happen.

"I thought the mission was a success," came a voice from behind him, but Jonas didn't flinch or jump. He'd heard the exact moment his friend and leader Isaac had come out of the main part of the lodge and headed in his direction.

"Objectives were accomplished."

Isaac came to stand next to him at the rail, looking out over the cove as the blustery March wind slapped at them both. There was a storm coming in, currently hunkered down over the mountain, so it smelled like rain and the deep tang of low tide.

Sometimes, if Jonas stood right here and breathed deep enough, he felt clean.

"How did August do?" Isaac asked.

"Excellent. As expected."

"No concerns about performance? Or team integration?"

"He performed well. I almost forgot he was new." Jonas looked at Isaac. "How are the others doing?"

Things were changing in Alaska Force. Isaac was settling down. He now split his time between Fool's Cove and the house he kept in Grizzly Harbor that was more convenient for his woman, Caradine Scott. She ran the only decent restaurant in town, and therefore on the island: the Water's Edge Café. Templeton was going back and forth between Fool's Cove and Anchorage with the Alaska State Trooper's special attachment to Alaska Force, his woman, Kate Holiday. Even ice-cold Griffin was domesticated these days, over in Grizzly Harbor with his no longer on the run Southern steel magnolia of a woman, Mariah McKenna. Blue Hendricks, former Navy SEAL and all-around badass, had gotten married in September. He and Everly, his wife, lived here in Fool's Cove, but the balance had shifted.

All four of them had more reason to go home than to go out on an op these days. Unlike Jonas, who had spent years on certain missions in his time and sometimes thought that was the only time he was really, truly himself.

When he was playing someone else.

But that was an identity crisis for another day.

Isaac was looking into more permanent outposts in the middle of ongoing operations abroad. And while he never recruited for Alaska Force, because it wasn't a good fit for someone unless they came and found it on their own—and he only took on about one in ten of those who made the trek—he'd found a crop of decent new members over the last six months.

August was one. A few weeks after Isaac had returned from a long few weeks in the Amazon last summer, Benedict Morse had shown up, maybe or maybe not a former member of the highly secret Task Force Black. Two more men had joined that fall: Jack Herriot, former Air Force Weatherman, and Lucas King, former ANGLICO Marine, among other things.

Isaac had a good eye. All the new men were distinguishing themselves on and off the field.

"Everyone is settling in great," Isaac confirmed. "In fact, Jonas, there's only one area of tension in the ranks, as far as I can tell."

He didn't sigh, because that was a tell. "Don't."

But Isaac ignored him. "Are you ever going to sort that out?"

"There's nothing to sort out."

"Because if it's a problem with women in combat, you should know we have an excellent female marine who's been dancing around coming out to see us for a while now. I have a feeling she's going to take the plunge in the next few months, and that will make it two."

"You know I don't have a problem with women," Jonas gritted out.

"What I know and what I've seen right here in Fool's Cove are two different things."

Jonas stared at his friend. "It's been a year and a half. We just completed a perfectly successful mission. What do you care if it's not all pop songs and rainbows?"

"I don't." Isaac's gray gaze was intense. And steady. "We might not have ranks here, but you're a leader. Hard to justify that when you've taken an obvious and undying dislike to one of our people."

"I don't dislike anyone."

Isaac almost smiled. "But you don't like them, either."

"I liked you until roughly five minutes ago."

"Good thing I don't need you to like me." And the way Isaac grinned, it was clear he wasn't particularly worried that he'd lost Jonas's hard-won affection. "You need to figure it out, whatever it is, because the next time someone asks me about it? I'm going to insist on mediation."

Jonas didn't reel around blinking in astonishment, because he had far too much control for that. He reacted only when he wanted to react. But it felt like a close call, when it shouldn't have been.

"Mediation?" Jonas caught himself the second before he actually scowled at Isaac. Another clear sign he needed to get a handle on himself. "There's nothing to mediate."

"Then it shouldn't be hard to fix it," Isaac said calmly. He nodded toward the storm gathering force up above them. "I'll leave you to your brooding."

But it wasn't the brooding that got to Jonas, he thought, when Isaac walked away. It was the ghosts.

And Bethan's ghost was the worst, because he couldn't snap himself out of it by telling himself that she was dead and gone like all the rest.

Because at any moment he might turn around, and there she'd be. Reminding him of when he was helpless. Vulnerable. That was bad enough.

It hadn't been the first or the last night he'd fully expected he might die before morning, but because of her, it had been the only night he'd ever been desperate to stay alive instead.

Desperate.

He thought that haunted him as much as she did.

Three

The next morning, Bethan woke up the way she usually did, without any alarm, a good two hours before dawn.

She stretched as she lay there, tucked in beneath the rafters in her cozy loft bedroom that opened up the downstairs into a comfortable studio. She took her time getting out of bed, because that first shock of her cold floor in the morning always made her gasp and remember the California beaches of her youth, more vividly with every step down the open stairs to the ground floor.

But once she was up, her body kicked in and fired up her brain. She threw more logs into her wood-burning stove, so her cabin would be nice and warm when she finished her morning routine of one hundred burpees as fast as possible right here in the center of her living space, followed by a cold shower.

She felt energized, wide-awake, and gloriously alive when she sat down in her compact kitchen and fixed herself a pot of strong, black coffee and a quick energy-boosting smoothie that was both easy to digest and quickly converted to fuel.

Her cabin was just off the wooden walkways, within walking distance of the lodge, unlike some that were miles into the dense forest. Bethan liked being remote, but not that remote. She preferred easy access to her cabin, because it was her refuge. Inside these walls, she could indulge in all the feminine parts of herself she kept locked up tight when working. Because nobody wanted a cuddly, cute Army Ranger.

Her cabin was soft and cozy, then, because she couldn't be. Everything in it had been chosen either because it was comfortable or because it made her smile. Her oversized armchair was piled high with the softest throws. Her couch was a soft, pastel nest. Her bed was festooned with approximately a thousand pointless throw pillows. There were bright, happy colors everywhere, scented candles, and thick, deep rugs thrown everywhere because she liked to sink her bare feet into them. Outside, on the private deck to the side of her cabin, sat her major indulgence. The wood-fired hot tub she'd built with her own hands, which was her favorite reward for those hard, often grueling days of pushing herself to her limits and beyond.

Bethan let no one inside her cabin. Ever.

When she was finished with her coffee and smoothie, she dressed in layers for the 0700 community workout and then headed outside, into a typically cloudy Alaskan morning. The woods around her were wet, thick with the scent of woodsmoke, damp pine, and the richness of the sea all around. She ran in place for a moment to encourage her body temperature to rise to meet the relatively warm near-forty-degree morning, then started down the steep hillside toward the beach.

She was at the end of her second winter here, and she liked the dark, barren months more than she'd expected she would. She knew that the Southeast Alaskan islands had it easy, comparatively speaking, to the rest of the hardy Last Frontier. *Balmy*, people liked to say when it was even marginally above freezing, because thanks to the sea, the islands never quite got the intense snow and blindingly negative temperatures that occurred farther north. She'd been told it was the relentless gray, clouds and fog and rain, that got to people over time, but that really wasn't a factor for Bethan. She had her bright, happy cabin to keep her spirits high.

And after spending a week in the blinding desert, she found the press of morning fog a relief. She followed the dirt path from her cabin toward the lodge but skirted around it, heading toward the water instead. Because it was down there, set back from the high-tide line, that Isaac had the Alaska Force community gym. They liked to call it their box of pain, and Isaac certainly delivered. He came up with torturous workouts that would make a drill instructor proud.

"Morning," Isaac said cheerfully when everyone who was off mission and in Fool's Cove had assembled inside the sprawling, stark cabin. "I sure hope no one had a big breakfast."

And no one groaned, because that only encouraged him.

Bethan wasn't particularly surprised when the workout consisted of a truly vile amount of cardio and then some heavy sled pushes down the unforgiving rocky beach to really make everyone feel as gross as possible. But that was the thing about gross workouts. Once you survived them, you felt like a god. She'd been chasing that high for years.

Once their solid hour of community hell was done, most people staggered off to deal with themselves before the standard nine o'clock briefing. But that was when Bethan took her extra hour to work on her fitness. Sometimes she pushed her cardio. Sometimes she worked on strength training. She liked to push her boundaries and intensity. Today she picked up a 150-pound sandbag and started walking down the beach with it.

Cursing the weight of it and her matching bad attitude with every step.

But she didn't care what attitude she had as long as she kept going. That was what had gotten her to apply to Ranger School in the first place. And then, far more demanding, to survive it. And graduate.

She was aware almost instantly that someone was behind her as she made her slow way down the stretch of beach with the weight that felt like it was crushing her flat. She assumed it was Isaac. Or Templeton, maybe. Both of whom sometimes stuck around with her after workouts.

When the screaming in her body overwhelmed her, she dropped the sandbag. That was the thing about a sandbag. You always dropped it, eventually. You fought and fought to keep from dropping it, dropped it anyway, and then instantly felt both the delirious relief of not holding it anymore and the kick of panic that you'd have to pick it back up again.

Sandbags were gritty little metaphors, and Bethan loved them in theory. Not so much when she was in the middle of carrying one.

She wheeled around to commiserate and, to her shock, saw that it was Jonas behind her. He did not drop the sandbag he was holding. Bethan forgot to keep her expression appropriately placid, and glared at him. "What are you doing?"

"What does it look like I'm doing? A heavy sandbag carry."

"Since when do you work out with me alone?" She hated that she felt so raw, and blamed him. He'd ambushed her—and given what he was capable of, she had to think it was deliberate. "Since when do you acknowledge I exist?"

A muscle in his jaw worked, and that was a shock. It

suggested this man who was stone straight through had actual human reactions, when Bethan had been reasonably certain he'd left them all behind on that op she knew better than to mention.

"Since today," Jonas said without inflection. "Before our debrief yesterday, Isaac told me that if we didn't start getting along, he was going to suggest mediation."

"Mediation." Suddenly the sandbag was looking good if her only other option was this maddening conversation with the most irritating man alive. "And why would I be involved in any kind of mediation? I'm not the problem."

He only stared back at her, those black eyes of his as forbidding and unreadable as ever.

And the truth was, Bethan did not give herself a whole lot of opportunities to stand around staring at Jonas Crow. Because there was no point, and it always felt too much like a Pyrrhic victory, anyway. She certainly never wanted him to catch her doing it. Besides, he was already etched inside of her, as if he'd laser-cut his own image into her bones. She might not like that, and some years she thought the things she carried might choke her from the inside out, but there it was.

But there was no getting away from the fact that the man was . . . an assault.

Jonas was inarguably beautiful in a particularly male way. Since she'd met him, his hair had sometimes been long and sometimes been cut to short military precision. Currently it was somewhere in between, but the deep, silky blackness of it only made the dark of his eyes seem more intense. Sometimes he sported a bit of a beard. Today it looked as if he'd shaved, which only accentuated the perfect brown line of his jaw. The sharp blade of his nose and his high, knife-edged cheekbones stood as a counterpoint to the impossibly sensual mouth he tried his best to keep forever in its stern, unforgiving line. So no one would notice.

But she already had.

Like everyone in Alaska Force, Jonas was in astonishingly good shape. Rumor was that one part of his deeply classified background was that he'd been a Navy SEAL, which would explain why he was never cold. And worked out on blustery mornings like this in athletic shorts and a T-shirt, seemingly unaffected by the March weather.

Which was unfair, because it was very, very hard for Bethan—who was a woman despite all the many ways she tried to pretend otherwise—to keep from staring at his muscled arms. His impossibly well-defined abs. The whole of him that was a finely tuned, masterfully honed weapon of destruction that was also, regrettably, as beautiful as it had been when she'd met him long ago. When they'd both been different people.

Meanwhile, he looked at her with the same disdain he always did.

Well, a voice in her said. *Not always.*

"I don't have a problem," Jonas said, and he actually sounded . . . stiff. "It's not unreasonable to prefer that the past stay in the past."

Bethan did not gape at him, because she had control of herself. Barely. "Could you refresh my recollection as to when, exactly, I ever so much as breathed a word of the past to anyone?"

That dark gaze almost made her shiver. "I don't like knowing that you could."

Bethan looked past him, back down the beach toward the gym and the lodge beyond, as if the cavalry might ride in to save her from this. But no one else seemed to be around. Because the fact that she'd stayed to work out by herself was completely unremarkable, and it would never occur to her teammates to save her from it.

She jerked her attention back to Jonas because, as usual, she would have to save herself.

"I joined Alaska Force a year and a half ago," she said,

fighting to keep her temper out of her voice, but not entirely sure she'd managed it. *Oh well.*

He looked like a carving of himself. "I know when you joined, Bethan."

She *would not* react to the way he said her name. She pushed on. "Since then, I've watched other people come into Alaska Force. So I can compare and contrast the way that you react to new hires. And I can assure you that if anyone has indicated that you and I have any kind of a past, Jonas, it's you. Because you don't treat me like anybody else, and you never have."

Bethan waited for him to reply. He didn't. Because he might as well have been one of the cold trees, and she knew all too well that he'd convinced everyone around him that how little he chose to speak was some kind of special ops virtue.

When all it really meant, in her view, was that every time he opened his mouth his words were treated like pronouncements from on high.

"Then again, maybe it's not the past that's the issue here," she said after a moment, and for once, did absolutely nothing to curtail the expression on her face. "Maybe you're just one more boring, run-of-the-mill sexist jerk who had no problem with me when I was in a subordinate, noncombat position, but can't cope now that we're on equal footing. You wouldn't be the first."

"This is what I'm talking about," Jonas growled, and he threw his sandbag on the ground, next to hers. It thudded against the rocky beach loudly.

And it took Bethan a moment to realize that the thing buzzing around inside of her was a very particular kind of high-octane anticipation. A hit of pure adrenaline, like when she was on a mission and things were about to go down.

It took her another moment to realize that she was pretty

sure she'd just seen Jonas Crow display his temper. Imagine that.

"I don't like the reference." His voice was that same cold growl, his dark gaze stark. "I don't need anyone on this planet knowing what happened on any of the missions I've been on. I don't talk about them, Bethan. And here you are, referencing one of the worst ones."

"No one is here. No one is listening to what I reference or don't reference."

"I'm here."

"Both Templeton and Isaac have been on missions with you, and I don't see you maintaining boundaries and border walls to keep them at a distance."

"That's different."

She narrowed her eyes. "Why, I wonder? What do both of them have that I don't? Oh, right. Penises."

Something flared in his gaze, and that muscle in his jaw flexed, but he only stared back at her. "If you want to believe that I have an issue with women, go ahead."

One of the most maddening things about Jonas was that Bethan did not, in fact, think he was one of those who couldn't handle female soldiers. She was intimately acquainted with the type. She knew overbearing males inside and out, and no one in Alaska Force had that particular stench around them.

Especially not Jonas Crow. She had no idea why he wanted her to think otherwise.

"Catch me up here," she said after a moment, folding her arms over her chest and resenting him. For . . . everything, including this interruption to her workout, because she could feel the cold again, biting at her in every place she'd sweated. "You're on a voluntary sandbag carry with me because . . . what? You thought you'd throw in a show of friendship to prove we don't need mediation?"

"I don't put on shows."

"Good, because rule number one of a performance is to make sure there's an audience," she shot back at him. "Maybe you can tell me why you sought me out, in private and off mission, for the first time since I came to Alaska, to deliberately be obnoxious. What's your endgame? Do you think that if you freeze me out long enough, or whatever it is you're doing, I'll leave?"

He studied her, and she doubted that she was the only one who felt that kick between them. It had always been there. She suspected it always would. But if he was going to act like he didn't feel it, she was, too.

"The window for peak physical performance at this level is small," Jonas said.

"Thank you for that non-answer," Bethan replied. "You've had over a year to get used to my presence here. You clearly haven't. That sounds like a you problem, not a me problem."

He took an audible breath, which from a man of his talents and skills was akin to watching him crumble. Bethan froze a little.

"I never expected to see you again," he said, clearly surprising them both. "All things considered, I think I'm handling it pretty well."

She couldn't let herself care that this was a huge admission for him. She couldn't let herself *care*. It never led anywhere good. "Do you."

Her sarcasm hung there between them, like more fog.

"Bethan." And the few feet between them seemed charged. Bright, when there was only fog and the crash of waves against the beach. "You know and I know what happened. That's more than enough."

"And here I was, hoping that I could write a book about it. Maybe make it into a Hollywood movie. Definitely do the talk show circuit."

"If that means I have to change my behavior, fine. I'm

happy to do that." He didn't exactly glare. He didn't have to glare to slice a person in half. "That's why I'm out here on the beach, carrying two hundred pounds for no reason."

She opened her mouth to snap at him, but paused. Considered.

Jonas was a master strategist. He could manipulate the sun into thinking it was the moon and then thank him for it.

This did not strike her as an effective strategy, unless . . .

"Is this . . ." She tilted her head a bit to one side. "Is this your form of an apology?"

That muscle in his cheek worked overtime.

"Okay. Wow. I think it is." There was a fizzy thing inside her then. It seemed to dance around, taking up more space than it should. "I don't really know where to put that."

"I'm not apologizing. I have nothing to apologize for."

Jonas eyed her sandbag, then picked his up, letting out a grunt at the effort to haul the thing up off the ground. Bethan made sure to pick up her own bag while making absolutely no sound, because he might or might not have considered this an apology, but there was always a pleasure to be found in petty victories. Another seemingly small truth that had served her well along her chosen path.

But standing around holding a heavy sandbag was even less fun than talking with him, so she turned and kept going toward the far end of the beach. Because she refused to cut her carry short because he was here, apparently dead set on annoying her even more than usual.

The next time she dropped her bag, because she literally couldn't hold on to it another second more, they'd made it down to the end of the long beach and halfway back again. Jonas dropped his, too, and they both stood there, panting.

And Bethan honestly couldn't tell if that racket inside her chest was from exertion or from him.

She definitely wasn't pleased that after a year and a half of hard work to keep herself from noticing that Jonas was a man, she seemed to have backslid. Right back into that traumatic space she didn't like to think about, right after that mission where she'd first met him but before she'd decided on a path of action to *do something* about those memories.

"This is great," she managed to get out, still trying to catch her breath. "Is this what friends do?"

"Pick up your bag," he growled.

And the last, long trudge was the worst yet, but she did it.

Because it was like most things. Or most things in her life, anyway. Sometimes Bethan ended up completing horrendous tasks not because she had such a stellar strength of will, much as she might like to think she did, but because she was entirely too competitive for her own good. And given that the people she was forever competing against were men of Jonas's caliber, that meant that if she wanted to compete at all, she had to force herself into levels of intensity she would obviously prefer to avoid.

But that was also why she was in such excellent shape.

Still, when she got back inside the box of pain, she threw her sandbag back into the pile with far more force than necessary.

"Well," she said, eyeing Jonas the way she might any enemy combatant, "this has been delightful. I feel super close. Let's do it again."

She headed for the door of the gym, ready to go back to her cabin and take a breather between her workout space and the briefing. Just a little moment to recalibrate.

"Bethan."

She remembered, suddenly, how she'd reacted out there in that terrible desert to her name in his mouth. It was worse now. It felt more intimate, here in an empty gym with only the fog outside as a witness.

"I never thanked you," he said, his voice low.

Bethan's hands curled into fists, and maybe it shouldn't

have surprised her that this man, who was the catalyst for so many things in her life—Ranger School, for example, and because of that, Alaska Force—should be the only person who could manage to get to her these days. The only person she saw regularly, that was. She'd been waiting for his hold on her to fade, but it had been years.

Maybe it's not going anywhere, she was forced to acknowledge.

And she didn't try to hide the fact that she was clearly fighting off her temper when she turned around to face him.

"You didn't," she agreed. "Because you're not thankful. You're furious."

"I wouldn't use that word."

"And I really hope you're not about to insult me by thanking me now, as if throwing me some bone you don't even believe in is going to make me feel better about something that *I* don't feel bad about."

Maybe he sighed. Maybe he said her name again. Neither was acceptable, so Bethan kept going.

"I don't have a problem, Jonas. You do. Maybe that's something you should figure out, but leave me out of it while you do, because I'm here to do a job. I don't need to be a part of your therapy sessions."

She expected the usual stonewalling. He was Jonas Crow, who could disappear while you were looking straight at him and make you question whether you'd ever seen him in the first place.

Instead, he nodded. Curtly. "Fair enough."

And she wanted to stand there a moment. Express her extreme surprise that he was suddenly being reasonable about something when that was so unlike him. But if she'd learned anything in the military, it was how to spot a tactical advantage when it presented itself. Not to stand around congratulating herself out of that advantage.

So even though it was the last thing she wanted to do, she turned around again and walked—sauntered, really, because she refused to pick up her pace in case he interpreted that as an emotional reaction on her part—away from him.

And the fake attempt at a long-overdue conversation he didn't want to have and she'd given up expecting to have years ago.

By the time she made it to the briefing, she had all her usual defenses back in place, where they belonged. And she'd made a vow to herself.

She was done with the Jonas thing. She would quit him the way people quit cigarettes—cold turkey, no matter how it hurt. She would treat him like he was a piece of furniture, or a wall. No need to look at him. No need to worry about him. No need for him to claim all this real estate in her head.

This needs to be over, she told herself, again, as she walked into the meeting.

Everyone who wasn't out on an active mission was crowded into the lodge in the big, lobby-like main room where they entertained clients and gathered themselves. The place was all *frontier chic*, as Bethan's friend Everly liked to call it. Comfortable, masculine couches, wood and stone, and Pendleton blankets. Everly was not here today, because while she was married to former SEAL Blue Hendricks, she was not herself a member of Alaska Force.

Besides, Everly had said once, *I work remotely so I don't have to sit in meetings anymore.*

Bethan smiled at Blue as she took her usual place, standing against one wall. She would have preferred to sit closer to the big stone fireplace, but she didn't allow herself unnecessary comforts while she was on the job. Too easy to get soft. To melt into complacence, and the moment she was complacent, she risked becoming average.

And *average* was unacceptable. Excellent was her average. She viewed it as failure.

She was aware of Jonas, drifting into the room like

smoke and standing apart from the rest of them, as suited the Alaska Force ghost. But Bethan didn't allow herself to look in his direction.

Isaac came in from the hall that led to the various offices and command centers, Oz in his wake. Bethan stood straighter, because neither one of them looked happy. Oz sat down in his preferred seat, flipping open his laptop. Isaac frowned at the tablet in his hand.

And suddenly the big flat screen on the wall was filled with the face of the scientist she'd personally helped deliver to his safe house in Montreal yesterday.

"Some of you will recognize Dr. Tayo Sowande," Isaac said.

Bethan caught herself looking at Jonas and pinched herself on the thigh. Viciously.

"Yesterday, after extracting his sister from Chile, we picked him up in Portugal and took him to a safe house in Canada." Isaac looked out around the room, his sober gray gaze making Bethan's stomach drop, because that was bad news. The whole room knew it—she could feel the air go taut. "The extraction team was concerned that the operation was a little too easy. And sure enough, it was. Because he's gone."

Four

"What do you mean, he's gone?" Jonas clipped out from his usual position in these briefings—or anywhere else. Back against a wall, egress points identified and in view, and ready to make his exit at a moment's notice.

Something he'd learned as a kid and that the service had only refined.

"The client called in thirty minutes ago," Isaac said, nodding at the screen. "After hearing nothing from Dr. Sowande or his sister all day, he went over to the safe house to check in on them. His expectation was that following their ordeal, they were both taking some time to recover. But the safe house was empty."

"No sign of forced entry or struggle," Oz said before anyone could ask the question. "It's as if neither one of them was ever there."

Jonas went back over every detail he carried around in his head about this particular operation. "The client is a highly placed academic with ties to the pharmaceutical industry. Could Sowande have decided the safe house wasn't as safe as advertised?"

Though he'd been there when the scientist and his sister had walked through the little house. They hadn't seemed anything but grateful. And deeply exhausted. Their reactions had been in line with what he'd expect to see in individuals who'd been through a traumatic experience and were wrestling with the possibility of hope—not runners.

But people were complicated.

"It's possible something spooked them and they ran," Isaac said. "But I wouldn't expect the safe house to have no trace of them at all if that was the situation."

The screen changed from Sowande's face to their client, an older man who looked like what he was. Rich, white, intellectual, and used to getting his way. That his way in this case involved what was supposedly a safe landing space for a renowned biochemist whose work had entirely too many military applications didn't change the basic facts. By the same token, those facts didn't make their intellectual client a bad guy. Necessarily.

"Do we think this could be another kidnapping scenario?" Templeton asked, tipped back in his chair. He let out one of his booming laughs. "Or do we think the doctor and his sister decided that all things considered, they'd rather set their own ransom?"

It wouldn't be the first time a victim had taken the reins like that, because why not make money on their own trouble if they could? But again, Jonas hadn't gotten that feeling from the Sowandes.

His feelings weren't always correct, of course. He just hadn't been wrong in a long, long time.

"All questions I would like to have answered." Isaac crossed his arms over his chest and frowned at the screen. "Here's what we know. Sowande is a brilliant biochemist. His research involves the behavior of a compound colloquially known as SuperThrax, anthrax's bigger, badder cousin.

He first came to the attention of various branches of the U.S. government and military while he was an undergrad at MIT. They really sat up and took notice when he was doing his doctoral research at Harvard. Throw in a few fellowships and postdocs and what you have in Sowande is the world expert on a new form of chemical warfare."

"So what you're saying," Blue said, sitting back in his chair, "is that our scientist is a popular guy."

"He's not just popular, he's the prom king," Isaac replied. "But he disappeared three days before he was supposed to deliver a paper at an international conference in Osaka, Japan. The buzz was, he was going to rip the field wide open."

"What he was," Jonas interjected, "was scared."

"More than scared," Bethan agreed.

Jonas allowed himself to look in her direction because this was work. This was part of the mission. This had nothing to do with regrets or memories or conversations he should have known better than to try to have on a cold beach. Alone. With no buffer between them.

"I got the distinct impression that while his sister was furious about what was happening, Sowande himself was more . . . beaten down," Jonas said, and told himself the tension in his voice was about their missing scientist, nothing more. "He repeatedly described himself as an academic, not a soldier. Not someone who wanted anything to do with weapons."

"The sister was furious?" Lucas King asked in a considering sort of voice. "Maybe that's what doesn't track? Wasn't the expectation that she would be a wreck?"

"I would say she was both," Bethan replied in that steady, even way of hers that Jonas always admired when it was aimed at someone else. "Those men drugged her and kept her knocked out after they found her in São Paulo, and she doesn't know how long it took for them to transport her to the Atacama. She also has no way to tell what they did to her. And yet throughout her ordeal, she didn't give up her brother. That takes a certain level of fortitude."

"Are we interested in finding out where she came by this fortitude?" Griffin asked from his preferred position, with his back against a different wall.

"We're interested in everything about this case," Isaac replied. "No detail too big or small when there's potential chemical warfare in play. But the client swears that the safe house was clean. No one except him knew the Sowandes were coming, no one knew when they arrived in Canada, and he swears that on top of that, no one even knew that the residence was a safe house in the first place."

"On our end, we swept the house, made sure there were no eyes on it, and triple-checked the access points." Jonas stood still and sure, not putting on a show of fidgeting the way Templeton did. "It would take a pretty high level of tactical ability to enter at all, much less enter and then leave with two potentially unwilling adults."

"Maybe the question to ask is if we trust our client," Bethan said. "Was this a distress call or step one in covering his tracks?"

Isaac shrugged. "Would I trust the guy to have my back? No. Do I trust that he's probably telling the truth as it relates to an asset I'm pretty sure he was going to use to make money on in one way or another? Sure. I'll trust that. To an extent."

Everyone started talking then, debating how much trust they could or should put into a client like this one. Intellectual, sure, but he didn't write poetry. He was deeply involved in an industry that could too easily be used to profit off the terrible wars and less publicized, sometimes more hideous skirmishes that everyone in this room had fought.

Jonas studied the image on the screen, now the biochemical makeup of SuperThrax. It never ceased to amaze him that people started down paths like the one their scientist had only to discover that at the end of it was a weapon that could be used for only one purpose—war. Killing humans on a grand scale. What had Sowande thought studying agents of chemical warfare would lead to?

He'd known people like this all his life. Standing on a path that was clearly signposted, baffled and a little outraged that it led exactly where it said it would. But that felt a little too much like diving into another part of his past he had no intention of revisiting, so Jonas shoved that aside.

"I want to know who hired the individuals we met in the desert," he said when there was a lull in the conversation. "It seems to me that they were working too hard to seem less cohesive than they actually were."

"They didn't make sense," Griffin agreed. "Bethan walked right into that house, but they took the trouble to wire up the whole town? Who were they expecting?"

Bethan nodded. "And if they were expecting us, why did they blow up an outlying shed? It was a diversionary tactic at best, but it didn't divert anything. So why not actually come for us?"

"Here's a question," Templeton said after a moment. "Did you get a sense that the sister was orchestrating the whole thing?"

Jonas had already considered that option. He looked over at Bethan, who was shaking her head. "She's certainly not a helpless bystander or any kind of wilting flower. But I would be very surprised if Iyara made that happen."

Oz was typing, and the big screen changed again, going dark.

"There are a lot of people who would like to get their hands on this guy," he said. "Some of them tried to recruit him, others were less polite with their overtures—and that was when he was still in college."

"Being prom king is never worth the crown," Templeton said. And laughed when everyone looked at him. "But you better believe I looked fantastic in mine."

Blue rolled his eyes. "Like they had prom in jail."

"I didn't go to jail, I joined the army."

"Like that's any better," Blue said with a snort, all navy.

"We can eliminate most of Sowande's suitors," Oz said, though Jonas saw he was fighting back a grin. "They would have to have a particular set of capabilities, like being able to track your extraction from a South American desert to Europe and over to Canada, all without any of you picking up on it. Then they would have to be able to penetrate security measures we had in place in the safe house, secure and abduct two adults and their things, and then disappear, all without leaving a trail."

"We don't know the scientist didn't do it himself," August said. "It might be unlikely, but we don't know he didn't."

"We don't," Oz agreed. "Except that he would have to have that same capability to remove himself and his sister from the safe house and then disappear into the greater Montreal area. Again without tripping over any of the safety measures we put in place, which I have to tell you is even more unlikely."

"And if he could do that, why would he have been hiding out in that flat in Lisbon?" Isaac asked. "You didn't find a single security measure. A toddler could have broken into that apartment."

"Unless he was setting himself up as a decoy," Jonas countered. "As bait for a trap that we walked right into."

Everyone sat with that for a moment.

"Anything is possible at this point," Isaac acknowledged, looking pissed. The way he did when things didn't go according to plan, because that wasn't how he rolled. It wasn't how any of them rolled. They liked successes, not failures. It was why they were all alive.

The screen changed. "If I map out the necessary skill set against all the known entities that sent Sowande into hiding in the first place, I come up with only five realistic possibilities," Oz said.

He flicked through a series of five headshots. Three

high-ranking military officers, all currently serving in the Pentagon, and two Fortune 500 CEOs, one on either side of the very thin line between certain pharmaceutical corporations and the military-industrial complex.

"Interesting," Griffin muttered.

That wasn't the word Jonas would have used.

"Bring it on," Templeton threw out into the room, with a big laugh. "It's going to be fun figuring out how to get a little sit-down chat with security clearances like theirs."

"I personally volunteer to break into the Pentagon," Blue offered. "Because who doesn't want to break into the Pentagon?"

"You need to let that *Mission: Impossible* fantasy go, brother," Templeton said with another laugh. "You can't *swim* into the Pentagon, no matter how impressive you were in the SEALs."

"Does Alaska Force break into places like the Pentagon?" Jack Herriot asked.

"*Can* Alaska Force break into the Pentagon?" Benedict Morse shot back.

"We can argue whether or not we're capable of it another time," Isaac said, but he was grinning. "For the record, of course we *could*. The question is whether or not we want to lower ourselves to such parlor tricks."

That set off several different spirited arguments, and it took a while for the room to settle again.

Jonas didn't engage in any of the arguments. He was too busy going through what they knew. They were all good at reading people, but that didn't mean they couldn't be played. Anyone could be played. And the minute someone had enough ego to think they couldn't be, they might as well sign up to learn that lesson the hard way.

That said, however strange that creepy mining village had been—not to mention the men there—Jonas could have sworn that Iyara Sowande's reactions, and later her brother's, had been genuine.

And the men Oz had presented them with were a very specific type. Three of them were actually in the active military and could send their own commando teams to do their bidding, officially. Two had enough money that they could hire their own. Either way, any one of them could have staged that fight in South America, then turned around and extracted Iyara and her brother from Canada.

When the room quieted, he said as much.

"True story," Blue agreed. "Fun fact, I've actually met General McKee. He didn't think the rules applied to him when he was gunning for his first star. No way that changed since."

"What's the mission here?" Griffin asked coolly. "Are we trying to locate the scientist again? And if we do, where do we take him this time that he can't be reached?"

"It's also possible that the client made a deal with one of these guys," Templeton said. "And we were just a delivery service."

Jonas eyed him. "Then why would the client call us to report them missing?"

Templeton shrugged. "Because people suck?"

Isaac frowned at the screen. "Any of this is possible. That's the problem. The ideal scenario would be if we could round up all five of them, get them in a room together, and ask a few questions."

"Good luck with that," Rory said, laughing.

But Oz and Isaac exchanged a look, and Jonas stood a little straighter.

"About that," Oz said, a strange note in his voice. "As it happens, we're about two weeks out from an event with all five of them on the same guest list."

Isaac nodded, not really looking at anyone, which was weird. "Ordinarily we would figure out the appropriate parameters and send in a team without a second thought. But this is different. It's . . . delicate."

Jonas realized Isaac was looking at Bethan. Both he and

Oz were watching her closely. And the longer they did it, so did the rest of the room.

"I can already tell I'm not going to like this," she said.

"It's your sister's wedding," Isaac said in a gentle sort of way that still felt like a bomb.

Jonas tried to evaluate why that was. Maybe it was the fact that Bethan looked so surprised, as if she'd forgotten she had a sister. Or hadn't planned on attending the wedding either way. Maybe it was that he'd forgotten she had a whole life outside Alaska Force that he'd gone out of his way not to know too much about. Then again, maybe he was the only one reading anything in her, because a quick glance around the room made it clear that everyone else was gazing at her expectantly.

"My sister's wedding," she repeated.

Bethan blinked but didn't otherwise betray any kind of reaction, and still Jonas had the ridiculous urge to dive in front of her as if he were saving her from a bullet. As if she would let him save her from anything.

Isaac's gaze turned considering, which didn't bode well. "Your sister, Ellen, is getting married on your family's estate in the middle of April. You're looking at me like you didn't know that."

"Oh, I know it." Bethan's voice was smooth then. Easy. "You don't know my sister. There has been no topic of conversation other than her wedding since she met the lucky groom six years ago. I've kind of been hoping that I'll be unavailable, on some mission far, far away, tragically unable to attend."

"Alaska Force is always here to stand as a buffer between you and your civilian life," Isaac said with a laugh.

And not for the first time, it hit Jonas that Isaac was . . . different now. Truly a different man now that he and Caradine had stopped sneaking around and could have whatever relationship they wanted to have right out in the open. It had made Isaac more open, too.

Jonas personally couldn't understand that kind of thing. Not the appeal, and certainly not the execution.

"My sister's great, don't get me wrong," Bethan said judiciously. "I'm delighted that she and Matthew found each other. Really. It's just that if you pictured the most over-the-top, fussy, dramatic wedding of all time, you would have to multiply that by approximately twelve million to even approach the level of the monster my sister and mother have planned. And that's not even getting into the fact my father is using the entire enterprise as an opportunity to impress his buddies from work. Who are, as noted, a *Who's Who* of some of the most powerful men in the nation."

She smiled then, a little bit wickedly, in Jonas's estimation, as the roomful of men gazed back at her in varying degrees of horror.

"I had to pretend to be a regular person at my sister's wedding," Griffin offered. "It wasn't the worst thing in the world."

"Not everybody has to pretend to be human," Templeton retorted.

"If you did, you all would have failed at my wedding," Blue shot back.

But Jonas was looking at Bethan. He could see the faint hint of color on her cheeks and remembered, against his will, the few self-deprecating things she'd said about her family over the years. Stitched together, none of them painted the picture of particularly healthy family dynamics.

Then again, who was he to judge such a thing? He'd cut his teeth on dysfunction.

And those were his happy memories.

"This provides us with an opportunity," Isaac said. "We could potentially walk right in the front door for a change."

"And by *we*, you mean me," Bethan said. "The front door in question being my parents' house. The one I've succeeded in not entering since I was eighteen."

"We can always come up with different strategies if this

is a no-go for you," Isaac said, still studying her a little too closely. Looking for weaknesses, as always.

There was no reason Jonas should hate that.

"Not at all." Bethan sounded the way she always did, Jonas thought. Steady, sure of herself, and committed. It had never occurred to him before that it was as much a mask as anything else. "I'm trying to adjust my thinking on this, from it being the one event I most wanted to avoid this year to something that will be significantly more enjoyable if I have a job to do. Other than, you know." She looked around the room and smirked. "My primary job, which is maid of honor."

"You were going to not attend your sister's wedding, where you're the maid of honor?" Templeton asked. "That's cold-blooded."

He sounded impressed.

Beth was gazing back at Isaac. Serenely. "The issues we have to consider are that my parents' house has excellent security that will no doubt be on high alert. My sister's fiancé's family isn't military, but they are wealthy. Between the two of them, there's no way they're not going to have the place locked down. And that's not even getting into which guests will come with Secret Service details."

"We've handled a lot worse," Griffin protested.

"I have no doubt that we can handle it," Bethan agreed. "But if we go ahead and handle it our way, there's no need to go to the front door. If we want to go through the front door, we need to come up with a softer, gentler footprint than usual."

Oz pulled up pictures of the kind of house that as a kid Jonas had assumed was simply a made-up Hollywood thing. A gorgeous, sprawling, gleaming white affair, with a tiled red roof that screamed Southern California. So many graceful arches and different wings that he found it hard to imagine that anyone had been a kid there. It sat at the top of a hill, surrounded on all sides by rolling fields, cypress trees, and vineyards. And in the distance, the Pacific Ocean.

Paradise, in other words. He didn't know why that bothered him. Why it mattered to him one way or the other how Bethan had grown up.

As if it mattered at all what different worlds they came from.

"Home sweet home," Bethan said, irony in her voice. She crossed her arms over her chest and looked like she was perfectly at her ease. But he remembered that raw expression on her face earlier. And he could see the difference. Maybe he'd always seen the difference. Maybe that was the trouble. "There will be too many guests for all of them to stay on the property, but if I had to guess, I would suspect that the highest-profile guests will probably take over that far left wing and the guesthouses. If you're looking for all five to be in the same place while not in the middle of the wedding ceremony, that's probably where they'll be."

"Do you rate a guesthouse?" Jonas heard himself ask.

When she looked at him, there was no trace of the woman he'd seen on the beach. She was pure soldier, completely contained, and it was his problem that he liked both versions of her, whether or not he wanted to admit it.

"I doubt very much that the black sheep of the family is considered high-profile enough to rate the stellar guest accommodations," she said.

"You're the black sheep of your family?" Isaac asked, with a laugh. "How is that possible?"

"My father's an air force man," Bethan said with a grin. "He would forgive me anything . . . except the army."

The briefing quickly devolved into the usual ribbing about which branch of the military was the best—a pointless conversation as far as Jonas was concerned, because it was obviously the navy—and when it died down, Bethan was grinning.

Jonas was not.

"This is the most excited I've been about my sister's wedding since I got the invitation," she said. "Viewing the whole thing as a tactical endeavor can only make it more enjoyable. All I need—"

"Is a date," Jonas said, his voice cutting through the room. And he didn't falter when every eye in the place turned to him. He was looking at Bethan instead. "No problem. I volunteer."

Five

Hours after the briefing had finally ended, Bethan still hadn't managed to get herself back under control.

She was aware that they'd sat around hashing out more things about the scientist, his sister, and the confluence of jackholes that would be at her sister's wedding, but she was unable to remember a single word of it. Much less the other scenarios and missions they'd run through afterward, one after the next, making sure that the plan they had in place—the one where she was going to basically go deep cover as herself in her family's home—was the best.

Bethan was . . .

Well. *Astonished* didn't begin to cover it.

She was perilously close to emotional, a state she avoided as if her life depended on it—because it often did. Men spent a lot of time substituting anger for fear. Bethan had learned a long time ago to do the same, because the alternative was to feel what she actually felt and cry, and she allowed *that* about once a year, and in private.

Though sometimes it happened more than once a year,

like when she'd finally found herself alone in a hospital in Germany after the transport that had lifted her and Jonas out of that terrifying hellscape that should have killed them both. She'd crumpled, right there against the nearest wall, sinking down into a ball of anguish. Her clothes covered in stains she didn't want to identify. Her hands smelling like him.

Sometimes she dreamed about all that and woke up with her eyes wet, but she told herself it was nothing more than a nightmare. Par for the course for anyone who'd spent any real time in the field.

Today she did not think she was at any risk of crying over Jonas Crow.

After the briefing had finally broken up, she'd avoided the subject by spending a couple of hours on the firing range, because she was sure that putting bullet holes through targets would soothe her the way it normally did.

But it didn't.

She wasn't any happier about things when she ran into Jonas in the lodge's mess hall come lunchtime.

"We'll need to sit down and hammer out our backstory," he said after dropping down at the table where she was very clearly sitting by herself. Not that anyone could read that poker face of his, but she could have sworn he looked . . . well, not alarmed and a little shaken, the way she was. "And I'm going to need more personal details about your family that a date of yours would know."

Bethan stabbed a forkful of the vegetables on her plate, and that, too, failed to make her feel any better. It wasn't violent enough. She suspected nothing would be violent enough to make her feel better unless it involved punching Jonas in the face.

But that would be unwise.

Probably.

"Are we in an episode of *The Twilight Zone*?" she asked, quietly enough, which felt like a victory because she wanted to yell. "Am I having a psychotic break? This morning, walking down the beach with me was too much for you to bear. But now you're volunteering to be my *date*?" She didn't like that word. It didn't seem to fit in her mouth, not when he was regarding her with all that implacable coolness, as if none of their history mattered, suddenly. "At my sister's wedding, surrounded by my family?"

"I volunteered for an op," he said mildly. A lot like he was attempting to control a crowd, not have a conversation. Like she was being irrational on the level of a *mob*. She would have snarled at him for that if she didn't think that was what he wanted. "Is that a problem for you?"

He knew that she was going to tell him it was no problem. Bethan was fully aware of that. She was almost convinced she could see a cool little gleam of challenge in his gaze.

"No problems on this side," she replied, trying to hit that same *wow, you should calm down before your craziness infects the world* tone he was using. She smiled when he seemed to stiffen just the littlest bit. "As we've established, I'm pretty much a problem-free zone. I'm a little more concerned about you, your feelings, and what it might do to you to be in such close proximity to me."

He wasn't the only one who could make a patronizing tone into an art form.

Jonas didn't laugh. It wasn't entirely clear if he knew how. But still, Bethan thought she saw a hint of it in that dark gaze of his then, if only for an instant.

"I appreciate your concern."

"Alaska Force is a family," she replied. And smiled. Kindly and with even more condescension.

That gleam in his gaze intensified. "Tomorrow."

And then he'd left her there, fully convinced that he meant that to sound like a threat. That it *was* a threat.

Not that there was anything she could do about it, except fume. There was no complaining to Isaac, as that would be as good as announcing that she and Jonas really did have personal issues requiring *mediation*, of all things. When Bethan had no intention of acknowledging that there was an issue, much less attempting to *mediate* it. The very idea made her shudder.

Jonas had boxed her in pretty well, she had to admit. What she couldn't figure out was *why*.

That evening, she jumped on one of the boats heading into Grizzly Harbor. Blue navigated the skiff around the jutting edge of the rocky coast, nimbly picking his way through the treacherous water like the navy man he was. And when they made their way into the main harbor on the island, Bethan forgot, for a moment, the enduring issue that was Jonas Crow.

She gazed out at the pretty fishing village that waited for her instead. Because she'd seen it almost two years ago and fallen in love at first sight. She'd stood out on the deck of the ferry as a summer day made the whole island sparkle, caught her breath, and that had been that.

Fool's Cove was quiet, tucked away on the other side of the island. Seaplanes came and went in accordance with Alaska Force's mission plans, but that was the only version of traffic they had. Sometimes they used the helicopter for faster response times. And there were a lot of satellite dishes around to keep them linked in despite being in the middle of nowhere.

In comparison, Grizzly Harbor was the height of civilization. There were no real streets, but there were enough people here that there were dirt paths and wooden boardwalks to connect the brightly painted, if often peeling, buildings. There was a general store, a post office, and the Blue Bear Inn. Other little shops that sold curiosities or fishing supplies or both. Tourists came here in the summers, though never in high numbers, as the island was off the Inside Passage cruise, and throughout the year the citizens threw themselves festivals, wallowed in the natural hot springs on the trail out of town, and built as tightly knit a community as was possible when everyone was a rugged individualist who liked their own company and space, or they wouldn't be living on an island off the coast of Alaska in the first place.

Grizzly Harbor boasted a couple of restaurants, assuming a person counted the hearty, down-to-earth food in the Fairweather—the dive bar in town that was also the only bar in town. And the scenic harbor wasn't just for show—it was used by the fishermen who lived there and was a stop along the Alaska Marine Highway, where a person could catch a ferry that could take them all over the state's coastline and down into the Lower 48, too.

Blue moored the boat at the docks and then they made their way up the hill toward the community center, where Blue headed up the weekly self-defense class. Bethan loved that the local women had taken to it. Rumor was, some of them had even used the techniques they'd learned in class when necessary, which just . . . made her happy.

Bethan had taken intensive training in self-defense methods on a much higher level and had a smattering of martial arts in her background, but she loved nothing more than teaching regular women that they weren't helpless. That they could fight back. And more, she loved that civilian women were always filled with what-ifs. That they typically had no trouble whatsoever stopping class to ask about the various scenarios they imagined, so Blue could show them what they could do to fight off their nightmares.

It was fun. And just the kind of fun that Bethan liked most, rough-and-tumble and dangerous besides.

She sometimes wished she could go back in time and tell the little girl she'd been that despite what her mother told her in tones of despair, it was okay to play rough. It was okay to be a girl who wanted to be tough and physical like the boys.

It was okay that she'd always liked playing with guns better than dolls.

"We're all going to the Fairweather," Everly said when

self-defense class was done. She nudged Caradine with her elbow when she said it, and Bethan was surprised that the deeply aloof owner of the Water's Edge Café not only allowed it but didn't actively scowl. Was that what taking her relationship with Isaac public had done for her? Made her more approachable?

But though she didn't scowl, Caradine did step out of range of Everly's elbow, restoring Bethan's faith in her famously bad temper.

"*We're* all," Caradine echoed, her eyes gleaming with what looked a lot like said temper. "We're a big *we* now. A group. What fun."

"She loves it," Everly told Bethan.

"Does she?" Bethan wasn't convinced.

"That's how she shows affection," Everly said with a grin. "The more outraged she pretends she is, the more filled with love she actually is."

"Or dead inside," Caradine countered, though she didn't walk any farther away. "And praying daily for deliverance."

Everly only laughed, her gaze on Bethan. "Come get a beer. Eat a burger. It's Friday night."

And that was how Bethan found herself sitting at a table of civilians, listening to Everly, Mariah, and Caradine laugh about what it was like to be in relationships with Alaska Force men.

"*Baby. Got to go,*" Caradine was saying in a credible impression of Isaac.

"*Wheels up in thirty,*" Everly said gruffly, as Blue.

"*Briefing at oh nine hundred,*" Mariah added, sounding remarkably like Griffin.

And that cracked them all up to such an extent that Everly cradled her face in her hands and Mariah wiped at her eyes. Caradine got so carried away she actually smiled.

"All of those are valid statements," Bethan said into the lull, but that only set them off again.

Bethan was grinning despite herself, but she wished

Kate were here. Kate Holiday was an Alaska State Trooper as well as being in a relationship with Templeton. That wasn't the same as what Bethan did, but it meant she wasn't a civilian, either. And best of all, she had a certain no-nonsense, refreshing matter-of-factness about her that always made Bethan feel comfortable.

Because it was different when you were a woman doing what was historically a man's job. That was just a fact.

"I wish I could relate," she told the group, though she did not, in fact, wish anything of the kind. Sex with a coworker was a risky proposition in any job, but in hers? It had always been catastrophic. Bethan had seen too many good women go down thanks to some guy who never seemed worth the fall, to her mind. She shrugged. "But I only work with them. I don't date them. Seems like a better plan."

"Here's my question," Everly said. She leaned across the table, shoving her beer out of the way. "Do you actually not notice that they're all ridiculously gorgeous? Or do you have to accept on some level that yes, they're remarkable male specimens, but yet somehow remain functional anyway?"

"If it's the first," Mariah drawled, "I salute you. But also have follow-up questions."

"And if it's the second," Caradine said, her gaze considering, "you're even more badass than I thought you were."

"I can't possibly answer that question." Bethan looked around the table. "We have more interesting things to talk about than my job, don't we?"

"Yes, yes," Everly said, and patted her hand. "What a trial it is for you to have a job like that, anyway. Constantly in the company of a legion of gloriously good-looking men who can also perform feats of skill and endurance on command, and you get to do it all with them."

"In fairness," Caradine said after a moment, "that does sound a lot like hell to me."

Bethan sat back in her chair and looked around the Fair-weather, which she'd first seen almost two years ago when she'd come to meet the myth that was Isaac. It looked the same. The rough-looking regulars who were, for the most part, sweethearts beneath all their bluster. The pool table that was always in use. The jukebox that was usually tuned to classic rock or country and was currently blaring out Creedence Clearwater Revival. The neon sign outside that flashed in the window, and the matching ones over the bar.

She'd come here chasing a story people in the service told one another but that she hadn't really believed was real. Oh, she knew Alaska Force was real. And she'd assumed Isaac was—whatever *real* meant for a man of his skill and background. But the idea that this place could actually be a kind of sanctuary for special ops soldiers? Or that it could be a group of the good guys—instead of some of the individuals she knew from all her years in the service, who she was never surprised to hear went into the kind of private security firms that everyone knew made them straight-up mercenaries.

Because Bethan might have been furious at the army. Or brokenhearted, maybe, and ready to leave. But she was no mercenary. She had always wanted to do good in the world. If she dug down beneath the skin of the eighteen-year-old she'd been, so determined to thumb her nose at her father by joining a different branch than his, that had been at the root of it.

That was still what she wanted.

But she was with civilians tonight. She could worry about doing good in the world tomorrow—with or without the looming complication of Jonas Crow.

"My personal hell is different," she said. "It involves big family weddings. Ones I have to be in, I mean, as the maid of honor, when my entire life has proven to me and my entire family that given the opportunity, I will shame them all."

"You're the maid of honor in a wedding?" Everly asked, as if Bethan had announced she was, in fact, Santa Claus.

"Like a real person," Bethan said, biting back her grin. "I know. I'm as thrown by it as you are."

"Have you tried *not* agreeing to appear in people's weddings?" Caradine asked. "That would be my first choice."

"Says the woman who catered mine," Everly retorted.

Caradine shook her head. "Food is not the same thing as all that matching-dresses-and-giving-speeches nonsense, and it's all such a hard pass I can't even think about it."

Mariah sat up straighter in her chair, the light of battle in her eyes. "When is this wedding, and who is getting married?"

"Two weeks," Bethan replied. She took a big gulp of her beer. Then a bigger one. "And it's my sister."

"Is she also in the military?" Everly asked.

Bethan laughed. "God, no. Imagine if a Disney princess became a corporate lawyer and lived in San Francisco. That's Ellen."

"Please tell me the wedding is Disney-themed and princess dresses are required." Caradine's smirk was evil. "And if there's a God, let there also be pictures."

Bethan smirked right back. "I have actually worn dresses before, Caradine."

"But a Cinderella dress?" she asked. Hopefully.

It occurred to Bethan that this was an opportunity. She really had been hoping that she'd be unavoidably called away on a mission. For the entirety of April, if possible. She loved her family, but it was never easy or relaxing to be around them. Or much fun, either. And part of that was because she never knew which version of her they wanted. The daughter they'd imagined she'd be or the daughter she was?

A debutante or an Army Ranger?

That Ellen's wedding was also an Alaska Force mission now made that a lot easier. She could be both.

And for the first time in her life, she actually had civilian female friends.

"The wedding party will be wearing tasteful, elegant gowns that we can use again and again," she said, and pulled out her phone. "Or so my sister assures me. I'm more worried about all the other events I need to attend, apparently *not* dressed in fatigues." She slid her phone onto the table with the picture Ellen had sent her of the dress she'd be wearing. "And yes, that was my mother's fear. That I would show up to a wedding in combat attire."

She laughed when she said that last part, expecting the table to laugh with her, but they didn't. Instead, the three of them gazed back at her with very similar affronted looks on their faces.

"She *said* that to you?" Everly asked.

Mariah was frowning. "And she meant it?"

Caradine got that dangerous look on her face that usually meant she was about to start banning people from her restaurant. "Is your mother aware that you're a grown woman who served your country and, in your spare time, made a little history? And therefore know how to dress for a formal occasion?"

"If you *did* show up in fatigues, it would probably be to save their lives, but whatever," Everly said with a sniff.

And Bethan was taken back, not only by how outraged they all seemed on her behalf but by how her heart seemed to get a little too big and too heavy in her chest. She had the almost overwhelming urge to crack a terrible joke, say something self-deprecating, even get up and leave—anything to stop it. Or make it less emotional, less intense.

She didn't *do* feelings. But tonight she sat there and let it happen.

Like it was a heavy carry she had no intention of dropping.

And when Mariah picked up her phone and studied it, Bethan did not reach over and swipe it out of her hand.

"Oh, sugar," she said, all that Georgia in her voice making her sound a little like she was purring. "We are going to make this *fun*."

Six

Bethan and Jonas made it down to Santa Barbara two weeks later with the rest of an Alaska Force mission team. But when the others headed away from the private airfield in an SUV to set up an on-site mission command in Santa Barbara proper, Bethan and Jonas climbed into the waiting convertible sports car instead.

If the bright and gleaming Aston Martin wasn't enough, the fact they were in civilian clothes certainly helped remind Bethan that they were really going for it—playing the parts they'd decided on in a series of awkward and tense meetings back in Fool's Cove.

Each more awkward and tense than the last.

Bethan could not say that she was having as much fun as her friends had made her believe she might over beers that night in the Fairweather. Then again, the outfit she was wearing—one of a selection handpicked by Mariah and subject to ruthless critiques by the rest until a consensus had been reached—made her feel amazing.

But then, Bethan had never been good at the serious girl

stuff. That had been her sister's place to shine, and Ellen had. Bethan had expected to feel as if she were wearing a Halloween costume, all dressed up in clothes she would never have worn if left to her own devices, but instead it felt like armor. For the first time in as long as she could remember, she felt as if she were actually pulled together in a way her family would understand.

They might even approve, a notion that carried a little more weight than it might have otherwise since she was back in Santa Barbara, where she had always felt that she only ever seemed to expose her belly—no matter how many tactical maneuvers she had under her belt. Here she wasn't a woman who had made history, a woman of integrity and strength. Here, she had only ever been the disappointing Wilcox sister.

Jonas shot her one of his patented brooding looks as he started the engine of the car, but didn't follow it up with one of his dark comments. She resented the fact it felt like a gift. But her resentment wouldn't program her family's address into the navigation system, so she did it with stiff fingers. Then sat back as Jonas drove her straight on into her past.

Downtown Santa Barbara was choked with college students and the usual tourist traffic. And the storefronts might have changed, but the general air was the same. Upscale boutiques on the same street with head shops, the buildings white with red roofs, and the Santa Ynez Mountains in the background. As they started to climb into the hills, Bethan was struck by the graceful dance of the palm trees, the deep blue Pacific forever in the distance. The road narrowed as they climbed, winding around typical Southern California mansions crammed into small hillside lots, with lush vegetation almost hiding the dryness of the land. There was a breeze today, but that didn't take away from how sunbaked these hills were already, on the upward slope toward fire season.

She breathed in deep. The hint of citrus and jasmine, rosemary and dirt, with salt and pine threaded through it all. The bougainvillea climbed here and there in flashes of glorious color, like the memories that teased her as Jonas drove. Road trips with high school friends farther up into the mountains, to Ojai. Excursions down into Los Angeles. The year she'd had a crush on a surfer and so had haunted places like Rincon and El Capitan every spare moment she had.

Bethan couldn't remember the name of that crush, but she could recall with perfect clarity what it felt like to harness the power of the ocean's waves and that sweet rush of riding them, so fast it felt like flying.

By the time Jonas made it to the long drive that led off the main road to her parents' house, Bethan was surprised to find that she was actually filled with nostalgia. Two days ago—even this morning when they'd left Juneau—she would have said she never looked back, because she hadn't. Because what was ahead of her was what mattered.

She took that as a reminder that what was ahead of her wasn't memory lane but a mission.

"We're approaching the house," Jonas said into the phone she'd been too busy excavating high school to see him pick up. "We're going into radio silence. Maintain positions until otherwise indicated."

She didn't have to hear the people on the other end of the line—Rory Lockwood and Jack Herriot, part of their California team—because Jonas wouldn't have ended the call if he wasn't satisfied.

He slid a glance her way as he took one of the curves that wound through the vineyards, getting ever closer to the sprawling white house that waited at the end of the drive. "They're in position and ready to run point and take queries. They'll stay in town until we need them. If we need them."

Bethan held out one hand to catch the warm California

afternoon in her palm, the other in her lap so she could keep enjoying the buttery feel of the dress she wore. "There's a part of me that would actually really enjoy watching an Alaska Force team infiltrate my father's house and possibly ruin my sister's wedding. But that is a mean, jealous, petty part of me that I'm not proud of."

"The world is built on mean, jealous, petty people. That's how it turns."

"You're a ray of sunshine, as always. I put it out there because now it's said, I fully accept that I'm that person, and now we can all move on."

Jonas grunted. "Everybody's petty."

She shot him a look, grateful that it was sunny and they could both hide behind dark glasses. "Yeah? What are you petty about?"

He didn't laugh because he was Jonas Crow, and a stray laugh might turn him to stone.

"Everything," he muttered.

Or maybe she only imagined he said that, because, Lord knew, Jonas was a great many things, but none of them *petty.* He'd reached the final approach and sat back in the driver's seat as the road before them straightened. And she was paying far too much close attention to him if she noticed the faintest twitch of his mouth.

She wrenched her gaze back to the marching column of cypress trees and the house that rose there at the end of it, all that glorious, gleaming white beneath red tiles, as if it were floating up above the vineyards and gardens.

Think about the mission, she ordered herself as her stomach dropped. *This is about the mission, not your memories.*

"Do you need to go over our backstory again?" she asked, shifting her attention back to him. In a tactical, strategic, professional manner, she assured herself.

He was playing a version of himself she'd certainly never met. The same Jonas Crow with the extraordinarily classified background in various levels of special ops, but instead of Alaska Force, Oz had made him a different background. This one far more high-flying. An office in Seattle and the kind of slick, private-security shingle that the men they were here to interrogate would understand. He'd dressed the part. No more regular Jonas, who might or might not disappear into the woods forever at the drop of a hat. This Jonas was downright sleek. He wore what should have been a totally unremarkable outfit. A sport coat over a button-down shirt and jeans over boots. The recognizable uniform of a certain kind of man.

But this was Jonas.

So instead of looking like any old guy, he looked dangerous. *Delicious*, a problematic voice inside her whispered. He'd cut his dark black hair so that it looked more CEO and less Delta Force. He wasn't entirely clean-shaven, though he'd made that look deliberate, which lent him a certain manicured ruggedness, as if he could be anything from a Hollywood actor to an off-duty king.

She had seen this man in a variety of roles. But all of them had been in combat. Bethan was forced to acknowledge that she was woefully underprepared for Jonas . . . undercover.

"I'm good on the backstory." He was driving like a different person now. Kicked back in his seat, one wrist hooked over the wheel. "We met through friends almost a year ago at a charity event. I fly you down to Seattle as often as I can. I'm traditional, though I would argue about it if anyone actually called me that, but privately think that the more serious we get, the less you should be doing the work you do. Anything else you want to add?"

She realized that even his voice was different now that he'd slipped into character. But it took her a moment to understand why it poked at her the way it did, and her stomach fell a bit more once she did. She'd heard this voice before. Filled with warmth. Life. In other words, not ice-cold Jonas.

This was the man she'd met in a far-off desert. Or a version of him, anyway, long ago.

There was absolutely no reason this should feel like a betrayal.

"Great," Bethan made herself say, no matter what it cost to keep her voice even. "Backstory is locked in."

And then Jonas was pulling up in front of the house in the wide, circular drive with a fountain in its center, and there was no putting it off any longer. Bethan needed to treat this the way she would any other op. *And you definitely need to ask yourself why that's a problem*, she snapped at herself.

As soon as Jonas put the gorgeous little car in park, she threw open her door and got out, the dress swaying after her like a new kind of shadow. For a moment, the sense that she was a terrible fraud washed over her like a sudden spate of illness, but she fought it back, forcing her lips into a smile she didn't feel.

Because there were eyes everywhere in her father's house. There always had been.

"Welcome home, Bethan," said a smiling woman Bethan had never laid eyes on before in her life as she bustled down the wide front steps to greet them. "I'm Charlotte, the housekeeper here. If you leave your bags and keys in the car, I'll sort it all out. Let me take you and your guest to your room."

"Your childhood bedroom, I hope," Jonas said, with a low sort of laugh, very male and suggestive and not him.

But Bethan hardly had time to process before he slung an arm over her shoulders, hauling her up against his side as they walked.

"Oh my God," she said, which was her actual reaction to both the display of Fake Jonas, who was some kind of a frat boy, apparently, followed quickly by her body's insane reaction to the *feel* of him.

First of all, he smelled good, which felt a lot like a personal assault. His arm was very heavy, though deceptively lean, and the way he was keeping her against his side meant she could feel entirely too much of that brooding power of his that informed every muscle and sinew, no matter how languid he was pretending to be.

It was like being surrounded by him, *drowned* in him, when she had done her level best to stay as far away from him as possible since she'd moved to Alaska.

But she remembered his scent. It was like getting walloped all over again, with memories she refused to entertain. Not here. Not now. Not ever. Still, the hint of something evergreen and spicy tugged at her, and beyond it, him.

If safety had a scent, it was Jonas.

Damn him.

Her heart was turning somersaults in her chest, and Bethan almost disgraced herself entirely. She almost pushed away from him, jolted as if he were attacking her, or otherwise did something that would indicate they were faking intimacy—but she remembered herself in the nick of time.

Because the housekeeper watched, still smiling so politely. And maybe she really was just a housekeeper. Then again, maybe she was something else.

"I sincerely hope that I no longer have a childhood bedroom here," Bethan managed to say with a light laugh. "How embarrassing."

Jonas laughed again, and Bethan ordered herself to concentrate on her job, not *scents.*

Charlotte beamed. "Your parents have asked me to place you and your guest in one of the suites. It will be so much more comfortable for a party of two. If you'll follow me."

"Where are your parents?" Jonas asked in an undertone he didn't do a whole lot to keep just between the two of them.

"The general will be flying in from Washington tonight," Charlotte said briskly as she led them in through the front doors, then into the foyer. "Mrs. Wilcox will be ready to greet you in the greenhouse once you've settled in."

Bethan was far too busy trying to focus on the job at hand with that arm still slung over her shoulders to do much more than make what she hoped was an assenting sound. Then, as they walked, she tried to imagine what this house looked like to Jonas. Whether in a tactical sense or otherwise.

It had always been fancy, and she didn't try to convince herself otherwise, but it seemed to have grown exponentially more fancy in the time she'd been away. She'd seen her parents and her sister at various holidays over the years, but those gatherings usually took place at the family home in Virginia. This house was the one they liked to call their beach house, when instead, it looked like something that belonged in a coastal magazine. As a hotel.

There was the sound of things happening in different parts of the house, but though Bethan and Jonas exchanged a look, they didn't investigate. They followed Charlotte down one hall, then outside along a porticoed walkway that provided shade but basked in the sea air. This was one of the newer parts of the house, built after she and her sister had graduated high school, but it matched so seamlessly with the rest that Bethan had to keep reminding herself that it hadn't been here when she'd lived here. The Spanish-style architecture flowed inside and out as they walked past a garden here or a gathering space around a fire pit there. And each and every part of the house was specifically designed to take in as much of the sweeping views as possible.

"Here we go," Charlotte said when they were inside again. She stopped at a door and opened it with more brisk economy than flourish. "Everything is ready for you. Please don't hesitate to call if you need anything, from either me or any other member of the staff. Just dial zero." She smiled again and stepped back. "I'll have your bags brought right along."

Once she left, Bethan wandered farther into the suite as if she really were in a hotel. Except the art here was significantly more impressive than anything you might find in a Hilton. There was an expansive sitting room that spilled out onto its own patio, with rolling hills and Santa Barbara below and the Pacific a dark blue presence far in the distance. To one side, through an arch that opened up into a short hall that seemed to exist purely for the purpose of letting in the sun through a skylight, was the bedroom. It contained a California king, a grand fireplace—as if it ever really got cold here—and two separate potential seating areas. The attached bathroom was suitably grand, including both a freestanding tub inside and a private hot tub outside. On the other side of the living area was a cozy little den, outfitted with all the entertainment devices a person could require and a small kitchenette besides.

When she turned back to the living room, Jonas was watching her. "You didn't tell me you were raised in a resort."

"That might just be the whole wedding thing." He only stared back at her. "Okay, I think the intensity of the hotel experience today is thanks to the wedding, but yes, Jonas. If you're asking, my father always had staff."

"Maybe someday you and I can visit one of the places I lived as a kid," Jonas said, and he was smiling, but she knew it was a fake smile. A fake smile he'd still made sure was edgy. "One time, when there was no money for food because they drank it away, my parents made us sleep in the car until payday. It was winter in Wyoming. Good times. Just like this."

She wanted to jump all over that, but she didn't. Because it was the first time he'd given her even a sliver of personal information since their doomed mission. And she saw the exact moment he was aware of it. His eyes got darker, which shouldn't have been possible. He stopped pretending to smile.

Bethan didn't pretend she knew how to process any of that.

"This is the general's world, Jonas," she said softly. "We just live in it."

There was a rap on the door to announce their bags, and she was happier than she should have been for the interruption. Happy to put a little space between her reactions to him, her extremely visceral memory of that arm over her shoulders, and how vulnerable it made her feel that he was here. Jonas. Here. In this world she could barely tolerate herself, no matter how much her parents had changed the house.

"Well," she said when they were alone in the room again, with bags, and her heart was still thudding. "I guess we should go find my mother."

"In the greenhouse," Jonas said, as if he'd previously thought greenhouses were myths.

"Birdie Gaines Wilcox is an avid gardener," Bethan told him as if she didn't hear his tone. "She's won awards for her roses all up and down the Central Coast, and she takes them as seriously as my father takes his military career. Mock her at your peril."

Jonas looked offended. "I would never mock your mother."

"She's mostly oblivious," Bethan warned him. "Until she's not."

She led him back into the main part of the house, past the lovely reception rooms that had all been designed to pour one into the next. She took him out into the back, where a green lawn eventually gave way to the slope of the hill. Below lay the pool and its guesthouses, then farther on, the vineyards. But she took him in the other direction, down a path lined with a trellis bursting with bougainvillea, to the greenhouse at its end.

Inside the glass building, it was as humid as she remembered, especially compared to the dry air outside. And her mother was there, right where Bethan had left her, repotting something with those elegant hands of hers that had always seemed too aristocratic for the dirt.

Birdie Gaines Wilcox had never been called her legal name of Elizabeth a day in her life. She had been raised in Marin and gone to school in Claremont, as befit the daughter of a sixth-generation Californian. Bethan looked at her mother and saw all the usual things. The serene fall of her mother's silvery hair that never took away from her elegant carriage, much less the steel beneath. She wore a pair of gold bracelets on one arm, and the sound of them gently clanking together was woven through every memory Bethan had of childhood. Bethan knew that when she moved closer there would be the faintest suggestion of Chanel No. 5, but only if she breathed in deep. Birdie's idea of gardening clothes was the same as it had ever been—the crisp white pants and pretty blouse she had probably been wearing all day, with a heavy sort of apron over the front, where her gardening tools peeked out.

Bethan felt all the usual things, too. A rush of complicated affection. Shock that this woman who she always imagined as larger than life and not to be trifled with by man or time was . . . older. More frail, though she knew her mother would object strenuously to the use of that word. And on the heels of all that, the usual jumble of the things she felt because she was Birdie's daughter and doomed to never match her in style or elegance. Bethan was the brutish, boyish one. The disappointing one.

"Darling," Birdie said, looking up. "There you are. And looking so lovely."

That was a dig, but Birdie pulled off her gardening gloves and held out her hands, so Bethan moved forward to take them. She leaned in to kiss her mother's cheek, and sure enough, when she breathed deep, she could smell the Chanel. She wouldn't be Birdie without it.

Part of her felt settled and soothed, while another part tensed.

That was also typical Birdie.

"Mom," Bethan said. "I'd like to introduce you to Jonas Crow, my . . ."

To her surprise, she faltered. Because she'd pretended to be a number of things at different points in her military career and had been given the opportunity to do some character work in Alaska Force from time to time, but this was her *mother*. And this was Jonas.

And none of the words that she should throw in there to describe him suited him at all.

"Boyfriend," Jonas supplied easily. In a friendly, engaging, *lively* manner that about floored her.

He made it worse by moving forward with a huge smile plastered across his face, his hand outstretched.

"Such a pleasure to meet you," Birdie murmured, taking his hand. And though Bethan was still thrown, she didn't miss the steel-eyed gaze her mother raked over Jonas. Her *boyfriend*. "I know the general is looking forward to meeting you, too."

"You have a housekeeper who led us through the house as if we were checking into a hotel," Bethan said, incapable of keeping herself from sounding like a glum millennial. She cleared her throat. "She said Dad would be home for dinner."

"Charlotte is a marvel," Birdie said, which Bethan took to be a faint reproof for mentioning her. Or that the "beach house" was like a hotel these days, which her mother would surely find vulgar. "Have you seen your sister yet? She and her bridesmaids are staying down in the vineyard house. You should go say hello before drinks." She smiled in her gracious, dismissive way. "At six. On the west patio."

Bethan didn't need another clue that her mother wanted her to leave, but when Birdie began to tug her gloves back on, she knew that was one. Jonas was still standing there as if he expected something else, like maybe freshly baked cookies or an inquiry into her well-being. So she did what any girlfriend would do and took his hand.

God, his *hand*—

But this was a moment to act, not *feel*. She tugged him after her, out of the greenhouse. Where she instantly dropped his hand as if she were scalded. But her fingers retained the heat of him. The strength. The fact he'd chosen to allow her to drag him anywhere.

"Does your mother always talk to you like you're a stranger?" Jonas asked.

Mildly enough.

The breeze was rustling through the palm trees. She could smell fire somewhere in the distance, but it was hard to tell if it was the charred remains of chaparral on far-off hillsides or a threat. It smelled precarious, just like home.

"She would never comment on a stranger's appearance." Bethan smiled at him because that was what she would do, probably, if he were her boyfriend. "Maybe you missed that she said I looked lovely."

"What? You do."

She couldn't let what sounded a lot like a compliment land. "Yes, but that was family code for *Thank you for not forcing me to remember that you're a soldier*."

"I thought this was a military family."

"Silly summer child." Bethan found herself grinning at him without having to force it. "This is General Wilcox's family. We exist to cast glory upon his name. Or not."

Jonas muttered something beneath his breath that sounded like the filthy, fluent sort of cursing that was some-times his only form of communication in the field. Oddly, it made her feel more at ease.

Bethan could see her own reflection in the greenhouse windows. The long black dress was tied at the back of her neck and came down in front, but showed nothing her mother might consider inappropriate. Meaning only her neck. The back was open and the dress even had deep pock-ets. Her hair was down around her shoulders, which she knew her mother also approved of, because it wasn't one of her on-duty slicked-back ponytails that caused Birdie despair.

"Today I look like the daughter my parents wish I was," she said, and for some reason it was a battle to adopt the wry tone she preferred when Jonas's too-dark gaze was on her. "That's a huge win."

Jonas shook his head. "I don't understand white people."

Bethan shrugged. "My mother and I are strangers. Sometimes more polite strangers, like today. Letting Mariah and the rest of them dress me for this mission was a good idea."

"She's your mother, not the mission."

"Are we really going to talk about our personal family dynamics?"

Jonas didn't answer that. But the deep flex of the muscle in his cheek did.

"We can't stop here," Bethan continued, trying to refocus. She started walking, heading down the path that led away from the main house. "You might as well get the full familial picture before you commit to a level of outrage about it. I wouldn't want you to feel you were misled."

She didn't have to turn around to know that he was following her. Bethan always knew exactly where Jonas was. She could feel him like he was a part of her—a notion she knew better than to share with anyone, or even indulge too much herself. The rest of Alaska Force liked to go on about what a ghost Jonas was—but not for her.

Unless it was just that he haunted her, specifically.

At the end of the path she led him down the stone steps to the little guesthouse—meaning it slept only six—set there above the vineyards.

She glanced over her shoulder at Jonas and smiled, though she couldn't have said if she was apologizing or enjoying herself. Both, maybe.

"Remember," she told him. "You did volunteer for this."

She knocked, braced herself, and moments later the door was swung wide open.

And there was Ellen, looking very much the way she always did, if ever more like a whippet with every passing year. Her strawberry blond hair was longer than the last time Bethan had seen her, but otherwise, she looked like what she was. Very well maintained, ruthlessly thin, and desperately in need of stress management.

A thought Bethan decided was uncharitable when her sister smiled hugely and enveloped her in a hug, even if she could feel every single frail bone in Ellen's tiny body. As ever, it made her feel hulking and thick.

"I really didn't think you were going to make it," Ellen was saying. "There were too many references to potential missions. But here you are."

"Here I am," Bethan agreed.

"And you must be Jonas," Ellen said, and she didn't actually push Bethan out of the way to get a closer look at Jonas, but she didn't . . . not do that, either. And her tone shifted straight into prosecutorial mode. "As far as I know, you're Bethan's one and only boyfriend ever. She's told me absolutely nothing about you. Care to fill in the blanks?"

Seven

The Jonas that Bethan knew would have frozen solid in dark, brooding disapproval, then disappeared. If not in a puff of smoke, by simply turning and walking away. But this was slick Fake Jonas. He burst out with a big smile and an even bigger laugh.

Then pulled Ellen into a friendly handshake.

"Not much to tell," he said in the sort of voice the man he was pretending to be would have. Confident and confiding at once. Everybody's best friend. Potentially also evil. "Was in the navy once upon a time, now in Seattle. Don't see enough of your sister, excited to meet her folks, and looking forward to celebrating your happiness this week."

He was doing his job beautifully. He was *smooth*. Ellen actually simpered a little as he grinned down at her.

There was no reason Bethan should want to punch him in the face.

"We just wanted to say hi," Bethan said, horrified that her voice was rising up a few octaves, the way it always did around her family. Because they were the only combat arena on earth where she felt uncertain. Consistently. "It was a long flight, and we want to pull ourselves together a little bit before Dad gets here."

Ellen sighed. "Good luck with that. He's been on a roll. You would think it was his wedding, not mine."

They talked for a few moments more. Then, finally, Ellen was pulled back inside by one of her friends. Family obligations attended to as much as possible so far, Bethan and Jonas could take their own little walk around the property, looking at the layout of the house and grounds from a far more tactical standpoint.

And the moment they did, Bethan felt better. Or more herself, maybe. Even if she was wearing a dress that swished when she walked.

"Some of the guests are here, and the rest will be coming in the next few days," Bethan said when they'd done a full loop at a leisurely pace and were standing in the lush grass out back, far enough away from everything that no one could overhear them.

And she almost jumped out of her skin—again—when Jonas reached over and ran his hands up and down her bare shoulders above her crossed arms. Over and over.

Her heart stuttered, then stopped. Bethan thought maybe she'd died. It was on the tip of her tongue to say something undoubtably embarrassing—

But, of course, he wouldn't touch her for the hell of it.

He wouldn't touch you at all if he could avoid it, she reminded herself tartly.

"We wouldn't want people to think that we were standing out here discussing strategy and tactics," he said, his voice mild and amused and without the faintest trace of ice.

Bethan knew that her feet were planted on the ground, because she could feel them. The tickle of the grass above the straps of her sandals. The evenly distributed weight of her body. Still, she felt as if she were tumbling, end over end, deep into those bottomless dark eyes of his.

And the abrasion, however faint, of his impossibly capable hands over her bare skin taught her all kinds of things about herself that she'd managed to lock away all this time.

Things she'd known before everything had blown up—literally—on that mission long ago. Things she'd long since decided she must have been imagining, all these years later, when there'd been not the faintest trace of them.

There were so many *things* that she didn't dare name, and it was as if he were rubbing them all back into existence. Or out of a deep sleep. One by one, right here on the vibrant green lawn that existed despite California's pervasive water issues, possibly in full sight of at least two of her family members.

It was the grass that got to her, tickling her ankles. Because she knew that if she reached down and tugged on it, there would be no roots to hold it in place. It was sitting in the topsoil, something that had disconcerted her when they'd moved here from Virginia.

All grass in California was more or less fake in the same way, because it shouldn't be here in the first place. It was fake, and Jonas was fake, and while the sensations that stormed around inside of her felt far too real for her liking, it didn't matter. They weren't a couple. Jonas had a head full of strategy, and she could be sure that if he was touching her, it had to do with that. Not sensation. And never *him*.

"Explain to me how you grew up here but ended up in a cabin in the middle of nowhere in Alaska," Jonas said, more command than conversation.

"That would be courtesy of the United States Army, of course. There wasn't a lot of staff in the barracks."

"You're supposed to be a debutante. Like your sister."

"You can only be a debutante before college, according

to my mother. After that, a certain number of accomplishments are expected. Pedigrees are great, but it's much better if they come with degrees from institutions with recognizable names."

"Most people consider the army an institution."

"Ranger School isn't the same as Yale," she replied. "It doesn't have quite the same cachet at the country club."

"Only one is useful."

"Not in this world, Jonas." His hands were still skimming over her upper arms, stirring her up . . . and she couldn't have that. Not here. She stepped back, trying to look as if she were filled with delight, and then started for the house. "But if you don't believe me, by all means. Bring up my accomplishments tonight. See what happens."

She thought it was a measure of her personal growth that she didn't even sound bitter when she said that. Because what was there to be bitter about? It was reality and this was a mission and it didn't matter in the slightest that she couldn't stop shivering deep inside.

Back in their suite, they took a few moments to sweep for listening devices. Then, when Jonas picked up his tablet and started sorting through all the pictures he'd taken of the house and grounds—all with Bethan smiling easily into the camera, as if he'd been taking pictures of her—she sat down, stared out at the sea, and asked herself why sweeping her parents' house for listening devices hadn't tripped a single wire in her. Was it because she wanted to believe that her family was capable of anything? Or was it that she knew they already were?

Not her entire family. That wasn't fair. Birdie was a whole thing, and Ellen was a little like looking at the road not taken, but neither one of them was actively malicious. They were who they were, and they had relationships with her that were complicated because relationships were often complicated and because fundamentally, they didn't understand her or her choices.

It was her father she wouldn't turn her back on in a darkened room. Even if she'd had nothing but warm and tender thoughts about him, Henry Colin Wilcox was a four-star general of the air force. Of course he was capable of anything. That was his job.

Her job was to act like she was the highly trained individual she was. Not her father's confronting elder daughter who had defied him at every turn.

"You seem tense," Jonas said when they headed toward the patio right on time, because punctuality was considered a virtue in this house, and woe betide the fool who kept the general waiting.

"That's because I *am* tense."

"I've seen you throw yourself into situations that would drop most people flat. You never flinch. But you're afraid of the man who raised you?"

Bethan felt her lips twist. "I wouldn't say I'm afraid of him. But ask yourself how many generals you've enjoyed spending time with." When Jonas grunted, she nodded. "Exactly. Now imagine that's your run-of-the-mill family dinner every night when Dad's home."

"Point taken."

"Do you enjoy spending time with your father?" she asked before she thought better of it.

And the Jonas she knew best slanted a look her way, his dark gaze a condemnation and a curse, and iced over besides. "We both know you already know the answer to that, Bethan. Is this really the night you want to start playing games?"

Bethan caught herself before she stumbled, a humiliation she wasn't sure she would have survived. "Was that an acknowledgment that we have a history *and* have had personal conversations? Impossible."

"I haven't seen my father in over a decade," Jonas said flatly. "Last I heard he was homeless in Vegas, but I can't confirm that."

She felt horrible for bringing it up, but she suspected that was what he wanted, so she kept her expression neutral. "Do you—"

"When the mission involves my family, I'll be happy to discuss them in detail," Jonas growled at her. "Until then it not only isn't relevant, it risks blowing our cover. Is that what you want?"

"We walked around the outside of the house to make sure no one could be lurking around, listening to us talk," Bethan said mildly. "I've been scanning the area as we go and have seen no sign that anyone is positioned to overhear a word. But I take your point. Feel free to stop glowering at me at any time."

And she took a little more satisfaction in that than she should have. But then, she'd warned him that she was petty.

They rounded the corner of the house and she knew, instantly, that her father had arrived. There was that hushed anticipation in the air. Staff hurrying this way and that.

Jonas reached over and linked their fingers together as they walked toward the small crowd on the west patio. And she obviously couldn't think too closely about *that*, so instead, Bethan tried to remember the last time she'd seen her father in person. Not for some time, she thought. Not since before she'd gone to Alaska. She'd worked through last Christmas, and though she'd seen her mother and sister in Washington, D.C., in the spring, her father had been unavailable.

The way he always had been.

When she and Jonas stepped onto the patio, Bethan felt a little charge that she was pretty sure was sheer relief that there were more people there, not just her immediate family. Ellen's bridesmaids and friends were there with their dates, all of them looking like the Ivy League hedge fund managers, bankers, and lawyers they were. A collection of people she instantly categorized as Santa Barbara residents—her parents' West Coast friends—because they looked the part, with their carefully curated effortlessness. Her mother and the women she'd gone to Scripps with, all dressed in different versions of the same outfit as they laughed and clinked their glasses together.

But Bethan's gaze zeroed in on her father, standing apart from the crowd as he usually did, because he liked to give the impression that the Pentagon might call him at any moment. In fairness, it might.

Jonas got instantly more intense as he walked beside her—something she likely would have sensed regardless but *felt* in her own hand because he was still holding it.

Do not think about the hand-holding, she ordered herself.

Instead, she focused on the scene before her. Because her father had two other men with him, and both of them were on their list.

"I guess it's go time after all," Jonas muttered around a smile.

"Rangers lead the way," Bethan replied automatically, because that was the Rangers' Creed.

"All the way," Jonas replied, giving the standard answer.

And then, suddenly, it was easier to pretend. Maybe because there were people here, some of them several drinks toward merry already, and they were a kind of buffer. Maybe because she had always pretended where her father was concerned.

Maybe because Jonas's hand tightened around hers before he released it, and she tucked that away somewhere inside her where she kept each and every one of his very rare real smiles.

But it was go time, so she jumped into her character. The version of Bethan Wilcox who would date a man who was not only a mercenary but ran a firm filled with them, who wore flowy dresses that proclaimed her femininity instead of her lethal capacity, and who was simply here at a cocktail party with her date.

She and Jonas wore matching smiles. He laughed and shook hands and was generally impressive. And when Bethan pretended this was just an op, not her family, she found it was a whole lot easier to sparkle along with him.

By the time they got around to her father's little power cluster, she had almost forgotten to be apprehensive.

"Hi, Dad," she said, shrinking a little and hunching her shoulders, making herself smaller as she smiled at him.

And it occurred to her, unpleasantly, that making herself smaller and looking ineffectual was something she did when someone had a gun on her. When they didn't expect her to fight back or mount a counterassault.

But this was not the time for unpleasant familial realizations.

"Bethan," General Henry Colin Wilcox said warmly. The warmth would have been surprising, but she knew he was always extra chummy when friends of his were around to witness it. "Gentlemen, this is my oldest daughter. Bethan, this is General Ambrose and General Darlington. Old friends of mine. Old friends."

"And this is Jonas Crow," Bethan replied after greeting the generals, and made herself smile in what she hoped was a suitably giddy manner.

She watched her father and his general buddies size Jonas up, then square their shoulders, indicating they were fully aware of at least some of his capabilities.

Meanwhile, Jonas slipped into character. There were various gradations of his characters, including Bethan's favorite: a drunken sports fan he could pull out in bars, complete with uproarious singing. The character he was playing tonight was the one he'd been leading up to since they'd arrived with his arm slung over her shoulders, that huge grin, and the careless confidence he wore like a suit tailored specifically to his body.

It was all part and parcel of Fake Jonas Crow, security expert, who maybe skated *just this side* of the kind of soulless mercenaries the Alaska Force team had determined were more than likely responsible for whatever had happened to the Sowandes.

Bethan knew that. She'd had her friends in Alaska outfit her with a suitable wardrobe for not only the daughter her parents wanted but the kind of woman that Fake Jonas would likely have on his arm. But that didn't mean she was prepared for the full-force version of it.

Because Jonas was so good at playing the *maybe not a good guy* that it almost hurt.

She accepted a glass of wine from a passing waiter and practiced her happy smile, as if she'd never been more delighted in her life than to stand around with a bunch of military men who were ignoring her service while falling all over one another to bro it up.

As usual, she found herself questioning whether or not she wanted to be mad about it. Because that was what it came down to, wasn't it? There were always slings and arrows. The only thing that changed was her reaction.

Earlier versions of herself would not have stood for this. She would have busted into the conversation to remind everyone standing there of her accomplishments, all of which she felt certain they knew.

But happy-go-lucky Fake Jonas pivoted from the conversation he was having about impenetrable male things, with a lot of supposedly salty male humor Bethan assumed was mostly funny when the men could patronizingly apologize for it. His hand found the small of her back, and she deeply regretted the backless gown the moment his palm slid into place.

She was dressed like a woman, not a soldier.

And his hand was on the small of her back, which wasn't the same thing as holding her hand for show, no matter what she tried to tell herself.

Her body couldn't seem to get the message that this was a mission, too. That his touch meant nothing. There was absolutely no reason for that fire to swell in her, to dance and flicker like an open flame, making her feel molten hot and heavy in places she normally preferred to pretend didn't exist on the job.

It wasn't like she didn't know that fire was there. She just never fueled it. Because there was no point.

He had always made his feelings about her perfectly clear.

Except tonight, standing in a loose collection of generals—one of them her father—Jonas slid her a dark look, and her stomach seemed to topple out of the bottom of her body. It was a sudden, shocking, hollow sort of feeling, because he clearly felt it, too.

She could *see* that he did.

And that only made everything . . . sizzle.

Bethan had to take another, longer pull from her wineglass to get a grip.

"We're ignoring the superstar in our midst," Jonas said. And there were so many layers to the tone he used. A hint of pride, but laced through it, that patronizing note that she knew the men who were all suddenly gazing at her would pick up on. "Not many who can say they made it through Ranger School. And what? A handful of women so far?"

Bethan watched her father. The other generals made appropriate noises, but her father did not. She found herself standing straighter, as if prepared for combat. On some level, it shamed her that Jonas, standing there beside her with his hand literally on her back, couldn't help but be fully aware of how conflicted she felt in her father's presence.

Because the general was not making suitable noises. He was looking the way he always did. As if Bethan's entire career were nothing but a bid for attention.

"Birdie and I are very proud," he said at last. He rattled the ice cubes in his drink. "Tell us more about this Alaska outfit you're involved with now, Bethan. Keeping you busy?"

Next to her, Jonas did nothing. He didn't shift. He didn't make a noise, or glare, or stiffen in any perceptible way. Yet she still knew that he was furious. She told herself it was Alaska Force's honor he was concerned with, not hers. Because he certainly couldn't have failed to hear that same patronizing note in her father's voice, as if he were asking after some childish hobby of Bethan's. Possibly finger painting.

It was her turn to flash a winning smile. "I keep my hand in," she said, with a self-deprecating little laugh.

Because the sad truth was that the army had taught her how to handle her father. Left to her own devices, they would likely still be fighting—even here. Still, it wasn't until she and Jonas made their excuses and left the little knot of high-ranking, practically interchangeable men that she felt that she could breathe again.

Especially since she seemed to be the only person at the party who could see the simmering fury written all over Jonas.

"Maybe your father is our guy," he said in an undertone as they stood together at the edge of the party where the patio gave way to the rolling fields, as if they were lovers taking in the view.

"He wasn't on Oz's list." Bethan smiled, not entirely for show. "That doesn't mean he couldn't know about it, of course."

Jonas's easy smile was in place, but his eyes were dark. "I like all of them for it. Pompous, smug, insufferable—"

"High brass comes with a high opinion of itself. You know that."

"What I know is that you're a remarkable individual."

Bethan could still feel the place where his hand had been on the slope of her back. Like a tattoo, she thought, except now it felt *alive*. Throbbing like a pulse. And some-thing chaotic was taking over her body, charging through her, that she knew she couldn't allow to take root.

She'd spent years telling herself that it couldn't. Ever.

But that was hard to remember with him looking at her like that. As if he were outraged on her behalf. And more, actually complimenting her.

She tried to find some kind of witty response, but she couldn't seem to find any words.

"You were already significantly accomplished in Army Intelligence," Jonas continued, a little too hot for the smile he was wearing. "But to take that and decide that you wanted to translate your experience into combat? And then do it?"

"They know all of that," Bethan said lightly. "You know they must."

"Not one of them has a special ops background. Or as much field experience as you do."

"Rangers lead the way," she said again, more softly this time.

Jonas didn't give the usual answer. "I guess I'm not sur-prised that a woman like your mother wanted a daughter in a certain mold. But your father should know better."

"You're making me blush," Bethan said, keeping her smile on her face. She was in no danger whatsoever of blushing, though that hollow thing inside her wasn't exactly comfortable. But she was terribly afraid that this conversa-tion might be the thing that would made her cry after all. And then she would never forgive him. "I had no idea you thought so highly of me. When you go to such epic lengths to make sure I think the opposite."

"I do nothing of the kind."

"Sure. Except that you do. Daily."

He wasn't smiling any longer. He was the Jonas she knew best, grim-faced and dark. "I'm perfectly aware of your accomplishments, Bethan. You're a valued member of the Alaska Force team, and I take a dim view of individuals who can't see that. It's not personal."

"Oh, certainly not *personal*," she said in mock horror. "Never that."

She would have sworn it was a flash of temper she saw in his gaze then, but it was gone in an instant. And then everything was cool and unreadable, as usual.

"I'm going to want serious intel on each and every one of those men," Jonas said, and smiled, in case anyone was watching them. "Now."

"Go call it in," Bethan said coolly. She held her wineglass like it was a weapon, because she couldn't handle any more of the pretend touching. "I've got this."

And she took it as a personal victory that she didn't watch him as he walked away.

Eight

"How's life up there in the hills?" Lucas King drawled when Jonas's call was connected, with his usual edgy ease. "Down here in the cheap seats, in Goleta, if you're interested—"

Jonas didn't quite sigh. "I'm not."

"—which is Santa Barbara's sad neighbor, we're living it up on weak motel coffee and a deep sense of our own martyrdom."

In the background, Jonas could hear the rest of the team—Rory Lockwood and Jack Herriot—issuing not-entirely-serious accusations about who was the biggest martyr, but he was never one to laugh it up. He scanned the area where he stood, far enough away from the house that no one could sneak up on him. Not unless he wanted them to.

"Martyrdom sounds uncomfortable," he said flatly when the noise died down on Lucas's side. "I want Generals Ambrose and Darlington examined on a forensic level. And General Wilcox, while you're at it." There was a slight pause at that, but he refused to explain himself or why he wanted Bethan's father looked at more closely. Mostly because he wasn't sure he could explain it rationally, and that only made his temper kick at him harder. "I don't like any of them."

"Are you supposed to?" Lucas asked, more edge than ease this time. "As far as I know, the entire purpose of a general is to be hated and loathed by the rank and file."

No one in Alaska Force had been considered true rank and file for some time, even before they'd left the service. But Jonas was already provoked. He didn't need to let it get the better of him.

"As far as I can tell, they all came in on the same transport at about sixteen hundred hours," he said evenly, instead of debating rank-and-file status with a bullheaded marine. "I want to know where they've been for the past two weeks. Any questionable meetings, any suspicious moves by staffers, any tense phone calls. Anything and everything. Got that?"

"Loud and clear," replied Lucas, with a chorus of assent in the background.

Jonas ended the call, but not before he heard more laughter, because everyone was always having a lot more fun than he ever did.

Unclench, he advised himself.

Which would have been excellent advice if he could see his way clear to taking it.

Because he was out of control. He knew it.

And it was all her fault.

Bethan Wilcox, the only woman who had gotten to him since his mother had relinquished that position by default. Because Jonas had disappeared into the navy and never returned, putting himself beyond her reach at last.

But even as he thought that, shoving his phone into his pocket and looking at that monstrosity of a house, he knew it wasn't fair. In his more charitable moments, he liked to think that Sabra Day Crow had done her best. It was just that her best sucked.

Hard.

Bethan's best, on the other hand, had never been anything but impressive.

It wasn't her fault that despite all the years he'd spent disappearing into various roles in support of whatever mission parameters he was following at the time, this one was messing with him. That was all on him.

Because the last thing he needed was the tactile, physical memory of the soft bare skin of her lower back imprinted on his freaking hand. Like he'd slapped it down on a stove, then held it there, like an idiot.

Jonas stared down at the hand in question as if it were on fire, flexing it and then straightening it again.

He had absolutely no desire to head back into that party. But since when did he pay any attention to his desires? Desires were for regular men. Jonas was about duty. And he was the one who'd volunteered for this mission.

It was on him if he was finding it a little more sacrificial than he'd imagined.

What did you imagine? he asked himself harshly then, as the plush laughter of rich men floated toward him and the last of the light flirted with the sea in the distance. *Familiarity hasn't bred contempt yet when it comes to her. It isn't going to start now.*

But that, too, wasn't particularly helpful.

The simple, indisputable facts were these: Bethan had been attached to the same unit he was. Jonas himself had been a plant, maneuvered into place because there were concerns that that particular unit, in that particular horror of a desert, was involved in shady situations. Or situations more shady than necessary, out there where *shady* was just a regular Tuesday.

He had been getting to the truth of what was happening when their convoy had been attacked. Everyone had died. Except Jonas and Bethan, and that was because Bethan had bodily dragged him from the burning vehicle, pausing only to take out the circling enemy with a few well-placed shots.

Then she'd held their position throughout a long, lonely night in a dangerously exposed area while they waited for help to come in the form of an air extraction.

It had taken Jonas a solid six months to recover from what had happened to him there. That night, he'd been certain that his number was up at last. That he'd beaten the odds too many times and fate had stepped in at last.

He'd been ready for that night since he was a kid.

And now he had to live with the fact that all this time, he'd thought that he'd face death like a warrior. Silent. Stoic.

When instead, he'd treated it like an opportunity for a deathbed confessional.

And Bethan Wilcox had heard every single word.

More than that, she'd soothed him. He had a perfect, viciously clear recollection of his head in her lap, her fingers in his hair, while his voice rang out as if it would never stop telling her his secrets.

Though he didn't know if he actually remembered that or if that was what they'd told him in the hospital. The story of how they found him. The story of Bethan with her weapon in her hand, keeping watch over him.

All those things he'd locked away inside seemed to shift then. Alarmingly.

Jonas made himself breathe, because history couldn't help them here. And she should know better, anyway.

He'd chosen a job—a life, a calling—where it never mattered what he felt, only what he did.

God willing, it never would.

Jonas sacked up, shoved his unpleasant memories aside, and walked back in to carry out his mission.

The way he always did.

The next morning, he wasn't at all surprised when Bethan came out of the bedroom in their suite on the dot of 0500 hours.

"Was the couch comfortable?" she asked in that even, impenetrable way of hers. Was she being sardonic? Was it a real question? It was impossible to tell.

"I slept on the floor," Jonas told her, because if it was a competition about who was more unreadable, he knew he would win. "Like a baby."

Her lips twitched, and he shouldn't have liked that. But there were so many things he shouldn't like. Including his own attempts to be entertaining when that was definitely not in his wheelhouse.

But then he stopped thinking about anything else because he finally noticed what she was wearing.

In some distant, rational part of his brain, he recognized that there was nothing particularly noteworthy about a pair of spandex running shorts and a tank top. *This is unremarkable running gear*, that distant, rational voice inside him informed him.

But this was Bethan. Whom he had never, ever seen out of uniform or tactical gear when she was engaging in physical activity.

And whom he had certainly never seen in *formfitting spandex*, God help him.

Jonas had prided himself for years on his ability to turn off all remnants of the kinds of things that made most people falter. But here, now, he was forced to acknowledge that despite all the work he'd put into locking himself down and turning into ice, he was only a man, after all.

Just a man looking at a woman.

That simple. That prosaic.

That much of a freaking problem.

Bethan didn't quite smirk at him. Not quite.

"I'm going to get some miles in," she told him as if she didn't notice the way he was looking at her, when the gleam in her cool green eyes told him she most certainly did. "Are you interested? *Boyfriend?*"

And that was how Jonas found himself wrestling physical reactions he hadn't allowed himself to have in a very long time, out on a run with Bethan Wilcox dressed in almost nothing, as the California dawn began to break.

They spent the first ten miles running at an easy pace. Then pushing each other to increase their speed, which forced Jonas to admit, once again, that Bethan was ridiculously fast.

She pulled ahead of him at one point, and he told himself he was admiring her form in a purely academic sense.

Though every part of his body protested that.

She was a pageant of lean, honed muscle. That she not only trained but took excellent care of herself was obvious in every single movement she made. She was fast. She was sleek and capable. She was a deadly weapon in clingy—

He ordered himself to settle down.

The final part of their run was a big loop around her parents' property, allowing them to truly case the place. Without discussing it, they maintained the same steady, leisurely sort of pace, running side by side around the edge of the vineyards and then looping back around so they could see the property spread out before them from above.

It was turning into a pretty morning—which he supposed was the entire point of California—when they saw another couple out running.

"My sister and her fiancé at three o'clock," Bethan said.

"I see them."

But Jonas saw more than that. His own body was a highly trained weapon, and the kind of training he'd had made him an expert on movement. Sometimes he wondered if civilians had any idea there were people on this earth who could simply look at them and see their choices, their hopes, and their fears, stamped all over them as if they were walking billboards. Because they were.

He knew that Ellen Wilcox was riddled with anxiety. That she starved herself and that she took pride in that, too. Just like he knew her bridegroom wasn't half the athlete he thought he was, which made Jonas wonder what other things he was overconfident about.

And Jonas wasn't exactly the reigning expert on the human heart. By choice, he liked to tell himself. But whether he liked it or not, he was surrounded by people in actual, objectively good relationships these days. Alaska Force was cursed with happy couples, and there was a certain body language to intimacy. To happiness.

Ellen and her man had none of it.

"Why is your sister marrying this guy?" he asked.

Next to him, Bethan shot him a look. She'd put her hair in a ponytail, but not the kind she wore when they were working. This one was high and bouncy and somehow lodged itself inside him like a fist. Like the California sunshine.

Like need, something in him retorted. Darkly.

"Ellen and Matthew have a great number of similar interests," Bethan said evenly. "She's very ambitious. He's very wealthy."

"Sounds great."

"The reality is that we moved around a lot when we were kids," Bethan said after a moment. "I think both Ellen and I made ourselves safe as best we could."

Jonas thought that was pretty charitable. He smiled brightly as the other couple waved to them but didn't stop.

"I thought we were going to have a family moment," Jonas said after they'd passed. "Isn't that what some families do? Get together and bang out 5Ks?"

Bethan snorted. "Ellen is very serious about running. There's no socialization."

Then, with another glance at him, she took off at top speed—so Jonas had absolutely no choice but to follow. And they raced each other all the way back to their suite.

Where Jonas absolutely did not watch as Bethan got some water from the kitchenette and stood there in the doorway, her head tilted back and that body of hers clad in so very little as she chugged it.

He was actually grateful when they broke apart for the day. Bethan was off to indulge in some kind of spa-and-beauty day with her sister and all the bridesmaids. Jonas, meanwhile, had been invited to golf with the military men.

Golf.

He knew it was not an invitation so much as a summons, so he presented himself at the front of the house at the appointed time. He smiled and he laughed, so a collection of three- and four-star generals who would never have given him the time of day before could all greet him and one another heartily, then trudge around a golf course together. Without any pesky civilian irritants.

And he didn't know why he couldn't quite disappear into the character he was supposed to be playing, the way he normally did. Not that his jovial, easy performance wasn't on point, but he couldn't quite get his head around it. Jonas Crow, who'd been given up on so many times in his youth, by so many different authority figures, family members, and his own bitter self, *golfing.*

At a country club he knew would never have admitted him had he been in less exalted company.

"Maybe you can give me some clarity," General Wilcox said when he and Jonas sat in a golf cart while a caddie drove them across the rolling green, which looked like it might topple off into the ocean if it had its way. "I understand that Bethan has something to prove. Seems to me she's proved it a hundred times over by now. It breaks her mother's heart to think of her up there in Alaska, of all places, running around like she does."

Jonas chuckled. Actually *chuckled*, because surely that was the kind of thing golfers in country clubs did with their chummy buddies in their funny, preppy clothes. "Well, she's good at it. Who doesn't like to do what they're good at?"

"We keep waiting for this obsession of hers to end," the general said. "First it was the army. Fair enough. In this family we're happy to support military service. But she kept reupping. And instead of moving out of the field when she could have, she doubled down."

"She did indeed." And it was harder than it should have been to keep that fake smile on his face.

But the general was clearly on a roll here. "Even Ranger School. Impressive, certainly. But surely the point has been made. When she left the army, we thought for sure she would finally settle down into real life. This Alaska Force nonsense is delaying the inevitable."

"The inevitable, sir?" Jonas asked.

General Wilcox gave him a shrewd look. "She can't do this forever."

Jonas shook his head like he didn't understand. "Sir?"

"It's not realistic, is it?" the general asked. "You're a sensible man. You understood that special ops comes with a sell-by date and got out before you were forced out. There are physical limitations to consider."

"I'm pretty sure she knows that," Jonas said, and it occurred to him that one of the reasons he was finding this so difficult was because he wasn't really acting. Not at the moment, when he was facing down a man who, in his view, should have been far more supportive.

Jonas had never had anything approaching a supportive parent himself. Just like he hadn't had fancy houses, staff, or the collection of advantages that Bethan might imagine she'd walked away from but were still right here, ready and waiting for her. He'd had none of that. Nothing was waiting for him, anywhere.

That was how he knew that this wasn't how it was supposed to go down. If she was going to have all the trappings of a Hollywood movie as a life, surely a little support from a father who was basically in the same industry should be part of the deal.

"I don't want to see my daughter chasing her ego until it's too late," Henry Wilcox told the man he thought was his daughter's lover. Jonas knew without asking he didn't discuss these things with Bethan herself. "Her mother worries about her staying safe, but not me. Every report I've ever read makes it clear she can handle herself. But I hate to see her miss out on life while she's out there trying to prove something no one needs proved."

Jonas had to remind himself that he wasn't, in fact, himself. He was the mercenary version of Jonas Crow. A version of himself who'd bailed on his friends, who'd sought glory and money instead of what was right, and most important, who was at heart the kind of man who would be at his ease playing golf with blowhards.

And more than that, at ease in this conversation about a woman he was with.

"I hear you, sir," he said with a wide grin that made all kinds of announcements. That he thought Bethan's life choices were *cute*. That he wasn't going to tolerate the cuteness forever. That he was in charge of her choices. Announcements he knew the general read, loud and clear. "And don't worry. I don't intend to let Bethan miss out on anything."

Next to him, the older man seemed to relax. He nodded, and even reached over and clapped Jonas on the arm.

Which was about as stellar a review of Jonas's performance as he could possibly have received, because the general might be a blowhard, but he wasn't a fool. And if Jonas had been presenting as dangerous as he actually was, no way would Wilcox have dared touch him.

"Birdie and I couldn't be happier that Bethan has found someone with a good head on his shoulders," the general said. "Couldn't be happier."

Jonas wanted to point out that Bethan was one of the most powerful and lethal individuals on the planet. That she did not stumble. That she did not need someone else's good head because hers was stellar. That he could not recall, in fact, any scenario in which she had been anything but fully on her game and performing at the highest level.

He wanted to knock the general back a few steps, or in

this case, straight off the side of the golf cart. He wanted to protest, at the very least.

And really, he should have let it go. He should have stayed in character. But he couldn't hit the older man, so he took what he could. "She has a pretty good head on her own shoulders, sir."

The golf cart was stopping near yet another hole, but the general didn't get out. He gazed at Jonas instead.

"I understand that, son," he said, and there was a different note in his voice. Jonas couldn't quite place it. Wilcox looked almost . . . resigned. "If she was any other woman, I'd try to recruit her. But she's my baby girl. And it doesn't matter how many combat zones she's capable of infiltrating, in my head she'll always be my baby girl. I can't help imagining that sooner or later she'll meet someone that makes her want to stay safe. Is that you?"

Jonas did not feel anything. He was incapable. His throat wasn't tight. There wasn't any steel band wrapped around his chest, making it impossible for him to breathe.

He felt nothing at all.

But he had to clear his throat as he met the general's suddenly too-canny gaze. "I believe so, sir."

The general nodded decisively, as if they'd settled something. Then he swung himself out of the golf cart, already calling out to his friends.

Jonas followed behind him, because he was playing the part of a man head over heels in love with Bethan Wilcox.

So it was lucky he didn't feel a thing. That he never had and he never would.

He told himself that over and over again as the afternoon wore on. As he assured himself that he was nobody's safe space, that he didn't have that capacity. That love was for people who knew what to do with the good things they found.

When all Jonas had ever been good for was war.

He was lucky straight on through.

Nine

Two days before the wedding, Bethan found herself sitting at a table of women at a ladies' luncheon hosted by one of her mother's oldest friends in the Santa Barbara Botanic Garden. It was a bright afternoon, a clear blue sky above, a faint breeze scented with salt and flowers, and beautiful in every way.

The sunshine was like a caress all over her face, but Bethan missed Alaska.

She smiled brightly and made small talk, because that was the job, but she was finding herself . . . homesick.

When she'd never been homesick. Not when they'd left their various homes over the years to follow her father's postings. Not when they'd left the semipermanence of Virginia to move here. Not when she'd gone into the army. Bethan liked to look ahead, not behind.

But she would have given anything to be in Grizzly Harbor right now, keeping a straight face in the Water's Edge Café while Caradine cooked and made snarky remarks, and outside everything was wreathed in grays, deep greens, and blues. She would exchange the California sun for a foggy winter morning in a heartbeat, and she suspected that said things about her she wasn't quite ready to acknowledge. Or even admit.

"It is *so* beautiful here," said the woman to her right. Lauren, she thought. Or Lori. Something along those lines. "I swear, if it weren't for the kids, Brent and I would leave Chicago tomorrow."

Bethan already knew more about Brent, Laurel, and their three kids than she wanted to know. Among the things she knew was that they would never leave Chicago. There had been entirely too many supposedly casual comments about Lara's mother's house *on the lakeshore.*

"I know," Bethan murmured over her salad. The eighty-fifth salad she'd had as a full meal in the last four days, by her count. She expected that at any moment, she might start sprouting kale out of her ears. And she liked greens as much as the next person, but unlike most of the guests at this wedding, she wasn't a stick figure. She liked her food. "Ellen and I are so lucky that we got to grow up here."

And her sister, sitting across the table from her and pretending to listen to one of their aunts, caught her gaze and smirked.

Reminding Bethan that nothing was ever as simple as she liked to think it was when she was locked away in her pink-and-fluffy refuge in Fool's Cove, with the better part of an Alaskan winter ahead of her.

She might find herself missing the slap of an Alaska morning, the particularly addictive grossness of Isaac's morning workouts, and the friendships she'd built around tables that were far stickier than the Botanic Garden's, in places like the Fairweather. But that didn't change the fact that Ellen still knew her in a way only a sister could. And therefore knew that she had lit out of Santa Barbara like she was on fire and had never had any intention of returning, no matter what she said to Laura from Chicago.

She didn't know if she liked that simple fact, or if it made her sad that it could be true when the two of them had never quite figured out how to be close. Not in any real way.

"I'll admit it," Ellen said on the drive back to the house when the luncheon was over. She'd waved off all her bridesmaids and had slipped into Bethan's car instead. Jonas's car, Bethan reminded herself. She had to think of it as Jonas's car, not hers, because he was supposed to be her boyfriend and she had to remember not to act like she was on a mission. "This performance of yours is impressive."

"I beg your pardon. I'm no actor. I'm a soldier, thank you."

"You told Aunt Sarah that you worked in *solutions*, and I heard her telling people that she thought you worked in IT."

"Aunt Sarah is famously dim. And I do work in solutions."

Ellen laughed. "Dad has literally stood there talking about sports teams he doesn't support rather than indicate he's even aware you were ever in the army, and you just take it. You never used to take it."

"What?" Bethan demanded, but she was grinning despite herself. "I can't mellow with age?"

"You?" Her sister shook her head. "No."

"This week is about you, El. Not me."

"Sure it is."

Bethan was saved from having to further explain herself by Ellen's phone, which was always ringing. And which she always answered, because you could take a lawyer out of the office, but you couldn't make them change their habits.

And despite herself, she felt guilty as she drove her sister back toward their parents' house.

Especially because driving her sister up into the hills over Santa Barbara felt a little too much like déjà vu. It could have been any scene from when they were younger, and Bethan and Ellen had been left to their own devices, as ever, while their parents were engaged in far more weighty matters, like roses and war games. Bethan had driven these same roads while, next to her, Ellen had chattered away, blithely unconcerned with whether or not anyone was responding to her.

There had been years Bethan had found that annoying. Sometimes, if asked, she would have insisted that her sister was the most self-involved creature on earth. But then, other times, it made her feel almost . . . affectionate.

Maybe that's just family, she told herself.

But whatever it was, she couldn't help but feel almost ashamed that she wasn't simply . . . here. That the only way she'd been able to do this was to come with a mission. A man who wasn't hers but was pretending he was. An entire strategy.

As if Ellen were the enemy, when she could still look across a table and see straight through her older sister.

Ellen was talking in that particular fast-paced way of hers that she always adopted when she was in work mode, making decisive gestures with her free hand that called attention to the flowy sleeves of the dress she wore. Bethan was wearing an actual sundress, all bright colors and *flouncy*, which had to be why she was questioning what she was doing here. It was all these *clothes*. She wasn't used to wearing dresses, day after day. She didn't *flounce*. She didn't keep her hair out of ponytails or put on eye makeup all the time.

A week of this would get to anyone.

She turned onto the long drive toward the house and had to squint against the glare of the sun. She slipped down the visor and as she did, saw a runner out of the corner of her eye. He was off the road, running down along the side of the vineyard, and she got only a quick glimpse of him as he moved, backlit and unidentifiable.

Her whole body went cold.

Ellen kept talking and Bethan held on to that, because her mind wanted to drag her back. Far back, to the flash of bright desert skies in the relentless, pitiless sun, and another figure, running toward the vehicle between them despite the flames and fumes—

She blew out a breath, trying to center herself. To feel her feet, her legs, her butt in the seat of this car. Her hands on the wheel.

The here and now, not then.

Everything in her screamed to turn around, off-road this car, and chase the man down, but she didn't.

It's a flashback, she told herself. *Something about the sun here, that's all.*

Besides, she couldn't imagine explaining it to her sister. *One of your wedding guests reminds me of a man who's supposed to be dead, El. A man I shot. Excuse me while I run him down in Mom and Dad's pinot noir vines.*

She blew out another breath that was more of a laugh, because that obviously couldn't happen. And Bethan didn't have that many flashbacks, generally speaking. But that didn't mean they couldn't kick in at any time. Like the nightmares that sometimes claimed her, because like it or not, that was part of the deal.

She'd seen nothing, she assured herself. She was safe. She was *here*.

Bethan kept repeating that to herself as she made it up the drive. She parked the car at the front of the house, where Charlotte was always waiting. *Lurking.*

"Hey," came Ellen's voice, not sounding quite as staccato as before. It meant she'd finished her call. "Are you okay? You look like you've seen a ghost."

A choice of words that had her gut telling her things she didn't want to hear. But Bethan made herself smile. "The ghost of high school, maybe. It's been a long time since I came back here. That's all."

Ellen laughed at that as they walked into the house and the cool grip of its air-conditioning. "I went to my last high school reunion, believe it or not. You don't actually know the ghosts of high school until you're face-to-face with them, discussing the so-called glory days."

"Why on earth would you do that to yourself?"

Her sister shrugged, still laughing. "We all have our preferred ways of proving that our lives are better. Yours was becoming Wonder Woman. Mine involves staring at the high school boyfriend who cheated on me with the woman he eventually married and reveling in their quiet despair. No one's perfect."

And Bethan found herself grinning all the way back to her suite.

Where Jonas was waiting, like a thundercloud.

Bethan eyed him as she walked in, feeling frothy and frilly and instantly safe from whatever ghosts had been haunting her out there. And something about that made her whole body hum as she beheld him. Dark. Grim. Serious.

It made her want to . . . *do* something. Not the kind of thing she knew how to do in a professional capacity, or even in some kind of training scenario. But far more intriguing and strange, the kind of thing she never, ever let herself do in a feminine capacity.

Like dance for him.

A thought that was so outrageous she couldn't keep herself from laughing. And when he looked up from the couch where he was sitting with his tablet, the usual query in his dark gaze, that only made it worse. She could dance for him. Or, if she were really his girlfriend, walk over to where he was sitting and slide herself onto his lap, flouncy and flowery, her hair down and her skin bared. She could loop her arms around his neck and make him smile whether he wanted to or not.

Suddenly, she could not only envision doing that but could *feel* it.

In such a tactile way that her inner thighs actually prickled, as if she'd settled herself astride him. But then, if she were astride him, she doubted she would be overly concerned about her thighs. Not when she would be able to rub herself *right there*, right where she needed him, right where she wanted him—

But she was not going to do that.

Just like she was not going to entertain certain dreams she'd had in the light of day.

"The look on your face," Jonas said, his voice dark. Clipped. Repressive in every way. Which he probably didn't know only made everything in her hum. "Rethink it."

She wiped her face clear of all expression. Or she hoped she did, anyway. Bethan had considered this suite spacious and over the top when she'd first walked in. But after a few days of carefully sharing the space with Jonas, it felt cramped. Tiny, in fact. Not only because he took up more space than he ought to, with all that brooding intensity of his. But because there was all that . . . *stuff* between them that neither one of them acknowledged.

Sometimes it did her head in. Other times her feelings about it seemed to be centered significantly farther south.

Today she decided she was far too feminine and silly in this dress to risk putting herself too close to him, particularly after that strange flashback on the drive in. Instead of sitting down in the chair she usually took across from him, she walked over to the sliding glass doors and looked out. As if the sea, silently watching in the distance, could keep her safe.

From herself.

"Any news?" she asked. "I was trapped with the ladies who lunch."

"Oz came back with a detailed account of the movements of two of our three generals," Jonas said, and she knew from the tone in his voice that whatever information he'd received, it hadn't been the evidence he wanted. "And your father."

"My father."

"I thought we should be sure."

Bethan was surprised at the pop of something like outrage at that, when she knew that if the situations were reversed, her father would not hesitate to investigate her. How strange that she'd come back here on a mission she was thrilled she could use as a buffer against her family, only to discover she cared a lot more than she thought she did.

"Not our guys, then?" she asked.

"Unlikely."

She glanced back to see Jonas frowning down at his tablet as he flicked through it. "Blue's favorite, General McKee, has an empty space in his schedule that can't be accounted for, but there are a lot of rumors that he's having an affair with one of his staffers. Oz is pretty sure there will be no love there, either."

"I know you wanted it to be one of them," Bethan said, and again, she was back in that desert. The pounding of her heart the only thing she could hear, and the heat all around. The terrible heat. The dizzying flash of something that made her look off into the distance only seconds before the explosion hit—

She rubbed her hands along her arms, willing the goose bumps to go away. "I guess I have enough of the army still in me that I'd rather not be forced to believe that they're all evil. That some of them might be bureaucratic, sure, but do their jobs."

"I always forget how idealistic you are."

Bethan turned, very slowly. Jonas was sitting back now, as close to lounging as she'd ever seen him, as he was such a precise, contained man. There was a dark, hawkish sort of look on his face that made everything in her freeze.

That wasn't quite the right word. She went still, but it was a highly charged stillness. A charge that was sparked straight through with all the things she never let herself feel.

Or never wanted to let herself feel, anyway.

"Why, Jonas," she said softly, taunting him, because the desert was in her head and Santa Barbara was in her throat and if she didn't hate her family, who was she? "Are you acknowledging that we share a past?"

His dark eyes gleamed. "I guess we all were idealists, once."

"Oh, sure." She didn't snort. Exactly. "Your idealism is what people notice first about you. It shines from you, like a beacon."

"If the generals aren't who we're looking for, that leaves the two CEOs," Jonas said, all business again, and she knew that she was supposed to see only that coolness. That armor of his that he wore so well.

But she'd known him for a long time, and more, she'd spent day and night with him here, not embroiled in a conflict with weapons. Or not their usual conflicts with her usual weapons, anyway. She'd seen him acting like one of the boys. She'd felt that hand against her lower back, and more, she'd seen the awareness in that black gaze.

More than once.

He wasn't as cool as he pretended to be.

And that made her feel something like . . . giddy.

She schooled herself to keep that giddiness under wraps. "I'm assuming this means you cozied up to Stapleton today, as planned."

Pharmaceutical bigwig Lewis Stapleton had arrived the night before. On their run this morning, Jonas had said his plan was to feel the other man out. Over another game of golf, which Jonas talked about as if it were literally torture. This from a man who had likely experienced the real thing.

"The major takeaway from my afternoon with Lewis Stapleton was that he takes great pleasure in describing himself as the *head drug dealer*." Jonas's voice was not quite disgusted. "I want to find that horrifying, but I'm impressed in spite of myself. He's got the Texas accent, the big voice, and if I wasn't looking for a reason to distrust him, I would think he was exactly what he appeared to be on paper. Rich as hell. The CEO of a pharmaceutical company that doesn't pretend to give a crap about anyone. The head drug dealer, son."

"That almost sounds like you admire him."

"It's difficult not to admire, on some level, a person so deeply unconcerned with the opinions of others."

Bethan was smiling at him, and they were alone. She shouldn't let herself do that. "I would have said you didn't care much for anyone else's opinion yourself."

"We're all drawn to the monsters we carry around inside, Bethan." Jonas's eyes flashed, dark and too watchful. "Aren't we?"

This time, her smile hurt. "And here I thought we were the monsters. We just happen to be the ones the bad guys fear."

"Every bad guy is the hero in his own story. Remember that."

There was a lump in her throat. She swallowed, hard. "I don't know how concerned I ought to be that playing golf with a man who was probably personally responsible for a wide swath of the opioid crisis has made you philosophical."

Jonas moved then, rolling up from a seated position to his feet in one of those impossibly graceful moves of his that were the reason he was half ghost. And the reason she, personally, had felt haunted by him for too long now to count. Too long to believe.

"I'm always philosophical," he said, an undercurrent in his voice she didn't understand. "You don't know me as well as you think you do."

Bethan laughed, more in surprise than in any real amusement. "I wouldn't dream of suggesting that I know you. Not after the seven hundred other times you schooled me on that topic. I wouldn't dare."

"If you didn't want friction, you shouldn't have joined Alaska Force."

But she knew all that ice and cold was a mask. Of course she knew. She'd just been thinking about it—but it was something else, she had to acknowledge to herself, to not only know it but to be the subject of all that frigid fire in his dark gaze.

She was too aware that they were alone here. In this soundproofed suite that no one was likely to enter. In a house that might as well be a hotel.

Where there was a bed, big and comfortable, right in the other room.

You need to get a grip before you humiliate yourself, she warned herself. No matter how dark and brooding and not quite . . . chained down as usual Jonas was today.

"As I told you a year and a half ago, I had no idea you were in Alaska Force when I joined," she told him, with a calm that felt like more of a disguise than any other one she'd worn. "How would I? The only person anyone in the service talks about in relation to Alaska Force is Isaac. By design. I followed the same rumor everybody else did."

"Whether you knew I was in Alaska Force or not before you arrived doesn't matter. Once you knew I was there—"

"What?" She jumped on that statement because there was a part of her that had been spoiling for this fight for over a year. If she was honest, for a lot longer than that. "You're not my ex-boyfriend, Jonas. You didn't get Alaska Force in the divorce. I understand that it upsets you that I exist, but I'm not planning to change that. And I don't know why you would imagine that I would. Because, again"—she waved a hand between the two of them, in case he wasn't already getting her point—"we have no situation. You do realize that every single person we work with thinks that we're basically Isaac and Caradine part two, don't you?"

He scowled, a tell that he wasn't in control of himself, but she didn't care. "Don't be ridiculous."

"Of course it's harder to imagine *you* having a secret relationship with anyone, because no one can imagine you having a relationship of any kind. It takes a significant suspension of disbelief to imagine you sneaking around the way Isaac did, for years, but Jonas"—she shook her head at him—"what other explanation could there be for the way you treat me?"

His scowl deepened, this man who had no tells. "I thought I was sexist."

"I almost wish you were. That would make this behavior make some kind of sense."

"I don't care what everybody thinks," he said, more gruffly than usual. And he lost the scowl, as surely as if he'd dropped a smooth mask onto his face.

Bethan hated it. "And now this conversation is beginning to feel circular."

"Very funny. But while on the topic, I don't think Stapleton is our man. Not that he wouldn't happily kidnap a scientist, or order someone to do it for him, but I don't think stealth is his strong suit."

It was an out. And she'd historically always taken the out. She always focused on the job. She always concentrated on what was ahead of her, because what was behind her couldn't matter.

But this was different for a thousand reasons, and most of them seemed tangled up in the way her heart couldn't seem to settle on a reasonable rhythm in her chest.

"Is this the part where I pretend that we weren't having a personal conversation because you're clearly done with it?" she demanded.

Because maybe neither one of them had their masks on quite as tightly as they normally did. Not today. Not here, where there was too much emotion in the air, like jasmine and rosemary. And things seemed to be far more complicated than they were when they were playing themselves.

Or maybe, came that voice inside her, *you both stopped playing parts. For a change.*

"If you can't keep things professional," Jonas began.

"Give me a break." She moved closer to him, which was likely a mistake, but she didn't check herself. She felt as unchecked, unchained, as he had when he'd scowled at her. "I hate to break this to you, Jonas, but you're actually a person. Can't help but get personal. It's right there in the description."

"Is that what you want?" he demanded, and there was heat and life and fury in his voice, which felt to Bethan like a victory. Like more than a victory. Like a kind of wild bliss, and she didn't have it in her to pretend otherwise.

"Since when do you care what I want?"

"Maybe a better question is what you want from me."

He moved then, and suddenly they were standing far too close to each other. All she could think about was his hand, hot and strong and low on her back, though he wasn't touching her. All she could see was all that fire in his dark gaze and the stern line of his mouth that did absolutely nothing to conceal the sensual curve of his lips.

"You're possibly the greatest soldier I've ever met," she managed to say, though everything in her was too hot, too tight, too *desperate*. "But you're a profoundly stupid man."

His grin was so dangerous it was practically serrated. "Say that again," he invited her. "I dare you."

"None of this has ever been about what I want from you," she gritted out. "It's about you. What you want. Or don't want. What you're afraid of and what you think—"

"Shut up, Bethan," he growled at her.

"Why?" she asked, a little wildly. Okay. A lot wildly. So wild it was like the words were appearing of their own accord. "I've already tried that. For years. And it still doesn't help. You march around, glowering and disapproving. You've let our colleagues think that we have some kind of sordid history. And why? Because once upon a time, one night in a war zone, you let another person take care of you."

"Fine," Jonas snapped. "I'll shut you up."

And then he did.

With his mouth.

Ten

It was that freaking dress.

Jonas could have ignored the provocation. He'd been ignoring it for years.

But the Bethan he'd learned how to ignore was always dressed like a soldier. Even when she was off duty in Fool's Cove, she tended toward the same kind of basic, essentially unisex clothing they all wore. Cargo pants. Tactical gear. Cold-weather staples. If he had to think about it—something he'd obviously avoided like the plague—he would probably conclude that she dressed the way she did deliberately, because she was a woman stuck deep in a job and a life otherwise populated by men. Bethan liked to outrun, outfight, and outshoot men, but she never seemed remotely interested in otherwise courting their attention.

Jonas had only ever seen her in a dress once before, at Blue and Everly's wedding, but it had been September in Alaska. The dress she'd worn had been long and billowy and she'd worn a long sweater on top of it, so all he'd really had to contend with was the sight of her hair down around her shoulders, too glossy by far.

This was different.

He could see her strong, beautifully shaped legs. And so much *skin*. And he was only a man, no matter how hard he tried to convince himself otherwise.

Kissing her was like running toward a cliff, then hurling himself off it at top speed.

He knew that the impact was going to hurt. That it might even crush him.

But the falling part was almost too good to bear.

He took her face in his hands and he angled his head, and it was already a disaster in the making, so he thought he might as well make it good.

And maybe, finally, give in to the voices inside him that had been clamoring for something like this for longer than he cared to admit.

She tasted like hope and heat. Her mouth fused to his, slick and hot, and it was almost like getting kicked in the gut.

If there was a way to get kicked in the gut in a good way, that was.

She flowed into him, and that made everything worse. Or better. Because the dress she was wearing was no reasonable barrier at all, and that meant he could feel her.

Everywhere.

Her breasts crushed against his chest. The sweet slope of an abdomen he'd always known was toned but had had the opportunity to study over the past few days, thanks to her running gear. Looking at her had been torture. *Feeling* her was worse.

Feeling anything at all was a disaster. Ruinous by any metric.

But he didn't stop.

Because there wasn't a single thing about kissing Bethan that Jonas didn't love.

The way she kissed him back. How strong and supple she was, telling him without words that she could take anything he brought her way. Take it, give it back, and together, make this fire burn even higher.

His hands didn't stay where he put them. He ran them down the length of her back, growling his approval when she arched into him. Then, finally, he got his hands on her bottom, another object of study over the course of years. He didn't know if she jumped or he hauled her closer, but then she was high in his arms, wrapping her legs tight around his waist.

He kissed her harder, deeper.

And somehow they staggered across the room, and he was tipping her back against the wall so he could hold her there with his chest and devour her.

Because there was nothing breakable about Bethan. He didn't have to hold himself back. He didn't have to be careful—and when he tried, because it was his instinct, she bit him.

"Ouch," he growled against her mouth.

"I'm not fragile," she replied, and yanked his mouth back to hers.

And there was no way anything should be this good.

It was asking for trouble. For fate to come in and set things to rights.

For once in his life, Jonas didn't have it in him to care when that other shoe might fall.

Because it wouldn't be now.

Holding her between him and the wall, he found the bottom of that dress she was wearing. It was frilly and feminine and too much for him to handle even as he pulled it up, over her head, so he could toss it aside.

And then, maybe, he died.

But his resurrection was glorious and he handled it by grinding the hardest part of him into the place where she was so soft she threw her head back and keened a little bit.

And meanwhile, he glutted himself on the view.

Because as he'd always suspected, and pretended he didn't notice, she was perfect.

Absolutely and utterly perfect, and he thought his mouth was watering.

Her breasts were surprisingly plump and lush, and he realized as he fitted his palms to them that she must spend a significant amount of time clamping them down. He marveled at that as he dispensed with the little bralette she wore, so he could finally hold the weight of her in his hands.

And below, the expanse of her belly was a wonder. She was toned and taut, not so much sporting a six-pack as the suggestion of one, and all of it tight. Pretty, he would have said. Because Bethan wasn't a skinny girl. She was a warrior. The thighs that gripped him were thick and strong, the way they would have to be. The way his were, too, because what they did demanded strong quads and fearless hamstrings.

He had never wanted a woman so badly in his life.

And for a moment, Jonas had to stop and take it in. That this was happening. That everything that had been storming around inside of him for years was real, that she shared it as he'd always known she did, and that there was only one place this was going.

He knew he shouldn't. He knew he should step away, set her down, and try to regain his equilibrium.

But he didn't.

He didn't want to.

"If you stop," Bethan said then, and there was nothing even or easy about her voice, "I'll kill you. Not metaphorically."

And despite himself, Jonas grinned.

Then it was a kind of race, but one where they were both going to win.

He tipped her against the wall again, and held her there.

She reached between them, hooked her fingers in the panties she wore, and ripped them straight off her own body.

Jonas didn't think he'd ever seen anything hotter in his life. His body shook with it.

"I don't have a condom," he managed to get out.

"I'm on LARC," Bethan replied. "Long-acting reversible contraception, suitable for the combat-ready female, of course." She smiled, wicked and sweet. "An IUD, Jonas. We're good."

He couldn't believe that he'd had the ability to get out a sentence, and that was before he found her sweet, slick center and tested her with his fingers. The evidence of how much she wanted him almost took him to his knees.

Almost.

Then it was as if he'd done this a thousand times before. With her, only her. As if this were a simple thing after all. He reached down to work his own zipper and Bethan lifted herself up, like they'd already plotted out all the angles.

As if their bodies had been ready for this for years.

He pulled himself free, positioned himself, and their eyes locked together.

And slowly, so slowly it made his head spin, he guided himself to her entrance and she lowered herself down to take him in.

It took a lifetime.

It was a revelation, a terrible mistake.

It was perfect.

And as he sheathed himself inside her, Jonas felt completely naked. Even though he knew that he was the one who was still dressed.

"Wait wait wait," she whispered fiercely, but she didn't quite make it through the last word before she was arching against him, shaking and shaking, crying out the kind of pleasure he would have said couldn't exist.

It was too real. Too raw.

Perfect, something in him said again.

When she rocked forward, dropping her head against his shoulder, she was half panting, half laughing.

And Jonas felt drunk on this. On her.

He could die right now and he would actually be happy, for once. Buried deep inside her, where she was so soft, so hot, so *his*. Her mouth against his neck, all of the power and strength that was Bethan Wilcox spent and sweet and in his arms.

He could hear the alarms inside, telling him to stop now. While he still could. Telling him that it was already too much of a good thing, and that always ended badly.

But instead, Jonas wrapped his arms around her, widened his stance, and began to lift her. Then lower her.

Slowly, at first.

Slowly, as she shuddered against him and flexed a little bit, as if she were going to fight him for control. He knew the exact moment she sighed, then surrendered.

He lifted her, then dropped her, and both of them groaned when the friction and sensation ignited between them, bursting into flame. Then burned, over and over again.

For a long while, there was only that fire. That friction. The look on her face, soft and intent and wild.

And that heedless, hedonistic roar inside him that he'd never felt before. He'd never let it out—he'd never let it get close to his skin. He'd never set himself free like this.

But this was Bethan, and there was no other way to have her. No other option.

Jonas built up his rhythm, prepared to carry on forever, and loving that though he was controlling the depth and the pace, she was anything but passive. He could feel the sleek muscles in her thighs as she helped lift herself, then gripped him hard on the downstroke.

God help him, but it was as if she had been built for him. Built for this.

And that knowledge didn't strike him like a bolt from the blue. It was obvious. Hardly worth mentioning.

If he was honest, he'd known that the very first second he'd laid eyes on her on a base in a foreign country when they'd both been different people. He'd made different choices then.

This was here. This was now.

If he could have, he would have kept going forever.

But her breath started to catch. All that California sunlight poured into the room and he could see the way a flush washed over her neck and breasts, a glorious tell.

And this time, when she tilted her head back, clamped down on him, and lost it, he found himself jumping off that same cliff behind her.

Because the bottom was going to hurt, he knew that, so at least they could fall together.

He staggered with her to the couch and sat down. Hard.

And for a long while, there were only the two of them, still wrapped around each other like that. He tipped his head back and kept it there, so he could stare at the ceiling as he fought to get his heart rate back within normal limits. Bethan was still gripping him. Her arms were around his neck, her legs around his waist, and she was still holding him deep inside.

He could feel her heart and his as they both beat wildly. It felt the way he'd always imagined joy would.

Then slowly, slowly, they both began to settle.

She sighed and sat back, making Jonas hiss in a breath as another jolt of sensation moved through him. He would have said it wasn't possible.

Bethan sat upright, a lithe demonstration of the sorts of things she could do with that body of hers. She shoved her hair back, out of her face. Jonas had no intention of making this worse but there he was, reaching over to take a chunk of it and wind it around his finger.

She did nothing to change the fact that he was still deep inside her.

Yet as they gazed at each other, he had to assume that the wariness he saw in her eyes was mirrored in his.

He remembered too much—that was the trouble.

What a gift it would have been if he'd been knocked into a coma. If the trauma had taken his memories from him, but it hadn't.

He'd been messed up after their vehicle exploded, but not so messed up he couldn't remember her. And the way she'd looked at him when she'd huddled down next to him and checked his injuries. She hadn't cried, but her eyes had gone glassy. Something about the way she looked at him now reminded him of that, when neither one of them was hurt.

Or at least, neither one of them had survived a deadly explosion *today*.

At least not the kind that came with physical scars and six months of rehab.

Jonas found himself sitting there with one hand resting in the crease of her thigh, the other in her hair, like he'd forgotten who he was. Because that could be the only explanation, even if he had the distinct sensation that for the first time, maybe ever, he was the opposite of lost.

But Jonas knew better than to let himself go too far down that road.

The silence dragged out between them. He realized he was expecting Bethan to jump in the way she did, into anything and everything. To say something smart. To say *something*.

But she didn't.

All she did was regard him as if it were the first time she'd ever seen him. As if it were that terrible day in that godforsaken desert where he should have died. And then slowly, as if she expected him to block her, she reached over. And instead of helping herself to his hair, she smoothed her fingers over his mouth.

Solemnly, as if she were learning him. Committing him

to tactile memory. As if it were an act of great significance, and all of this was—

"I guess this was always coming," he gritted out, though his voice felt harsh in his throat. And sounded worse, hanging there in the air between them.

Bethan sighed with her whole body, though notably without an actual release of breath. "Are we doing this? Now?"

Everything inside Jonas protested, but it was time for action. Setting his jaw at how little he wanted to leave the hot clasp of her body, he lifted her off and set her aside, then rolled up to his feet. He zipped himself up, ordered himself to get a grip, and it was like it never happened.

Until he turned around and saw that Bethan was just . . . naked. Kneeling on the couch where he'd put her, looking perfectly at her ease. And watching him with a kind of knowledge in those distractingly green eyes of hers that he did not like at all.

"I accept that this was likely inevitable," he said, as coolly as he could. "I think we can both be grateful that this happened when there were no other Alaska Force members around. Easier to keep a lid on it that way."

"And keeping a lid on it is our goal here?"

He didn't like her tone. Because it was too much like a drawl with something like humor in it, and it took an act of supreme will to keep his hands from curling into fists.

"I'm not in the habit of sleeping with people I serve with."

"Good news, then. We're not serving."

"It's the same thing."

"I think you know it's not."

His jaw ached. He stopped gritting his teeth. "That's a debate with no end. Alaska Force is what you put into it. For me, it's the same."

"I'm not surprised to hear that," she replied quietly, and he wished that she would get up and put some clothes on.

That she would show any hint of the storms that were going off inside of him, one after the next, like a chain of apocalyptic events.

But instead, she just knelt there. Beautifully naked. He could see the flush on her skin. Her nipples were still hard. But while he was wound so tight he thought he might detonate, she looked . . . relaxed.

And worse, if he wasn't mistaken, concerned. For him.

"After all," she continued softly, "if you weren't beating yourself up about something, holding yourself to the highest standard, and denying yourself anything that might bring you comfort, would you even be alive?"

He ignored the buzzing in his head, cutting through it the way he did all extraneous noise—with his very own personal windchill. "You don't actually know anything about me, Bethan. I don't know how many times I have to tell you that."

"I don't have to have personally experienced a scary night of near-death and intimacy to know how determined you are to set yourself apart from everyone else, Jonas," she replied, seeming notably unaffected by the arctic blast he was aiming her way. "We work together, in case you forgot. I see it with my very own eyes, right there in front of me, every single day."

"The fact that we work together is another reason this was a mistake."

She shrugged. "It didn't feel like a mistake to me."

"What do you want?" he demanded then. "What do you think is going to happen here? Because I can tell you right now, it won't."

"It isn't about what I want." And there was a bit more emotion in her voice then. Jonas couldn't decide if that pleased him or if it made him loathe himself all the more. "What has what I want ever had anything to do with what you do?"

That shouldn't have stung, but it did.

He remained, still and unassailable, because that was what he knew. That was what had saved him, more than once, long before he'd enlisted. "I know you think you have some ownership over me, or some insight, because you saved my life. But here's a newsflash. I would have been perfectly happy if you hadn't. If you'd left me there with the rest."

And the look on her face almost killed him. Because Bethan looked as if she wanted to get up from where she sat, come over, and hold him the way she had that long, terrible night. Worse, her eyes were getting that glassy look again, and he didn't think he could handle it.

"Do you really think that's a newsflash?" she asked softly.

But he couldn't take that on board. "Maybe this was always going to happen. Maybe you really don't think it was a mistake. Either way, it's still just sex. It's not unusual for the pressures of a mission to get to people."

"Really? Oddly, I've always been able to control myself in the past. Are you saying you haven't?"

He knew the look he was giving her then was filthy. "This isn't any run-of-the-mill operation. Your family is involved. It's no wonder emotions are heightened."

"Because I'm definitely the person in this room suffering from heightened emotions."

"It's not going to happen again," he told her, all command and fury.

But it was Bethan, who still hadn't seemed to notice that she was absolutely stark naked. She . . . stretched. She lifted one arm over her head, then the other, and arched a little bit, too. And when she was done, she rose to her feet in an easy manner that made his throat go dry.

"Okay," she said.

"I mean it. We're human." Technically. "One mistake is allowed."

"Human. Got it."

When she sauntered toward him, he stiffened, sure that

she was going to launch herself at him. Whether to kiss him or strike him, he couldn't say.

Instead she only smiled, stepped around him, and swept her clothes up off the floor. He couldn't even say it was a particularly seductive movement. She just did it, then carried on. Heading, he realized after a moment, for the master bedroom.

"I'm going to need you to acknowledge—"

But when she turned, gazing back at him over her shoulder, his words failed him.

"Acknowledge what?" she asked, lightly enough, though he didn't mistake the edge in her voice. "That you're freaking out?"

"I do not freak out."

"Maybe you're in character, then. And your character is having a panic attack. Whatever. I'm sure you're right. I don't know you at all." And he could see that same edge in her gaze. "But do you?"

"That's a stupid question."

"If you say so."

"Of course I know myself," he gritted out.

"You know how to punish yourself," Bethan replied, and what struck him most was that she didn't sound as if she were trying to hurt him. Or even slap at him. Her voice was entirely too matter-of-fact for that, and it made his ribs hurt. "You know how to make yourself pay. It's your life's work, clearly. But whatever debt you think you have left, after all this time, don't you think you've already paid it?"

She didn't wait for him to answer. Instead, she walked away, back into the bedroom, taking all of her warmth, nakedness, and fire with her.

And worse, the hope he hadn't known he'd had until it was gone.

Eleven

She wasn't surprised at Jonas's behavior. But that didn't make it any easier to deal with.

Bethan took a very long shower, and when she emerged, her character was firmly in place. The character she was playing had not succumbed to a long-term attraction with a man she knew better than to touch. The character had certainly not let herself get emotional, because if anything, she was even more locked down and compartmentalized than usual.

That was the best way to survive pretty much anything. She knew that, no matter what character she was playing.

When she came back into the living room, Jonas's dark gaze met hers with all the force of a sonic boom. Bethan wondered if she'd broken something, so determined was she to keep her expression bland. As if nothing had happened.

Because she had no idea how else to keep going.

"Ready to get back to work?" he asked, and she allowed a small part of her brain to process the fact that Jonas Crow was actually doing the provoking for a change, rather than standing about doing an impression of a granite slab of stoicism. But the rest of her flatly refused to be provoked.

"There's actually no wedding event tonight," she said in reply. "That means it's an excellent time to rendezvous with the rest of the team."

"Terrific."

And with that brisk exchange, they both settled down with their tablets to compile all the information they had so far.

"There's still no sign of the Sowandes in Montreal," Bethan said at one point, after a long phone call with Oz back in Alaska. "Blue is on the ground there, trying to shake some trees, but there's no love."

"The only reasonable conclusion is that someone got their hands on him, took him and his sister to a laboratory somewhere, and are currently making him put his research into practice." Jonas's tone was dark, but it was hard to tell if that was just him or if he was deliberately directing all that darkness her way. She told herself she didn't care. "It follows that it's the kind of laboratory that was built deliberately to be hard to find."

"We should meet our final candidate tomorrow." Bethan frowned at the schematics of the Montreal safe house she'd been studying, as if what had happened there would simply pop up on her screen like those old videos, if she stared long enough. "But maybe we should take a moment to think about what we're going to do if he doesn't fit."

"Oz hasn't been able to dig up anything on him," Jonas said, sitting back. He almost looked relaxed, which Bethan found . . . surprisingly infuriating.

Because it was one thing to understand, on whatever level, that this man simply could not deal with her unless it was about work. Or sex, apparently. But after actually having sex with him—something she'd never thought would happen and which had actually been far, far more spectacular than she'd imagined it could be all these years—it turned out that she felt a whole lot less forgiving of his issues than before.

Still, she would rather die than crack where he could see it.

"Nothing outside the available résumé," she agreed. "Dominic Carter, which is almost certainly not his real name according to Oz, has every second of every day thoroughly alibied. Almost as if he expects he might be called to account for it at any time."

"Suspicious in itself."

"Sure. Then again, he's the CEO of one of the slickest private military companies in the world. His people regularly trick governments into giving them lucrative defense contracts and are rumored to like a little regime change of an afternoon. Keeping his hands clean is probably just everyday best practices."

Jonas studied her for a moment, and she did not react to that dark gaze of his. Externally.

"Why doesn't Oz think Dominic Carter is his real name?" he asked.

Her shrug felt as if someone else were doing it with her body. "He said he had a feeling."

"Oz's feelings usually turn out to be facts."

"That they do," she agreed, maybe too brightly, then cursed herself. But there was nothing to do but immerse herself in her reading until Jonas finally went to take his own shower.

It wasn't until she heard the water running that Bethan let out a long, hard breath.

She thought she'd acquitted herself as well as could be expected, after her long shower, of entirely too much raw reaction, which she'd decided to keep to herself. But Bethan had never slept with a man she worked with before. She couldn't think of a single time she'd even been tempted. She'd always been far too focused on the job. On what she wanted to prove, maybe. And she was far too aware of the ways sex could bring a woman down in her chosen profession. Not the man she slept with, of course. Just the woman.

She'd *laughed* at the idea that she could ever be so dumb.

And yet she hadn't simply *let this happen* with Jonas. She'd enthusiastically participated. She'd practically done it herself.

The crazy part was that she didn't regret it.

There was no shame. No self-recrimination. She found he was increasingly more on her nerves, but maybe that was only to be expected. She certainly wasn't beating herself up about it.

Her entire body was still buzzing. She felt raw and deeply sated, as if she'd just had an intense, deep-tissue massage. She wanted to curl up in a ball and sleep, blissfully. If she were a cat, she would've been purring.

And the grumpier and grimmer he got, the giddier she felt inside.

Try as he might, he wasn't going to get her to think it was meaningless. Or anything but a natural progression that would have occurred a whole lot earlier if he hadn't first ordered her away from the hospital in Germany, or second, literally gone out of his way to avoid ever being alone with her like this since she'd turned up in Alaska.

She was turning that over in her head when he came out of the shower, dressed as Fake Jonas and looking as shut down as she'd ever seen him.

Which was to say, typical Jonas.

"Why did you volunteer for this?" she asked him.

Without really meaning to. *Oh well*.

That dark, unreadable gaze burned where it touched now. "It was obvious that you were going to need a date. It was obviously the best and most effective way to have two team members infiltrate this situation."

"Agreed. But why did *you* volunteer?"

She thought she saw something flicker on that beautifully cold face. "Volunteering to put myself in the line of fire is my life's work, Bethan."

"In the line of fire, sure. But this?" She lifted her chin to indicate the two of them. "You've been avoiding being alone with me in any significant way since you woke up in Germany and refused to see me. So what changed?"

"I thought we agreed we were back to work," he retorted darkly. "Or let me rephrase that. I don't have any interest in further personal conversations."

"Tough."

He sighed, then settled his hands on his hips. Both of those things were so unlike him that Bethan almost laughed. Because Jonas didn't fidget unless he was in character or trying to throw someone off their game. He was very, very still. Preternaturally still, in fact. It was one of his defining characteristics.

"I'm going to go ahead and nip this in the bud," he told her.

She shouldn't have been smiling. "Is there a bud to nip? That's news to me."

"I have nothing to give," he said, so calmly and with such precise chill that it made her stomach hurt.

Because she had no doubt that he meant that. Fully. From the very depths of his battered, dark soul.

And it made her want to cry. For him.

"I didn't grow up like this," he said, his voice cool. "Like you. I would hardly call what happened to me *growing up* at all, except I came out on the other side of it and I was no longer a child."

"Jonas," she began. "If this is about my parents' house or my sister's wedding, you should remember that I did basic training like any other—"

"It's not that I come from a different social class," he said, cutting her off—but again, without the slightest bit of heat or temper, as if all of this was a boring dictionary entry that he hadn't bothered to read aloud before. "I'm talking about a different world. My father was an abusive drunk who had a soft spot for narcotics, and those were his good days. My mother was a junkie. My little sister was born addicted to heroin and OD'd when she was sixteen. There were rumors of an older brother they surrendered to the foster system, but they only talked about him when they were wasted. We lived in cars. Tents. Or we squatted in structures I wouldn't bother to call houses."

She found she was holding her breath.

"My sister was three years younger than me," Jonas said. "I wouldn't say my parents cared about us, but they fed us occasionally because we were useful. People are more likely to give their spare change to a couple of kids. I joined the navy the day I turned eighteen because I wanted to go to war. Not because I wanted to do good, Bethan. Not like the rest of you. I wanted to go to war because it felt safer."

He said all of that in the same matter-of-fact way, but his gaze registered the bleakness of what he was telling her.

Bethan wanted to contradict him. To argue. But she knew that if she did, he would somehow twist it and take it as confirmation of everything he was saying. Because he could believe whatever he wished, but she did know him. Better than he thought.

Some years, better than she wanted.

"I doubt you're the only one who feels that way," she said after a moment. "We might have grown up in different worlds, but the army felt a lot more comfortable to me than this place ever did. I understand it's not the same."

"Do you?" His dark gaze seemed to intensify. "You're not the only one who remembers that night, Bethan. The difference between us is that I might have saved you from a burning truck, but I never would have tried to soothe you. I never would have nurtured you in any way. I would have accomplished the task and then moved on to another fight. Because I don't isolate myself for my own protection. I do it for everyone around me. None of you need to know how empty it is inside. None of you can handle it."

"That's an interesting take," she said quietly, her eyes on his as if this were a challenge. When all she wanted to do was go to him. Touch him. Convince him, somehow, that his heart was right there inside his chest where she'd felt it pounding earlier. "Because the story going around Fool's Cove is that you went off into the Alaskan interior to get up close and personal with how empty you are. Until Isaac and Templeton dragged you back."

"You all want that to be meaningful." Jonas actually laughed then. Not one of his fake laughs. But not because he thought anything was funny, either, clearly. Because the laugh sounded as bleak as he did. "What I'm trying to tell you is that it makes no difference to me. Dancing with my weapon in the cabin alone, or here with you after all these years. It's all the same thing. I don't have what you do inside. I don't feel things the way you do. And no, before you ask, I never will."

Bethan had to bite her tongue so hard she tasted copper to keep from arguing with him. She made herself stand. She smoothed out the front of yet another dress she was wearing—this one, happily, less flouncy than the last—and kept her smile polite. Engaged, but not sympathetic.

Anything but sympathetic.

"If that's true, then what do you care if we have sex again?" she asked. Mildly. She could have been asking the time. "We could have sex all the time if you don't feel anything. Because if you're empty inside, why would it be a problem for you?"

Fidgety Jonas was gone then. And in his place was the one she knew best. So still, so deadly, that part of her thought that if he so much as blinked she would take it like a bullet to the chest.

Accordingly, she smiled more broadly. "It's a reasonable question."

"I'm not protecting me, Bethan."

"Oh, right. Got it. You're being noble on my behalf. Protecting me from all the girlie feelings that might have their way with me. Because, obviously, one taste of Jonas Crow and my world will never be the same."

She watched, fascinated as ever, as that muscle in his cheek pulsed.

"In my experience," he said in that deadly way of his, "you are almost certain to get emotional. I won't."

"How many Army Rangers have you slept with?"

"I'm telling you my experiences. With women. Regardless of their profession."

"So, zero, then. And of the Army Rangers you know, how many of them are prone to outbursts of uncontrollable emotion?"

"The fact that you're offended by this is proving my point, Bethan."

"You've worked with me in two completely different roles, neither of which, as far as I'm aware, involved a whole lot of emotional breakdowns on my part. If anything, I would say you're the one who's having emotional difficulties here."

"Great," he bit out. "That's not you. Crisis averted."

She made a meal out of shrugging carelessly. "Again, Jonas. You're going to great lengths to convince me that you don't feel anything, but you also were quick to tell me that this could never, ever happen again, because . . . reasons. You'll understand if I'm not convinced that you're the most reliable narrator."

What exactly are you trying to do here? she asked herself. *Do you really want to throw yourself into a physical relationship with a coworker? Even if it's Jonas.*

Her heart was beating so hard in her neck that it took everything she had not to press her fingers against it, which would show him far too much about what she was hiding.

Especially if it's Jonas, that voice continued, darkly. *Do you really think you can handle him?*

Maybe that was why she was pushing. Because she knew she couldn't, but she also knew she was in no danger of finding out.

And meanwhile, she was so busy compartmentalizing everything that had happened this afternoon that if she thought about it, she was sure she would be unable to contain her reaction. That strange flashback. Sex with Jonas. And then the story he'd told her, that would've broken her heart into pieces if she let it. That would, she knew, the moment she was alone.

All of this and she was standing in her parents' house in Santa Barbara, with more family shenanigans looming ahead of her, no matter how she assured herself that what mattered was the mission. That might be true, but it was still Ellen's wedding.

She shoved each part into its own cordoned-off area inside her, made sure the walls were standing high, and locked the doors up tight.

And when Jonas did nothing but stare back at her, still, steel, and as approachable as a wicked knife, she inclined her head toward the door.

"After you," she said, taking pride in how calm she sounded. "Unless you'd rather stay here and continue to pretend you're not the one having a breakdown."

The look he gave her was scathing. It took all she had not to glance down and check to see if he'd actually flayed all the flesh from her body that easily.

A victory, she told herself stoutly, as he stalked from the room.

It was a victory, all right, but the kind that claimed far too high a cost.

Because Bethan was good at what she did. She prided herself on that. That meant that she didn't display any kind of reaction when he casually took her hand as they walked into the main part of the house and were confronted with Ellen and all of her bridesmaids. Bethan smiled and leaned closer into him. Even when he slid his arm around her shoulders as they talked to the various groups of people who were gathering in the foyer to set off for different dinners down in Santa Barbara. Or for the more adventurous, over the mountains to Solvang or even down the coast to Los Angeles.

He touched her as if they'd just had sex. That they really had was something for her to carry inside her until there was a safe place to examine it.

She wasn't sure such a place existed, so she snuggled in close and smiled dreamily.

But when they finally drove away from the house full of wedding guests, she shifted seamlessly into her usual persona. Because even that was a series of masks, she was well aware. She could no longer separate herself from what the army had made her, but there was a version of her no one else ever saw. Her cabin in Fool's Cove was a monument to that Bethan.

And it was only here, driving through another gold and deep blue Southern California evening, keeping so many armored little pieces of herself walled off inside, that it occurred to her to wonder how long she could keep all that up.

How long could one person splinter themselves into so many pieces and expect to ever be whole again?

But she had no choice but to shove that away when they met up with the rest of the team in the motel where they'd set up camp in the neighboring town.

"I had no idea you cleaned up pretty, Bethan," Rory said with a laugh as they all crowded into the motel room.

"Not something you need to worry about, Lockwood," she shot back, so everyone would laugh at him and stop looking at her legs.

Everyone did. Except Jonas.

After several hours of throwing possibilities around and outlining potential scenarios, all they'd really succeeded in doing was annoying themselves. Because Dominic Carter was in town, supposedly, but caught in meetings until the rehearsal dinner. Until then, everything was waiting around and conjecture.

"We're sitting in a motel room in Goleta, and who knows if the scientist is even in North America any longer?" Jack Herriot muttered as Jonas and Bethan got ready to leave.

"I told Iyara Sowande to trust me," Bethan shot back, one of her walls toppling inside, leaving nothing but the anguish she usually knew better than to show. "I intend to make sure she can."

She kicked herself all the way back toward the house, through a night gone thick and ripe with jasmine and rosemary. Somehow that seemed to match the man beside her, so silent he ached with it.

He reached for her hand when they left the car out front. And once again, Bethan had to have full-scale intervention with herself as they walked through the house, because it didn't matter how it felt with their fingers laced together like that. It didn't matter what her body was telling her, because she couldn't act on it. She already had, and she was therefore looking forward to a nice, long night alone, locked away in the master bedroom of their suite, where she could process her emotions.

And maybe scream into her pillow while she was at it.

Inside their room, Jonas flicked the lights on, then paused.

No one who didn't know him would have thought anything of that pause. They probably wouldn't have noticed it.

But to Bethan, it was like he'd suddenly gone electric. She was in the process of slinging the fussy little clutch she'd been ordered to carry around, because that was what civilian women did, onto the coffee table. When she straightened, she had no notice. She saw only that look on his face, fierce and delicious, enough to make her heart seem to catapult from her chest to her feet and back—

In the next second, he was on her.

He hauled her against him, taking her mouth with a sheer ferocity that made her entire body feel weak and wild at once.

Jonas kissed her with so much passion she wasn't sure her body could contain it, but God, she wanted to—

It took her a moment to realize that he was saying something, there against her mouth.

Her heart was too loud in her ears. She thought she might combust.

Jonas moved his mouth from hers and made his way along her cheek, her jaw. He lay a trail of explosive fire that made every part of her go tight and soft, as she could do nothing but helplessly arch into him.

All her walls were in rubble around her. All her *compartments* were wide open.

All he had to do was kiss her and she betrayed herself completely.

Then his mouth was at her ear.

"Camera," he said, a low growl that she could feel work its way through her, like pure need. "On the painting."

Jonas didn't give her a chance to look, or respond.

He took her mouth again, long and drugging and demanding. "We're being watched."

Twelve

It was hard to keep his mind where it should have been, something that had never happened to Jonas before. Ever. Yet even as he recognized that he was being pulled out of his usual level of focus on the operation, he could feel a different kind of intensity click into place between Bethan and him.

She smiled at him as if he'd just handed her the California sun in the middle of an Alaskan winter, then arched her body into his. And he was sure that to anyone filming this, she looked abandoned and seductive. All about pure sensation.

But he could feel every bit of tension in her body.

And somehow, that made it all that much hotter. *More dangerous*, something in him insisted, because he couldn't seem to help himself from responding. But this wasn't the time to worry about these things that shouldn't be happening between them. The things he certainly shouldn't be feeling. Or wanting. Or *needing* when God knew, he'd learned long ago never to *need* anything, because that led straight to the kind of addictions that had laid waste to his entire—

Bethan leaned in and bit his ear.

Hard.

And when he stared at her in amazement—and the kind of temper he could feel pulse in him, everywhere—she only grinned.

"I want to go get in the hot tub," she said.

Jonas was horrified to realize he was having trouble keeping track of all the things that should have been like second nature to him, because there was that sting in his ear and her body against his, and he was . . . short-circuiting.

Because, of course, utilizing the hot tub out on their patio was an excellent idea. Such an excellent idea that he wasn't sure why it hadn't occurred to him already. If their rooms had cameras in them, that was one thing. People who bugged rooms, in Jonas's experience, rarely bugged outside areas as well, because the quality of received sound was so inconsistent.

That all flashed through him, the way it should. But what he was really thinking about was the fact that Bethan was . . . playing with him.

As if that were what was important here.

And he couldn't seem to think about anything else as she spun around, executing a delightfully girlie sort of spin that belonged in the kind of romantic movies he didn't watch. It brought home how lithe and pretty she was. How perfectly shaped—and not just to run missions or carry heavy things or decisively end attempts to assault her.

She was graceful, as tough as she was lovely, and Jonas should never, ever have touched her. Because now that he had, he couldn't seem to shove her back where she belonged. He couldn't seem to access that space in his head where he could gloss right over how beautiful she was every day, and focus only on what she could do as part of the Alaska Force team.

Bethan grabbed his hand, tugging him with her, and it took him a moment to process the sound she was making while she did it.

Giggling.

Bethan Wilcox was *giggling*, which in any other circumstance he would have taken as clear evidence that the world was ending. He had to remind himself that she was in character. She was playing this flirty, giggly role to the hilt, and he knew that meant that he should be doing the same.

His job was all he had. All he was. So why wasn't he doing it?

This was the trouble with all those feelings he'd told her with such confidence he didn't have. He didn't want any part of them. This confusion. These signals canceling each other out, so he couldn't entirely tell if he was playing her lover, or if he only wanted to be her lover when he shouldn't, or why it seemed he had to choose between that and the capacity to *do his freaking job* the way he should.

It was that last part that got through to him, finally. He didn't actually slap himself across the face, because that would hardly play well on camera for whoever was watching. But he followed her willingly enough as she tugged him into the master bedroom, flicking on lights as she went, then led him out onto the patio and the hot tub that waited there.

Jonas waited until she turned on the jets, then pulled her close, getting his face near enough to hers.

Near enough that it made him think that kissing her again was a great idea, when he knew better. *Handle yourself.* "There's another camera in the bedroom."

"The patio looks clear," she responded, apparently not hearing the growl in his voice.

And they both grinned widely at each other, as if they were whispering words of sex and devotion.

She ran back inside, still giggling madly, calling out something about towels. Merrily.

While she did, Jonas stood on the edge of the patio with the room at his back, looking over the lights of Santa Barbara far below. He shot off a text to command center in Alaska, looping in the rest of their local team.

Our suite suddenly has eyes on it, he texted. *Two rooms so far. Can someone hack that feed?*

There was a pause, and then Oz texted back. *On it.*

Behind him, Jonas heard Bethan come back outside. He had to admire the way she tripped a little bit over her own two feet as if she were tipsy, when he knew she was no such thing. But he braced himself when she came closer, tipping herself against his back and sneaking her arms around his waist.

And he absolutely did not reflect, for even one second, on how good and right it felt to have her there, where she also fit entirely too well.

He held his phone where she could see the screen and kept typing.

Tell me where the feed originates, but don't cut it yet, he wrote. *I want to know what angles they have on this suite.*

He let Bethan do her thing, telling himself it was like a trial by fire and he'd passed every one of those yet. With flying colors, thank you. She rocked a little bit with her arms around him, as if she were making him dance with her. As if she were coaxing her *always busy, always on the phone* lover to set it aside for a second to pay attention to her. Jonas could envision the scene she was setting all clearly in his head.

But *feeling* it was something else.

And he wanted to rage. He wanted to shove her away from him. Every second she touched him it was worse, and he'd known that for years now, hadn't he? He'd woken up in Germany wishing he hadn't. The body he relied on was a mess, and the heart he'd given up on when he was still a kid was a disaster in his chest, and while he needed the former to do the only thing he was any good at, he wanted no part of the latter. Ever.

He'd thought, *No. None of that.*

He'd ordered her sent away, having no idea that she would take what had happened to him—*with* him—as some kind of calling. He'd forbidden himself to look her up in the intervening years. He'd never so much as asked after her.

No one was more surprised than Jonas when Isaac had flashed her face up on the screen in the lodge for the usual Alaska Force new-member vote.

He'd thought that was as bad as it could get.

He should have known better.

Because he was waiting for Oz to hack into the video feed, aware that the very existence of those cameras indicated that there was a distinct threat. More, it showed that all this pretending at a family wedding had been the right thing to do, no matter how odd and disconnected it had felt these past few days. He was keenly aware of those things, the way he should have been.

But all he could really think about was the soft weight of her breasts against his back. The scent of her that already haunted him, that he couldn't imagine getting any worse until she made his head spin. But then there was the heat of her. The shape of the impression she made against his back, like he was changing his form to fit hers.

She made him feel like he was drunk, a state he had never experienced and never would. Still, he'd watched enough drunk people to get the idea. He felt the way they'd always looked. As if his head were fuzzy. As if his legs didn't quite work beneath him.

As if she were leaving her mark on him, so hot and right that it would be visible from space.

The screen of his mobile lit up, and Jonas felt like breaking out into a chorus of hallelujahs.

He did not.

Two feeds, Oz texted. *One takes in your living room. The other is focused on the bedroom.*

What's the sight line out the sliding doors in the bedroom? Jonas texted back.

Zero, was the reply. *It's all bed and bathroom and what looks like a walk-in closet.*

Jonas could feel Bethan's body tighten at that, as if she were processing how best they could use it. But another text came in then.

Key point, Oz texted. *It's a local feed. I traced it to the house you're in.*

Jonas's body shifted, the way it always did, into combat readiness. He felt Bethan do the same. And if he was pathetically grateful that he wasn't ruined forever by *feelings*, he kept that to himself.

En route to perimeter, Rory texted. *Backup will be on hand in approximately twenty minutes if needed.*

Roger that, Jonas texted back.

He shoved his phone into his pocket and waited for Bethan to let go of him. But she didn't.

"We don't know if there are physical eyes on us," she murmured, and it was like torture. Her lips moving against his back. He could *feel* them. What was he supposed to do with that?

Especially because she was right. It was dark. All kinds of things could be lurking in the dark.

He turned to face her, though that wasn't better. All it did was create a new host of problems, especially when she slid her arms around his neck.

"I want to find where these feeds are originating," he muttered. His hands found her hips a little too easily, too naturally. But if anyone was looking at them, they would look like lovers in an intimate, private dance. That was the point, he reminded himself.

"I want to know what changed," Bethan replied.

He lifted his head enough so he could see her expression.

"There weren't cameras this morning," she said, though she looked dreamy. Nothing like the highly trained operative she was, and he should have had absolutely no reaction to it. She was doing her job. The way he should have been doing his. "What happened today that we became a threat?"

"Good question."

Jonas smoothed his hand over her hair. Standing like this, not kissing her and not rushing to get inside her, felt a little too much like battering himself with information he really didn't want. Like the way she *fit* him. He couldn't get past it. It was too easy to hold her. His hands liked being right where they ended up, wrapped around her hips like she was his.

He had the terrible notion that this game they were playing wasn't a game at all. That it was more like an infection, and once it set in, he was a goner.

But he'd been a goner before, and here he was anyway. He ordered himself to stop worrying about *fitting* and to start treating the situation they were in with the respect it deserved.

Or at least with the benefit of his full freaking attention.

"I don't think that Oz is going to be able to narrow it down any further than this property," he said, like an imitation of the ice-cold, strategic genius he was supposed to be.

"That's no worry at all." Bethan grinned. "I was a teenager here, remember? Trust and believe that I know how to sneak around this house."

She stepped back from him, pulling him with her toward the hot tub. She made a show of kicking off her flat sandals as if they were high heels. Then she went over to the side and pulled out a screen he'd thought was purely decorative. Maybe it was, but Bethan arranged it like a privacy screen. For the benefit of whatever silent audience they might have watching them, she tugged it across the front of the hot tub, blocking off any lines of sight. Better still, it was wide enough that it covered over a good foot to the side of the patio, giving them an exit option.

And once the screen was up, Bethan instantly looked neither giggly nor tipsy at all.

Something thudded through him, unpleasantly, because he understood that while Bethan leaning into her femininity had disarmed him, none of that was the real problem.

This was the problem. His no-nonsense soldier, the one who impressed him and everyone else in Alaska Force daily. The one who, long before she'd tested her mettle in Ranger School, had held off insurgents single-handedly while he was too injured to do anything but babble out his life story.

Even tonight, while she was wearing one of those dresses of hers, this one a sleek sort of a shape that both emphasized her figure and yet did not cling to it, she looked like the Bethan he knew best. Her gaze was cool, considering. She was all business.

She was so beautiful it actually hurt. Particularly where he was already too hard and ready.

"There are too many guests in this house for us to be rolling around with visible weapons," she said, which he took to mean she had nonvisible weapons stashed on her person. Like he did. "Agreed?"

"Agreed," Jonas replied.

As shortly as possible, for fear that what was happening inside him might show in his voice.

Because now the blinders were gone. All the walls he'd built up were in rubble.

He was screwed.

But there was no time to think about that. She nodded at him, shoved her hair back behind her ears, and slipped into that foot-long space overlapping the patio next door. She was already at the glass doors by the time he followed her.

He expected her to pick the lock, but she tested the handle first, and then soundlessly slid the door wide. Jonas was impressed with the way she did it, confidently walking inside even though the lights were on and there was the sound of the television from the next room.

He followed, knowing that whoever was staying here would never know that they'd had visitors at all. He and Bethan were both so quiet, they might as well have been the kind of ghosts he'd always considered himself.

A notion that sat on him a little strangely tonight.

Once in the hallway, Bethan didn't head toward the main part of the house the way they normally did. Instead, she looped around, leading Jonas up a short flight of stairs and then into a second-floor gallery that stretched from this new addition into the old. He followed her silently, on alert for signs of life in any direction, but it was quiet.

They were lucky that it was late. Or late enough, anyway, for the guests staying here. He doubted they would have found the place so quiet if the wedding party were staying here.

Bethan led him to a door and paused, cocking her head as if she were trying to hear through the wall. She opened the door slowly, carefully, then poked her head through. The jerk of her chin was his only indication that he should follow her, and so he did. And found himself in a more narrow, less openly splendid part of the big house.

"These are the servants' quarters," she told him as they moved. And he knew she was deep in mission space, because she didn't even make a rueful remark at that. Or about the fact she'd grown up like this. Like a princess, when he was—

It doesn't matter what you were, he snapped at himself. *There is no you and Bethan to worry about.*

And she was still talking. "I figure we can either go rifling through guest rooms, or I can go straight to the source."

"What's the source?"

She looked back at him then, smiling faintly. "My mother is very particular, especially about parties. Which means I know that she keeps a master list of which guests are in which rooms, and that list usually includes likes and dislikes, gifts left for them if my father's trying to make an especially big impression, and any other hostess information she deems important."

"You want to break into your parents' room?"

He was fine with that. Just surprised that it was her move during this wedding week.

"I could." And he thought she might have laughed if they hadn't been standing in this strange little hallway, whispering. "Ellen and I used to do it for fun. Mostly to prove that we could, because it felt like a major rebellion. But no, I'm not going to drag you into the general's bedchamber. My mother's office will do just fine."

And then he was following her again as she moved nimbly down this back hall, making almost as little noise as he did. Something he had the impression she hadn't learned in the army but here. In this very same hallway. A general's daughter who wanted to make sure she could conduct her mischief as she saw fit.

It made him feel something like nostalgic for a childhood he'd never had. For this notion, on parade this whole week, that this was what family was supposed to be. Not the pretense of endless harmony, or even mandated friendliness. But that no matter what, they could make each other laugh with old stories like this one. That they could come together and act right, however briefly. That there was a shared idea of what the family was, and everyone participated in it.

When he thought about his family it was never a shared thing. It was always solitary and sad, no matter who else was there. It was always hunkered down in the back of a crappy old car, wishing the temperature would drop low enough that he would just die and get it over with.

He was seized with the urge to shout that at her, as if it were her fault—

Or maybe you're tired of holding on to it, something in him suggested. *Like some kind of sick vigil for people who forgot you. Regularly. While you were right there.*

And that was even worse.

But there was no time to think about it. Because Bethan was moving swiftly, and she was just as lethal in bare feet and a dress that ended above her knees as she was in full tactical gear. She wasn't holding a weapon, but the intensity of how she held herself and how she moved made him think that a gun or knife would have been entirely superfluous.

And he supposed it was his curse that the Bethan that turned him on most of all was the lethal one, and he couldn't pretend otherwise now.

She led him out of the servants' hall and into part of the house he hadn't been in before. It was obvious that this wasn't for staff. The halls were too airy. There were suddenly fancy rugs, art he didn't have to be able to make sense of to know was priceless, and the faint sound of classical music from somewhere he couldn't quite identify.

She took him down from the second floor to the first. He wasn't surprised to see that they'd circled around so that they were closer to the greenhouse out back. Rugs and polished wood gave way to graceful stone, and she led him toward what appeared to be a wall of windows. During the day he imagined he would be able to look out at the greenhouse and the hills that rose up behind the house. But tonight, she led him down the airy hall of windows set with glass on hinges, all open to let the night air in. And at the end of it, she opened a large wooden door, very carefully.

"It squeaks," she whispered over her shoulder.

She waved him in, then carefully closed the door behind them. There was another, shorter hall, and then Jonas found himself in the kind of elegant room that likely had a name, because all these sorts of places did. *Solarium. Conserva-*

tory. Something normal people didn't have. There were books arranged, not shoved in tight, on shelves. Low couches in vibrant fabrics with throws and pillows just so. Incidental tables piled high with collections of books and objects that all managed to create a kind of harmonious feel without giving the suggestion of clutter.

"Why does your mother need an office?" he asked.

"You have no idea how much time she spends handling the various boards she's on," Bethan replied. "It's a full-time job. Besides, sometimes I think she just wants a little space that's only hers. I can't blame her."

She headed for the desk that stood against one wall and bent over it, looking through the items on the desktop with purpose.

Jonas found himself drawn against his will to the fireplace on one end of the seating area. It was a decorative number with a huge flowering plant where there ought to have been logs, but it was the mantel that got his attention.

Because it was cluttered with pictures. The general and Mrs. Wilcox when they were young. And later, accepting awards and commendations from various military and political superstars.

He filed those away, but what interested him were the family pictures. Not the family—her.

Bethan as a girl, all freckles and that madcap grin of hers. Bethan in her army uniform, clearly straight out of basic training. Bethan and her sister, mugging for the camera on some bench with the sea in the background.

Bethan throughout the ages, captured forever in these pictures. And collected here, as if to taunt him.

He didn't think a single picture had ever been taken of him as a child, much less saved. Or displayed. And he didn't feel sorry for himself about that, because he'd always thought such things were silly. That no one really cared that much to look at them anyway.

But here, standing in this room while Bethan rifled

through her mother's things, it all struck him in a different way. Because seeing her in all her different phases made him . . . Well. It was that same nostalgia for things that weren't his. That same longing that seemed to bloom into a kind of ache, because there was something about the progression. From a little girl with a gap-toothed smile and pigtails to the sleek Army Ranger. He could see the little girl in the Army Ranger's face. And the suggestion of the Army Ranger to come in that little girl, too.

It had never occurred to him that memory could be more than a grim, harsh weapon. That it could be a bow, tying things together and making them shine.

And he thought, again, that it was possible he wasn't going to survive this after all—that she had already taken him out when whole wars had tried and failed to do the same—when he heard the sound of that big wooden door creaking open.

He wheeled around and found Bethan doing the same. Their eyes met in a flash, and Jonas didn't think. He hit the ground behind the couch, hoping that whoever came in wouldn't head for the fireplace the way he had.

He froze, still and silent, as someone charged down that short hall, aware that Bethan hadn't tried to hide herself, which meant she was facing the intruder.

There was a silence. But not a good one.

An indrawn breath.

Jonas tensed.

And then, "What on earth do you think you're doing in here?"

Thirteen

Bethan smiled blandly at Charlotte, the housekeeper, who was literally bristling where she stood at the end of the hallway.

"Oh, hello, Charlotte," she said mildly. "I didn't think you worked this late. I hope my parents pay you a lot of overtime."

"I'll ask again," Charlotte said, and it was very interesting to watch the woman without her customary polish. Without that obsequious smile, or all that service she clearly prided herself on. Or usually did, anyway. "What are you doing in your mother's office?"

Jonas had been over there looking at likely embarrassing pictures over the fireplace, and that had given Bethan the idea. She didn't glance in his direction, because she didn't want Charlotte to see that he was hiding there, so Bethan only smiled down at the picture she'd swiped from her mother's desk.

"This was taken on their first date," she said softly. It was true. She held a picture of her parents taken approximately a thousand years ago. They were both so young they practically squeaked. And more, they glowed with the off-handed attractiveness of youth. He was handsome and she was pretty, and it was hard to reconcile these strange, bright creatures, who looked as if they were up to a bit of mischief, with her far more restrained parents.

She set the frame back down and turned that smile back on Charlotte. "I remember when I was much younger than they are in this picture. Now I'm older. I guess that's the way of things, but it feels weird."

But the housekeeper was staring back at her, still bristling with affront, and did not look particularly charmed by Bethan's reminiscing. "Mrs. Wilcox does not like anyone in her office."

Bethan didn't have to think about her *character* in this instance. Her smile faded a little as she regarded this woman who looked ready to storm over, put hands on her, and bodily remove her, if necessary.

"Charlotte." Bethan reminded herself to be kind. "This is my parents' house. I understand that you work for them, and clearly they have certain expectations of you. But if I want to come in here and look at family pictures because I'm full of nostalgia, that's what I'm going to do. With or without permission."

"I'm afraid that's not acceptable."

"My little sister is getting married. I brought a man home to meet my father, for the first time ever." It occurred to her that both of those things might, in fact, be factors in how she was feeling—and she wished she hadn't said them with Jonas listening. But she pushed on. "It's an emotional time, Charlotte, and having you try to tell me how to behave in the house where I grew up does not help."

"The general and Mrs. Wilcox take their privacy very seriously," the other woman said stiffly.

"They're welcome to take it up with me, then," Bethan

retorted. But then she summoned her smile again. "Don't worry, I'll let myself out."

And then there was a bit of a staring contest. Bethan felt her eyebrows inch higher and higher on her brow, and for a moment, she thought Charlotte wasn't going to give in. It made her wonder what the other woman's actual job here was.

But the longer the silence between them dragged out, the more she could see Charlotte waver. Until finally, she inclined her head sharply, turned with near-military precision, and then stalked away.

Bethan waited until the door closed behind her. Then went over to make sure that she hadn't simply opened and shut it but stayed inside. But the small hallway was empty. When she came back into the room, it was just in time to watch as Jonas rose from his hiding place.

Like some kind of mythical creature. Lethal. Glorious. A song to be sung, an epic tale to be told.

Settle down, she ordered herself.

"Way to handle the staff," he said dryly. "I bet they taught you that in finishing school."

Bethan opted not to argue about the kinds of schools she'd attended. "Something about her rubs me the wrong way. It's not that I think she's some kind of operative, necessarily. But I'm their daughter."

"Did you get what you needed?" Jonas asked in his usual cool, unbothered way. As if the petty concerns of mere mortals were beneath him.

Maybe someday she would understand why she found that so compelling.

Maybe someday she wouldn't look to him for all the things the two of them would never be.

But none of that mattered. Not tonight.

"As expected, my mother has a spreadsheet," she said instead, briskly. Professionally. "How much do you want to bet our favorite CEO likes to keep tabs on people's bed-rooms?"

Jonas's eyes gleamed. "Seems as good a place to start as any."

If she was interpreting laconic Jonas-speak correctly, that meant he was thrilled.

They made their way back into the main part of the house, skirting what sounded like security doing a sweep—or Charlotte the housekeeper, Bethan thought, wandering around and sticking her nose in.

There were two likely culprits staying in the house, according to her mother's notes in elegant handwriting that Bethan could have identified from a mile off. Lewis Stapleton was here with his full-on Texas wife and his staff, up in one of the expansive guest suites on the second floor of the main house. Dominic Carter and two of his aides had been accorded similar accommodations on the opposite side of the same floor.

But since Dominic Carter was the newest arrival, and they hadn't been surveilled by Lewis Stapleton or anyone else before now, they decided to start with him.

"The Carter party is in the Bougainvillea Suite," she told Jonas.

He grunted. "You grew up in a hotel suite?"

"Certainly not." Bethan stopped before she led him up the side stairs. Not the staff stairs, but the family stairs. The sweeping grand staircase was far too dramatic for daily use. "Most of the suites are part of the renovation. I think my childhood bedroom still exists, but I also think it's been repurposed. As the sitting room, or possibly staff quarters."

Jonas studied her in that way that always made her fight off a shiver. "The way you say that makes me think you're not a fan."

Bethan knew that he'd been faking it for the cameras this last time, but that didn't change the fact that his mouth had been on her. All over her. She knew what that felt like now. She knew where it could lead when there were no cameras involved. And she thought she was holding herself together pretty well, all things considered. After all these years and everything that had happened between them, to find out that she'd been right all along about what was beneath that dark gaze of his was . . . spectacular.

But she remembered herself. And more to the point, she remembered that he'd decided to act like all he'd done was scratch an itch.

"I left here and never meant to return," she told him, pleased with how calm she sounded. "I don't really care what they did with the room, if that's what you're asking."

His gaze moved over her. "Seems like you had a lot of rooms to choose from."

Bethan rolled her eyes. "Do you expect me to apologize for the house my parents bought when I was a teenager and renovated when I was gone?"

"I don't expect you to do anything."

"Of course not. Because then you might have to admit that you actually have a feeling about something. And obviously, the whole world would immediately explode."

All they had to do was go up a flight of stairs. Dominic Carter was staying in the suite directly above them. They could do what they'd come here to do—create the necessary diversion, sweep the rooms, and cut the feed if this was where it originated. If the feed wasn't coming from his rooms, they could check the rest of the guest suites and then fan out to the cottages. A whole night of tasks to complete—possibly while all the suites and rooms were occupied. It was right up their alley.

But neither one of them moved.

Jonas's eyebrows rose on that stark, stunning face of his, all those sharp brown planes and the impossible sensuality of his mouth. That she'd now tasted.

She couldn't say she had regrets. But she couldn't seem to get past it, either.

"Is this about what happened earlier?" His voice was cold. "While we're in the middle of an operation?"

Bethan didn't think. She surged forward so she could get her face as close to his as possible, without actually poking him in the chest like a cartoon villain.

Though she thought about it.

"Don't you dare patronize me," she clipped at him. "I get that it's convenient for you to pretend that you're somehow above all this. But the only real difference between yesterday and today in terms of operational functionality is that we're being honest about this situation. You've been treating me differently from the rest of the team as long as you've known me. And yes, I'm including way back when. It has nothing to do with men and women in combat roles, and it never has."

She pulled in a breath, not expecting to see anything on his face. Not expecting anything at all. "It has to do with you, Jonas. And me. That's always been a thing. It always will be. And it's certainly not going to change now, while the operation in question is in my parents' house."

"Bethan," he began, and she took a strange sort of solace from the fact that he didn't sound as frigid as he usually did. How sad was that?

But he didn't finish what he was about to say, because a door opened. Directly across from the small hall where they were standing.

"There you are, Bethan," her mother said in her cultured tones. "We've been looking all over for you."

Bethan was still seething inside, whether she wanted to admit it or not, and more than spoiling for a fight. Jonas was maddening. The situation was worse, though she supposed it was the same as it always had been. Maybe that was *why* it was worse.

But she couldn't deal with any of that—with *him*—because she had to plaster a smile on her face and try to look as if it made all the sense in the world that she was standing here, in the little back corridor that was for family only. Where they could go back and forth without staff or guests any the wiser.

"Looking for me?" she asked lightly, though it cost her. "Why?"

Birdie opened the door wider, and Bethan saw that her entire family was gathered in the sitting room adjacent to her father's office.

"We're having a family summit," Ellen said, waving the tumbler in her hand a little too carelessly. Next to her, Matthew was looking on indulgently while rattling the ice cubes in his own drink.

"We've been trying to contact you all evening," Birdie continued. "It's not like you to have your phone switched off."

Because it was never switched off. Which was how Bethan knew her mother was, at best, exaggerating. If she'd texted Bethan, it could only have been in the last hour—while her cell phone was back in the room in the clutch she'd discarded once she and Jonas had returned from town.

"My fault," Jonas said from behind her. Bethan wished she had a word to describe what it was like to be this annoyed by someone and yet absurdly comforted when his hand came around to rest on her hip. Like a real couple. "We've been out to dinner, and I'll admit, I like to keep her attention on me."

If Bethan let herself think about that—about all her attention on him, or his insisting upon it in some alternate reality where this relationship they were faking was who they actually were—but she couldn't. She couldn't go there.

He ushered her into the room with his hand a faint weight in the small of her back, and she let him do it while her mind raced. It was impossible not to wonder if, after all, her family was responsible for those cameras. But as she scanned all the faces around her, no one seemed to look anything but mildly interested that Jonas had a phone rule.

No one seemed to think that they ought to have been tucked up in a hot tub, even now, but she figured it wouldn't hurt to cover their bases.

"We've been having a very Santa Barbara evening," she told them, lying brightly. "We had dinner in town. Then we wandered State Street, looking at all the shops. We went down to the beach to say hello to the Pacific Ocean, then came back to make use of that hot tub on our patio. Then I decided it was a fine time to take Jonas on a nostalgic tour of the house I grew up in. Although to be honest, so much of it's changed now that it's hard to be too sentimental."

"It's practically a hotel," Ellen agreed. She eyed their mother. "A very pretty boutique hotel, of course."

Jonas pulled his phone from his pocket, making a show of checking to see if it was switched on. She saw him send a swift text and knew that he was making sure Rory and the rest handled those cameras. If she had to bet, she'd say he told them to create some kind of disturbance in that feed because they weren't going to be able to track it as planned.

"Sit down, sit down," her father said in his overly hearty host voice. He handed out drinks, then settled back in the armchair he'd vacated, smiling a bit indulgently. "We're plotting out a war, apparently."

"Not a real war," Ellen said with that smirk of hers that it turned out Bethan was very fond of. "Down, military people. No need to call in the cavalry."

Bethan found herself exchanging glances with her father and Jonas, which unsettled her. They were two of the most maddening men she'd ever met, she had complicated relationships with both of them, but if she wasn't mistaken, all the soldiers in the room were . . . having a moment.

She didn't know where to put that. She would have said—she *had* said, repeatedly—that her father bent over backward to act as if he didn't have a daughter who had ever gone near the military.

"It's time to separate," Matthew intoned. "Since the girls

are doing their thing, I'm hoping you'll join my groomsmen and me."

It took Bethan a long moment to realize that her soon-to-be brother-in-law was addressing Jonas. And if it took her a long moment, she could see that it was going to take Jonas a whole lot more than that.

"Are you and your groomsmen doing something exciting?" Bethan asked when Jonas only stared.

"Matthew and I thought it would be fun to split things up for the last time," Ellen said. Bethan watched the way her sister smiled at her fiancé. She'd always thought that smile had to be fake. A show of some kind, but she was revising her opinion. Because when Ellen smiled at Matthew, it was softer. Her nose wrinkled. She didn't look like the Ellen that Bethan knew, but maybe that was the point. "All the girls and all the boys are going to split up. We'll see each other tomorrow night at the rehearsal dinner, then again at the wedding."

"What do you mean by *split up*?" Jonas asked, sounding utterly baffled.

And he made Bethan's heart ache. She suspected he really was baffled. By everything that was happening here.

"A reasonable question," the general said, getting a sharp look from his wife in return.

"I think it's a lovely custom," Birdie said, as if that settled it. "Bethan, just throw a few things in a bag."

"You don't need anything in a bag," Ellen protested, clearly not seeing the way Bethan blinked at that. "You can just come back to the vineyard house with me. You can share my bed. And don't worry, I'm no longer the cover hog I was when I was a kid."

"It will be fun," Matthew was saying in an undertone to Jonas, because none of these people seemed to understand that both Bethan and Jonas could kill all of them. With very little effort. "Maybe a hike, maybe shoot some pool. Stuff like that."

"Matthew and his groomsmen are staying in a hotel about ten minutes away," Birdie chimed in. "Now that we've found you, he can give you a ride tonight."

"To the hotel that's ten minutes away," Jonas said, sounding . . . wooden. Maybe only she could see that he was as baffled as he was horrified. "So that we can . . ."

"Bond," Bethan told him, suddenly seized with a sense of what she could only assume was mischief. Yes, at his expense. It felt like the logical response to all these years of nonsense. "How fun, honey. Don't you think?"

And she smiled sunnily at him when he shifted that dark, murderous glare to her.

After they'd all sat around in that sitting room talking wedding details to death, and after Jonas had been forced to smile and tell his loud jokes before heading off with Matthew, Bethan found herself bundled off to the vineyard house with all her sister's friends—and a shared bed. Which she lay in while her sister snored gently beside her and tried to imagine Jonas doing frat boy things.

She fell asleep with a smile on her face.

The following morning, all the bridesmaids got up and insisted that it was time for a morning run.

"Fun run!" one of her sister's blonder friends squealed.

Bethan's halfhearted protests that she had to go back to her room to get her running stuff were ignored because they could lend her everything.

"Lucky me," she murmured while Ellen snickered at her.

And then off they all went in a giant pack of giggles to do their fun run, which bore no resemblance to any kind of run Bethan ever did on her own.

"Zoe runs a 5K every two years and thinks she's a marathoner," Ellen muttered under her breath as they all ran about the property like a herd of prey.

"Amazing," Bethan said in return, trying to fit in, but her sister only smirked at her.

"Yeah, yeah. You're a badass and you probably run six marathons every morning."

"I didn't say anything!"

"You don't have to say anything," Ellen retorted with a laugh. "Your entire body says it all for you."

"I do not, in fact, run marathons. Any morning, thank you."

"How many miles do you actually run, then?" Ellen asked, and Bethan recognized the competitive look on her sister's face. As it was so often the same look on her own.

She thought of Isaac's hideous workouts. "I don't only run."

Her sister tilted her head slightly. "All right, then. Let's race."

Bethan let out a laugh before she thought better of it. "I'm not racing you."

Ellen snorted. "Are you afraid I might actually be better at something than you?"

Bethan nudged her with her shoulder. "You're better at a lot of things, El. But probably not physical things."

"Coward," her little sister threw at her, and then took off.

And for a moment, Bethan was torn. She didn't want to race Ellen. Well, that was a lie. She was highly competitive, especially with her sister, and would enjoy nothing more than kicking her butt. But was it worth it? This was Ellen's weekend.

"Who's the badass now?" Ellen yelled over her shoulder.

And that decided it.

Bethan took off. She rounded the bridesmaids and went after Ellen, who was running full out down the side of the vineyard toward the house they'd left earlier. When she got closer, she realized her sister was laughing maniacally as she ran. And when Ellen glanced back over her shoulder, her face was filled with glee.

It was like toppling back in time. Bethan picked up her speed, catching up to Ellen easily and then keeping pace with her. But she found that she was grinning ear to ear herself, because she could remember a thousand races like this one. Ellen, who so often looked ruthless and severe, was lit up.

Bethan was, too. And she found she didn't have it in her to crush her sister the way she knew she could have.

Maybe knowing was good enough.

She stayed at Ellen's side, laughing louder the closer they got to the house. It wasn't the kind of run that should have challenged Bethan at all, but at the same time, she didn't spend a lot of her time laughing this hard while she was running.

Bethan checked her pace right at the end, almost as if she'd stumbled. Ellen screamed out her victory, her arms up in the air, as they both staggered to the door of the old stone house.

For a long moment, there was only panting, laughing, and Ellen grabbing her sides.

"That was amazing," Ellen managed to get out. "I don't even care that you let me win."

"Let you win?" Bethan asked innocently. "Me?"

Ellen launched herself at Bethan then and hugged her, tight.

"I'm glad you're here," she said. A little bit fiercely.

And there was too much *stuff* inside her. All of it a little too unwieldy. Love. Regret. Nostalgia. Hope. Stuff that had everything to do with home, her family, her sister—and nothing to do with Alaska Force.

"Me, too," Bethan said, though it felt inadequate at best.

But the strangest part was, as the day wore on, she found she meant it.

Fourteen

That Jonas might not want to spend all day and into the evening with Matthew and his buddies did not seem to occur to anyone. It was, apparently, one of those ritualistic domestic agreements everyone else seemed to take on the chin. No one questioned it. They all went along with it because . . . that was what people did.

Jonas never felt more like an alien than when watching rational humans respond—usually in the same way—to irrational cues that bypassed him entirely. But while he was irritated with this unexpected, and astounding, wrench in his plans, he didn't have it in him to disengage from the groomsmen the way he knew he could have.

Almost as if, somewhere inside of him, he wanted Bethan's family to think that he really was with her. The way he was pretending he was.

That was the only justification he could come up with to explain why he trailed around Santa Barbara with Matthew and his largely boneheaded friends, engaging in activities he would normally avoid like the plague.

Thus far those had included surfing at the crack of dawn; an enormous breakfast composed entirely of carbs and sugar, which had led to an impromptu pancake-eating contest; immersive video games; a lunch that was more booze than burgers; and now what appeared to be a cutthroat pool competition in a questionable bar.

Jonas had voluntarily done exactly none of those things before. Ever.

He would have opted out of the whole male-bonding experience today, but once Matthew had dragged Jonas back to his hotel the night before, his friends had welcomed Jonas as if it had been their idea to have him as part of their rowdy little gang all along. They reminded him of a litter of puppies, wriggling about, all of them irrepressible and remarkably soft.

But once they incorporated someone into their group, they expected that person to stay with them at all times. Something they policed with the tenacity that would have impressed some battalions Jonas had observed.

"I had to see it for myself," Rory said, grinning widely at Jonas in a dive bar outside the Santa Barbara city limits. The location for the pool tournament, which Jonas could easily have won already. Instead, he was pretending to have the same level of hand–eye coordination as the rest of Matthew's "boys," an experience that was a lot like burying himself headfirst in wet concrete and allowing it to dry all around him. "You said you were in the wedding party now, but I didn't believe it."

"I'm a frat boy now," Jonas replied with a huge grin, slapping Rory on the back. Perhaps harder than necessary, though it fit with his bigger than life, everybody's best friend in a sports bar persona.

"Was there hazing?" Rory asked. "Templeton won't stop texting me, asking if there was hazing."

Jonas was entertained by the notion that Templeton Cross was handling whatever missions he was working on up in Alaska, not to mention his trooper, but was no doubt lighting up rooms with that big laugh of his as he imagined Jonas doing exactly this. Not that he showed it.

"I'm assuming the amount of drinking they do is a form of hazing," he said.

"It's not living unless it's liver failure," Rory agreed.

"What was the situation with the feed?" Jonas asked. He knew that if any of Matthew's friends were watching, as he was sure they were because they were all obsessed with making sure Matthew was appropriately and constantly celebrated, all they would see was friendly, happy Jonas making a new friend at the bar.

"We're interrupting it at random intervals," Rory said, settling in like he was half watching the game on the television and half paying attention to the stranger beside him. "The one in the living room we're keeping steady, but we're making the bedroom one temperamental. It should be impossible to tell if it's a software issue, something about its placement, or even if you're messing with it."

"Perfect."

"Oz did say that he's finding the source of the feed mobile. You know what that means."

"It's on someone's phone." Jonas laughed like Rory had told him a great joke. "Okay. Keep tracking it."

"Will do," Rory replied, signaling the bartender for a beer. "But first I'm going to sit here and watch the game for a minute."

His bland smile made it clear that the game he planned to watch was Jonas pretending a bunch of drunken frat brothers could take him at pool. Or anything else.

Jonas laughed, because all he did in character was laugh, and made his way back to the group of groomsmen to lose in style.

"How was your day as a run-of-the-mill groomsman?" Bethan asked him later that evening, smirking.

The smirk was a gift. It was grounding. Because Jonas was still recovering from the shock of the sight of Bethan dressed in a skimpy little thing that hugged her body and *sparkled*. Little boots that made him remember, in excruciating detail, all the things she was capable of doing with those legs of hers. And her hair a deliberate sort of tousle that he knew perfectly well would have any man who looked at her thinking about what it would be like to get his hands in there.

It was certainly all he could think about.

As if he'd actually gone and turned into a regular man today, despite himself—but Jonas knew it wasn't the frat boys or the beer. It was her.

Always and again, it was her.

His chest felt uncomfortably hollow, which was the last thing he needed at this rehearsal dinner for a wedding that had already required more attendance at various events— not to mention war plotting the night before—than entire years of missions he'd executed.

"I'm apparently an honorary member of Pi Kappa whatever," he said. "Be amazed."

But he couldn't seem to keep himself from smiling at that, and it wasn't as fake as it should have been.

Bethan threaded her arm through his as they walked with everyone else into the grand courtyard of the space Matthew's parents had rented for tonight's dinner. "I really didn't expect there to be quite so much family stuff. Here at this family wedding. I know that sounds ridiculous, but I was under the impression that my family had all agreed on a hands-off policy. Years ago."

Jonas didn't point out that all the hands-off policies he'd ever known about had failed. Spectacularly. All around him.

"This is the part I don't get," he said, even while inside him there was something far more worrying than the usual ice and stone. Or even that hollowness. It was as if something had melted, or the stone had crumbled, but he didn't know what to do about any of that. He'd been playing a part all day, and playing it well, but now she was here. And the way she looked at him, her green eyes too bright and every last inch of her delectable and lethal at once, made him . . . *feel*.

And left him disarmed.

Not a state he enjoyed. Or had experienced very often.

In fact, he'd experienced that sensation more often with her than with anyone else alive, because he usually got the better of individuals who actually disarmed him. And made certain they didn't repeat that favor with anyone else.

"The rehearsal dinner?" Bethan leaned in closer to him, so he could note that she smelled of sunshine and flowers. *Not helpful, idiot.* "Some people only invite out-of-town guests to rehearsal dinners, which is supposedly all that's required. Others don't do anything at all, depending. Matthew's family has obviously taken the opposite approach."

"I don't mean that."

Inside the white-walled courtyard there were flowers bursting everywhere, cheerful lanterns strewn about overhead, and a Spanish-style fountain in the center. It was all very festive and brightly lit, with deferential waitstaff circulating among the guests, bearing platters filled with delicious finger foods and drinks at the ready.

Jonas was used to feeling out of place. Usually he used whatever role he was playing to ease his way, but that felt harder when it was only the two of them. Much harder than it should have been. "You've always made it seem like you don't get along with your family at all."

Bethan wrinkled up her nose. "I don't, really."

And maybe it was something about how intimate all this already was. She was standing so close to him, hugging his arm the way she might have if they really were a couple. And he'd succumbed to that ache inside of him and given in to his darkest yearnings after years of containing those things within him—and the world hadn't ended as he'd expected it would. If anything, all that longing and yearning was worse.

A small taste had only made him want to drown himself in her.

But where he normally might have said something cold or cutting to put them back on footing he understood, tonight he studied her face instead.

"Maybe you don't want to live with them again, but you all seem to get along just fine," he said. The way a boyfriend might because he was *concerned* about his girlfriend and *invested* in her feelings. About anything and everything. It should have felt as foreign to him as all the rest of the parts he played on demand, but it didn't. Because it was Bethan. "Even your father."

"Did you see it when the general actually acknowledged me like I was a fellow soldier?" She laughed. "He must have been drunk."

"I don't think he knows what to do," Jonas heard himself saying, still acting like he was this alternate version of himself, who not only *cared about things* but cared about them to such an extent that he was conducting an entire conversation about feelings. Other people's feelings that didn't affect him in any way. "He knows how to treat soldiers and underlings, but you're his daughter. I don't think he knows how to feel about it."

Bethan gazed at him in wonder. "Are you, Jonas Crow, talking about . . . feelings? Of your own accord?"

He regretted it. Deeply. But now he was in it, so he kept going. "He told me—"

"He *told* you? You had conversations about your feelings? With my father?"

His jaw ached from gritting his teeth so hard. "He said he would hire you himself if you were anyone else. But instead, he worries about you, because you're his . . ." But he was doing the thing, wasn't he? There was no point avoiding the meat of it. He cleared his throat. "You're his baby girl. That's a direct quote. And if you keep looking at me like that—"

"He really said that?"

Jonas didn't know what to do with all of this . . . stuff. Like the way Bethan, the toughest and most dangerous woman he'd ever known, was suddenly staring at him with her eyes wide and soft when he knew she was showing him the deepest, farthest reaches of her heart.

He didn't want that. Surely he didn't want any part of that. Because he didn't know what to do with any of these things, and he certainly didn't know what to do with his own heart, stomping wildly and uncomfortably in his chest.

"Jonas," Bethan said then, her voice soft, too.

He was terribly afraid that she was the thing that was melting him and changing him. That she was the thing that was turning him inside out, and if he didn't do something about it, what would become of him? Where would it end? He needed to shove her away from him. Physically, mentally, and certainly emotionally. He never should have volunteered for this role in the first place.

The list of things he never should have done was getting far too long. And she was the only item on that list that made him want to repeat the same mistake. Jonas had never had regrets before. Not until her.

But he couldn't seem to do anything but gaze down at her, soft and sparkly tonight, and wait to see how she would ruin him next.

"I'm going to have to steal her away," came a singsong voice with a giggle.

Jonas watched—as if he were underwater, the way he'd spent a significant portion of his military career—as one of Ellen's friends took Bethan by the hand, her high ponytail bobbing but not quite matching the high-pitched elevation of her voice.

He saw the same bemused sort of amusement in Bethan's

gaze, very similar to the expression he was pretty sure he'd been wearing all day.

"Oh, right," Bethan said. Her lips curved. "Important bridesmaid stuff."

"Don't worry," the other girl said brightly. "We'll make sure you know the whole song."

Bethan looked back at him as she let the other girl drag her away, her eyes wide. *The whole song*, she mouthed.

And he supposed it told him everything he needed to know about his current untenable emotional state that he stood there a moment *gazing after her*.

He shook himself, hopefully not visibly. When he was a man widely praised for his stillness. *Get yourself right*, he ordered himself darkly. *Now*. Because it didn't matter what Bethan was doing. Jonas was now left to his own devices in the middle of a fancy cocktail party, and he wasn't here to enjoy the appetizers.

What galled him was how long it took him to decide to stop standing around, thinking about his *feelings*, God help him, and get back to work.

He made his way around the courtyard, happily slipping back into his loud, carefree character, because that was a hell of a lot easier than navigating whatever was happening inside him tonight. He reassessed every general and high-ranking military officer there, including General Wilcox. He paid closer attention to all of Matthew's buddies now that they were dressed and composed after their long day of frat boy shenanigans. He found himself engaged in a long conversation with self-proclaimed *head drug dealer* Lewis Stapleton, because despite himself, he liked the man's Texan bluster.

He had a long conversation with Birdie about the alchemy of roses and a particular rosebush she'd grown from a cutting taken from her grandfather's garden.

"I had no idea roses were their own histories," he said.

"Roses are whatever we allow them to be," Birdie replied with a smile he found particularly enigmatic, especially when he followed her gaze across the party to where her daughters were standing next to each other, laughing, looking like two unique renditions of the same theme. "Thorns and all."

Jonas told himself he didn't *want* to know what that meant.

The friendly staff was just rounding up the guests, asking them all to proceed from this courtyard to the next in this particularly Southern California space, when he came face-to-face with Dominic Carter.

At last.

Jonas didn't know what he'd expected, but it wasn't what he got. The other man grinned broadly, reached out his hand, and looked absolutely delighted to see Jonas.

As if they were long-lost friends.

"I hear we're in the same business," Dominic said. Jovially.

He looked exactly like every picture Jonas had studied of him, which was rarely true. He was neither overly jacked with muscle nor soft and paunchy. He had the sort of face that could belong to either a middle-manager accountant from a pleasant suburb somewhere or a CIA agent. He was perfectly friendly—so friendly, in fact, that it took Jonas a moment to process that they were roughly the same size.

An interesting tidbit, because if asked, Jonas would have docked the man a few inches and some width based on the khakis he wore and one of those strange collared T-shirts that made Jonas automatically consider a man soft and useless. But it also had to have something to do with the way the other man held himself.

Meaning it had to be deliberate.

Then he took Dominic's hand to shake it, and he knew instantly that everything about the way this man presented himself was a lie.

Because there was something about the way he shook Jonas's hand. There was a certain tension, maybe, or understanding that flared there between them. The kind of knowledge that could be transmitted only physically—and that couldn't be concealed. Dominic Carter was going out of his way to appear soft and meek, but he'd seen some action.

More than *some*, Jonas would bet.

"Were you in the service?" Jonas asked.

The other man grinned self-deprecatingly. "Not me. I work with a lot of military folks, but never had the honor of serving myself."

But Jonas didn't believe him.

"I'm based in Annapolis," Carter continued conversationally. "I don't get out to Seattle much, but I'd love to get a good foothold on the West Coast. We should sit down sometime, throw a few ideas around."

"You looking to expand?" Jonas asked, grinning widely, the way he would if he were running a security company.

Dominic Carter laughed. "Always looking to be better, friend. Isn't that the meaning of life?"

Jonas did not say that as far as he knew, life had meaning only if it was lived honestly, because that seemed a little hypocritical under the circumstances.

They both laughed heartily, then shook hands again, which was the universally preferred method of communication among a certain set of wealthy, connected men. But when Carter got caught up in another group of far more important people making their way to the next stage of the party, Jonas held himself back.

He waited until most of the crowd had vacated the first courtyard, took out his phone, and went out into the street.

Where he did a quick head-to-toe check to make sure no one had planted any listening devices on him with all that shoulder-slapping and handshaking, and then he called in.

"Report," Isaac said when he answered.

"This is a gut feeling," Jonas replied, looking back toward the courtyard he'd just left as if there were eyes on him, even now. "But I think we found our guy."

Fifteen

Bethan woke up early on the day of the wedding and crept out of the vineyard house before dawn. Her sister was still sleeping off the rehearsal dinner's slight overindulgence in the vast king bed they were sharing, and Bethan thought Ellen might wake up when she moved—but Ellen only flopped over, then began to snore.

Bethan slipped out into what was left of the night, taking another moment to breathe in what could only be California, smelling sunbaked even in the dark. The last of the night-blooming jasmine, the hint of sage and rosemary, and the rich earth all around. Maybe not the place she wanted to call home, but part of her nonetheless.

Jonas met her by the pool house, as arranged. And if anyone saw them, they would look like lovers who couldn't bear to spend a night apart. Bethan told herself that attempting to get into *that* character role was her hardest challenge yet.

"I think he's hiding something," Jonas said after he gave her a breakdown of his interactions with Dominic Carter the night before, and what he and the rest of the team had concluded while Bethan had been off singing ridiculous sorority songs and generally making a fool of herself.

That she'd laughed a whole lot and actually valued getting the opportunity to spend time with her sister—more than she'd thought she would—was neither here nor there. Bethan wasn't supposed to feel these things while she was on a job. She did her best to shove it all aside.

And while she was at it, also not ogle Jonas in his running gear.

"Like, hopefully, our scientist and his sister?" she asked instead, the way an operative who was focused on the mission might.

"I wouldn't be surprised." Jonas moved closer to her and took her hand, which Bethan knew perfectly well was about optics, not inclination. She knew that. And still his touch jolted straight through her. "He's lying about his background, and I don't understand why. Not in this group, anyway. He must have known that pretending he didn't have any kind of serious action in his background is unbelievable."

"Wouldn't we know if he had military service in his background? Even if he tried to downplay it?"

"Not if he didn't have military service," Jonas said flatly. "There are a lot of would-be washouts who take it upon themselves to sell their guns and wannabe Delta Force egos to the highest bidder."

Bethan didn't waste her breath condemning that course of action. Her views on mercenaries should have been perfectly clear. Because she wasn't one, when she could have been. They all could have been.

"Okay," she said instead. "Ellen grew up with a military dad. I don't think it's going to be too surprising to her if I have stuff to do that isn't about her wedding day. Kind of par for the course around here."

"You don't have to do anything," Jonas replied. Gruffly,

Bethan thought, but she was ignoring that. She was ignoring anything and everything that wasn't the job, because if she didn't, she thought the fact that they'd actually, finally, kissed and had sex might kill her. "You're doing what you're supposed to be doing."

"What I'm doing is killing time being a part of the bridal party, Jonas." She was not remembering what it had felt like when he'd driven himself inside her. She was *not.* "That's not exactly following the operational handbook."

"It's your sister's wedding." And Jonas looked unduly fierce when she frowned at him. "We already have a team on the ground here. It would be unnecessarily risky to infiltrate the house during the wedding—but even if they went ahead and risked it, I find it hard to believe they could find anything we didn't. If Carter is our guy, I have to think that the cameras in the room were only a part of it. He went out of his way to let me know he knew who I was. I expect he'll do the same to you."

"I hope he does," Bethan replied.

"Not sure what message that is, but he's sending it."

"I can't wait."

And for a second, just a stray second there in the darkness, she thought she saw all kinds of things in Jonas's gaze. As if they were both remembering the way he'd kissed her. The wildfire that had exploded between them—

But in the next moment he was gone, melting off into the shadows like he'd never been there at all. And it took a little while for Bethan to start breathing again, much less breathing normally.

She took her time walking back to the vineyard house as the sky above her started to lighten, a band of bluer dark beginning to spread above the eastern hills. Bethan was aware of entirely too many competing emotions rocketing around inside her as she moved. She wanted to go back to Alaska, where she could sink back into her preferred routine and stop feeling all these . . . *things*. She wanted to go back to the person she'd been when she'd left Alaska, so absolutely certain of where she stood in this family and what they all meant to her—or didn't. The past few days here had shifted everything around. Instead of showing her that she'd been right about her family, what she kept being shown was that her family was . . . just a family. No better or worse than anyone else's. Just particular to her.

It was funny how she found that a whole lot harder to take than the notion that her father might be involved in something evil.

And all of her family stuff was a lot easier to consider—a lot less dangerous and far less explosive—than what had happened between her and Jonas.

She crept back into the house and crawled into her side of the bed again, so that when Ellen woke up a few hours later she would never know that Bethan had been gone.

"Hey," Bethan said, grinning when Ellen finally blinked her eyes open. "Do you really want to sleep in today? I feel like there's something you're supposed to be doing."

Ellen smiled, a slow sort of brightening that took over her whole face and made Bethan feel guilty she'd ever thought her sister was marrying Matthew for his money and status. Or only for that. "I can't believe I'm getting *married*."

"In style," Bethan agreed.

"I guess I better get up, then." Ellen threw her arms over her head and stretched. "I'm pretty sure I have about two hundred hours of hair and makeup to sit through." Her smile widened when Bethan made a face. "And don't go imagining you're immune, big sister. So do you."

She wasn't kidding. Hours upon hours later, Bethan had subjected herself to more time than any human being should ever spend getting ready for anything. She had personally gotten ready for wars with less prep work.

Which only meant that it was time for pictures.

"So," said her mother as they stood around watching the

photographer arrange and then rearrange Ellen's train beneath a brace of scenic palm trees.

"That sounds ominous," Bethan murmured.

Birdie arched a brow. "Ellen looks very happy. I only wonder if you might seek the same sort of happiness someday."

Bethan opened her mouth to shoot back the usual retorts but paused instead.

"Probably not the same happiness," she said softly, after that pause. "Because El and I aren't the same, Mom."

"Of course you're not the same," her mother said with her usual brisk impatience, done up as genteel disapproval. "I think you know that wasn't what I meant."

And a week ago, Bethan would have shot back something about how she was perfectly happy as she was. She would have figured this was the perfect opportunity to extol the virtues of her very active, occasionally violent life, complete with its solitude and risks.

But she thought of what Jonas had said about her father. About the possibility that what she'd always seen as his disinterest in her military career was something else entirely. Was it really possible that she'd been misreading her parents her whole life?

Why not? asked a voice inside. *You've been absolutely positive that they've been misreading you.*

She slipped an arm around her mother's trim waist, smiling when Birdie looked startled. "You don't have to worry about me, Mom. I figured out a long time ago how to make myself happy, so I do."

And if she ignored all the Jonas-shaped things in her life, that was true.

"You've always been like that," Birdie said with what actually looked like a fond smile. "So determined and individual since the day you arrived. It was always Ellen who fell apart when things didn't go her way. Never you."

They both looked toward Ellen then. Bethan blinked a

bit, because she thought of her sister as unflappable. A rock. Then again, there was all that anxiety and the obsession with her own eternal skinniness—a hallmark of control issues. Maybe the real lesson here was that no one was the same as Bethan had thought they were when she was a teenager, herself included.

"I don't like to think about what you do for work because it's hard to imagine you out there, involved in the kinds of things you must be involved in." Birdie shook her head. "But it's thinking of you all alone afterward that truly worries me."

"But I'm not alone," Bethan protested.

Her mother patted her hand. "Not now. Your father and I are quite impressed with your Jonas. The general says that he might walk a line or two, but never crosses it."

Bethan wanted terribly to tell her mother that it was all an act. That the real Jonas Crow went nowhere near any kind of line and never would. But she didn't. She couldn't.

Just like she couldn't tell her mother that it wasn't just Jonas—who wasn't hers, not that way—who kept her from feeling alone. It was all of Alaska Force. Because of them she'd found a home, at last, where she could be everything that she was without apology.

But she knew if she said that, it would sound far too much like an accusation, so instead, she smiled at her mother and didn't correct her. And knew full well that the Bethan who had arrived here a week ago would not have made the same choice.

Then, finally, Ellen was getting married.

Bethan stood beside her, there on the altar they'd created, with a perfect rolling view of the lovely Santa Barbara vineyards, hills, and sea, and for that short little slice of time, she took pleasure in being nothing at all but Ellen Wilcox's sister.

But she was happier to see Jonas than she probably should have been as the reception began.

For purely operational purposes, she assured herself.

But it wasn't operational oversight that had her throat going dry as she wound her way through the crowd that was already gathered under the big tent the staff had set up on the far end of the grass, up above the vineyard house, with spectacular views in every direction as the sun sank toward the sea.

Jonas was dressed in a dark suit that made the most of his stupendous form. It had obviously been made to his precise specifications, and she tried to take that on board. But it was too much. The idea of Jonas Crow submitting himself to a tailor's ministrations, much less acknowledging that such things as *bespoke attire* existed in the first place, refused to come together in her head.

But however it had happened, there was no denying the fact that he eclipsed every other man there.

That dark hair of his gleamed, his brown skin making his black eyes and high cheekbones almost too beautiful to bear. And he was playing his role to the hilt, so that the sensual mouth she knew the feeling of now was curved into all kinds of improbable, smiling shapes.

Jonas and yet not Jonas, with every last inch of him shown off to perfection.

It really wasn't fair.

Bethan was a healthy woman. She had healthy desires. And yet the only object of those desires was the one man in all the world who wanted nothing to do with her, and had still turned her inside out with a single kiss. Good thing she'd been trained, because no matter what turmoil might be going on inside her, she knew there was a smile plastered across her face, as befit the maid of honor at this wedding.

When she arrived at Jonas's side, that black gaze of his was hot in a way that made everything inside her seize, then shiver. He handed her a glass of wine with a certain proprietary air that played up more of that intimacy that he was entirely too good at faking.

Not so good at doing, *though*, she thought. Then ordered herself to stop thinking.

"What's the report?" she asked as she lifted the glass to her lips.

"Oz is deep-diving into Carter's past. But obviously the smart take is that no way did he stash Sowande anywhere near his base of operations in Annapolis. That would be a rookie move, and no one who can disguise his real identity like this is a rookie."

"Agreed." She tipped her head back, like Jonas was whispering sweet nothings her way, and smiled. "Do you think we're going to flush him out this weekend? Seems unlikely."

"I don't like him," Jonas said flatly. "Everything about him was off. If he was threatened enough to bug our rooms, I have to think that means he's on edge."

"*On edge* is something we can use," Bethan agreed.

But in the meantime, there was the wedding reception to survive. There were all her parents' friends who found their way to Bethan's side to exclaim over her—and get an eyeful of Jonas while they were at it. There were her sister's friends, from childhood and beyond, whom Bethan felt compelled to charm as best she could, as if she were a hostess alongside her parents.

She wondered how the Bethan she'd been a week ago would have handled this—without Fake Jonas as a date tonight and without her mission identity to protect her—and suspected that she would not have been nearly so gracious. She would have found it necessary to assert herself with her sister's friends on the off chance they didn't already know what it was she did for a living. She would have done the same with her parents' friends, even more pointedly, and really, it wasn't pleasant to see herself *quite* so clearly.

Not when it came to her behavior, and certainly not when it came to her poor heart.

"Are you nervous about your speech?" Jonas asked

sometime later, when the initial celebratory cocktail hour had ended and they were all being politely directed toward their seats.

"Public speaking doesn't make me nervous." Bethan grinned at him. "It's not getting punched in the face, is it? Or having a sniper lay down fire from some unreachable post."

"Amen," Jonas replied, the smile on his face not making his tone any less taciturn.

It was the *touching* she resented. He was playing a part, as she had to continually remind herself, but there she was, reacting like a real girlfriend every time he leaned too close. Every time he put his hand on her leg, or around the back of her chair, or played with her fingers on the table.

There were too many weak and desperate places in her heart, she understood. Filled with *maybes*. And *almosts*. And *what abouts* . . .

But soon enough this wedding weekend would end, and everything would go back to the way it usually was. Jonas would disappear in plain sight. He would speak only in the context of missions or to Isaac and Templeton. He would keep his distance from her everywhere except in the field, and even then only when under literal enemy fire.

And Bethan would have to find a way to accept that. Again.

But first she had to stand up beneath this tent and give a little speech. She and Matthew's best man exchanged glances down the length of the wedding party's table, pantomimed what she assumed was a schedule, and then she rose as all around her, glasses were clinked together. The smiling wedding planner handed her a microphone. A sea of faces shimmered there before her.

"For anyone who doesn't know me," she said into the mic, smiling broadly—and this time, not because she was playing a role, "I'm Bethan. Ellen's older sister. The maid of honor, but you already know that because all my sister's ladies are dressed in that glorious magenta but I, and I alone, get to wear this violet."

She swished her dress in emphasis. Ellen was smirking at her from the center of the high table, but the rest of the crowd was laughing. Bethan let her gaze move over the nearest tables, and then stopped, because she found Dominic Carter.

Who was not laughing. He was staring straight at her with an intensity that made her entire body take notice. A prickle ran down her back, but she fought to keep herself from reacting visibly. She made herself keep looking around as if she hadn't noticed him.

But there was something off all right. There was something wrong.

Because Dominic Carter was looking at her as if she were a significant personal threat. When all she should have been to him, at best, was a member of a team he'd somehow played—assuming he was behind the Sowandes' abduction from Montreal.

The way her gut twisted, she had to believe it was more than that.

But she was in the middle of her freaking speech. She glanced down at Jonas, who looked like he was smiling up at her supportively, but she could see the intensity in his black gaze. He saw Carter, too. That was something, even if they couldn't do anything about it.

"I've had the pleasure of knowing Ellen for my entire life," she told the wedding guests. "But somehow, it feels as if Matthew has known her longer, and loved her so well, all that time. Which is hard to imagine, since I know they met in college, while El was in her sorority sister phase."

Her bridesmaids broke out into one of their sorority songs while the crowd applauded. Ellen and Matthew exchanged a look, smiling brightly at each other.

And this was Bethan's life in a nutshell, wasn't it? Some potentially dangerous individual in front of her, her family—and the man she shouldn't care so much about—all around her, and her forever balancing between the two things. Something she'd never done well, she could admit. She'd usually chosen one or the other. She lost herself in the army, and that had felt too immersive to come back to her family much. But wasn't that what her father did? Maybe she didn't love all of his methods or all of his choices, but somehow, he'd always managed to have a military career and a home life.

She didn't pretend not to know that it was the man beside her who was making her question the way she'd compartmentalized her entire adult life. Because he made her want too many things at once. Sex, sure. But also that intimacy that she knew was the last thing in the world he wanted. Everything she saw in her sister's smile. All the things she'd thought she didn't want, and still didn't—unless it was with Jonas.

And somehow, Dominic Carter giving her the hairy eyeball at her sister's wedding reception while the bridesmaids kept singing their sorority song seemed . . . perfectly normal.

"Then there was her law school phase," Bethan said when the singing wound down. "Which I personally thought was overkill, given that Ellen managed to win every debate that ever happened around the family dinner table." There were more laughs. "Of course, looking back, one of the things that's most impressive about my baby sister is that she always knows what she wants, how to lay out a path to get there, and crucially, always keeps her eyes on that prize, come what may."

Ellen and Matthew laughed at that. All of Ellen's friends were applauding wildly. Even their parents were looking at each other a little ruefully, possibly because there were other words to describe the kind of focus Ellen possessed, and most of them seemed to come back around to *bullheaded*, one way or another.

It occurred to Bethan that might be a family trait.

"I was going to stand up here and take you through a tour of embarrassing Ellen moments," Bethan told the crowd. "That is, after all, my solemn duty as maid of honor."

She looked at her sister, who was shaking her head as if to warn Bethan off—but smiling big and bright, clearly not at all afraid of what Bethan would say next.

Bethan glanced at Dominic Carter to find that yes, his gaze was still on her like a nasty touch.

"But then I remembered that I'm not married yet." Bethan grinned. "And if there's one thing everyone here knows about my sister, it's that she's a very firm believer in consequences. And swift, merciless judgment rendered on any and all betrayals."

"Old Testament, baby," Ellen said from her place at the table, and everyone laughed.

Beside her, Bethan felt Jonas shift, though she was sure no one else could see him move. It was more a coiling of all of his power and strength, the finest weapon she'd ever seen.

Bethan raised her glass. "Please join me in a toast to my marvelous sister, her amazing husband, and all the years of happiness they have ahead of them."

Everyone toasted and cheered as Ellen rose from her seat in an elegant rustle of white to hug Bethan, tight.

"I love you," Ellen said fiercely in her ear.

"I love you, too," Bethan replied.

When she finally sat down again, after more hugs to Matthew and some of the bridesmaids, she could see her parents gazing at her. Fondly, she was forced to conclude. There was no other word for it.

And the revelations kept slamming into her.

If she accepted the possibility that her parents and sister had always been fond of her, she had to accept that a huge part of the awkwardness she'd felt with them was of her own doing. So determined to make herself different. So sure that they had nothing in common.

When the reality was, this wedding, her family—these were the things she fought for. Love. Hope. The possibility of a bright future. How had she spent all this time thinking that what she was doing was no more than proving a point? Bethan knew better than that. Most of the soldiers she'd known were wild, unbridled idealists. At least at first.

Something shifted in her as she thought that, sitting there next to the brooding man who'd told her that he'd enlisted because he was a nihilist.

She didn't believe him.

"What?" he asked when she looked at him, his dark gaze moving over her face.

"Dominic Carter," she replied, because there was no other possible way to answer that question.

"Oh, I see him," Jonas replied. "Seems a little over the top."

"What fascinates me"—and Bethan leaned in close so it looked like she was whispering little love words into his ear—"is what would make a man like him look so personally outraged at us? If it's an Alaska Force thing, theoretically he already won. He should be smirking, not glowering."

"What else could it be?"

But Bethan had no answer for that. And there was nothing to be done about it in the middle of Ellen's wedding reception. There were more speeches, food, and laughter, and then the dancing began.

"I know we didn't discuss this," Bethan said then, leaning closer to Jonas than strictly necessary. "And I don't know how much attention you were paying at the rehearsal. But you do know that as part of the wedding party, I'm going to have to dance in a minute. And when I finish dancing with Marcus over there, who walked me down the aisle—"

"Marcus"—and Jonas's voice was dark—"can't hold his liquor. Or shoot pool."

"When we're done, you're going to have to come out

onto the dance floor. And then dance." He was staring back at her, steel and stone, so she smiled wider. "With me."

"I understand the responsibilities of my position," he said. Perhaps a bit grimly.

"I don't know what that means, Jonas. Not with you."

His grin felt real when she knew better. "I can do anything in character. You should hear me sing."

"Just get ready to dance, swabbie," she told him.

Bethan suffered through the indignity of best man Marcus's too-warm hands and propensity to step on her feet. But soon enough the music changed, and Jonas was there.

And nothing changed. Not the mission, not the party. Not the fact that Dominic Carter was lurking around, doing God only knew what. It was just one song. Three or so short minutes in the grand scheme of things, and nothing more than a performance.

But Jonas pulled her into his arms so easily, it was as if they'd danced together all their lives. His hands moved to the small of her back. Hers moved over his fine shoulders. Then he swayed with her, holding her close, his black eyes lit up from within.

"Jonas . . ." she began, because her heart was beating too hard.

"Just dance," he rumbled.

And that was what they did.

It was like a dream. The music and their bodies swaying together, creating their own melody. There was heat in his eyes, something stark on his face. And her heart kicked her over into the final revelation of the night, but it came in softly. Because she already knew. She'd always known.

And there was no point in saying things he wouldn't hear, so Bethan danced with him instead.

When the music changed yet again, he took her hands from around his neck, lifted them to his mouth, and pressed a kiss there that she told herself was fake.

But she knew it wasn't.

"I'll go get us some drinks," he said in that dark way of his she felt all over, inside and out, and melted off into the crowd.

Bethan had time to take in a single, steadying breath, and then Dominic Carter was there before her.

"Wonderful speech," he said, and he was no longer staring at her the way he had been while she'd given it. Now he was grinning, ear to ear, with his hand extended.

Creepily.

"Thank you." Bethan switched roles—realities—in a heartbeat. She took his hand and shook it, the early-warning system in her gut and down her back in a ruckus. There was nothing specifically wrong with his handshake, but she felt what Jonas had the night before. That it was wrong. *Off*, somehow. Because the man in front of her didn't look like much, but he was shaking her hand in a way that told her, clearly, that there was far more to him. Everything about him was just slightly off, from the rumpled suit to the scuffs on his shoes. She realized she believed none of it. "I'm sorry, I don't know everyone here . . . ?"

"Dominic Carter. I sometimes do business with your father." He chuckled knowingly as he let go of her hand. "Defense stuff, you know. Too boring for a party."

"It's not a party unless we're talking business," Bethan said with a laugh. "At least for me."

They were still on the dance floor, but she made the flash decision to simply stay there. If it was uncomfortable, let him fix it. She would act completely at her ease.

"Oh, right," Carter said, something about his tone getting to her. "I heard about you. You're the sister who enlisted. That must've been something."

Bethan let out a cocktail sort of laugh. "You know basic training." She felt certain he did not. "It's always something."

They were discussing absolutely nothing of significance, and yet she felt as if they were in a deadly battle. She didn't waste time scanning the crowd for Jonas. She knew it was impossible he wasn't aware this was happening.

"Well," Dominic said, still holding her gaze in an aggressive manner completely at odds with the grin, the body language. "A pleasure to make your acquaintance, Bethan. Really."

"You, too," she said sweetly. Innocuously.

They both beamed at each other, fake and weaponized, and Bethan was so tense she was surprised her teeth didn't shatter in her jaw.

The lights in the tent changed with the music, sliding through the crowd and backlighting the man before her. He was turning away, then moving around the bodies before him, the light catching him as he went.

And everything in Bethan screeched to a halt.

She understood then.

In a flash, a vicious scrape of terrible understanding, she got it.

Her heart was pounding. Her breath was coming in short pants that would have scared her, but she couldn't allow that. Not now. Not when the desert was in her head again. The aftermath of the explosion. Crawling out of the wreck, not sure if she was alive or dead, the world gone to dust and fire.

She was hardly aware of it when Jonas appeared beside her.

"What happened?" he demanded.

But Bethan could hardly manage the riot inside of her. The shock. She'd had that flashback the other day, and it hadn't been random.

None of this was random.

"What did he say to you?" Jonas growled, his voice hard.

She made herself turn to him. Focus. "It's him."

"I know. I think it's him, too. He's the only—"

Bethan reached over and took his hands. She knew that

if she ran her fingers up along his arm, she would feel some of his scars. She knew that there were more down one side of his marvelous chest, marking him forever, badges of honor, and memories he had to wear on his skin.

But there were bigger scars.

"Dominic Carter isn't just any random guy," she told him, tense and sure. "He's the individual who blew up our convoy, killed the rest of our squad, and tried to kill you and me, personally. I never saw his face, but I saw him move. Just like tonight. It's *him*, Jonas."

Sixteen

Something thudded through Jonas like a grenade, with no hope of avoiding the coming blast. And when it followed, he was surprised he'd stayed on his feet.

"You killed him," he told Bethan shortly, in case she might have forgotten the long night he'd been only half-conscious for.

"I shot him," she countered. "But I obviously didn't kill him. Because he's here."

Jonas stared down at her, too many fires inside him and no possible way of controlling them. Not if their past was coming back at them like this. Not if this had suddenly gotten a whole lot more personal.

"The other day I was driving back from a lunch with Ellen," she was saying fiercely, as if maybe she needed to convince both of them. "I saw some guy running in the vineyards, and I was suddenly fighting off a flashback. The first I've had in a long time."

"Why didn't you tell me?"

She blinked. "It didn't occur to me to tell you. I'm not in the habit of showing my weaknesses to anyone. Are you?"

Jonas acknowledged that with a faint nod of his head.

"You've looked at a million pictures of this guy with no triggers."

Bethan swallowed, hard. "I never saw his face that night. He was backlit, though I swear he was grinning. Ear to freaking ear. No one else had gotten out of the vehicle fire. But then he came around the side of the vehicle and saw you lying there, and I didn't even think. I fired. Then I dragged you to a more defensible position. But I never saw what happened to his body."

The following morning air support had arrived and taken them to Germany. Jonas had refused to see Bethan and had been sent to rehabilitate himself. Bethan had been sent stateside, no doubt to spend some time debriefing the powers that be about the losses incurred.

He'd spent a lot of time and energy since then trying not to remember the parts of that mission he *could* remember.

Jonas rubbed a hand over his jaw, realizing while he was doing it that the fact he was making strange little gestures meant he was more shaken up than he wanted to admit. Worse, he was sure Bethan knew it, too. "It's unlikely, isn't it? You don't miss."

"I didn't say I missed," she retorted. "I said he's alive. And here at my sister's wedding, deliberately introducing himself to both of us. Almost like a test to see if we recognize him."

He tried to tamp down the raging fire inside him. "You know as well as I do that PTSD can warp things. Any and all things."

"I don't have PTSD," she snapped at him, and then modified her expression into something more smiley and appropriate when the people nearest them glanced in their direction. Her hands were still on his, and he should stop that, too. But it was like he was in quicksand and, for once, had no idea what to do. "And I don't regret shooting the man who tried to kill us. What I regret is that he's alive and well and clearly knows who we are."

Everything in Jonas rejected this scenario. Because it wasn't possible. Because it put Bethan at personal risk, and something in him . . . couldn't handle that.

Really couldn't handle it.

Day-to-day risk was one thing. They were highly trained. Risk was part of their job. And the job was often intense, but it was never personal. Yet if this was the guy she'd shot in that desert and he had as much of a hard-on for Bethan as he'd seemed to throughout her speech, this was an entirely different level of risk.

An unacceptable level.

Bethan moved closer, keeping their hands tucked there between them. "Do you trust me?"

She asked the question softly, almost carelessly, but he was looking at her. And he could see far too much in those eyes of hers.

None of this was safe. None of it was smart.

He wanted to chalk this up to the same nightmares that lived in all of them, and too often snuck their way out into the light of day, no matter how well-adjusted they might have been otherwise. It was one of the burdens they carried. *Chose to carry*, he liked to tell himself.

Jonas would have told anyone else to talk to a therapist first. Or, barring that—because he, personally, would rather punch himself in the face than talk about his thoughts and feelings for any reason—to do a few seriously killer workouts to pump up the endorphins and see things a little more clearly.

But this was Bethan.

"With my life," he said gruffly.

"You trust my instincts in the field, if nothing else, or we wouldn't be able to work together."

"I trust you," he repeated, more darkly. "Whatever else, that's always been true."

"Then trust me," she said urgently.

Something in him seemed to break apart, though he couldn't have said what it was. More fire. More hand grenades he suspected he was throwing himself. Because like most complicated things, in the end, it was really simple.

He had trusted her before they'd gone off in that convoy that fateful day. He'd watched her work, able to access certain assets through their women because she was more than happy to sit down, get to know them, and figure out who they were. She'd been good at psyops. She'd been an excellent attachment to special ops forces, which for a long time was as close to a combat role as she'd gotten.

If he'd had any doubts about her, or her capabilities, she'd cleared them all up that night she'd saved his life. More than once.

And he might have kept his distance from her since she'd turned up in Alaska, but that had always been about him, not her. He didn't want any of that intimacy to spill over into his present-day life, maybe, but he certainly trusted her to do her job and have his back in the field.

Who was he kidding? He'd trusted her all along.

The person he didn't trust was himself.

"I do," he told her, hardly recognizing his own voice. "I do trust you, Bethan."

And he knew—the way he always knew—that the same electricity jolted through her then. It lit him up. Because it felt like far more of a vow than it should have.

The quicksand kept sucking him in deeper.

But all she did was nod. "Okay, then. It's him. You need to call this in. And I need to dance with my sister. Then, Jonas, we need to end this guy. For real this time."

She didn't wait for him to respond to that. She swept up that violet dress of hers and charged back into the thick of the dance floor, where her sister and all the rest of the bridesmaids and assorted other friends were dancing to the band's medley of '80s classics, entirely unaware that anything was happening but this.

It was as it should be. Civilians were supposed to live without the crap he carted around. It was *why* he carried it.

But seeing Bethan out there in the middle of a sea of heedless civilians made something in him . . . break open.

He told himself he had no idea what it was.

Jonas made his way through the reception tent, pulling himself firmly back into character. He smiled and shook hands. He laughed with the groomsmen, who now considered him a buddy. He played his part to the hilt, even when he saw Dominic Carter chatting with one of the generals.

Chatting, when some of the blood on his hands was Jonas's.

He envisioned about seventeen ways he could take the man out, right now, but he didn't. Not only because it would ruin the wedding Bethan clearly wanted to go well, but because they still had a scientist to find.

Once he left the tent, he put significant distance between him and the party, then called into command back in Alaska. And braced himself when Isaac answered.

"You sound like you're at quite a party," his leader and best friend said, clearly enjoying himself. Which he did a lot more lately—something Jonas supported more in theory than when it was aimed at him. "Now I'm trying to imagine you at a party, Jonas. In my head, it's a lot like when we're doing mission breakdowns in the lodge and you stand with your back to a wall, staring blankly."

Jonas waited.

Isaac sighed. "Fine. Report."

Jonas broke down what Bethan had told him as succinctly as possible. And when he was done, there was a silence.

If he were the kind of man to close his eyes and sigh deeply, he would have.

"Tell me that again." Isaac sounded significantly more

intent than he had a moment before, which only boded ill. "You think that Dominic Carter is the individual who blew up your convoy in the desert. Then tried to finish the job, only to be taken out by Bethan, who was not yet an Army Ranger. Is that what you said?"

Jonas glared at the dark night before him, seeing Isaac's face entirely too clearly even though he was all the way north in Alaska. "That's what I said."

If he listened carefully, he was sure he could *hear* his friend's expression. Of pure and unholy glee.

"And you were doing what, exactly, while Bethan was having a little firefight with this guy who might or might not currently be the CEO of the sort of so-called defense outfit that fights its own wars when they feel like it?"

"I remember her shooting him." Jonas's voice was tight and telling, but he couldn't seem to do anything about that. "Or I think I do. I kept going in and out of consciousness."

There was another silence. And Jonas waited for it, because he could feel Isaac's delight from some three thousand miles down the Pacific Coast. As if it were a seismic event.

"Jonas," Isaac said very carefully. And without doing much to hide the laughter in his voice. "Did Bethan save your life? Did she . . . rescue you from the bad man?"

Isaac stopped restraining himself from laughter, assuming he'd even tried to keep it in. Jonas made a few pointed suggestions about both his parentage and potential solitary activities he could enjoy while he laughed it up.

Isaac declined. "Is this why you've been gunning for her since the day she arrived in Alaska? Because she had the bad manners not to leave you to die in your own misery? And then worse, *thrived*?"

"It wasn't misery that was killing me. It was more the C-4 and the secondary explosions."

"This is the best story you've ever told me. I can't wait to tell Templeton. He's going to lose his mind."

There was no point asking Isaac to keep this to himself. He wouldn't have, even if this little slice of history hadn't turned out to be important to their current mission.

"Not much to lose, then," Jonas muttered.

"Obviously I assumed you had a history, but I was thinking more the naked kind," Isaac said. "Not this. Not that she dared see you in a compromised position and live to tell the tale."

Jonas wanted to break things. He wanted to let the quicksand have him. He wanted to turn around right now and go deal with Dominic Carter, because he owed the other man a world of pain, and it would be deeply satisfying to deliver it.

He mostly wanted not to be having this conversation.

"We need to figure out who this guy was back then," Jonas said with as much quiet dignity as he could muster. "And how he got from mercenary work to defense contracts and, more important, weddings like this one."

"I have a lot of follow-up questions," Isaac said.

Jonas couldn't seem to maintain his cool, and that was the most galling part of this whole thing. He'd lived through one of the worst missions of all time with Isaac and Templeton without once losing his cool, despite how very many times he'd thought they were well and truly screwed. But throw Bethan into the mix, and he was a disaster.

"I'm not answering your questions," he snapped. "Things that happened out in the field should stay in the field. Bethan showing up in Alaska complicated that, and I resent it. I don't understand why that requires so much commentary or speculation."

There was a pause. And as it stretched out, Jonas got to think about how incredibly foolish it had been to show his hand like that.

To Isaac Gentry, of all people, who knew him better than almost anyone else alive.

Another reason Jonas preferred to remain unknowable.

"I meant follow-up questions about Dominic Carter's rise to power," Isaac said calmly. Much too calmly for Jonas's peace of mind. "Although now I definitely have other questions, too."

The worst part was knowing he'd brought all this on himself.

"We'll be finishing up the wedding portion of this mission tonight," Jonas managed to say, doing an admirable rendition of the version of him who would never have shown a crack in his armor in the first place. "I think both of us are more than ready to get back to reality."

Or maybe that was the worst part. That he could say things like that, believe them, and also have this other thing in him. The part of him that couldn't seem to let go of how she'd felt in his arms, swaying gently to a love song. The part of him that couldn't get past the way she tasted. The way her scent moved through him, brighter than all those California flowers.

He didn't know how he was going to lock all that away once they made it back to Alaska and returned to form. He only knew he would.

Because what other option was there?

"Listen to me," Isaac said then, and Jonas braced himself at that particular note in his friend's voice. "I know you think that if you allow yourself even one stray second of anything like humanity, it'll be the end of you. I'm going to tell you right now, it's not."

Behind him, the tent was filled with light and music and the sounds of happy people. But Jonas stood outside in the dark, in this place where even the stars hid themselves. Alone.

He reminded himself that this was better. This was normal.

This had always been where he belonged.

Everything else was playacting, and he knew that even if no one else did.

"I have no idea what you're talking about." He was pleased to hear he sounded cool and unbothered, as he should.

"None of us are unmarked," Isaac said quietly. "None of us walked through those fires and came out the other side unscathed. That's not how it works. But all that means is that you were marked. That you have scars. They're part of you, but they're not you, Jonas."

But Jonas had always known exactly who he was. He hadn't had the benefit of a before-and-after scenario. He had no fond memories of a portion of childhood without darkness. He had no fond memories at all until the service.

He wasn't like these people who called him *friend*, and he never had been.

"I have no problem with my scars," Jonas told the man who had led him into more hells than he could count, yet still didn't understand whom he'd had at his back. "I was little better than dead when I started. The fires we walked through didn't mark me any, Isaac. I was born ash, crushed into coal, and never had a single thing to lose when the service made me a monster."

And that, too, felt like another solemn vow he could feel in every part of him. A part of the very shape of his face. His true reflection, the one he'd always been brave enough to face.

It was other people who objected.

"Let's say any of that is true, which it isn't." Isaac almost sounded mad, somewhere beneath that calm tone he was using. "So what? You have a hell of a lot to lose now, my friend. Are you willing to do that just to prove you can?"

Jonas hung up, which was kind of like standing naked in the middle of the lodge in Fool's Cove and offering a three-hour theatrical performance of all his issues.

He knew Isaac would see it as more or less the same. With popcorn.

There was nothing he could do about that.

There was nothing he *wanted* to do about that.

He called the local team next and ordered them to stand down, break down the command center, and get ready for an early-morning return to headquarters.

"The party's that good, is that it?" Jack asked.

Jonas hung up on him, too, before he started making derogatory remarks about flyboys.

And if he was grateful that the local team on this op was made up of newer guys, none of whom would ever dare challenge him on anything—much less confront him about his *feelings*—he was wise enough to pretend he didn't.

Because there was only so much quicksand he could take.

He turned his back to the comfort of the dark and ducked back into the wedding tent. He found Carter in another little knot of high-placed, highly ranked people, and it took everything he had to keep from going over there and handling the situation here and now.

He knew it would be foolish. It would be acting from emotion instead of any tactical advantage, and that wasn't him.

That hadn't ever been him.

Jonas forced his carefree expression back into place on his face as he weaved his way through the reception tables. He found Bethan where he'd left her, still with her sister out there in the middle of the dance floor.

And there was no time for this. They should be plotting, planning, coming up with strategies and backup strategies—

But he knew, whether he planned to admit it or not, that the real reason he didn't get her attention and indicate that it was time to go was because she looked so happy.

Happy.

His beautiful Bethan with her arms in the air and sheer joy on her face.

Jonas didn't have it in him to cut that short.

He pulled out a seat at the nearest table, smiled at the other guests as he sat himself down, and . . . waited.

Because he wasn't sure he'd ever felt much in the way of joy, but she made him think it was possible. Even for someone like him. And he was going to sit here and bask in it a while, because deep down, Jonas figured that quicksand or not, Bethan was the only human thing about him.

And she wasn't his.

Which meant this was as close as he was ever likely to get.

Seventeen

They were back in Alaska by early afternoon the following day.

It was pouring rain in Juneau, the clouds so low and tight they blocked out all but the faintest suggestion of mountains or sea.

As homecomings went, Bethan found the gray, soggy weather perfect. It matched her mood.

They'd left her parents' house at 0600 hours, swinging down into Goleta to rendezvous with the rest of the team. And then they'd been on their way to the airfield shortly thereafter to board the Alaska Force jet for a few hours' direct flight north.

For the first time in a long while—maybe ever—it was hard to pull on her usual version of casual tactical gear. To wear a deliberately restrictive sports bra, cargoes, and boots, rather than a sundress. To secure her hair in her preferred ponytail, low and tight, instead of letting it fall past her shoulders.

As if the soldier were the costume.

Or at least as much of a costume as the version of herself she'd been playing all week, and Bethan didn't know quite where to put that. It was easier to march along with the rest of the team, pretend Jonas was nothing more to her than the leader of this mission, and sit quietly during the little jumper flight back to the island, counting down the minutes until she could finally be alone to decompress.

Landing in Fool's Cove took her breath away, the way it always did. First the cheery lights and bright-colored buildings of Grizzly Harbor, then the hidden bit of water carved into the rocky base of the cloud-shrouded backside of the same mountain. She felt her whole body relax as they came in for their landing.

And by the time Bethan made it to the top of the wooden stairs that led up from the dock, she felt like herself again. It was something about the air. The moody Alaskan spring. And the pleasing slap of the lodge doors as she opened them, like the old fishing camp was welcoming her back.

Isaac came out from the offices in back as they dropped their gear, all smiles. Because he might be the leader of Alaska Force and therefore one of the most dangerous men alive, but he liked to pretend he was nothing more than an average, relatable boy next door here in his hometown.

Maybe these masks they all wore were as much to protect themselves as anyone else, Bethan thought. Because they were all lethal. They were all at or near the top of their games. If they walked around showing all of that all the time . . . it would make this place a battlefield, not a refuge.

"Oz has some thoughts," Isaac said. "Jonas, Bethan, come on back."

That cut the rest of their team loose, so Bethan took a moment to say the usual *good op, good job* good-byes that followed fieldwork. Jonas did not. Bethan caught up to him and Isaac in Oz's lair, where the team's technology wizard was going back and forth between his series of huge monitors and only glanced at them quickly as they came in.

"Dominic Carter is clean," he said without preamble.

As usual, Bethan took a moment to reconcile herself to the fact that most computer nerd types did not look the way Oz did, as if he could win wars as easily with his own two hands as he could online. But that was one more thing to tuck away.

"But that's not surprising," he was saying. "He would have to be to maintain such a public profile with so many government ties. The mercenary group we think was responsible for what happened to you two in that convoy back then, though, is another story."

Bethan repressed a shudder, because it was one thing to make that connection and know it was real. It was another to stand here with the colleagues she admired and have that connection treated as fact. It made her stomach feel a little fragile.

That only made her stand straighter.

Oz typed something, and one of the monitors filled with photographs of men. Pseudomilitary men posing with various weapons, tanks, and backgrounds. "This particular outfit had a bunch of different names but distinguished itself pretty quickly. Mostly by doing things no one else would touch. That means we're talking about scraping a pretty low barrel."

"That sounds right," Bethan said, cool and professional, which was her preferred method of self-soothing. "There are certain hits you take and accept that's just how it goes. That's what being in a war is, like it or not. But this one wasn't strategic or necessary from an enemy perspective. It was mean. Punitive."

In the doorway, Isaac shifted, though that cool, assessing gray gaze of his didn't come to Bethan. It moved to Jonas instead.

Who said nothing. He might as well have been a slab of granite.

"We lost the whole convoy." Bethan heard her voice change as she spoke, becoming less civilian by the syllable.

She handled the things she'd done, the things that had happened to her while she was doing them, *because* she'd been a soldier. That was how she made those things intelligible. Palatable.

Or that was how she tried.

"The irony was that it was an aid mission," she said. "Or maybe that's not ironic at all. Maybe that was the point."

Oz moved in his chair, turning from one monitor to another. "The group we're talking about wasn't official in any capacity. Just a group that liked killing people and blowing stuff up, as far as I can tell. They took no sides. No loyalty at all. It was all about the money."

"Men like that are always the same," Jonas said quietly, and Bethan was certain she wasn't the only one in the room startled that he had said anything at all. "They serve war. They like chaos. And they particularly like it with a body count."

Bethan bit her tongue, because she knew it would serve no one if she lashed out at Jonas for what sounded a lot to her like another one of his appallingly self-lacerating autobiographies. Especially not if she had to explain how, why, or when he'd told her more details about his past. That would be even worse.

"There was a core group of about eight individuals," Oz was saying.

A fuzzy picture filled one of his screens, bursting with what looked to Bethan like a pack of Grade A jackholes. But that wasn't a purely professional response, so she shoved it aside and looked more closely. Eight men, all in good physical shape, though some of those muscles leaned toward steroids. They were all toting guns and ammo as they gathered around an all-terrain vehicle in some indistinguishable place. It looked hot, which made her imagine it was another desert, but then again they could have been squinting anywhere.

"The resolution sucks," Oz said bluntly. "It's very unlikely that I'm going to pull facial recognition off of this picture. But it's an overview, anyway. And there are other ways to narrow down the members here."

"Death records, I can only hope," Bethan said.

Oz nodded, his hands flying over the keys. "Yes, as a matter of fact. Three of these men are dead. If we get no love combing through the rest of them, we'll revisit the deaths and see if there could be any shenanigans. We all know how easy it is to fake a death."

Especially following a tour of a war zone, Bethan thought. She'd met so many soldiers who were out there trying their best to cling to an ideal in the face of almost unimaginable horrors, day after day. But then there were the others, who'd found human misery an excellent *opportunity*. To profit. To make a grab for power. Then to wield it.

She found it was usually pretty clear who was who.

"I don't like how much time is passing for our scientist while we're digging around in all this ancient history," Isaac said, his arms folded across his chest. "It's coming up on a month since he and his sister have been God knows where. I don't like it."

"I told Iyara Sowande that she could trust me," Bethan said, the way she had in California. It didn't get any less bitter. "So far, that's nothing but a lie. And I'm not a liar."

Jonas looked at her, black and steady, but said nothing.

Isaac nodded. "Understood."

"Two more of these guys are easy enough to find," Oz said, his voice as calm as it always was while his hands moved like liquid over the keys. "They both work for bigger security firms. Though not Dominic Carter's, interestingly enough."

"That leaves three men," Isaac said. "If we can't find them, we have to assume that might mean we already have. That one of them could be, for example, hiding in plain sight at Bethan's family wedding."

"What happens to aging mercenaries?" Bethan asked, allowing her spine to soften slightly as she stood there. "That's not a philosophical question. I'm honestly curious.

What's the typical career path after you finish selling your soul for money?"

"Tropical island," Oz replied.

"Easily accessible bank account in the Caymans," Isaac countered.

"Hit man," Jonas offered.

Everyone in the room looked at him, and he did that thing where he gave the impression of shrugging without actually moving.

"Your average mercenary generally goes for a squad so he can pretend that he's the same as the military, only better paid. I figure it would have to be easier to go solo later. When you can't keep up with the demands of work-for-hire wetwork and air-assault insertions into enemy territory."

"You've given this a lot of thought, have you?" Isaac asked from beside him. He shook his head. "That really warms the heart."

"Seems like a natural progression," Jonas replied.

"Better get on that, then," Bethan said, ostensibly talking to Oz, though her gaze was on Jonas, too. "I'm sure they have social media for sociopaths, don't they?"

"Yeah," Oz said. "They call it social media."

"I have a lot of questions for this guy when we find him," Isaac said while Bethan was still grinning at Oz's grumpy statement. "How they got into the safe house, then abducted two grown adults, is a puzzle, sure. But I want to know how he knew we were coming for the scientist. I want to know how they tracked us without our knowing it. That's what's keeping me up at night."

It was possible that was a joke, too, as Isaac famously rarely slept. Though maybe that, too, had changed now that he had a life outside of Alaska Force to cuddle up with at night.

"They didn't track us," Bethan said when no one else responded. "They tracked her. Iyara. I would say they injected her with a microchip and set her up as bait."

She smiled faintly when they all looked at her. "Maybe it was keeping me up, too."

"There's still the possibility she wasn't bait against her will," Isaac pointed out. "That she's been in on this from the start."

Bethan thought of the other woman in that battered old structure. Her bruised, determined face. "It's always a possibility. But that has to be how they did it. And from a distance, because otherwise we would have made the tail."

Isaac considered her for a moment, then turned his gaze to Oz. "You think you can narrow down these identities anytime soon?"

"It might take me a little while," Oz admitted, as if it hurt him.

"Consider it a number one priority," Isaac said.

Then the three of them left Oz to it, walking back out into the hall that led to the command center, Isaac's office, and down around the corner to the kitchen and mess hall.

"I have a developing situation." Isaac inclined his head in the direction of the command center. "Is there any reason we can't postpone our debrief until tomorrow?"

"That depends on how quickly Oz finds something," Jonas said.

"But in the meantime, there's no reason we can't take a closer look at Carter's legitimate enterprises," Bethan added. "I think it's pretty unlikely that he mixes streams, but you never know."

"I'll call you all in when my situation resolves itself," Isaac said. "But I have a feeling we're looking at tomorrow."

Jonas only nodded.

And Isaac slid a look his way then. That was all he did. He didn't throw Jonas back against the wall. Jonas didn't take a swing.

Still, Bethan tensed as if she were suddenly in the middle of a bar brawl.

"You enjoy that wedding?" Isaac asked him.

"I always enjoy observing rituals," Jonas replied. "From my usual distance."

Bethan laughed as if that could dispel the tension. "Except you weren't distant. You were my date. My parents *approved* of you."

Jonas merely shifted that dark glare of his from Isaac to her. But all she did was rock back a bit on her heels and smile wider.

"They approved of him?" Isaac asked. "Ouch."

"I executed the mission parameters," Jonas said. Fiercely, for him, when he was in stone-cold mode. "Appropriately."

"It's true," Bethan told Isaac. "He was so charming that my brother-in-law considers him a *bro*."

Isaac laughed at that, reaching over to wallop Jonas on the arm, something Bethan was fairly certain would get anyone else killed. "Good thing we're debriefing tomorrow, then. You can run back into the woods, freeze that leftover charm right out, and beat all the humanity right out of you."

He was still laughing as he wandered off down the hall, his too-smart border collie, Horatio, emerging from his office as he passed, eyeing Bethan and Jonas suspiciously, then following him.

Bethan stayed where she was, there in yet another hallway with Jonas glaring fire at her.

"Well," she said.

"Well," he replied.

It was tempting to read a whole lot into that. But all she saw was that wall coming down, as if there'd never been anything else.

But she couldn't help herself. "I know that if I say anything at all you'll fall all over yourself to tell me that you were in character. That none of it meant anything more than aiming at your mission parameters, like you said." She held up a hand when it looked like he was going to speak. "I want to thank you, that's all."

That muscle in his lean cheek flexed. "You have nothing to thank me for."

"That's where you're wrong." She wanted to reach out to him. To take his hands in hers the way she would have this morning. The way she had yesterday.

The way she had again last night when they got back to their suite and made sure there were no cameras on them, when she'd led him into that big wide bed.

And she could tell that he was remembering the same thing.

But this was Alaska. They were back at work, back to being themselves, and there were no blurred lines in Fool's Cove.

No matter how blurry she, herself, might feel.

"I expected my sister's wedding to be an inconvenience," Bethan told him. "But it turned out to be a complicated sort of wonder, all its own, and a large part of that was having you with me."

"It was the job."

She tried to swallow the lump in her throat. "You did it very well. I won't forget that."

Bethan turned then, not happy to find that her vision was blurry, too, but she blinked that back. She headed for the door to the main lobby, so she could go back to her cabin, hide away, and do something about how thin her skin had become while she was wearing a different version of it.

"Bethan."

She stopped, but she didn't turn back. She didn't want him to see her face and whatever it was doing. Whatever it showed.

"I wish you would," Jonas said, his voice dark. Bitter.

She kept going, because the other option was to turn around and fight this man for his own soul. Right here in the hallway in the beating heart of Alaska Force's operation, something she doubted he would forgive.

Truth was, she felt later—after she'd taken her gear back

to her cabin, unpacked all the frilly, flirty clothes she had no idea when she'd have occasion to wear again, and then headed back down to the lodge to see if anyone was headed over to Grizzly Harbor—while Jonas would hate her for it, everyone else might applaud the effort.

Templeton and his trooper provided her with her ride, out in a little trawler that hugged the coastline as Templeton navigated the moody swells, the sea not quite ready to let go of winter.

They all huddled there in the little bit of inside space the boat had to offer.

"Rumor is you got Jonas to dance," Templeton boomed, and then laughed as if that were a joke in and of itself.

Next to him, Kate rolled her eyes. Though with affection.

"It was a wedding," Bethan said judiciously. "Not like he spontaneously started dancing in the middle of a regular op. That would be far more interesting."

Templeton shot her a look, then returned his attention to the water. "I've been on a lot of ops with Jonas Crow, and the only dancing I've ever seen him do involved making like a ghost and taking the enemy out inside their own camps. Not, you know, a waltz."

"There was no waltzing," Bethan assured him.

It wasn't a lie. Not precisely.

Once they docked in Grizzly Harbor, Templeton stopped to take a call, leaving Kate and Bethan to hike into town on their own.

"Are you headed somewhere particular?" the trooper asked.

"You know." Bethan shrugged. "Caradine's."

"Is there . . . a meeting?" Kate asked, with a sudden, aggressively neutral expression on her face that made Bethan laugh.

"You mean like . . ." Bethan started.

"Don't say it."

". . . *intimate friend time*?"

Kate grinned. "I don't know. You just got back from a mission. Maybe you require an infusion of . . . whatever you would call that."

"Girls' night?" Bethan teased her, given that neither one of them was a likely candidate for the sort of *girls' night* people tended to mean when they used that term.

Bethan would rather die than drink a cosmopolitan in a world where whiskey existed.

Kate made a face. "I still don't know how these things work. There are always mysterious calculations, but I never know the math."

"The Alaska Force math is pretty simple. There are a lot of dudes. Therefore, both of us who aren't dudes hang out."

"I get that part." Her eyes gleamed. "Templeton made me watch *Bridesmaids*, claiming that I could view it as the definitive text on female friendships."

"Really?"

"My people skills might be remedial," Kate said dryly. "But somehow, I have a hard time imagining Mariah McKenna succumbing to food poisoning in the middle of the street."

There was nothing to do but laugh at that, because their friend was polished and elegant no matter where she was. Even if it was here, in the dark of winter.

"Does Templeton know that you pretend to be less capable of human interaction than you really are?" Bethan asked as they approached the new version of the Water's Edge Café, after the old version had been burned down last summer. Bethan had personally helped rebuild it with the rest of the community.

"Only when it suits him," Kate said, biting back a grin. But that cop's cool gaze landed on Bethan then. "But I'm not the only one around here who pretends to be a little bit less than human. It's not the act that matters half so much as why."

Bethan stared back at her, willing her face blank. "I don't know what you're talking about."

"Of course you don't," Kate agreed. "But I bet it was a really fun dance all the same."

Inside Caradine's new café, which was brighter than before and far more open and welcoming—and she would include the owner in that, despite the fact she still clattered her pans around, threatened tourists, and issued lifetime bans for minor infractions at least three times a week. Bethan found Mariah and Everly hunched over their laptops at their preferred table, as usual. As if Grizzly Harbor were a big city with coffeehouses people liked to use as their offices.

And she told herself it was because she found herself missing her sister and all her sister's manic, alien, and somehow endearing friends, but Bethan didn't feel truly back home until she sank down at a table and tried to place an order with Caradine that was ignored with a rude gesture, because Caradine served what she wanted.

Later, as the light began to change outside, she and Everly walked through town, up the hill, then followed the trail out to the hot springs. The town had long ago built a few cabins around the naturally occurring springs so that they could keep some lockers there—cubbies, more like—so no one had to carry wet bathing suits or soaked towels around in the worst of the winter weather. Tonight it was the women-only hour when they arrived, so they nodded around at the familiar faces there and sank down into their corner of the large, hot pool.

"How does she know she's pregnant again?" Nellie Oberlin, who worked in the Fairweather, Grizzly Harbor's dive bar and greasy grill, was asking.

"She claims she knew upon conception," Madeleine Yazzie, who could usually be found at the front desk of the Blue Bear Inn, confided, her red beehive rising from above the water like a shark's fin. "Don't get caught up on that. Get caught up on this: once again, no one knows who the father is."

Bethan and Everly exchanged a look.

"The continuing adventures of Maria and her hipster boyfriend plus Luz with her fisherman husband," Everly murmured almost reverently, her eyes sparkling. "Why can't I get enough of it?"

Bethan shook her head as the hot water bubbled around her. "At a certain point, isn't it time to accept that everyone is sleeping with everyone and stop pretending that there are two separate couples?"

"But then you can't stand around in the middle of a public festival, intensely discussing your sex lives." Everly grinned. "Where's the fun in that?"

Maria and Luz, who had both been pregnant at the same time once already—and apparently unable to determine paternity—were the closest thing Grizzly Harbor had to a soap opera. Especially because the two of them and their apparently interchangeable men seemed determined not to drift off into quiet obscurity or part from one another. They lived off the grid halfway up the mountain and were apparently still swapping partners, and more babies were on the way.

Bethan had no idea why that made her feel so cheery.

Afterward, soaked so warm that she half thought she was back in California, she and Everly walked back down to the docks to catch a ride back to Fool's Cove. Because someone was always heading one way or the other.

"I'm glad you enjoyed the wedding," Everly said as they waited for Benedict and Blue to load up the boat. "I know this might not be a popular opinion these days, while everybody's wandering around canceling everybody else, but I think family can be a good thing. That it's worth building bridges if you can. I don't think we're supposed to go through life with people who agree with everything we say and do and are always easy to get along with."

"It was nice to be pleasantly surprised," Bethan agreed.

When they landed back at Fool's Cove, she headed back to her cabin.

Once inside, she stripped out of her utilitarian clothes a lot more quickly than she normally did. She'd gotten too used to dresses and sandals, clearly. She'd become far too accustomed to her hair down.

It was April, and certainly not as cold as it could be, but after a week in California she felt chilled anyway. She stoked the fire, so the cabin would be extra toasty. She started the fire out on her private deck to heat up her hot tub, thinking she might enjoy another long soak, this time with only the stars as company. Then she padded around, changing into her coziest, most luxurious pair of pajamas. They had been a Christmas present from Ellen one year, in a creamy cashmere. The bottoms rode low on her hips and the sweet little top tended to droop over one shoulder. But they felt like a hug, and Bethan opted not to think too much about why she might need one.

She was thinking about making herself a cup of tea when there was a knock on her cabin door.

For moment, she stared at the door, because no one came here. She had never encouraged visitors once, not as long as she'd been here.

She glanced at her phone, because surely the only reason someone would actually come and physically seek her out was if she'd missed an important call. But there was nothing on the screen. She was tempted to grab one of her weapons, but she knew better. No one turned up in Fool's Cove unannounced, so whoever was on the other side of the door had to be friendly.

But that didn't mean she had to be.

She went over and cracked open the door, already scowling.

Something that didn't change when she saw who was standing there. Jonas.

And something in her . . . cracked. Shattered, maybe.

But she couldn't seem to make herself stop and worry about that. She stepped back, opening the door wider, but she didn't invite him in. But she didn't tell him to stay out, either.

He paused, there on the threshold, as if he wasn't sure what he was doing there, either.

Then he came inside, his movements almost jerky, which made her stomach flip.

Because this was Jonas, who moved like silk. Like a whisper. Like a ghost.

He brushed past her, and she closed the door behind him, because that was what people did. Then her head was spinning and her knees felt strange, so she leaned back against the door she'd closed and stared at him.

Her heart started to clang, hard, against her ribs.

Because he was so *male*. He was a wicked blade of a man, thrust into the middle of the one place she was soft.

He was in all black, as ever, and her cabin was a festival of pastels. She couldn't imagine anyone alive would be more out of place here than he was. He seemed to look around him for a very long while. And only when she thought her heart might actually have made a dent on the inside of her chest did he turn back around and face her.

Unreadable as always.

"What are you doing here?" she asked, and she couldn't do anything with her voice. It was too soft, too thready.

Too obvious.

But Jonas was staring at her like it hurt. Like she wasn't the only one who couldn't quite handle this. Whatever *this* was. And while she watched, his expression changed.

She thought that he looked tortured. Wrecked.

And even as something in her reveled in that, because it so closely matched how she felt, the rest of her despaired.

"Jonas," she said again. More urgently. "Why are you here?"

And when he spoke, his voice was as ravaged as his gaze. "Damn you," he said, a dark lash that swelled in her like a kiss. "I don't know."

Eighteen

Jonas should not have been so surprised by Bethan's cabin.

He'd had enough clues in California. She might have put on a good show about dresses and hair care being unlike her, but she'd taken to it all easily enough.

Maybe he should have expected that the woman who had once held him through the night would make her soft heart an actual, physical place. That she couldn't possibly keep all of that inside her. That she might have gone through Ranger School, but she was still the same person she'd been throughout the longest night of his life.

He hadn't meant to come here. Jonas had spent the hours since he'd last seen her in the lodge, trying to do exactly what Isaac had suggested he would. He'd alternated running laps up the most punishing trail he knew with cold plunges to reset his nervous system, but he couldn't seem to find his equilibrium. No matter how many rounds he did.

He'd headed down to the gym to throw some weight around, but all it had done was make the gnawing, aching thing in him worse.

After he'd accepted that he couldn't conquer it with iron, he'd eaten dinner in the mess hall in the hope carbs and sugar could settle what sweat couldn't. But he hadn't had it in him to listen to the usual off-color jokes and typical banter that passed for conversation with the Alaska Force crew.

Clearly he needed to be alone.

But sitting in the dark of his cabin only made it all worse.

When he'd decided he needed to go for a walk, he'd pretended he didn't know where he was heading.

And then he'd hoped she wouldn't let him in.

But she looked like dessert.

She was wearing something that looked too soft, too much like a cloud, to be sleepwear. Her hair was down again, and the buttery light that filled her cabin brought out all the shades of red that he'd spent a significant amount of time pretending he didn't notice down there in the California sun.

The longer he looked at her, the pinker her cheeks became.

And that didn't help, because it reminded him of last night and that big king-sized bed where she'd laid him down, told him to lie back and think of England, and then had her way with him.

Twice.

And what he'd thought about had not been the least bit British.

"I must be missing something," she said, her gaze a little flinty on his. "Because you greatly resemble a coworker of mine who stood before me at oh five hundred hours—naked, but who's counting—and told me that anything of a personal nature that might have happened between us had to stay in California. Was that you, Jonas?"

"Your cabin," he managed to grit out. "It's very . . . pink."

And she matched it more by the second as the color in her cheeks deepened.

"That was a trick question. I know it was you."

"And . . . *fluffy*."

"There's a reason I've never let any of you in here," she snapped at him, trying to pull herself up into an imposing stature there against the door, but she was pink in the face and covered in a cloud and *soft*. "I'm sure you have your own cabin done up to suit you, which I assume means a bed of nails, a selection of hair shirts, and a martyr's pyre or two. With cold water and gruel as a treat."

That was a little too close for comfort, but he couldn't focus on that. Not now.

"Deep down, beneath the tough-as-nails Army Ranger, you're . . . a pink-and-fluffy unicorn, Bethan."

She vibrated away from the door. "Incorrect. I have always been a unicorn. That's how I *became* an Army Ranger. Some people relax with whiskey. I prefer fluffy pillows and a calming color palette. You can go now."

Jonas could see her reach for *indignant*, because that was probably easier.

Anything was probably easier. But since when did either one of them do anything the easy way? He moved toward her, and he saw her startle at that, because she probably thought he really was leaving.

But instead, he trapped her there against her own door, carefully flattening a palm on either side of her head.

"I graciously allowed you to have your way with me this morning," he said, and if he stepped back and thought about this, he would stop. So he didn't.

He could see her pulse beat hard and fast in the crook of her neck. The scent of her was in his head again, warm and addictive and encouraging him to do all kinds of things he probably shouldn't. And the look on her face, naked and needy, almost did him in.

"I'm not sure that I would use the word *gracious*," she countered, though her voice was soft.

"It's unlikely that we'll have that briefing before tomorrow morning." He bent, then, and traced her pulse with his tongue, pleased when it made her break out in goose bumps. Everywhere. "That's a long, long while."

"All night," she agreed.

"I don't remember our first long night," he said gruffly. "Not in any detail."

"Jonas," she whispered, her voice strangled. And he knew it was because he was rarely the one to bring up that first night at all.

"We've had a lot of missions since then," he said. He lifted his head from the temptation of her neck. "And then last night, which was hardly a night at all. The reception didn't end until two."

"I thought we did okay."

"Tonight," he murmured, his mouth so close to hers, "I'm going to take my time."

He could see the questions in her eyes. They were in him, too. But he didn't have the answers, and he was tired of looking.

All he had was this. The breath between them. The night stretching out before them.

And a soft, pretty cabin dressed in pink.

He found her mouth and somehow kept himself from letting all the wild need in him out at once. *Play the long game, dumbass*, he ordered himself.

Jonas tasted her as if she were a delicacy. He took his time, learning her mouth.

He kissed her until she was trembling. Until he thought he might start shaking, too. And somehow, somewhere in there, they were both laughing. Breathless and beautiful, there against the door, with only that kiss between them.

"Are you trying to kill me?" she asked, her voice in a whisper.

"Not necessarily," he said.

Then he got his hands on her. The pajamas she was wearing were so soft it made him shudder, but her skin was even better. And he couldn't get enough of her, flushed and hot and *his*.

He knew better than to let that word take root, but he didn't have it in him—not tonight—to fight it off.

This time, when he took her mouth, it was harder. Deeper. Wilder. He got a hand in her hair. He had the other one down the back of those distractingly soft bottoms, and she responded in kind. She surged into him, pressing herself against him so that all he could feel was the temptation of her breasts against the T-shirt he wore.

And she was as hungry as he was, finding her way beneath his T-shirt, her hands against his abdomen and then, better still, at the waistband of his trousers.

"No," he told her, and found himself laughing again. Like a normal person—but he wasn't going there, either. Not tonight. "We're taking it slow."

"I did not sign up for slow."

"Tough," he said against her mouth, like a different sort of kiss.

And then he bent down and picked her up, enjoying the weight of her in his arms. She was far more solid and dense than she looked, because she was made of lean muscle. And those sweet curves. He never wanted to put her down, especially because she looked at him that way, a little bit starry-eyed, like no one else had ever bothered to try to lift her.

Idiots.

He carried her over to the couch that waited across the room, deep and soft and unquestionably girlie in all the ways he would have sworn were part of that mask she'd worn in California. Something cracked in him at the notion that she was always both versions of herself—it was just a question of what she chose to show.

Jonas settled her on the couch and then knelt down before her, taking in every last detail about this woman who was his torment. His temptation. His treat. Her eyes were gleaming now, with the same lust and longing that flared so hot in him.

He'd messed up her hair so it was tousled, still begging for his hands. Those pajama bottoms were a little too low and falling off one hip, which matched the way her top drooped down her arm, showing him the better part of one breast.

Jonas thought he might explode.

She was the one thing on the planet that threatened his control, and here, with his hands on her body and that look on her face, was the only place that it didn't bother him.

He smoothed his hands down the soft fabric that covered her thighs, then pulled it along with him, grinning when she greedily lifted her hips to help him along. Underneath, she was naked.

That went to his head like a bullet.

"Sometimes," he told her, though he shouldn't, "you're so beautiful it distracts me. Out on a job."

She blinked. And then, while he watched, a smile spread over her face. Until it seemed to him that even her freckles were glowing.

"Careful, Jonas," she murmured. "All these hearts and flowers might go to my head."

He didn't answer her with words. Instead, he slid down to his knees at the side of the couch. He slid his hands beneath her, hauling her forward to the edge of the cushion, and then he buried his face between her legs.

Because he had to know if she tasted the way she looked.

A moment later, he knew. She was much, much sweeter.

Unimaginably hotter.

And he was a goner.

But if this was the way he was finally going to go, he was more than happy with it. He licked his way into her, determined to drown.

It was almost easy to ignore the clamoring in his own body as Bethan softened and shook beneath his mouth, his hands. The noises she made, greedy and sweet, went straight to the place he was hardest and only spurred him on.

And only when he'd made her call out his name a few times did he move on, peeling off her soft cloud of a top so he could finally see all of her in the warm, buttery light.

"You, too," she ordered him, though her eyes were glassy and her voice was rough.

He'd done that to her. And he liked that so much it made him ache even more.

Jonas stood, making short work of his T-shirt, trousers, and boots.

He was not a self-conscious man. He'd viewed himself as a weapon since the age of eighteen. A useful tool, nothing more, and before that—well, he'd been the same, but he hadn't much liked the people who'd had their hand on his trigger.

It had been dark in their room last night in California, for the few, scant hours between the end of the reception and the cruel inevitability of the alarm that indicated it was time to head back to reality.

But it wasn't dark now. And Bethan was staring at him, her mouth slightly ajar and her eyes wider by the moment.

It was enough to give him a complex.

"I have never understood," she said softly.

She rose from the couch and swayed toward him, and then her fingertips were gently moving over the skin of his chest. And he couldn't breathe.

His scars, he realized with another jarring beat of his heart.

She was touching his scars.

"What didn't you understand?" he made himself ask.

"How a man so harsh and cold can be this beautiful," she whispered. "Always too beautiful."

And before he could take that on board, she bent. She pressed her lips to the top of the mess of scars that started near his shoulder and then splintered, mapping out a record of the explosion they had both survived. Then she began to follow those scars down.

Jonas wasn't prepared for this.

The cool brush of her fingers was like a prayer and a penance in one, and it lit him up as if he'd been waiting his whole life for the bright kiss of sunshine only she could give him. He thought he could muscle through it somehow, but as she kept going, it dawned on him that she intended to leave her mark on every last one of his scars.

Particularly the ones she'd watched him get.

"Bethan . . ." he began.

But her name sounded like a song, a poem. Something lyrical and unlike him.

Because he wasn't playing any character tonight. He wasn't wearing a role, immersing himself in a part, doing what he had to do for some broader purpose.

He was here by choice. He was here as him.

And he might not know exactly who that was, but Bethan did.

She told him with every kiss, every brush of her hand. She smiled, her mouth against his skin as she followed his scars to his back, and she knew how to identify each and every mark she found in his flesh.

As if she were the one singing. A song of battles won and lost. Knives and guns, grenades and shrapnel, and explosions of all kinds.

When she made it all around him, in a big circle to his front again, he wondered if this was what it felt like to be reborn.

Made new in her eyes.

"Absolutely beautiful," she whispered.

"Not compared to you," he managed to say in return. "Nothing compares to you, Bethan. Nothing ever has."

Her eyes gleamed. "Here's hoping nothing ever will."

It was hard to say who moved. It was her, or it was him, and somehow, she was in his arms again. His mouth was on

hers, she was twining herself around him, and they were
tumbling back down onto that couch that was like its own
caress.

But this time, they were skin to skin. With all that light
between them, so there was no hiding.

There were only the two of them, naked. Maskless.

And Jonas lost himself in the only place he'd ever been
found.

He took it slow, making sure that he returned the favor
she'd given him. He got his mouth on every last inch of her
body.

And by the time he finally pulled her beneath him again,
her breath sounded like sobs. She'd taken to cursing him,
and he grinned at her, braced there above her.

"Patience, Bethan," he told her. Piously.

He loved it when her green eyes blazed fire at him. And
when she went so far as to call him a selection of ugly
names.

"That's remarkably impolite," he chided her.

"Why don't you go f—"

But he thrust in, deep.

She arched against him, the curse she'd been throwing
at him shifting into a kind of scream.

And only when she finished shaking did he begin to
move.

He still took it slow, but he didn't take it easy on her.

Because this was Bethan, perfect in every way. Beautiful beyond imagining and every last part of her strong, capable, and gorgeous. She could amaze him with her hair
down to capture the light, and she could take him and all
his dark demands.

And he knew with every impossibly deep thrust, every
time she met him and groaned out her pleasure, that this
was real.

Raw.

Something like magic, changing them both by the second.

She wrapped her legs around his waist and held on tight.

Jonas lost his pace, his rhythm.

Then he burst into flame, consuming them both, until there was nothing but the glory of it. And her voice in his ear as they both hurtled straight on into the center of the sun, whispering his name.

He could normally track time to the second, but he lost any claim on it as they lay there, tangled up together in the warmth and brightness of this soft, sweet cabin of hers. He wanted to protest when she stirred, and had no idea how he managed to keep it to himself. Particularly when she sat up, then looked back over her shoulder at him, smiling at him in a way that made his heart hitch.

Another thing he refused to think about. Not now.

"Stay there," she said as she got to her feet.

He obliged, watching her as she moved, swift and lovely, over to the side door of her cabin. She pulled on a long coat that hung on a peg there, stamped her feet into boiled wool boots beneath it, and grinned at him when all he did was stare.

"I have my own hot tub," she said. "We never got to use the one in California, did we? I started the fire earlier, but let me check the water."

She slipped out the door. Jonas rolled to his feet, then stood there, naked. All the pastels were getting to him, because he found it all . . . soothing.

Meanwhile, his heart was a problem behind his ribs. His head was spinning, like he was drunk again. When he was never drunk.

Only with her, something in him whispered.

She came back in, bringing a gust of cooler air with her, and only grinned at whatever expression he had on his face as she shrugged out of her coat and kicked off the boots.

He braced himself, because surely now would be the time for discussions he didn't want to have. Surely she would demand . . . more vulnerability, if that were possible. Things he didn't have in him. Places he couldn't go.

But instead she came and took his hand, tugging him with her across the cabin and into her small kitchen.

"I don't know about you," she said, not even looking at him as she busied herself in her small refrigerator. "But I'm starving." She paused as she assembled simple ingredients on her counter. "Does the mighty Jonas Crow admit hunger?"

"Occasionally," he said, and found he was actually smiling back at her. "I'm starving, myself."

The strangest part about it was that he actually was. He did whatever was required of him when he was playing a character, but here, back in Fool's Cove, he usually adhered to a strict eating schedule that he used to maintain the ratios he preferred in his body's lean mass.

None of which he could bring himself to care about while Bethan set about making sandwiches.

He recognized the bread as Caradine's. It was the same bread she baked daily and used in her café.

"Oh yeah," Bethan said, glancing up to see that he was looking at the loaf she was cutting hearty slices from. "Caradine sells bread. But you better believe she charges three times the going rate for it. Still." And she sighed a little, a bit like the way she had when he'd been inside her. "Totally worth it."

She finished making two sandwiches, not skimping on any of the ingredients. They were piled high with what looked like anything she happened to have in her refrigerator. A refrigerator she must have restocked at some point today, with what looked like items pilfered from the lodge.

She levered herself up and onto her counter, then sat there, cross-legged, to eat, which she did with the same greedy abandon she'd used on him. Jonas thought he should have felt out of place. Awkward and strange, standing there naked an inch or so away from her, but he didn't.

It was hot in an entirely different way. There was no awkward conversation. There were only the two of them, clearly enjoying the hell out of the sandwiches she'd made them.

It was only when they were both done, and Bethan was licking her fingers with sheer relish, that he understood that this, too, was another intimacy.

Only with her. Always with her.

She led him over to the side door, and he had no idea why he was permitting her to tug him around like this, only that he didn't have it in him to stop her. He didn't *want* to stop her. Not tonight.

Outside, the air was cool but the wooden cistern she had out there, just large enough to hold the both of them, was steaming.

"How did I not know that you had this here?" he asked when they were both in the water and he'd gone with an urge he couldn't identify and pulled her onto his lap with her back against his chest.

"Because I like to keep my private life private," she replied simply.

But she'd let him in.

Jonas didn't have to ask her to clarify what that meant. He knew.

And for a long while, they simply soaked there together. The hot water was another caress, soothing the body he'd worked so hard to beat into submission earlier. And all around them, the Alaskan spring night was dark, cool, and wet. Like a secret.

Jonas could hear the water in the distance, waves against the rocky shore. He heard a cabin door slam, somewhere on the hill. There was the sound of Horatio barking, which meant Isaac and Caradine were spending the night here, rather than in their house in Grizzly Harbor. There was the hum of generators. The rush of the wind up above as it tangled with the evergreens.

The crackle of the fire in the stove heating the water. And each and every breath Bethan took.

There were so many things he should have said. But he couldn't begin to imagine how he could go about it. Any of it. He wasn't built that way.

So instead, he showed her.

He shifted her in his arms, tipping her back so he could kiss her the way he wanted to. Hungry and reverent, sweet and wicked.

And when they started to get hotter than the water, he picked her up again. He carried her out of the tub, grinning when she yelped at the blast of cool air against her warm skin.

Jonas brought her inside and toweled her off. Then he carried her up the open, wooden stairs to her sleeping loft. He laid her out on her soft bed, flushed and ripe in the middle of what looked to him like approximately ten thousand pillows.

"What are you doing?" she asked, but she was smiling, stretched out before him like a lazy sort of cat.

"I'll show you," he told her, crawling onto the bed.

And then he taught them both how to want all over again, as if it were new.

Nineteen

Bethan woke the way she always did, happy to be in her bed. Home at last.

Except today, when she sat up in her bed to start her morning routine, she realized almost instantly that she wasn't alone.

And even as her body responded with a kick of alarm, she remembered.

Jonas.

My God, something in her sang out, *Jonas*.

Jonas, who shifted from what looked like a sound sleep to total alertness by simply opening his eyes.

Her breath shuddered out of her.

Because Jonas had always been a beautiful man. Bethan had been known to appreciate that beauty in any number of inappropriate places.

But today he was *in her bed*.

And as it turned out, that was a fantasy she hadn't known she had.

Especially today, when she could remember—distinctly—

each and every thing they had done together in this bed. Each touch. Each cry. Each long, hot, gorgeous hour.

She found herself smiling despite herself. Or because of him. Either way, she did nothing to curb the impulse.

"You looked like you were headed somewhere," he said after a moment, that dark voice moving over her and in her like a new caress. And her body was so attuned to him now that she felt herself shudder into instant awareness. Ready and greedy, just like that.

"I have a morning routine," she managed to say, without letting that greed color her voice. She knew she probably shouldn't reach over and touch him, but he was *in her bed*. Right there in front of her. What was she supposed to do? "I'm going to guess you probably have one, too."

His dark eyes gleamed. "We are who we are."

Her smile widened in delight. "Did you just make a deliberately amusing remark?" She shook her head in mock astonishment. "I really have corrupted you."

He sat up then, a swift, efficient movement that made her breath catch. Because he was all smooth muscle and leashed power, and she wanted him like she'd never tasted him at all. Like the hunger for him was in her now, on a cellular level, and would never, ever leave.

"Come on," she said briskly, to cover it. "A hundred burpees before coffee."

He arched a dark brow. "Is that all? I thought that surely, one of the world's few female Army Rangers, would do a full Ironman before breakfast."

She grinned. "Only on alternate Tuesdays."

Bethan thought this should feel weird and awkward, but it didn't. She'd never allowed anyone inside her cabin, much less let a man spend the night here. Much less *Jonas Crow*. But it felt . . . perfectly normal. She told herself it was because they'd spent a week pretending this was who they were in California.

Don't make this something it's not, she ordered herself.

Jonas went downstairs ahead of her to pull on his discarded clothes, and he was already stoking her fire by the time she met him there. As if he knew how she liked to start each day.

And then, with only a faint curve of that mouth of his, he did her morning burpee routine with her, side by side, with a race to the finish. A cold shower, then coffee.

As if they'd done all this together a thousand times before.

As if this were their life.

It was California. It had to be. It was all those long jogs they'd taken, just the two of them together, that made this all feel so easy and familiar.

But somehow, she thought it might be a little bit more than that.

He left her a little bit before the community workout, gruffly telling her that he'd meet her there. And then he shocked her to her toes when he curved a hand over her neck in a hard grip and kissed her.

Swift and knee weakening, leaving her smiling foolishly after him once he left.

And for a moment, alone in her cabin again, she could only stare off at nothing in particular, try to catch her breath, and try her best not to read anything into . . . anything.

She'd made that mistake before.

And thinking about that night in the desert—and Dominic Carter—was sobering. Like another cold shower. She fought to keep those images out of her head, but they lived in her. The fear and the adrenaline. The grief, the determination, the will to live no matter what. They were all still a part of her.

Just like he is, she thought, as she made her way down to the beach.

And she welcomed the opportunity to stop *thinking* so freaking much for a brutal hour.

After the workout, when she decided to go on a run in a

heavy weighted vest, because that sounded like the kind of awful she needed after glutting herself on Jonas all night long, Jonas went with her.

He didn't seem to care that everybody watched him do it.

Bethan fought her feelings about that for almost the whole of her run down to the far end of the beach and back. Then she remembered the last time the two of them had been on this beach together. The evil sandbags and the fact that he'd come out here against his will because he'd wanted to avoid whatever Isaac's mediation might look like.

She stopped running and looked at him, panting, a sudden dark suspicion taking her over. "Is all of this because you don't want mediation?"

Jonas gazed back at her, implacable and unreadable as ever. "No."

"Because the last time we were out here, that was what you were worried about. And now . . . all this."

And ordinarily, she would have wanted the earth to open her up and swallow her whole, because her voice cracked on the last two words. But today she didn't seem to care about that as much as she should have.

Jonas's jaw tensed. "Mediation was one of the things I was thinking about when I volunteered to be your wedding date. But I haven't thought about it since."

A knot throbbed to life beneath her ribs. "Everybody knows this story, Jonas. Dumb girl lets some guy get one over on her to save himself. Loses everything in the process while he's fine. Is that what's happening?"

That muscle in his lean jaw pulsed. "No."

"Because I can't help noticing that for someone who was deeply concerned with making sure no one knew what had happened between us only days ago, you sure didn't mind letting everybody see you come out on this run with me. What do you think they're going to think? Or is that what you want?"

"Who do you think I am?" he asked her, that dark gaze of his an indictment.

But she refused to let that get to her, no matter how it made her heart pound.

"How would I know?" she asked, forcing herself to stay quiet. Calm. Focused. When what she wanted to do was scream. "You could be anyone. Isn't that your job?"

"As often as it's your job."

"Don't think it hasn't occurred to me that you play a role here the same way you do everywhere else, Jonas. Maybe your biggest role of all."

She didn't realize that she was holding her breath until he slid his hand over the nape of her neck again. And she nearly gasped.

That impossibly dark gaze moved over her face, and she should have jerked away. She should have tried to hide. She should have done *something* to keep him from seeing too much . . . but she didn't.

He saw everything. She let him. "You let me into your cabin. You feel vulnerable."

"Or played," she countered. "One of the two."

"And if I played you, you can lean into the anger here. I get it."

She thought he did, and that was . . . worse and better at the same time.

"You're right," Jonas said after a moment. "I play all kinds of roles wherever I go. But not with you, Bethan. Never with you."

And he didn't kiss her. He only gazed down at her, his mouth an unsmiling line and his gaze so intense she felt as if it were carving out her insides as she stood there.

He didn't kiss her, but the weight of his hand on her neck felt like some kind of brand, or maybe that was his gaze, and everything inside her seemed to pull too tight even as it broke apart.

And still, all they did was stand there on a windswept beach, waiting for the morning fog to lift.

"The briefing's at nine," he reminded her after a lifetime or two. And then he broke her heart by dropping his hand and stepping back. Breaking whatever it was that hummed there between them, like their own personal electric charge. "I'll race you back."

When she walked into the briefing in the lodge at precisely 0900 hours, Bethan had erased any possible trace of the night before and, while she was at it, everything personal that had happened in California.

Every *visible* trace, anyway.

Once inside the big, cheerfully masculine room, she nodded and smiled faintly at her colleagues before taking her preferred place over against one wall, next to Kate Holiday.

She and the trooper were the only women in the room, which would have made them friendly by default. Good thing Bethan also happened to like her enough to count her as a real friend. That wasn't always the way it went in primarily male spaces.

"One of these mornings you need to come to the workout," Bethan said as she settled into her usual stance.

Kate smirked. "I keep meaning to. Then I remember that I hate group activities."

"Everyone works out alone, Kate. Nobody lifts the weight for you. You have to do it yourself."

"And still a hard pass from me on that one," she replied, the way she always did.

When Isaac and Oz walked into the room, the whole group fell quiet. They all pulled out their own tablets and paid close attention as Isaac laid out the active missions, the potential missions and clients, the new candidates who'd impressed him—including, Bethan was delighted to see, another woman—and any other orders of business.

"Let's circle back to the scientist," Isaac said then.

And when he flashed a picture of the Sowandes on the screen, Bethan forgot Jonas, her family, kidding around with Kate, and all the rest of it.

Because looking at Iyara Sowande made her feel nothing but guilty. She'd made her a promise, and so far, that promise was broken.

"To bring everyone up to speed," Isaac was saying, "we all feel pretty sure the person responsible for the disappearance of the Sowandes is this guy. Currently masquerading as a squeaky-clean CEO—"

"*Is* there such a thing?" Blue asked.

"Not in this lifetime," Templeton replied.

"—without a single red flag on his record." Isaac nodded at Blue and Templeton. "This seemed unlikely from the get-go, because nobody collects that many defense contracts without a little mess in there somewhere."

"In this case, it's a very well hidden mess," Oz added from his spot near the front, his laptop making his face look blue. "I had to do some seriously deep diving to figure out who this guy used to be."

"Way back when he was blowing up convoys in a land far, far away," Bethan added, not doing a great job of keeping the tension out of her voice.

"About that," Jonas said from his place across the room, and the way his dark eyes moved to hers made her belly tighten. "Bethan shot that guy once already. And he came back, created a new identity for himself, then acted like he didn't know who we were at Bethan's sister's wedding."

"While putting cameras in your room," Jack added.

"And going to great lengths to make himself look like some pencil pusher," Lucas agreed.

"I don't like resurrections," Jonas told the room. "Particularly not secret ones. No one does that for a good reason."

"Amen," Isaac muttered, and he probably wasn't the only one thinking about the situation Caradine had been in last year. Though Bethan figured he was probably still angrier about it than anyone else in the room. He cleared his throat, a sign of emotion that Bethan absolutely was not comparing to Jonas's complete lack thereof, because why torture herself when she needed to concentrate?

Oz kept going. "Pre-resurrection, our friend was better known as Judson Kerrigone. Born in Delaware and raised mostly in New Jersey, with a couple of years in Philadelphia as a kid. Tried to enlist in the army, the navy, and the marines in three consecutive years but was rejected every time. Debt, drugs, and a criminal record. Tried to make a lateral move to the police but failed the psych eval."

"He sounds like a real winner," Templeton drawled.

"Obviously, the next step was to embrace that mercenary life," August agreed.

"One thing I'll never understand," Jonas said in that dark way of his that resonated inside Bethan, even from across the room, "is why anyone would think it's easier to kill for money when it's hard enough to do it for the right reasons."

"Everybody in this room knows how hard it is," Isaac said, sounding as pissed as Bethan figured they all felt. "Just like we all know what kind of loser prefers to turn it off just to make a dime."

"Translation," Griffin said coolly. "We don't like this guy."

There was a rumble of agreement throughout the room, because everyone here was still a little idealistic, or else they would have quit when they left the service. Even Jonas, Bethan thought, whether he knew it or not.

"He made my skin crawl," she said when the rumbling died down. She did her best not to look at Jonas. "And that was before I knew who he was. Before I knew that he'd tried to kill me once already. I couldn't get my head around the timing. What changed between our arrival and the appearance of those cameras? Then I remembered that I'd had a flashback of what happened to our convoy." She couldn't keep herself from looking at Jonas then, which was better than paying too close attention to all the other very serious gazes trained on her. "I thought it was random, but then I remembered there was a man, running away, off in my peripheral vision. The cameras appeared later that same evening."

"You think he saw you doing a drive-by?" Isaac asked.

Bethan shrugged. "The options are that he already knew who I was, or that he saw me in that car before I saw him. Both are possibilities. Either way, he installed cameras in the room and then, at the reception, went out of his way to come up and get in my face."

She let that sink in.

"Yeah," Templeton drawled, and let the chair he usually kept tipped back thud to the floor. "Not a fan of this guy."

"Judson Kerrigone doesn't have a lot to recommend him," Oz agreed. "Probably why he decided that after meeting Bethan in the desert—"

"Bethan and her gun," Jonas said, with a lethal satisfaction.

Everyone else nodded at that, even Griffin, the best sniper Bethan knew.

"That seems to have been a turning point for our guy," Isaac said. "Because after somehow surviving Bethan, Judson Kerrigone disappeared. And not long after, Dominic Carter took his place. With a bright-and-shiny interest in the sorts of things that Judson Kerrigone would know all about but could no longer touch, because everybody knew the kind of nasty character he was."

"I spent a lot of time digging into the life and times of our boy Judson," Oz chimed in. "He left a trail of petty destruction behind him, a couple of kids, and overlapping wives. The individual the wives knew was all about the steroids, pumping iron in the gym, and a lot of strutting around, making himself the center of attention."

Kate shook her head. "It fascinates me that he made this re-creation of himself so . . ."

"Soft," Jonas supplied, his voice like a whip. The word *soft* sounding like a curse. "He deliberately makes himself seem smaller than he is. He wants to be mistaken for an easily forgotten pencil pusher. But he must have known that a single handshake would blow his cover."

"Does that mean he made you, too?" Benedict asked.

Jonas considered. "Not much to make. I wasn't pretending I didn't have a military background. He was."

"Whatever he's doing, he was playing with us," Bethan added. "I can't shake my interaction with him. It was too deliberate. And again, the options are that he either suspected I already knew who he was and rolled right up to me like that, or thought it was entertaining to flaunt himself in front of me knowing that he almost killed me. Either way."

There was another low sound throughout the room, the kind of growling male assent that Bethan knew was about the highest level of support these colleagues of hers had to offer.

Which was why Alaska Force was so much more than a job. It was home.

Oz changed the photos on the big screen. "I looked for the kind of places Judson Kerrigone might stash not just our scientist and his sister but a lab where Sowande could create any practical applications of his research. Two possibilities jump out."

"Two?" Templeton laughed, loud and long. "I don't have a single place in my life that could contain a science lab. Didn't realize it might be required."

"Only if you're a psycho," Blue said.

That only made Templeton laugh harder.

"As an at-risk teenager, he spent some time at his uncle's orchard in Upstate New York," Oz told the group. "It was supposed to cure him of petty theft, vandalism, and truancy, but it didn't take. And for about six months while he still thought he could convince a branch of the military to let him enlist, he spent a lot of time making like Rocky in a warehouse in New Jersey."

"A warehouse in New Jersey?" Templeton asked. "Isn't that a fate worse than death?"

"It *is* death. Straight up," Lucas retorted.

Kate laughed. "I'm happy to say I haven't spent enough time—by which I mean any time—in or around New Jersey."

"Yeah, yeah, you're an Alaskan by birth, we get it," Templeton rumbled at her, which made them both grin.

A great many aspersions were cast upon the great state of New Jersey then, while Lucas, the only person in the room who had spent any time there—or would admit to it—mounted what could only be called, at best, an anemic defense.

"Everyone's feelings on the Garden State are noted," Isaac said when that had gone on for a while. "We're going to break this up into two teams, because I think we have to get a move on this, and also, I'm pissed. I don't like that Dominic Carter, Judson Kerrigone, or whoever he is, tracked us. I don't like him at that wedding, I'm not happy about biological weapons that close to a major metropolitan area, and mostly, I want to personally express my feelings about an individual who almost killed two people standing in this room."

"Hear, hear," Templeton drawled.

And the rest of the group echoed him, while Bethan found herself lost once more in Jonas's dark, deep gaze. She wished it didn't feel as much like finding herself at the same time, because she should know better.

Isaac issued assignments, ignoring the heated argument that sprang up over who got to go. Because everybody wanted in on this one. Bethan was back on the original team that had gone into the South American high desert, plus Blue, which suited her fine. They all nodded at one another, then focused on the rest of the briefing.

"I'm downloading schematics and mission parameters to your tablets," Oz told them. "Go take care of your personal business, and then let's be back here after lunch to really dig into it."

"We'll fly out tonight," Isaac added. He nodded at Jonas, and thereby the rest of the California team. "Let's do the wedding debrief in thirty."

Then there was the usual flurry of activity that followed mission guidelines as everybody went to sort themselves out. Some people had to talk to significant others. Others simply had to pack their go bag and make sure anything that needed switching off in their cabin was taken care of. Others had to make phone calls.

Bethan went back to her cabin, packed and closed up in an easy ten minutes, then headed back down to the lodge, where she planned to find a quiet corner and study what Oz had sent to her tablet before the debriefing.

When she got to the lodge's front doors, Kate and Caradine were standing there, while Horatio sat at Caradine's feet. They were talking while leaning against the rail that looked over the cove, the water still draped in ribbons of fog.

"I would've thought you'd be back in Grizzly Harbor," Bethan said as she joined them. "Aren't you usually open for lunch?"

"Otis Taggert pissed me off," Caradine said with her trademark smirk. "So I closed for the day. If people are mad about it, they can take it up with him or snack on whatever treats he offers in the Bait & Tackle."

"He's the one who has that grudge against Isaac, right?" Kate asked.

Both Bethan and Caradine were well aware by now that Trooper Kate Holiday very rarely asked questions she didn't already know the answers to.

But Caradine didn't seem to mind. "Apparently he has an epic generational grudge against all members of the Gentry family. Whatever. He can explain to all the fishermen why they couldn't get their coffee this morning."

"To be clear," Kate said, not quite grinning as she met Bethan's gaze, "she didn't just close the café. She put up a sign in the window stating exactly why."

"Of course she did," Bethan said, and couldn't keep her own laugh back.

"He said some things about Isaac I didn't care for, three seats away from me in the Fairweather." Caradine smiled a lot more now than she used to, but that didn't mean it wasn't an edgy affair. "One of the benefits of small-town life is being able to respond in kind."

As the other two started talking about the particular Alaskan flavor of small-town life here, Bethan couldn't keep herself from thinking about last night. It had been a dream come true and a nightmare in the making all at once, because Bethan didn't know how on earth she was going to live here, in the one place she'd ever felt like she belonged, when Jonas was here, too.

Because unless she was missing something, while he might have enjoyed having sex with her, he not only had no plans to take it further than that but probably wouldn't even know what that looked like.

Sometimes she thought about the things that man had faced, long before he'd joined the service and become his own personal war machine, and she wanted to cry. Sob out loud. And then break things.

A sentiment she doubted very much he would appreciate.

"You have a very strange look on your face," Caradine said, snapping Bethan back to the here and now.

"It's just my face," Bethan said, but she wiped her expression blank.

Caradine looked unconvinced.

Kate, on the other hand, looked far more speculative. "How was it? Playing wedding dates with Jonas?"

"How do you think it was?" Bethan adjusted the duffel bag she was carrying on her shoulder, though it didn't need adjusting. "Always the life of the party, that one."

"If I was the kind of person to ask questions like this," Caradine said, as if to herself, "I would want to know why you have a little mark. Right here." She pointed to her clavicle, making Bethan freeze.

Somehow she managed to avoid slapping her own hand to her collarbone. "I don't have a mark there," she said flatly.

Kate laughed. "You don't. But now you're blushing."

"I don't blush," Bethan gritted out.

"Good thing," Caradine said then, an evil little glint in her eyes. "Because if you did, you'd be bright red by now. And sooner or later, if you were in the presence of your other friends, who are far less restrained than Kate and me, it would be like an interrogation."

"I prefer only to interrogate suspects," Kate said. "As a rule."

"Great chat," Bethan replied brightly. Desperately. "Girl power, intimate friend time, whatever. Glad we could do this. Now, if you'll excuse me, I have to go chase bad guys."

Her friends laughed at her as she turned to go. And it took every bit of training Bethan had ever had to keep from breaking into a run to get away from that knowing sound.

Or worse, to stay right where she was. And unburden herself, when she knew better.

Because talking about what had happened between her and Jonas would only make everything worse.

It might even make it real.

Twenty

Jonas couldn't sleep.

It was one more indication of what a goner he was, not that he needed further evidence. He was 100 percent screwed, top to bottom, and he knew it.

Because soldiers of his caliber didn't have insomnia. They couldn't afford it. He slept when there was time to sleep, because there was no telling when that kind of time would come again. Chances were always high that it wouldn't.

But here he was, wide awake as the jet hung somewhere over Canada, en route to New York. Staring out at the moon.

Questioning what the hell he was doing.

His bad decisions kept intensifying, and there was a part of him that resented the fact that while his world seemed to be inside out and getting worse by the second, Bethan was currently sleeping like a baby. Six feet in front of him, in one of the reclining sleeper chairs in the main part of the jet. He resented that he knew for a fact that when the jet was packed like it was tonight and sleep space was at a premium, she never went and took a place in one of the state-rooms. Because that meant no one would go in and get a little shut-eye next to her the way they would if she were just another guy claiming one of the wide beds. Not that she'd ever drawn that boundary, but everyone tended to give her that respect whenever possible.

Bethan, of course, didn't want it.

And Jonas would have said that he'd spent his life learning how to keep himself from wanting anything.

Because it was better that way. Safer.

Now he couldn't stop.

Templeton was sacked out across from him, but Jonas noticed the moment the other man's breathing changed. He wasn't surprised to find his brother-in-arms suddenly completely alert, as if he'd downed a pot of coffee in the time it took most people to open their eyes and remember they were alive.

"You're thinking too loud," Templeton said, and not in that trademark booming voice of his that would have woken up the entire plane. "It's giving me nightmares."

Jonas didn't bother to respond to that. Or crack an expression of any kind, for that matter. Not that it bothered Templeton.

"The funny thing about you keeping me awake," Templeton continued, shifting in his comfortable seat that could easily sleep most men but was a little snug for his huge frame, "is that it's not how you normally roll, is it? You could be freaking out and no one would ever know it, because you're too busy making like a ghost."

"I think maybe you're talking in your sleep," Jonas replied.

Templeton grinned. "Nice one. But no. I've seen you sleep through regime changes. Why are you awake tonight?"

"A better question is why you think that's your business."

"Wide-awake on a routine overnight flight, unnaturally

chatty, and on top of that, snippy?" Templeton shook his head. "I don't know, buddy. That adds up to a whole lot of brooding discontent, which I didn't think was your thing."

"I've never trusted army math," Jonas replied coolly. "Not thinking I'm going to start now."

Templeton grinned his appreciation of that one. And for a moment, he was quiet.

But Jonas didn't relax, because he knew better. Templeton liked to act like he was everybody's best friend, but the reality was, he was a remarkably tenacious individual. And scary good at getting information out of people who didn't want to give it.

"To the casual observer," Templeton said after a while, "it seems like maybe playing Bethan's boyfriend for a week isn't sitting too well."

"That or I'm preparing myself to meet the man responsible for putting me into a hospital rehab center for six months of my life."

"You mean after Bethan saved your life. From the big, bad wolf, while you were as helpless as a baby. Just to clarify."

Jonas did not actually give Templeton the finger, because he was above such things. Also, it would only entertain his friend. Still, the sentiment seemed to hang in the air between them.

Templeton grinned. "I've known you a long time, Jonas. In and out of too many versions of hell to count. And I think you and I both know that you're not apprehensive about getting a chance to express your feelings on that subject to Dominic Carter. You can't wait."

"I'm only good at one thing," Jonas replied, meeting his friend's gaze steadily. Even though he didn't want to. Maybe especially because he didn't want to. "And I'm really, really good at it."

He didn't say that thing was war. He didn't have to, not to Templeton, who already knew.

"I know you think that," his friend said quietly. "But I'm one of the few people who's seen you fall apart. In case you forgot."

"I never forget."

Not that he particularly wanted to remember the cold winter he'd spent in the Alaskan interior. He, Templeton, and Isaac had walked away from their last official mission when no one else did. Then they'd walked away from the service. After they'd left the usual Washington, D.C., circus behind, Isaac and Templeton had decided they were going to head out of there and figure out civilian life.

Jonas hadn't bothered. He was no civilian. He'd barely been a member of society before he'd become what the navy had made him, and all his years playing dangerous Delta Force games had nailed that down tight.

But what did a man made to make war do in peacetime? What did a loaded weapon with an inconvenient pulse do with himself when he had nowhere to aim?

He'd spent a dark season in a crude cabin with nothing but his guns and his thoughts, puzzling that one out. He knew that Isaac and Templeton believed that he'd been in despair, that he'd been a mess. He hadn't been. He'd been in a hole, sure, but he'd been deciding if it was worth climbing his way out.

"That wasn't me falling apart," he said now. "There's a reason we lock up certain members of society. It's for the public good. I was quarantining myself until I figured out where I fell on that."

Templeton rolled his eyes. "I don't need a lecture on the benefits of the prison system. You think I don't know that particular dance? You think I don't have my own dark nights of the soul? Of course it's easier to pretend you're some kind of machine. Everybody gets that."

"If you get it, then I don't understand why we're having this conversation."

"You get to be human," Templeton said, so softly that

there was no reason Jonas should have felt the other man's voice go through him as if he'd shouted. Or punctuated that sentence with his fists. "You are flesh and blood and mortal, no matter what you do to pretend otherwise. And there's nothing wrong with that."

"I appreciate the biology lesson."

Templeton shook his head. "Your parents sucked. Your childhood was a war zone. Believe me, I relate. The world isn't going to end if you let yourself be happy now, brother. I promise."

And whatever Jonas might have said to that, Templeton cut off the possibility. He shut his eyes again, shoved his headphones into his ears, and gave every appearance of falling immediately back into a deep slumber.

Leaving Jonas even more unsettled than before.

It wasn't that there was too much noise inside him suddenly. He was good at blocking out noise. He didn't allow distractions.

But Bethan was more insidious than that. All he could think about was pink. Pastels and pillows. That cottage of hers, soft and cozy, both unexpected and entirely her.

She was like sunlight, reaching into parts of him that had never seen the light of day. He didn't know if he resented it or thirsted for it, but whatever it was, he felt poisoned. Altered.

Except this was the kind of poison he didn't think was going to kill him.

Maybe he only wished it would.

He was something like relieved when they landed in a private airfield outside New York City. Everyone was awake and ready to set about the process of deplaning, splitting up into their two separate teams, and taking possession of the waiting vehicles.

Isaac was leading the warehouse team. He and Jonas, leader of the Upstate New York team, conferred for a moment while everyone else threw their bags into the back of their respective vehicles, checked their weapons, and handled their adrenaline.

"I have a bad feeling about all of this," Isaac said quietly. "You?"

"No more than usual." Jonas kept his gaze on Isaac. He did not look around to see what Bethan was doing. He did not need that, because he shouldn't need anything. "This guy already took a shot at messing with our heads. I'm not sure what else he has to go on."

"We'll see," Isaac muttered. He jerked his chin at Jonas, and then they all headed out.

Jonas took the wheel of the SUV and headed north. At this time of the morning, just before rush hour and headed away from New York City—and therefore the worst of the congestion—it was an estimated two hours to the old orchard near the Hudson River, in a typically old East Coast town with one of those Dutch names.

No one talked much until Blue announced he was studying the schematics. That led to talking through various options for taking the perimeter. Then the farmhouse and assorted outbuildings.

"I don't think it would be that hard to renovate the place on the down-low and get state-of-the-art lab facilities in there without anyone being the wiser," Blue said.

"Does it have to be state-of-the-art?" August asked. "Or does it just have to be usable?"

"I would think it has to be secure, first and foremost," Bethan said, from directly behind Jonas. "How unstable is this SuperThrax? Is that a factor in the kind of facility Sowande would need?"

"I guess we'll find out," Rory said with a laugh.

No one else laughed.

Sometime later, Jonas turned off the main highway. He let the navigation system lead him through a series of winding, pretty back roads, circling around the old orchard to drop them on the far side. A good mile or so back from the various structures identified on Oz's latest map.

He stashed the car and they all rolled out, then prepared to take their previously agreed-upon positions.

"We're in position in New Jersey," Isaac said into everyone's comm unit. "Updates to follow."

"Roger that," Jonas replied. "Approaching the perimeter of the farmhouse."

The team fanned out and began to move in. The sun had come up while they were driving, and it lit up the budding, gnarled trees that made up what was left of the old orchard. They went in fast but carefully, because everyone was certain that if this was the right place, it had to be alarmed—if not outright booby-trapped.

That only meant they needed to be both swift and sure.

For a solid ten minutes, there was radio silence as the whole team moved into place.

"I'm around to the front of the building," Bethan said into the comm unit, not sounding the least bit out of breath, even though she must have run full out in tactical gear, plus weapons, to get there. Because of course she wasn't out of breath. Jonas ordered himself to listen to her, not her breathing. "There are no cars in the drive, but there's clear evidence of significant recent activity. It's a little muddy and there are tracks. At least four vehicles, by my count."

"Any visible signs of life from within?" Jonas asked.

"Negative," Bethan replied.

Jonas had taken the rear of the farmhouse. He settled into the best vantage point he could find while the others called in their various positions from the outbuildings.

No signs of life all around.

But that could mean anything. Including the possibility that they were being watched right now. More than a possibility, to Jonas's mind.

He scanned the back of the farmhouse, seeing no movement. Then on his second scan of the scene before him, his gaze caught on a window on the second floor. It was cracked open, and he knew instantly that wasn't right.

"I don't see anything out back," he reported. "But there's a cracked open window on the second floor."

"This part of the world can still get cold this time of year," Rory replied. "I don't think people leave windows open if they're not planning to come back real soon."

"Agreed," said Griffin. He had taken a position high on the barn's roof, with an overview of the house. "I'm in position and see nothing moving anywhere, but I don't like it."

"Do any of those outbuildings look the least bit scientific?" Bethan asked.

"Negative on that," Blue said. "There are three. Two look like sheds. Unused sheds with overgrown vegetation in front. Still a possibility that they could be entrances to some kind of subterranean situation, but my gut says no. And the third doesn't have four walls. It's wide open; I can see straight through it, and there's nothing there."

"Same on the west side of the property," August chimed in. "The old barn is missing windows and has ancient cars packed inside. Unless it's all Hollywood-level misdirection, I don't think anyone's been in this place in years."

"Ditto the garages down by the main road," Rory said. "Locked up tight and dusty."

Jonas scanned the back of the house again, his senses telling him that this was the place. Even if there hadn't been tire marks on the front drive, he had that feeling he knew well enough to treat like another piece of navigational equipment. He just knew.

"We have to take the house," he clipped out. "Rory, stay down by the road. Bethan and I will take point. Blue, August, get into position to cover, then join us."

There was a quick series of assents, and then it was on.

Jonas felt himself slip into that particular space that he'd always liked best. The heightened danger. The adrenaline and cortisol. And all the grueling training that let him use all that to do things regular people couldn't.

He didn't have to see his teammates. He knew where they were. He knew them, so he knew how they would move, how they would cover him, how they would follow orders when necessary and take their own initiative, too.

These war games were the only time he felt alive. Or connected.

Or they were, something in him suggested. *Until Bethan.*

But this was emphatically not the time for such thoughts, especially if they were true. He assured himself he'd handle it all later. He'd face what needed facing, honestly. That was who he was, whatever else he wasn't.

Here, now, there was the mission.

He headed toward the farmhouse's back door at a low run, not liking the fact that he had to expose himself for a little too long while he made the break from the surrounding trees. He assumed Bethan was experiencing the same problem, and there was nothing for it. Some situations required stealth and cover. But this one wasn't one of them.

Jonas made it to the back door, automatically checked his weapon, and then took approximately three seconds to work the lock.

He opened the door, that prickling sense of his on overdrive as he stepped in.

It just wasn't right. He didn't believe that an individual like the one they were chasing would leave a door like that. So easy to open. *Too* easy, when the same person had tracked Alaska Force without their knowledge and abducted the Sowandes without a trace.

But he shoved that aside as he conducted a sweep of the first floor. He found nothing interesting in the kitchen or the living room, and he was finishing an initial walk-through of the dining room when he met Bethan coming down the stairs from the second floor.

Because she'd known he would handle the first floor, so

she'd gone upstairs without asking for confirmation. Working with her had never been anything but seamless.

Not now, he growled at himself.

"I found your window," she said in a low voice, her eyes still scanning around them, as if she were waiting for an armed response team to leap out at any moment. Just like he was. "There's nothing personal in the room, but it was recently used. The other rooms on the second floor are stripped of any bedclothes, pillows, and so on. That particular room has two made-up twin beds, one of which looks more rumpled than the other."

"Someone's been staying there."

Bethan nodded. "The window is typical for an old house like this and is too swollen to open fully. Now it's stuck. This might be going out on a limb, but my guess? They stuck Iyara in there, she tried to escape, and couldn't."

"Why the sister? Why not the scientist?"

"Just a feeling." Bethan didn't quite grin at him, which still felt more personal—more intimate—than it should have. "It doesn't feel like a man was in there. Also the twin beds are kid-sized. Sowande is not a small man."

Jonas nodded, tucking that away. "Attic?"

"Crawl space," Bethan replied.

And then they waited. Until they both heard the faint, almost to be confused for some far-off bit of wildlife sound that Jonas knew was the others joining them.

Sure enough, moments later, first Blue, then August, materialized.

Jonas nodded at them. "Get ready for whoever was here to come back. Rory, if they show up, don't stop them. Let them come. Meanwhile, Bethan and I are going to take a look in the basement."

"Check," Rory said over the comm unit.

"You got it." August was already moving to take a position overlooking the front drive.

Blue nodded, then melted off to the west side of the

house, where a private dirt lane wound around and came in from the orchards.

"Ready?" Jonas asked Bethan.

She jerked her chin in an affirmative. Then she fell in behind him as he headed for the back of the house and the door to the basement he'd seen on his first pass through the kitchen.

"Old houses like this are creaky," Bethan murmured as they moved. "If anyone's down there, they already know we're here."

Jonas's personal alarm system was still working overtime.

"It's too easy," he muttered.

Bethan made a noise of agreement. "The front door was unlocked."

That didn't sit right. Jonas considered as they went into the kitchen, then nodded toward the basement door. "I guess we know we're in the right place."

And there was no choice. That was the way missions like this went. It wasn't about identifying the threat. It was about neutralizing it.

They stood at the door to the basement, and the look they shared seemed to swell in him—

Later, he told himself sternly. He would deal with all this, somehow, later.

Bethan nodded jerkily, like she was in his head. Then she went and put her hand on the doorknob.

At the same moment, the comm units went wild.

"Abort!" came Isaac's voice, louder than usual. "Warehouse, abort! Bomb set to detonate. *Repeat, abort!*"

Two hours north, Jonas and Bethan froze. No one on their team spoke, and still, Jonas was sure he could hear their agony, loud and clear.

They could hear their friends and colleagues shout to one another down in that warehouse, a state away.

Then thirty seconds later, everything went silent.

Another thirty seconds passed, but Jonas stayed where he was, frozen in place. Watching all the shock and sickness in him wash over Bethan's face, though she didn't let them land. And he had the stray thought that there were some intimacies no one should have to share.

"One minute since detonation," he bit out in the comm unit, his voice flat and commanding, because that was all he had. That was all there was. "Warehouse, report."

But there was nothing.

Another whole minute dragged by.

"The blast could've taken out communication in all directions," Blue growled from his position.

"Two minutes out," Jonas replied. And there were protocols. Their line of work required it. He shut his eyes for a moment, but only a moment. "We have to move. Rory, get Oz on tracking duty and proof of life. Blue and August, maintain your positions. Griffin—"

"Anything so much as breathes too loud," came the sniper's voice, even colder than usual, "and I'll drop it."

When Jonas's gaze found Bethan again, she swallowed. Making him wonder what look was on his face. He didn't know, which was telling enough.

She reached out and touched his arm. Briefly. And then, before he could comment on that or lash out at her or grab her tight, she turned to the basement door again. She eased it open with no visible shake in her hand, then stepped inside.

Bethan slapped on the light switch and moved double-time down the stairs. Jonas was at her back, taking in the situation as she moved. They made it to the foot of the old unfinished stairs without incident, then paused. He looked around, finding the place cramped and damp, with a musty smell thick in the air.

It looked like every basement he'd ever bothered to imagine.

It was also a lie, he realized in the next instant.

"This basement is the wrong dimensions," Bethan said in an undertone.

"Check," Jonas replied. "Also, no dust or cobwebs."

She was already moving, skirting the wall that held an old sink, laundry facilities, and an open cabinet packed tight with what looked like gardening supplies. The wall next to the cabinet was smoother than it should have been. Out of place. She squatted down, and Jonas came up behind her to look over her shoulder.

On the ground, there were clear signs of a door swinging open and closed.

It took her only moments to look around and find the lever, almost hidden behind the cabinet.

"You're covered," Jonas told her.

"Any reports?" she asked, because it was possible he might have heard something on a private channel.

"Negative," he said.

And he couldn't think about that. He couldn't think about the explosion, or what might have happened at that warehouse. This was what they trained for. The ability to do their jobs no matter what.

No matter who they lost.

Bethan threw the lever, then pulled open the heavy door. Jonas was unsurprised that behind her, on the other side of the door, there was a high-tech medical facility. Unsurprised, but suddenly a lot more alert.

Bethan moved inside, looking around, taking in the lab. It was a large place, stretching out much farther than the foundations of the house. Everything looked sterile.

And more, empty.

They went in farther, looking around as if they expected the Sowandes to appear out from under a lab table. But there was nothing. Only medical supplies and cameras everywhere, telling Jonas that this place was under surveillance. Live surveillance, if the red lights were any indication. He didn't bother pointing them out to Bethan, sure that she'd seen them, but decided to go and see if he could disable one.

Until behind them, the door swung shut. And the air-conditioning switched on with a hum.

"Well," Bethan said after a moment. "That's not good."

And they both turned when a large screen on the wall nearest them crackled to life.

A moment later, there was Dominic Carter. A smug, disembodied head.

"Oh, hey, Judson," Bethan said casually. Jonas had the deeply uncharacteristic urge to hug her, but didn't. "Weird that you keep turning up in the strangest places. Like a basement in the middle of nowhere."

The other man bared his teeth, looking nothing like the smiling fool he'd played in California.

"Congratulations," he sneered, and laughed. A creepy sound Jonas did not want to hear again. "You've just been infected with SuperThrax. I hope you enjoy the rest of your life. The current estimate is forty-eight hours before you start getting sick, and then a brutal, painful race to the finish. I can't think of any two people who deserve to suffer more."

And then, with another laugh, the screen went blank.

Twenty-one

After the screen went dark, neither Bethan nor Jonas moved.

Bethan could feel her heart in her chest, and her pulse hard in places like her wrists. Her neck. Her temples.

And all she could see was Jonas.

He looked the way he always did, stern and austere and stark—except for his eyes. They were far too dark. Ravaged. Filled with a ferocity she'd never seen before.

She didn't know whether that should scare her. When what she really felt was something like guilty and grateful at the same time that if this thing were really happening to her, he was here to share it.

"What's happening down there?" Blue asked.

"Not like he's a trustworthy source," Bethan said. She didn't speak into her comm unit, but even as she said the words out loud she knew she was hedging. Trying not to say something for fear the act of saying it would make it real.

Suddenly, that seemed foolish.

"We're going to need to contain this," Jonas replied, his voice gravelly, and also not broadcast to the rest of the team. "Whatever the situation is."

But neither one of them moved.

Bethan could feel the very air around them pressing in on her, like a big hand tight around her throat. She tried to breathe, deep. She tried to push that hard grip off, gain an inch or two of space, because she couldn't allow herself to break down. Not now. Not if all she had left was forty-eight hours and a grim finish.

That's more than Isaac had—

But she couldn't go there.

Jonas didn't reach for her. He didn't wrap his arms around her, put his chin on the top of her head, or do any of the things he had done what felt like a lifetime ago in her cabin. And still, the way he looked at her, that pressure on her throat eased. She managed a decent breath.

"We have a situation," he said into his comm unit, his eyes still on her. "Bethan and I have been potentially exposed to SuperThrax. We're going to need a containment unit, medical personnel, and if I'm making a wish list, an antidote."

There was a long silence. Not unlike the one that had followed the explosion earlier.

Bethan refused to let herself think about that. She couldn't afford it. Not now.

"On it," Blue said eventually, his voice forbidding.

Bethan knew that if she stayed where she was, looking at Jonas like this, she would do something they would both regret. Right here in this sterile death lab where Dominic Kerrigone, or whoever he was, was clearly watching their every move. But this was no place for emotion, so instead, she went over to the door to see if it had sealed them in when it shut. She studied the latching mechanism as best she could but didn't pull the door open, because there was no need to expose everyone else in the house.

"I don't think we're actually locked in here," she told Jonas. "But I don't want to take the risk."

"Understood."

For another moment, their eyes seemed to catch. Bethan could feel her heart speeding up, that grip at her throat, but she knew there was no point in acknowledging it. Anything she said would only make this worse.

"Okay," Jonas gritted out, his dark gaze flashing. "Let's see if we can find anything in here, since we're not going anywhere."

A task was good.

They each took a separate side of the lab space and explored. They opened drawers, rifled through notes. Looked for anything and everything that might give them a clue as to what had gone on here.

While they were at it, they disabled the monitoring system. And once that was done, Jonas picked up a wastebasket from under a desk and shook out a few balled-up pieces of paper. He spread them out on one of the lab tables between them, ironing out the crinkles in the paper with his big hands, forcing Bethan to remind herself that the point was the paper and what was written on it. Not his hands.

She ordered herself to focus. One looked like some sort of scientific equation. The next was an address in New York City. The third was a little bit of doodling. The longer Bethan stared at the curly little doodles, the more she thought that they were actually numbers. She reached over and traced them with her finger, and Jonas's gaze sharpened as he took pictures of each of the three papers and sent them to Oz.

"Threes," he said.

"Could be a clue." Bethan traced one of the bigger ones. "Or it could be a doodle."

"A containment unit is mobilized," Blue said into the comm unit in a brisk, furious voice that was almost as bad as something sentimental. "ETA is forty-five minutes or less."

"Let's hope for less," Jonas replied.

Bethan didn't expect an immediate response from Oz, not with so much else going on. But that left the two of them, standing here. Locked in this room. Maybe already halfway dead, though she still felt fine. She took another breath, to test it.

Nothing was happening. Nothing was wrong, yet, and still she felt as if she were being squeezed too tight to breathe.

Because she wasn't sure SuperThrax was something she could fight off. She couldn't shoot it. She couldn't disarm it. She couldn't strike it in the face and bring it to the ground. She wouldn't have let herself think such a thing before the explosion, but it was possible she was really done this time.

"Jonas," she said very quietly. "Everything is terrible. But I want you to know—"

There was a loud, shocking noise.

It took her a panicked moment to realize that it had come from him. That Jonas Crow had pounded his fist into the lab table between them.

"*Don't*," he belted out, a harsh one-word command.

"I only want—"

"I have spent my entire life more than ready to die," Jonas told her, not raising his voice. But then, he didn't have to raise it. Not when it seemed to fill the room. "I signed up for it. I courted it. And I would have been perfectly happy to go at any time. But not now." His gaze was so dark it made her heart kick at her. "In three days you can tell me anything you want, Bethan. But not here. Not now."

And Bethan thought that her sister and all her sister's friends, or her mother for that matter, might not appreciate those words. They might not understand them for what they were.

But she did.

Jonas had ripped out his heart, placed it on the table between them, wrapped it in a bow, and made it hers.

"I love you, too," she told him quietly.

And he looked . . . haunted. Wild and electric. Furious.

But he reached across the narrow table, fitting his hand to her cheek in a manner she could not quite describe as tender. It was too hard. Too intense.

His gaze was boring into her so intently she almost thought that look alone might save them. She was surprised it didn't.

"Don't you dare say that to me when you think you're going to die." It was possible he was whispering, harsh and low, but she heard every single word like a shout. Deep inside her and all around her, so loud it drowned out the world. "Don't you throw it at me like some kind of Hail Mary."

"I felt like it needed to be said."

"Love is for the living," Jonas growled at her. "Which is why I've never wanted any part of it. You want to love me, Bethan? Figure out how to keep us alive."

Some women might like flowers. Chocolates. A sonnet or two written in their honor.

But Bethan got Jonas, big and pissed off and more animated than she'd ever seen him while he was fully clothed, ordering her to *live*. Then love him. In that order.

If she were the kind of woman to swoon, she would have, but she was too afraid she might not come out of it.

"I'll love you any way I want," she told him. "But you're right. I would like to do it for more than forty-eight hours and a steep decline."

"Bethan," he began, and she could see the torture on his face. All over him. All the things she'd always known had lurked there beneath that cold facade of his. "You have to know—"

There was a crackling burst of sound in their comm units. They both jerked back, each putting a hand to the ear where the noise was coming from. Once again, their gazes were locked together.

Another long, loud crackle.

"Who has an open channel?" Griffin demanded, sounding arctic. "This is not the time."

There was a pause. Then a long, fluid, creative string of curses.

But Bethan's heart leapt inside her chest. Because there was only one person she knew—

"Templeton," Jonas said, his voice cracking slightly. He coughed to cover it, but it didn't matter. Bethan felt the same.

"Templeton, you beautiful bastard," came Blue's voice, sounding as suspiciously intense as Bethan felt. As Jonas looked. "Tell me some good news."

There was another long crackling sound, another loud spate of swears and invocations, but again, all clearly Templeton.

"We are all present, accounted for, and intact," came another voice, cool and measured.

Isaac. Bethan sagged a little against the lab table, while across from her, Jonas dropped his head for a moment.

"The warehouse was leveled, and it blew up our vehicle," Isaac said. "Kicked out the comm router."

"Would've taken us with it," Templeton said, sounding mildly irritated and a little bit lazy, and Bethan had never been so happy to hear him being perfectly *him* in all her life. "But there were some disgusting bunkers to hide out in."

"Old garage bays," came Lucas's voice. "I think this place used to be a chop shop."

"I'm a little banged up," Isaac said, sounding clipped. *Pissed*, Bethan thought, and that was enough to make her straighten her spine. "My ears are still ringing. I thought I was about to bite it, and I have to tell you all, the idea that this lowlife could take me out remotely did not sit well. I want him ended."

"Hear, hear," August said.

"But first," Isaac continued, all leashed rage and tempered fury, "what's this I hear about a containment unit?"

"Oh, just SuperThrax exposure, no big deal," Bethan said.

She could see the half smile on Jonas's stern mouth. The hope in his eyes where before it had been nothing but that darkness. "Bethan and I have forty-eight hours. Then the painful death begins."

"Before that party starts," Bethan continued, "I'd kind of like to find this guy and hurt him. And while we're at it, locate the Sowandes and see if maybe they have an antidote."

"That works for me," Isaac said, sounding official and *alive* and in charge, the way he was supposed to be. "You two hold tight. Everyone else, lock down that house. Then tear it apart. I want anything and everything. We'll be there within the hour."

"We found a few things of potential interest here in the death lab," Bethan said, because Jonas was too busy smiling. "I'm guessing that now Oz knows we're all alive and kicking, he'll get it all out to everyone shortly."

"You all need to hurry up and figure this out," came Oz's voice, all the way from Alaska, and he, too, sounded different. Because the worst had happened, but then hadn't, and they were all still reeling. She knew she was. "And then come back to Alaska, where you're all obviously safer with the grizzlies."

Templeton's laugh boomed in Bethan's ear then. Miles away, she and Jonas smiled at each other, the way they had when they were locked up tight in her cabin. And she knew that everybody here in this farmhouse probably had that same half-goofy smile on their faces.

And for the rest of that hour, it was almost easy to forget her own death sentence. Oz kept feeding in updates and clarifications as he worked overtime to track the transmission that had come into the lab, find the remote detonation trigger down in New Jersey, and try to run diagnostics on the clues they'd sent in.

Inside the farmhouse, the team tore each and every room apart, looking for anything that could give them a clue as to what had gone on here. Bethan and Jonas had to sit it out, trying to out-calm each other when she knew he was probably as close to coming out of his skin as she was.

Then the containment team arrived, and everything was hazmat suits, invasive checkups, and stripping down naked while pretending not to notice or care that Jonas was doing the same, so they could get sprayed down. Repeatedly.

Anthrax wasn't contagious. SuperThrax showed no signs of being contagious, either—people couldn't share it between them like a virus; they had to be exposed the way Bethan and Jonas had been. Still, *abundance of caution* was the watchword in situations like this.

By the time they'd been hosed down enough to start taking it personally, examined repeatedly, and tested so many times that Bethan was surprised she still had any blood left in her body, another few hours slid by.

Given that she currently had so few left, Bethan found she resented that. Deeply.

She and Jonas had been moved from the lab to a makeshift quarantine unit set up out in the field in front of the old farmhouse. It looked like a crime scene. Isaac and the warehouse team had taken a chopper up, allowing medical attention only once they'd arrived. The containment team had come in a different helicopter, and an Alaska Force support unit in a third, so everywhere she looked, there were very serious people doing very serious things, while her life had turned into an hourglass.

And she was sure that she could feel each and every grain of sand as it slipped away.

"They need to let us out of here," Jonas growled from behind her.

They'd been issued new clothes because theirs were potentially contaminated, and Bethan chose to focus on how annoyed she was by that. She'd had to surrender her weapons as well as her clothes, each and every item of which she had personally selected and, more, relied on. Better to let herself feel grumpy about that outrage than to focus on her own impending death.

They were both wearing gray T-shirts and cargo pants now, but Jonas looked much better in his. The shirt wasn't quite big enough for him, so his biceps were doing the Lord's work, there against the sleeves that strained to fit him.

If that was the last thing she was going to get to see, Bethan couldn't complain.

"Here's what I keep thinking," she said before she lost it and either touched Jonas or broke down into sobs. "Why dose us with SuperThrax?"

Jonas looked suddenly intense in that way he got when his head started spinning out strategies.

Bethan pushed on. "That was a sealed room. If he wanted us dead, surely there were more efficient ways to do it."

"Good point. Why two to three days?"

She considered. "I guess it's possible he just wants to torture us."

"Back in the desert he blew up the convoy, then came in on foot to finish the job. He doesn't strike me as a hands-off kind of a guy. In Santa Barbara, he made sure he shook hands with both of us."

"Literally hands-on," Bethan agreed.

While Jonas turned that over in his head, Bethan watched their friends and colleagues outside. All a little bit battered and bloody, maybe, but alive. Her comm unit had been confiscated with the rest of her gear, and a part of her wondered if that was for the best. No chance for sentimentality that way. Isaac had come and put his hand on the other side of the thick plastic walls that kept Jonas and Bethan quarantined. Jonas had lifted his in return. Bethan had only smiled, so bright and wide she thought her jaw might crack.

Templeton was putting on a show out there, laughing

good and loud while Blue pretended to be irritated, and that, too, was comforting.

"I have to think that he didn't leave random pieces of paper behind by accident," Jonas said. Bethan shifted around to look at him.

"Maybe it's an invitation," she suggested. "That address at three o'clock."

He nodded. "I'm sure we're supposed to think that the recipe is an antidote, but I'm betting it's not."

"That would be easy," Bethan agreed.

Jonas's mouth crooked up in one corner, as if that were easier for him now. "Isaac specifically told us both to stay put."

Bethan grinned. "That he did. He seemed pretty serious about it, too."

Let us figure out how we're going to handle this, he had said. And then he'd looked each one of them straight on and ordered them to let that happen.

"Good thing this is a private security company," Bethan mused, still grinning. "And not the United States Army, where I would feel duty-bound to obey that order."

"I couldn't agree more." That crook at the side of Jonas's mouth deepened. "We're losing our hours here, Bethan. You ready to go rogue?"

Bethan did not say, *I would follow you anywhere.*

But she thought that was implied when that was what she did, moving swiftly after him when he picked up one of the medical implements the doctors had left behind, cut a slit through the plastic sheeting, and made a break for it.

Twenty-two

They were a good forty-five minutes down the Taconic Parkway when the call came in, lighting up the SUV's console. Jonas debated ignoring it, but a few hours ago he would have killed half the world to have a pissed-off Isaac in his ear. He couldn't bring himself to squander any opportunity, whatever it looked like.

"What exactly do you think you're doing?" came Isaac's voice, not in the least bit cool or controlled.

"I'm not dying standing still, brother," Jonas replied, switching lanes and taking the curves of the winding highway with far too much speed. "I can tell you that."

"Then I hope you and Bethan are taking a little joyride," Isaac retorted. "Taking in the sights, maybe."

"I've always wanted to see Niagara Falls," Bethan piped in from the passenger side.

Isaac grunted. "I don't believe you."

"That's why you're the boss." Bethan laughed. "I actually saw the falls when I was in high school. Very loud, it turns out."

Isaac sighed. "I don't suppose there's any point in asking you to turn that vehicle around and return to the containment facility."

"I can't do that," Jonas replied. "For one thing, the containment facility is no longer contained."

"You mean because you cut your way out of it?"

Jonas and Bethan exchanged a look, because that was a lot more temper than Isaac normally displayed.

Then again, it had been a long day.

"We think there's a personal component to this," Jonas said after a moment. "I'm betting if you look at the air-filtration system in that basement, you'll find that there were other options available to our guy."

"Actually, yes." Isaac made a sound that wasn't *quite* a sigh. "The support team just finished testing down there, and there was cyanide, loaded and ready to go."

Bethan was nodding. "That would have killed us right away, wouldn't it?"

"Correct," Isaac said.

"But he chose option B." Jonas passed a slow-moving sports car. "There has to be a reason for that."

"You can't really think this guy went to all the trouble to kidnap a scientist, build a secret lab, activate fail-safes, and create a biological weapon, all to flush the two of you out."

"I think we're the icing on the cake," Bethan said matter-of-factly. "It's no secret that I work for Alaska Force. All he had to do was ask my father what his daughters do for a living and he would've gotten chapter and verse. And there's no way he didn't know it was Alaska Force out there in that high-desert ghost town."

"That doesn't justify—" Isaac began.

"So you're this guy," Jonas interrupted him. "Years ago, you have a near-death experience out in the desert, but you don't think better of your life choices because of it. You double down. You go underground, nurse your grudges, and wait. And then, look at that, the perfect opportunity presents itself."

"I understand that this guy has a hard-on for the two of you," Isaac said. "But I have two competing issues. First is the fact that you have a death sentence on your heads. I don't really think you should be running around and encouraging your bodies to process all that poison even more quickly."

"That's a legitimate concern," Bethan said in her soldier's voice, basic acknowledgment without offering a solution. Why did that make him want to smile?

Isaac clearly chose to ignore that. "The second issue is bigger. It's that this man, proven unstable already, has a biological weapon in his hands. Maybe he was just testing it out on the two of you. Either way, where will he test it next? I'm thinking, if I'm in the business of war and defense contractors and I'm out here on the East Coast, I'm going to take down to New York City, create chaos, and profit from it."

Jonas made a low noise. "That's why we left. You focus on saving the world. Bethan and I? We're going to focus on taking this muppet down."

Isaac muttered something uncharitable.

"We have a death sentence coming at us," Jonas reminded him. "We're not contagious. What's the harm?"

Jonas knew his friend could think of all kinds of harm, but all he did was blow out a breath. "You know where our safe house is in Manhattan," he said after a moment. "I don't want you out of contact. And the minute you start feeling symptomatic—"

"I have no intention of dying today," Jonas growled, and he was aware of how Bethan reacted to that, beside him. He could feel Isaac do the same. "Or tomorrow, while we're at it."

He knew he might as well have declared himself reborn. Resurrected, even. Or someone else.

"Okay," his friend, leader, and brother-in-arms said quietly. "Then get to work."

Jonas was already driving well over the speed limit, but at that he went even faster.

"Where's the safe house in Manhattan?" Bethan asked, leaning forward to program the navigation system.

But Jonas waved her off. "I know where we're going."

And he drove even faster. Because time was running out.

Once they made it into the city, he stashed the SUV in a parking garage. Then he and Bethan walked out, blending into the sea of humanity that was Midtown Manhattan on a random, sunny workday.

New York, in Jonas's opinion, had nothing to recommend it. Crowds made him itchy. The tall buildings blocked out the sky, when he liked it visible—and big. There were too many smells, all of them the complicated result of too many human beings packed into too few square miles. Refuse. Despair. Garbage, literal and figurative. Food, mixing with all of that, and body odor, everywhere. He didn't like concrete. He didn't like traffic, stoplights, and the neon carnival that was Times Square.

But somehow, today, all of those things seemed to move in him like a kind of poem.

He looked over at Bethan as they stopped, thirty people back in a tight scrum waiting for the crosswalk to get clear of the jolting traffic. She felt his gaze on her the way she always did, glancing over and smiling slightly. But he could see the emotion in her eyes.

All these *people*. So much *life*, careless and unheeding, right here on this corner.

Jonas reached over because he couldn't help himself. Because she was the only person in his entire life who had ever told him they loved him, and he wasn't ready to deal with that. But he couldn't forget that she'd said it, either.

He took her hand, loving the way she gripped him back.

immediately. And the way her smile changed, her eyes getting soft and bright.

The light changed, and they let the crowd carry them along to cross the street that smelled like exhaust and the subway system rattling below. They were jostled, pushed, and crowded, but their fingers stayed tightly laced together. Her hand in his, skin touching skin. The most solid bond he thought he'd ever known.

So many people all around them. All that life.

And Jonas . . . *wanted*.

He wanted everything.

He wanted the noise. The smells. The wild, pointless laughter. The flashes of joy. The sharp elbows, the muttered curses.

All of it.

Most of all, he wanted Bethan. This. No words, but her gaze catching his in the middle of the crowd, deeper and better than all of those conversations he'd never bothered to have with anyone else.

When they finally made it to the utterly unremarkable apartment building squashed on a side street, Jonas wished the walk had taken five times as long. He wished that they really were off on some kind of last-day joyride.

But that wasn't who they were.

He led her inside, making himself let go of her hand as they stood in the vestibule. It was overheated and much too small, and the loss of her fingers in his felt like a flesh wound. He keyed in a code, waited for the buzzing sound and the lock to release, then pushed his way inside the second door.

Together, he and Bethan jogged up five flights of stairs to the very top floor, where he keyed in another code to the only door on the landing.

"Wow," Bethan said as they walked inside. "Isaac really knows how to live. In all these places he doesn't actually live."

"I don't actually know if he owns this one." Jonas shut and locked the door behind them, then input his fingerprint and security code into the system. "But he likes to keep safe spaces wherever he goes. Or we might go."

Bethan walked farther inside. Turning a circle, she took in the big windows, the simple but comfortable-looking furnishings. And when she turned all the way back around and faced him again, he almost thought that she would say something. The way she had back in the lab. And he braced himself, because he couldn't allow it. He couldn't process it, not yet. Not now.

But instead, her eyes glinted. "Where are the weapons?"

"That's my girl."

And she grinned, but she shook her head. "None of that. It's day three or nothing. You made the rules."

Jonas nodded, but he discovered that he was smiling, too. And that it didn't feel new, or unused, or unusual. He knew that was all her doing.

They made short work of the safe house's offerings. They upgraded their clothing to better tactical gear, because the closets were fully stocked and ready. They found and activated new comm units. Then they both loaded up on weapons, as many as they could reasonably conceal.

By the time they hit the streets again and headed south, it was almost possible to forget that they were running on borrowed time. Jonas reminded himself that forty-eight hours to the onset of symptoms was a madman's estimate. At best.

They arrived at a converted brownstone in Chelsea a little while later. Once a private home in some distant, historic version of this city, it was now visibly broken up into apartments. It sat on a block lined with more of the same, a line of once-grand brownstones with big staircases out in front of all of them, looking steep and unwelcoming to Jonas's eye.

"This is the problem with New York City," Bethan said

mildly, gazing up at the building before them, flush against its neighbor. "With a little more time, maybe I could find a way in the back. Otherwise, there's only the front door."

Jonas eyed the door. "But no need to announce ourselves."

He had every intention of picking the lock. But when the two of them made it up the front steps, a harried-looking woman in business attire came out, flinging the doors wide in front of her. Bethan smiled brightly, in a way that reminded Jonas of California, and held the door for her.

And that easily, they were inside the building.

"Do people in these apartments think they're safe?" Jonas asked when the doors to the outside were shut tight behind them and they both stood there a moment, listening. Getting a feel for the place.

Bethan shrugged. "I think they expect the outer door to be a barrier, but I also think they have numerous locks on their individual apartment doors."

He didn't quite make a face, but it was close. "I prefer living in the woods."

She grinned up at him. "You prefer being the most dangerous thing around."

"If you can't be the apex predator," Jonas said, scanning the small hall they stood in. It smelled like someone's meal. He headed for the stairs. "You'll get eaten by the apex predator."

"You should make that your Christmas card," Bethan said sweetly, and followed him up.

The address they'd been given indicated an apartment on the second floor. Jonas moved swiftly and silently up the stairs, Bethan behind him. He glanced back and wasn't surprised to see she had a gun in her hands, ready to protect their rear should anyone approach.

There were two apartment doors on the second-floor hall. Jonas stopped at the first and listened, hearing the faint sound of a television set from within. Then he moved on, soundlessly, to do the same at the second door. Where everything was ominously silent.

Bethan melted into place, covering him. Jonas flattened himself against the wall. Then he reached out laterally to test the doorknob, expecting to find it locked up tight.

But when he turned the knob gently, it gave. The door swung open.

He froze, waiting for a gunshot. A shout. Some indication that someone was on the other side, waiting, and using the open door as a trap. Because what else could it be?

Very slowly, he counted to five in his head.

"Good news," Bethan said very quietly from her watchful position. "We're already infected."

There was really nothing about that he should have found amusing, he knew. But Jonas still found himself biting back a laugh as he pushed the apartment door the rest of the way open.

He still waited at the threshold, thinking that the opening of the door could be the signal Carter was waiting for to launch his attack. But nothing happened.

Jonas eased himself inside, like the shadow he was. The door opened into a reasonably sized living area, with a kitchen on one end and a dining area tucked off on the other. Jonas checked it all in a quick sweep as Bethan moved around the island in the kitchen to weed out any lurking threats.

Everything was clear. Jonas pointed down the small hallway off the main living space.

With a nod, Bethan went first, moving with equal parts power and grace. First she checked out the bathroom to the left, but it was empty. She glanced back at Jonas before pointing to the left of the two doors that waited at the end of the hallway. He nodded, and she did the same thing he'd done at the front door of the apartment. Waiting, testing, and then quietly pushing the door open.

But the room inside was completely bare. Hardwood

floor, two windows at the far end overlooking a courtyard filled with green, and nothing else save a lightbulb in an open light fixture in the ceiling.

There was nothing about this Jonas liked. He backed up, jerking his chin to indicate that Bethan should come back out into the small hallway and then repeat the same steps on the last remaining door.

He noticed everything. He always did, but he'd become so good at shutting off the parts he didn't wish to acknowledge. Like the assured way she did her job, as if she were made of butter and steel.

She bent her head to the thick wooden door. She listened. Then carefully, soundlessly, tried the doorknob. It gave the same way all the others had.

When she pushed it open gently, carefully, Jonas expected another empty room.

But as the door widened, both he and Bethan froze.

Because the room wasn't empty.

Tayo Sowande was tied to a high-backed chair in the center of the otherwise completely empty room. His mouth was taped shut with an abundance of duct tape. His wrists and ankles were similarly restrained, taped to the chair he sat on.

There were unpleasant-looking sores—lesions, Jonas corrected himself, if he correctly remembered the anthrax informational packet the containment crew had given them—on almost every part of the man's skin.

Jonas did not need a medical degree to understand that he was looking at his own future. At exactly how he—and, more incomprehensibly, Bethan—would die. And soon.

He was so focused on that he almost missed the cherry on top of this sick, staged scene.

There was a piece of paper on the floor at Sowande's feet. Written on it, in block capital letters, it read: *TOO LATE*.

Twenty-three

Bethan instinctively moved toward the poor scientist, who was so still she couldn't tell whether he was alive or not—

But Jonas held her back with a hand on her elbow.

"Careful," he warned her. "SuperThrax isn't contagious, as far as we know, but all bets are off with an open wound."

Bethan tugged her elbow away from him. "What do you think he's going to do? Give me *more*?"

She moved across the room, going to her knees next to the chair. She pulled out one of the knives she'd taken from the safe house and sliced through the duct tape but didn't pull it off Sowande's wrists, afraid there were more sores beneath the adhesive. It was as she was trying to ease the tape off his mouth that the man blinked, then moaned.

"You're alive," Bethan said as evenly as possible. "That's the good news. The bad news is that I expect you're in a lot of pain."

"You must not touch me," Sowande said, sounding panicked. "You must not—"

"It's okay." Bethan tried to sound soothing. "We've already been exposed. We're in the same boat."

Sowande moaned again then, and this time it sounded deep. Broken. As if his pain were internal.

"It's too late," he said, tears gathering in the corners of his eyes. "It's all over now."

Bethan glanced back over her shoulder. Jonas was talking quietly into his comm unit, and she knew that he was summoning medical help. And notifying the others that they'd found their scientist, at the very least.

"I don't know if it's too late or not," Bethan said matter-of-factly when she turned back to Sowande. "Help is on the way. I assure you they will do all that they can. But you would know better than anyone. What's the likelihood of survival once you've reached this stage?"

"You don't understand," Sowande said. Then he swallowed in a painful manner that produced a deep, horrified kind of shudder move inside of her. Because she understood that the lesions she could see on his skin were inside him, too.

And would very soon be inside her.

But this was not the time to lose her ability to compartmentalize. She shoved the inevitability of her own coming doom away and concentrated on the man before her. Or tried to.

"Tell me what I don't understand," she encouraged him. "I'll try my best."

"No," she heard Jonas say from behind her. "No sign of the sister or Carter. Or anything else."

"He has Iyara," Sowande said. "He will kill her, of course. But first, he wants to test the weapon." His face crumpled as he fought whatever was working inside of him. Grief. Loss. Fear. Guilt. "I dedicated my life to this research to *fight* these weapons, and this is how I will go. The destroyer of worlds, despite everything."

"Listen to me," Bethan said then, in a voice of command that made the man before her blink. "If we survive, I would be more than happy to sit down with you and have a long conversation about your research and its noncombat applications. But right now we have to know what Dominic Carter has planned."

"Destruction," Sowande croaked out, his gaze dull. "Complete destruction."

"How?" Jonas demanded from behind her. "There are a lot of ways to cause destruction in New York City. Which one did he pick?"

Sowande's head canted to the side, his eyes fluttering closed. Bethan threw a panicked sort of look Jonas's way, even as she felt for a pulse and found it. Faint, but there.

"We have a medical team arriving any minute," Jonas said. "If necessary, we can use adrenaline."

"What effect will that have on a system that's already overloaded with SuperThrax?"

Jonas's fierce gaze settled on her. "What choice do we have?"

Bethan didn't like that. But then it didn't matter, because Sowande came around again.

He focused on her with obvious difficulty. "It's too late," he said again.

"Tell me where they went," Bethan urged him. Trying her best not to sound as panicked as she felt.

Sowande shook his head, despairing. "He's waiting for rush hour in Grand Central. He wants to make a big splash, kill as many as possible."

And though it cost her, Bethan stayed where she was while Jonas relayed the target to the team. Crouched down, murmuring encouragement to the man until the medical unit arrived. They came in wearing hazmat suits, clearly prepared for what they were about to find.

Jonas caught her gaze and jerked his head. And like that,

they backed away from the medical team, let themselves out, and found themselves back out on the street.

"I feel like I've seen this movie a thousand times," Bethan said as they walked away from the building that was now a crime scene. "Madman goes to some New York landmark, causes mayhem. Repeat as necessary."

Jonas didn't give her even that half smile, which made the panic in her build. He activated his new comm unit as they walked down the block. "The real question is, Do we call in the threat to the NYPD? Or do we hold off, because once we do that, they'll lock it down and our guy might walk away?"

"We're forty-five minutes out," Isaac replied, back to sounding fully in control and in command. "But I'm going to call some of my contacts and give them a heads-up. I'll let you know if I think it's going to turn into a lockdown."

"Give us twenty minutes to get into position," Jonas said, and Isaac agreed.

"I'm patching in to the cameras in and around Grand Central," Oz cut in from Alaska. "I'll start running facial recognition and see if we get any hits. But it's only coming up on four o'clock now. If I was going to target a rush hour, I would wait."

"That's what we're banking on," Jonas said darkly.

He nodded at Bethan, and they started walking north and east toward Grand Central, a mile away. Bethan had the urge to break into a run, to get there as quickly as possible, but she restrained herself. The last thing anyone in New York needed to see was the two of them running with deadly intent, like the assassins they very well could be, out in the open on an otherwise pleasant spring day.

So they walked, covering the distance in a swift fifteen minutes. They'd just reached the entrance to Grand Central on 42nd Street when Isaac was in their ear again.

"Calling in now," he said. "Are you in position?"

"Heading into Grand Central," Bethan replied, dodging a food cart to follow Jonas's long stride toward the entrance. Then pausing when he did.

"Copy that," Isaac replied.

And there were too many clocks competing inside of her. There was her prematurely shortened life span, coming at her much too quickly, and now with visuals. There was the countdown to rush hour and whatever horror Dominic Carter intended to dump on all these unsuspecting civilians. And there was whatever response Isaac would get from his call, which could complicate the situation even further.

It was tempting to give in to the panic churning around inside her.

Instead, she grinned at Jonas. "Army Rangers lead the way," she said, then set off into the terminal at a jog.

"All the way," she heard him say from behind her, and then they were moving fast and hard into the heart of Grand Central Terminal.

Over their comm unit, Oz was dripping in statistics. The number of people who went through Grand Central at rush hour each day. That it was the second-biggest train station in the United States. How many trains went in and out of the station.

"Hey," Bethan said as they made it to the main concourse, where there was already enough of a crowd to make her stomach twist. "Wikipedia. Put a lid on it."

And she thought that if she died then and there, it would be worth it just to see Jonas look at her like that, then laugh. Not in that private way he'd done when the two of them were alone, but the way she'd heard only one other time before. Smack in the middle of another intense situation.

Whatever it was, was a gift, and it went out over their comm units, and she loved it.

"Let's split up," he said when they found a spot near the

information desk and the famous clock. "What do you think? Is he going to go for a vantage point? Or blend into the middle of the crowd right here?"

"Who could possibly say?" Bethan asked. A touch sourly, she could admit.

She nodded at Jonas, and wasn't surprised that the next time she glanced in his direction, he was gone.

Bethan stood where she was, with the famous giant clock counting down the minutes to certain doom, one way or another. She made herself breathe, slow and deep. She tried to make her usual senses do twice the normal work. She scanned the crowd around her, looking for anything and everything.

Anything that snagged her attention. Anything that felt like some kind of flag.

"I feel like we're missing something," she said into her comm unit, directly to Jonas. "Is this all a setup? Is he actually climbing the Empire State Building as we speak?"

"Anything is possible," Jonas replied, unhelpfully. She didn't look around to see if she could spot him. Even if she could, she knew that it would only be for a moment before he disappeared again. If there was one thing Jonas Crow was particularly good at, it was making himself scarce when he was right there in front of you. Even if she'd always found it far too easy to see him, wherever he was. "But I don't buy it. This guy likes a show. Or we'd already be dead."

"What's the narrative here?" Bethan slowly, carefully turned in a circle as she stood there, never letting her eyes stop moving from this commuter to that. From tourists in their oversized backpacks to a group of schoolkids. "He bears a grudge. Here's an opportunity to take us out and make it operatic. I'll take that to mean I hit him pretty hard back in the desert."

She could hear the sound of loud talking from wherever

Jonas was. "The kind of man he is, I'm going to go out on a limb and assume he's not a big fan of women. Particularly women in combat roles, who made him look like a wuss. No wonder he changed his name. Hid himself away."

"And no wonder his friends from his old outfit haven't signed up with him in his new one," Bethan agreed. "They must know who he is. Someone had to take him out of the desert that night."

"Once again," Jonas said. "I have to think he's in this for the show."

But another quarter of an hour dragged by, and the only show around them was a typical New York rush hour.

"Maybe he's not focused on the commuters," Bethan mused at one point. "There's a whole food hall downstairs."

"I'll do a walk-through," Jonas replied.

Five minutes passed. Ten.

"No sign," Jonas reported back. "I'm going to keep doing laps. I have a feeling he's here. Watching."

"Watching paint dry," Bethan muttered.

Another five minutes limped by.

Her comm unit buzzed in her ear, indicating the broader channel was in use.

"Sowande's being transported to a secure medical facility," Isaac said, a note in his voice that made Bethan's bones feel unpleasantly hollow. "But I need to update you on the incubation period."

"I'd really prefer that you didn't," Bethan replied.

"Forty-eight hours is a very generous, very unlikely estimate," Isaac said anyway.

And Bethan adored him for many reasons, but chief among them was this. That matter-of-fact voice of his. As cool and devoid of emotion as it was possible for the human voice to be. She opened her mouth to ask him how long, then, but she found that her head was buzzing a little bit.

And suddenly she was horribly aware of her skin. Everywhere. She was afraid to investigate, for fear that prickling feeling was actually the beginnings of those sores she'd seen all over Sowande earlier.

"What's the updated estimate?" Jonas asked, sounding completely detached.

If she wasn't already ridiculously in love with that man, that would have pushed her over the edge. Because the question was so unemotional it allowed her to breathe. To get some air past the tight band that had suddenly taken over her chest. The great weight crushing her ribs.

"That depends," Isaac replied. "Factors include the size of the subject and activity levels."

No one said the next part. Because they all knew. The more activity, the more the blood pumped that poison all over their bodies.

And the smaller the body, the quicker all that infected blood would turn around and start causing trouble.

In a way, Bethan thought, it was clarifying.

"Spitball the window for me here," she said, and she was proud that she, too, managed to sound nerveless. As if they were discussing a lunch order.

"Sowande says he was infected last night," Isaac said. "Around eleven P.M."

And there were too many silences on this comm unit today. Bethan stood there in Grand Central Terminal, surrounded by strangers, but she knew that her friends and colleagues were right there, in her ear. She knew their silence was fury. That they were all filled with the same impotent rage that she would feel if the situations were reversed, in any one of them.

No one called for a moment of silence, because that wasn't who they were.

This is who I am, she thought, her eyes catching on a little girl who reminded her of herself, a thousand years ago. Clinging to the hand of an important and busy-looking father. A little girl who grew up and became her own hero.

A little girl who went from gazing up in awe at her father in uniform to wearing her own.

Bethan didn't want to die. But all things being equal, her life had been pretty great.

She couldn't feel the poison that was inside her even now, killing her where she stood. If asked, she would have happily signed up for a far more active death than this, with something invisible eating at her from the inside.

But she had chosen her path a long time ago. She had become the soldier she wanted to be, and then more. She'd rejected all the ceilings and limitations that others had put before her, and while she might not have joined the air force like her father, she had damn well figured out how to fly.

If she'd known how short a time she was going to have here, she would have figured out how to love her family a little better, a lot sooner. But still, she'd had the wedding. She'd had that week, and it occurred to her now, standing here in this unknowing crowd, that she'd been so busy telling herself she was playing a role in front of her family that she'd never stopped to consider that maybe she hadn't been. That instead, it had been the first time she'd allowed them to really see her. Without her trying to prove anything. Without her trying to hurl her accomplishments in their faces, as if they were whom she was fighting.

All in all, she thought, she couldn't regret a thing.

She scanned another quadrant, then stopped, dragging her gaze back to that little snag—

It was Jonas.

He didn't speak into the comm unit. He didn't come closer. He was a face in the crowd, nothing more, but she knew why he was there. Why he was letting her see him.

And they'd agreed.

So Bethan didn't say anything. She didn't tell him she loved him. She didn't say, *I fell in love with you a long, long time ago, sitting in tents in a makeshift base while we were different people.* She didn't tell him how much she admired him. How he had been her hero even then, and more as the years passed. How often she'd thought of him while she'd trained to take her shot at Ranger School, and how much more he'd been in her head while she'd been in and somehow surviving.

And now he was her hero more than ever. The more she knew about him, the more she loved him.

Bethan couldn't regret that, either.

Because they'd had this last week.

And if she'd learned anything, it was that trying to pretend she had no feelings was the weakness. Not the feelings themselves. Because what she felt made her feel stronger, not weaker.

Maybe she wished she'd understood that sooner, but on balance, she had nothing to complain about.

His gaze was so dark it hurt. And she was sure that he understood all those things she couldn't say, because he always did.

They had been exposed hours ago, and they'd spent a lot of that time running around New York. Bethan likely had very little healthy time remaining.

They both understood that they were very likely saying good-bye.

Because they had chosen not to be regular people. There would be no crumbling into a heap, sobbing about how unfair it was, or trying to figure out an exit strategy.

Because first, they had to do their job.

"Okay, then," Bethan said, at last. Five seconds had passed, though it felt much longer. "Then this time, when I shoot him, I'll make sure it takes."

Her gaze was still fastened to Jonas's. She could see too much there. All the nights they wouldn't have. All the days they should have had.

All that wasted time when they could have been who they really were.

It ached. It hurt like a mortal blow. But she let it go.

Because they'd had so much already. And wasn't that the point? They'd had more than some people ever would.

She blinked, her eyes too full, and he was gone.

Bethan turned, wondering what the clock looked like now. Not the famous one before her but her own personal clock. She both wanted and didn't want to know how much time she actually had left.

She started another scan of the crowd, turning incrementally, and went still when a woman staggered into her. Then lifted her head.

"Iyara," Bethan whispered.

And even as she did, something stung her. Like a hornet, making her entire arm burn. She jerked back, but the other woman was holding her by the elbow and yanked her close.

"Do you remember what you told me?" And though Iyara's voice was cold, there was something about the expression in her eyes. Almost as if she was pleading. "In that hut where we met?"

"I said a lot of things," she hedged as Iyara pocketed the syringe she'd just used.

Iyara moved closer, still holding Bethan's arm. "You should have known that I would take my revenge, then."

That didn't make sense.

But as Bethan frowned and opened her mouth, Iyara shifted. And as she did, the open collar of her T-shirt moved slightly, so Bethan could see the wire taped there.

He was listening.

And even as comprehension dawned, she realized something was wrong with her body. Deeply wrong. Her head was starting to feel upsettingly fuzzy, and her limbs worryingly thick.

"This is my revenge," Iyara said, louder, then began to walk.

When Bethan stumbled, she propped her up, wrapping one arm around her back.

Bethan laughed as the crowd around her dimmed, and her vision blurred, so there was nothing but that clock, ticking away the breaths she had remaining.

"I saved you," she told Iyara. Or maybe she only dreamed it. Maybe she was already dead. "And you killed me."

She heard a sound in her ear that she couldn't identify. She thought about Jonas in her cabin, his hands flat on the door on either side of her head, and both of them laughing because kissing wasn't enough.

Nothing with Jonas was ever enough.

Then everything went blank.

Twenty-four

You killed me, Jonas heard Bethan say, over and over again in his head, and that was unacceptable. Flat wrong.

He couldn't bear it.

Worse, he'd lost sight of her. By design, he assumed, because he couldn't spot Iyara Sowande, either.

He understood that meant Carter was his to find. His to stop. His to take apart, when what he wanted right now was to charge the crowd, find Bethan, *do something*—

Or, barring that, rip down Grand Central with his bare hands.

And he had already had entirely too much practice with the fury and anguish storming through him. Too much practice *today*. He had thought he'd lost his two best friends and all the rest of his colleagues, and he and Bethan had been exposed to this poison inside them, and all of that he'd handled the way he was trained to do. More or less.

But not this.

He was actually sweating. Breathing too hard. Acting like some newbie instead of who and what he was—

Jonas found himself hoping that was the SuperThrax, because otherwise, he was imploding on his own emotion, and he had no idea how to handle *that*.

"Jonas," came Templeton's voice in his ear. "We have your back, brother. Believe it."

"Look out for the NYPD and Fed response," Isaac said a moment later, so cold and precise that Jonas knew he, too, wasn't handling this well. *You killed me.* "They have every intention of taking control of the situation."

The laugh Jonas let out then was bitter. It made an older man near him flinch. "Then they'd better find him before I do."

And then, the way he had in water, jungle, city, desert, and mountain too many times to count, he went on the hunt.

Grand Central was packed, and getting more crowded by the minute. And Jonas wanted to go find Bethan more than he wanted to take his next breath. But he also knew that if she lived through this—*You killed me*—she would never forgive him if he didn't handle Dominic Carter when she couldn't.

The way she had done for him without hesitation all those years ago.

And as he melted through the mass of people around him, scanning the main concourse as he went, the fragments of that night that were still with him rose up like a wave. The endless dark of the desert night. The heat like its own implacable weight. The pressure in his head and the pain that rose and fell inside him like a tide—going out or coming in, but never letting him be.

He remembered his own voice spilling out into the space between them. Telling her things he had never said out loud before or since.

He remembered her fingers moving through his hair, gently. Cool, somehow, despite the heat. He remembered the tension in that body of hers—different then, but still spectacular—as she'd lifted her weapon. As she'd fired off a few rounds when necessary and held both him and their position through the night.

Jonas did a loop around the information booth and that clock that stood there, counting down what was left of his life, but there was no sign of her now. Not the faintest trace that she had ever been there. And it took all the self-control he had not to throw back his head and let out his rage and his grief, loud enough to shatter all three of the great windows that hung there above him and let in the last of the day's light.

He didn't see the point of light without Bethan.

Years after they'd survived the desert, entirely thanks to her, he'd looked up to see her face on that big screen in the lodge in Fool's Cove. He'd told himself it was resentment that had washed through him at the sight. His past coming to haunt him, when he preferred to be the ghost in any given situation.

And when she'd arrived that first day and smiled at him with pure delight, there on one of those wooden walkways, there had been no audience. It wouldn't have hurt him any to say hello, explain his position, then treat her the way he had no doubt she would have treated him. But he hadn't been able to do it.

He remembered how quickly her smile had frozen and gone blank when he'd stared at her as if he didn't know her, then kept walking.

He also remembered how hard he'd worked—for years—to pretend that didn't bother him. That she didn't.

Jonas had spent his whole life putting himself at risk without a second thought, because he'd been prepared to die since long before he'd lived on his own. Since he'd sat in the back of one broken-down car after another and wished for death before morning, because that way he'd escape. In all the years since, he'd never cared much if he went home or not.

Until now.

Until her.

And if he couldn't have her, if she was already gone, he would do the damn job anyway. The way she would. The way she had.

He would take care of her the only way he had left.

Everything inside him was a howl of rage. A black, crushing grief and a white-hot fury.

Jonas used it.

The rest of his team kept talking to him, but he wanted none of it. He pulled his comm unit out of his ear and shoved it into a pocket. Then he leaned in, hard, to all the training he'd had. All his instincts honed to a vicious, wicked edge. All the things he'd learned to become who he was, a ghost in any crowd.

He cut through the mass of people surging around him like a wicked blade, and they hardly registered he was there.

Inside, his strategic brain took over. If Dominic Carter had sent Iyara into the center of the main concourse, that meant he wasn't there himself. Jonas moved to the edges of the expansive halls, looked up toward the balconies, and then he knew. There were three grand, arched windows at the top of each stair. And on one, an ever-growing cluster of tourists pouring in from the street outside.

If Jonas were going to drop something deadly into a crowd, he would do it from there. Because not only was it a nice height and packed tight with victims already, but the constantly revolving doors behind him would push the air around and do the work the air-filtration system had done in that basement.

Not to mention, it was splashy and self-aggrandizing, just like his quarry.

Jonas moved for the stairs, passing people who stared straight at him and never knew he was there. He could have touched them and they still wouldn't have registered his presence. It was his gift. His curse. His most formidable weapon.

He melted up the stairs toward the balcony, winding his way in and out of busy commuters and clueless tourists snapping photographs, searching every face and every stance, looking for a man who could very well have disguised himself—

And then, at last, he saw him.

He'd dyed his hair since California, into a shocking red that was clearly meant to hide him by calling attention to the difference that would automatically disqualify him. But it was still the same man. Judson Kerrigone. Dominic Carter.

Once a mercenary killer, always a mercenary killer.

Jonas knew that Carter didn't expect to be recognized. He wasn't the steroid-slurping maniac he'd been in the desert. And he wasn't the overly smiley CEO, all about handshakes and that fake aw-shucks grin, either. Today he was dressed in a hooded sweatshirt and jeans, both far rattier and thicker than anything he'd worn in California. And he stood differently, so that he looked thicker himself. Not muscled and ready, but pudgy.

Not a great disguise, maybe, but Jonas knew full well the best disguise was often as simple as a shift in a facial expression. A change in gait. He was doing the same thing himself.

He looped around, concealing himself behind a loud group of men with pronounced local accents. And when he came around the other side of the surge of bodies there at the landing at the top of the stairs, he was face-to-face with Dominic Carter.

At last.

And had the distinct pleasure of watching the man stare straight at him, then jolt, as if at first he hadn't recognized Jonas at all.

But then he did.

"One step closer," Carter said conversationally. And the gaze Jonas had found unsettling enough at Bethan's wedding seemed even more intense. Downright unpleasant. "I dare you."

Jonas ignored him. "What are you going to do?" he asked mildly, moving closer. "Kill me twice?"

Carter's face twisted. "You should have died the first time. That bitch shot me."

"If it hadn't been her, it would have been someone else," Jonas said pitilessly. "You weren't exactly a popular guy, Judson. I'm betting you still aren't."

But Carter sneered as if that were funny. "Says Jonas Crow, who, turns out, doesn't own any company in Seattle. All talk to impress the crowd and General Wilcox, I'm guessing. Maybe you should ask yourself how valuable you are."

"To who?" Jonas asked. He was aware of distinct movement in his peripheral vision, and he glanced over quickly to see Templeton on one side, Isaac on the other. He knew without having to ask that Griffin had a line of sight. And Blue, no doubt, was already tracking Iyara Sowande and Bethan.

But he couldn't let himself think about any of that.

Even when Templeton pointed to his own ear, then gave Jonas the finger.

"You were a highly trained asset to your government," Carter was saying, seemingly unaware that Alaska Force had closed in around him. "But now what are you? Just another mercenary. Disposable."

"We're all disposable," Jonas replied. "The only thing you have, the only thing you ever have, is your honor. But you wouldn't know anything about that."

"You can keep your honor," Carter snarled at him. "I have a Fortune 500 company and the most powerful biological weapon known to man."

"That's what I can't figure," Jonas said, and he adopted a little bit of a character while he did it, almost grinning. Far friendlier than he felt. "What's your plan? You must know you're going to inhale a little bit of your cocktail. Then what? You don't strike me as the suicidal type."

But when Carter only sneered at him again—like he was stupid—Jonas knew the answer. He thought about that scrap of paper with all the chemical compounds on it. And suddenly, things got a lot clearer.

Because if there was an antidote and Carter had it, that meant all Jonas needed to do was relieve him of it. Then give it to Bethan.

And if Jonas had to kill Carter in the process—well, that wasn't the kind of thing he was likely to lose any sleep over.

Out of the corner of his eye he read Isaac's hand gesture, obliquely telling him that there were other eyes watching this interaction. Officials, no doubt. None of whom would hesitate to take him down if he gave them a reason.

He decided he might as well give them one. As a little party favor, so they all felt good about their roles here today.

When the next big knot of tourists came in the door, heedless and loud, he hurled himself at Carter. There was no contest. The other man had spent too long behind a desk, counting his money, and it showed. Jonas was on him, his knife at a kidney from the back, ready and waiting for the first opportunity to gut Carter like a pig.

"Empty your pockets," Jonas ordered him. "Now."

He heard Templeton's voice in the background, and while he couldn't hear the words, he knew that tone. It was crowd control. If he had to guess, Fed and SWAT control.

"I don't care if everybody dies," Carter threw at him, all bravado.

But he yelped when Jonas pressed the knife against him, the blade so sharp it easily went through the layers of his sweatshirt and pricked into his flesh.

"You talk a big game." Jonas spoke directly into the other man's ear, holding him so it looked like an intense conversation, nothing more. "You think if you watch enough movies it might make you something you're not. You think if you swagger around enough it will make you what you could never become on your own. But the truth is, you're a coward. Just a coward."

"Says the man who let a dumb bitch rescue him."

"She's good at that," Jonas said with dark intent, and had to fight his own urge to end this right now.

He had to fight to keep his hand steady and not let his grief make him anything less than what he was. Not that he cared—but he knew she would, if she knew.

If she lived.

You killed me.

Jonas forced himself to talk. Not act. "She's so good at all the things you pretend to be that she makes you look pathetic. And deep down, you know it." His voice was low. Insinuating. "You know exactly what kind of low-life disgrace you really are. And you're worse than most, Carter. Kerrigone. Whoever you are. You weren't satisfied with all the double-crossing and murder when you were nothing but a gun for hire. You had to run off and up the game. Now you think you can kill innocent people and profit from it."

The other man shook with rage. "There's nothing you can do to stop me."

"You disgust me," Jonas said with quiet menace. "You seem to be under the impression that because I'm not a lowlife like you, I won't kill you. You're reading me all wrong, friend. I have enough honor to know when extermination is the only solution for a cockroach who just won't die."

He stuck the knife in, just a little bit deeper.

And had the distinct thrill of listening to the other man hiss in pain.

Fun as all this was, time was running out. It was almost certainly too late for him, not that he cared to pay attention to the messages his body was sending him. That he was warmer than he should have been. That he wasn't as steady as he usually was. Worse, he didn't know what Sowande's sister had done to Bethan. It could be all over by now.

But Jonas didn't accept that. He couldn't.

He shoved Carter forward, knowing that to the untrained eye, they looked like friends who were roughhousing a little. He even grinned to show it was all in good fun.

It wasn't.

Carter hit the balustrade, and as he did, Jonas employed one of the few skills he'd acquired in his childhood. The pickpocketing his parents had made him learn when he was a lot more feral than he felt now.

He shifted back, glancing down at his hand. One syringe. And what looked like an aerosol tube of colorless air. It didn't take a genius to figure out which was which.

"Now what," Carter snarled at him, hauling himself around to face Jonas. "You understand what you're holding in your hand, don't you?"

Jonas bared his teeth. "I do."

"Are you really going to try to convince me that you're altruistic?" The other man laughed. "Give me a break. I've known guys like you my whole life."

"I sincerely doubt that," Jonas said.

"So moral. All about the high ground. But when push comes to shove, and it always does, you choose the easy way just like anyone else." Carter jerked his chin at the items in Jonas's hand. "Do you have any idea how much either one of those things would go for on the open market?"

Jonas assumed his expression was lethal when the other man flinched. "I don't care."

"If you take that antidote, you'll live," Carter sneered. "But your girlfriend is already dead. Is that really what you want?"

You killed me.

Jonas was already plotting out his next move, made harder by the presence of the authorities. But harder wasn't impossible, and impossible was all in a day's work for him. Even if he happened to be a little more impaired than usual today.

He focused on Carter. "It doesn't matter who dies as long as I'm rich, right? Isn't that the way you operate?"

"Spare me the lecture, you sanctimonious prick," Carter snarled at him, his face getting red. "I've scraped better men than you off my shoe. Just crawl back into your little hidey-hole in Alaska and leave it to the big boys to figure out—"

"Enough," Jonas interrupted him. "I'm done with you."

"What are *you* going to do?" Carter demanded. "Knife me right here in Grand Central? Is that the high road you think you're on?"

"Technically," Jonas pointed out, "I already did."

Then he lifted his hand with the tube in it.

Everything sped up all around them. He heard shouting. The kind of loud, abrasive commands that only cops made, because they wanted to clear the scene, take control, get everyone down on the floor.

Jonas looked to his right, expecting to see Isaac there, and sure enough, his friend was right on target. So he threw the tube that he knew was full of the SuperThrax that was even now eating him alive. He didn't wait to see if Isaac would catch it.

Because he knew he would.

Instead, he banked left, knowing that Templeton would do what was necessary to give him that opening—

He did. Templeton theatrically tripped over his own two feet, knocking back half the SWAT team gunning for Jonas.

Jonas dived for the stairs, plunging into the crowd and shoving his comm unit back into his ear as he went.

"Where is she?" he demanded, not bothering to look over his shoulder, because he was fairly sure most of the New York Federal Bureau of Investigation was behind him, with a few SWAT teams from the NYPD thrown in for good measure, and there was no point clocking their positions because he didn't intend to get caught.

"The corridor to your left," came Blue's gruff reply.

Jonas ran.

He didn't care if they shot him in the back. He'd keep running.

He didn't ask if she was alive, because that wouldn't help him go any faster. And if he was too late, he would deal with that once he found out one way or another. Likely by tearing the entire building down around him.

He ran and, for once, didn't do a single thing to disappear while he did it.

Every eye in Grand Central was on him, and he didn't care.

He vaulted over luggage, shoved a few clueless young men out of his way, and, for perhaps the first time in his entire life, was making a freaking spectacle of himself.

But it was for Bethan.

He would do a lot more.

Jonas threw himself into the corridor Blue had indicated and saw them there, halfway down the gentle incline. Bethan was slumped against a wall, down on the ground as if she'd crumpled there. Iyara Sowande was next to her, also sitting, while Blue was standing guard over them.

And it wasn't until Jonas slid to a stop, going down in a roll that ended with him up on his knees before Bethan, that he realized he was light-headed.

Exertion, something in him told him matter-of-factly. *You made that run in less than a minute, but it came at a cost.*

"I have the antidote," he managed to get out past the panting as his lungs worked overtime.

But his hands were already on Bethan. He checked for her pulse. He looked at her face. She was paler than she should have been, her eyes were glassy, and she didn't look right—

"Jonas," Blue began. "Brother—"

Jonas paid no attention.

He pulled out the syringe, sparing only a single, ferocious glare for the woman next to Bethan. He would deal with her later, in whatever time he had left.

But something happened to his hand as he lifted it. It was like there were suddenly two of them.

He thought, *This is how it ends. This is how it goes.*

But he shook it off, fumbling to get the syringe into position—

Bethan's hands were moving then. He would recognize her touch anywhere. Her hands were on his, keeping him from administering the antidote while everything was dimming all around him.

And her gaze was cool, green, and the only thing he ever wanted to see. The last thing he'd see, he thought, and he was okay with that.

"Stop," he told her, though his voice sounded far away. "I'm trying to save you."

"Too bad," she replied.

And he knew he was dying because though her voice was thready, she sounded . . . amused?

He tried to make sense of it, but he couldn't seem to focus past what he already knew. What he was here to do.

The antidote. Her. That was all that mattered.

"Jonas," she said, his name like a bright, happy thing in her mouth. He wanted to take that with him. "I've already had the antidote. I'm fine."

She pulled him closer, smoothing her palm over the inside of his elbow, and then she smiled. He would do anything for that smile.

When Blue laughed, it occurred to him that maybe he'd said that out loud.

Jonas felt a sharp prick in his arm, then a kind of buzzing sensation that spread out from the point of impact.

Bethan leaned closer, gripping his chin in her hand, so the only thing in the world was her face. Her gaze. Her. "I know you're going to hate this, Jonas, but I just saved you. Again."

Twenty-five

Things got very official, fast.

The authorities—city, state, and federal—were deeply unamused with the day's events. Bethan and Jonas were placed under strict quarantine. The CDC descended and, forewarned about the escape from their previous quarantine, treated Bethan as if she'd been incarcerated.

"This is like prison," Bethan complained to one of her nurses, a solid week into her quarantine, which had so far involved parades of doctors and long stretches of boredom and inactivity.

"You're not dead," the woman replied serenely. "I'd focus on that."

Both Sowandes were also detained. Tayo was in a different hospital, where a team of specialists had fought day and night to save his life, and were optimistic he'd make a full recovery. Iyara, on the other hand, didn't require hospitalization—but several levels of law enforcement and government were deeply interested in talking to her.

"It turns out she's her brother's research partner," Isaac

told Bethan, having somehow finagled his way past all her levels of security to stand there at the foot of her bed on the last day of her confinement. And apparently *he* didn't have to wear a hazmat suit. "She doesn't have any official degrees, which is how she flew under our radar, but she's his level if not higher. They do the work together and publish under his name. They never expected anyone to go after both of them at the same time."

"She was supposed to kill me." Bethan remembered that expression in Iyara's eyes. How close they'd stood, with that clock above them all the while. She'd been so sure it was counting down to her death. "And he wanted to listen while she did it."

Isaac nodded. "She convinced Carter that because of South America, she wanted her revenge on you. I don't know how she made that sound reasonable, but he believed it. Let's face it, he would kill anyone. For fun."

"What's going to happen to him?" she asked, though even thinking about that vile man made her feel sour straight through. He'd been at her sister's wedding, plotting this all the while. She felt violated in retrospect.

"There are a number of agencies and individuals interested in the man formerly known as Judson Kerrigone," Isaac said with an edgy sort of smile. "And not in a way he's likely to enjoy."

Bethan shared that smile. "It couldn't happen to a nicer person."

She didn't ask about Jonas.

Because she'd saved his life. And she already knew how that went.

When she was finally discharged after her observation period was up, it was time for her own debriefing sessions in Washington, D.C. Day after day of explaining herself and her actions, over and over again. Sometimes to people she recognized, but more often to strangers who didn't always introduce themselves.

Though she could have made some assumptions about the kinds of things they did.

Isaac had brought her replacements for the contaminated items that had been confiscated from her back at that farmhouse, not that she'd been foolish enough to try to use a smartphone in her debriefing sessions. But once the Pentagon was finished with her, she started to call in to the command center back in Alaska to report in.

Then stopped herself. She was in Washington, D.C., which happened rarely. And when she'd thought she was dying, one of her final thoughts had been a wish that she'd been better to her family.

So instead of heading home, she called her parents and went out to their place in Virginia.

"Are you well, dear?" Birdie asked when she arrived, faintly creasing her brow over the window box of tulips she was fiddling with, out in what she called her mudroom. "You look a bit peaked."

"I had a little cold," Bethan told her. "No big deal."

Birdie's brows rose, but she didn't argue. After all, Bethan thought, her mother had been a military spouse longer than Bethan had been alive. She knew when—and when not—to ask questions.

That night at dinner, she and her father eyed each other over their plates. Bethan suspected he knew exactly what she'd been up to lately, but he didn't ask. And she didn't volunteer it, because officially, none of it had ever happened.

Instead, she found herself talking about her favorite sports teams.

And maybe because she no longer felt like she had anything to prove, it was the most fun she could remember having at dinner with her parents. Possibly ever.

This is your second chance at your life, she told herself that night when she climbed into bed in what had once been her childhood bedroom, though it had long since been upgraded. *You get to do it right this time.*

All told, it was a solid month before she finally found herself landing in Fool's Cove again.

Finally, she thought, as the little seaplane came in for a bouncy landing.

She climbed out of the plane, waved off the pilot, and took a moment to appreciate the way her feet felt as they hit the wooden dock. She followed the straight line of the dock toward the stairs that led up to the lodge, breathing in deep as she moved.

Because she was finally home.

It was low tide, and she could smell the rich scent of the sea all around her. Woodsmoke and pine. Though it was May now, it was still colder here than it had been back East. It looked as if it had rained earlier, but the sun was putting on a little bit of a show up there above the mountain. It filtered down through the evergreens, lighting up all the cabins hidden away there on that hill.

Everything was precisely the way she remembered it. And while Bethan's heart might hurt a whole lot more than it had when she'd left here, because she already knew how Jonas would handle her saving him all over again, she still felt that same pull she had felt the first day she'd arrived.

She'd known from the start that this was the right place for her.

Her bones told her it still was, regardless of the state of her heart.

Bethan ran up the steep stairs. And as she got to the top, she heard a chorus of gruff male voices, welcoming her back.

They all stood there outside the big lodge doors. Her friends and colleagues, as close to emotional as any of them ever got, welcoming her back like . . . Well. Like family.

Bethan was terrified for a moment that she might disgrace herself by crying.

They'd all come out to greet her. To slap her on the shoulder, which was their version of a hug. To shuffle their feet and mutter things in their deep voices that were nothing much in and of themselves. But added up all the same to something like, *About time you showed up. You almost died. That was not okay.*

"Didn't think you were coming back at all," Templeton drawled, his voice booming loud enough to disturb a few seabirds perched on the railing some distance down the walkway. "Figured you'd cut and run."

"Army Rangers lead the way, Templeton," she replied, grinning wide. Because, of course, he'd been an Army Ranger, too. A real one, to her way of thinking, since he'd actually gotten to serve in the 75th Ranger Regiment.

"All the way," he replied.

And the way he looked at her made her stand a little straighter. It let her know, in no uncertain terms, that as far as he was concerned, they were the same.

She held on to that. Especially when Jonas didn't make an appearance.

Once again, Bethan didn't ask after him, because she knew better. She'd spent the time since Grand Central trying to talk herself into the reality she knew would be waiting for her here. When the greeting party was finished and she felt unduly pleased with her teammates, she headed for her cabin.

Reminding herself fiercely all the way that what truly mattered was the work. The job. Getting to do it in company like this, where she was not only valued but cared for, was a dream come true.

She did not intend to let one man color that because she'd been foolish enough to save him.

Again.

Even if she was desperately, foolishly in love with him.

Bethan had survived that before. She would again.

She let herself into her cabin, shivering as she got the fire going. Then she stood there for a moment as the flames started to warm the place. Waiting for her return to this private space to soothe her. To ease whatever pain she brought with her. To help her leave it at the door.

But it didn't work.

Because the last time she'd spent the night here, Jonas had been with her. And it was as if all she could see was him now. How easily he'd fit into a space that had only ever been hers.

"This is exactly why you never let anyone in here before," she muttered at herself.

There was something about how loud her voice was in the quiet of the cabin. How loud she felt, personally, after all this time spent out there in the Lower 48, mixed up in all that noise and commotion.

This was her sanctuary, and she would reclaim it. But she was done with secrets.

She'd risked death too many times to count, but what she had not done was see it come at her the way it had that day in New York. The deaths she'd risked in the past had always allowed her to fight back, one way or another. But Super-Thrax had been relentless. Irrevocable. Fighting the onslaught of the toxins in her body had been entirely hopeless.

But she'd survived. Bethan had been given a wake-up call, and this was her second chance. She was going to do it right this time.

She picked up her phone and shot off some texts she should have sent years ago.

And by the time they all arrived, she was ready. She'd liberated what she needed from the lodge. She'd cooked a simple dinner, pulled out a few bottles of wine, and when the first knock came on her door, she stood back. Then let her friends in.

"I knew it," Everly said, crossing the threshold and grinning widely as she looked around at all the softness and candlelight. "Underneath, you're *just like us*."

The old Bethan would have argued that point. But then, the old Bethan would never have let Everly through the door in the first place.

"Let's not get carried away," she said.

"One of us! One of us!" Everly chanted lightly, drifting farther inside as if summoned by the soft, deep couch.

"This is downright cozy," Mariah drawled when she arrived, sweeping in like a cloud of perfect hair and cashmere. "I'm not going to lie, I was expecting a CrossFit gym."

"I wasn't aware that you knew what a CrossFit gym was, Mariah," Bethan replied. "But since you do——"

"Don't even bother, sugar." Mariah grinned. "I will never run all over Isaac's beach, slinging tires around, or whatever it is you all do. Never."

Caradine came next, smirking as she carted in two heavy tote bags. She slung them on the counter, crossed her arms, and aimed that smirk directly at Bethan. "I brought dessert."

"You've become so domestic, haven't you," Bethan couldn't seem to keep herself from murmuring, even though she knew that was risking Caradine's famous temper. No wise person did that more than once.

But Caradine was different these days, too, and she only laughed. Then indicated the cabin. "Says the woman who lives in shades of pink."

Which Bethan had to take, because it was true.

Kate came last, her usual cop's smile turning into something much wider and more real as she came inside and looked around.

By this point, everyone had found a place to sit in the living space of the cabin. On the cozy couch, the inviting chair, and even the soft, cushy rug on the floor.

Bethan handed Kate a glass of wine without asking if she wanted it. She knew Kate did.

"Yes, it's pink," she said. "And cozy. And yes, I hid here this whole time, only soft in private."

Kate looked faintly appalled. "Where else are you supposed to be soft?"

Bethan beckoned for Kate to go sit and followed after her. And then, there they all were. Her four friends, who she never would have met if she hadn't come here. Who wouldn't have met her if they hadn't come here for their own reasons. They would be connected by Alaska Force no matter what, she supposed, but they'd made their own connections, too.

She might have had the bad luck to fall in love with a man who couldn't handle it, or her, but no life was ever perfect. And looking around at her friends as they sat in her home and prepared to eat her food, laugh and tell stories, and share this life no matter what it looked like, she knew that no matter how imperfect it was, it would be okay.

She was going to be okay.

"Welcome to my soft, pink underbelly," she said, lifting her glass. "Which, yes, I've deliberately concealed from you since I got here."

Her friends lifted their glasses, then clicked them together.

"To not dying at the hands of assorted madmen, criminal malcontents, and your average homicidal dirtbags," Caradine said, and maybe it was the candlelight that made her smirk look almost friendly. But Bethan thought it was probably the same thing that had her grinning so wide herself.

"I'll drink to that," Mariah said with a laugh. "Long and deep."

"Here's to the Alaska Force Survivors' Club," Everly said, and they drank to that, too.

Bethan knew what Kate was going to say even before she lifted her glass, her eyes gleaming.

"And to Bethan's favorite thing," Kate said merrily.

"Don't say it," Bethan warned, though she knew it would do no good.

And it didn't. "*Intimate friend time*," Kate intoned, and that sent them all laughing.

It was a theme that continued throughout the evening.

Hours later, when Bethan was full of sugar, pasta, wine, and friends, the cabin felt right again. Not a secret anymore, but a safe space all the same. Because she could be herself with her friends, within and without these four walls, and that made all the difference.

She finished straightening up so she wouldn't have to face it when she got up before dawn the next morning, then settled down onto her couch while the fire crackled happily.

"Home sweet home," she said to herself, sighing.

And then, somehow, managed not to jump out of her skin when the door to the cabin was slammed open.

Jonas stood there, grim and dark.

It was raining out there, and he looked as damp as he did furious. She was fairly certain she could see the steam coming off him.

He didn't wait for an invitation.

Jonas stormed inside, slamming the door behind him and heading toward her with a look on his face so starkly ferocious that if she hadn't already been sitting down, she thought she might have lost the use of her knees.

Her heart, always excitable when he was around, began to pound. Hard and dangerously slow.

"Hi, Jonas," she said, pleased that she managed to sound perfectly calm when she wasn't. "How nice to see you when neither one of us is being poisoned to death."

But that only seemed to enrage him.

"Three days," he belted out at her.

And as he came closer, she could see that there wasn't a trace of the usual stark, austere chill that she associated with him. His gaze was a black fire. His expression was . . . something she couldn't identify. Something she'd never seen before.

Her stomach twisted, and then, below, she could feel the pulse of it—of him—between her legs.

"What?" was all she could manage to get out.

"*Three days,*" he repeated, sounding even darker and more menacing. "That was the deal. If we survived. If we even made it to three days."

She remembered that conversation in the lab. She remembered everything.

"You don't like it when I save your life," she replied as coolly as she could. And there was a part of her that wanted to surge to her feet. Fight him. Fight *something*, anyway, because that was better than accepting reality. But she didn't have it in her. Not tonight. Not with him. "I've already played this game once."

"This isn't a game," Jonas growled at her. "Did you really think that after all of that I would just . . ."

He didn't finish. Bethan was glad she'd put her wineglass down, because her hands were trembling. Maybe she was trembling, now that she considered it. She couldn't seem to pull her gaze away from his.

"Yes," she said quietly. "That's exactly what I expected you to do."

He was standing in front of her then. She couldn't seem to breathe as she looked up at his beautiful face. That face that she'd never been able to get enough of. That face that she'd loved so long now, and knew so well, that she would know it by touch even if she were blind.

"I'm sorry to disappoint you, Bethan," he told her darkly. "But I can't go back to that."

And when he was right there before her, she expected him to *do* something. Something physical, some explosion of his strength, some mighty noise to remind her what he was capable of—

But instead, Jonas Crow sank down on his knees.

Twenty-six

Jonas had expected Bethan to come find him.

She hadn't.

He'd come back to Alaska after quarantine and a round of Pentagon games. He'd ignored his friends' good-natured ribbing. He'd dedicated himself to regaining his lost fitness levels and had almost managed to convince himself that he wasn't just killing time.

But then she'd come back.

He hadn't joined in her impromptu welcome party, but he'd watched it from higher on the hill. He'd told himself that what really mattered wasn't whether she came looking for him but that she was alive.

That was all that mattered.

But deep down, he'd still expected her to come find him. Instead, she'd invited all her friends over for a party.

He was coming out of his skin.

"I can't function," he told her, not sure if he was angry at her, angry at himself, or just so filled with whatever this heavy, panicked thing was inside him that he'd lost any ability to determine his own state. "I'm a menace to myself and others."

He expected her to spark at him. Bite back. Like all the times before.

But instead, her lips moved into a soft smile. "You always are. It's part of what makes you beautiful."

He wanted to reach for her, but it was as if he didn't know how to operate his own limbs any longer.

And he made himself say it.

"If you only thought you loved me because you knew you were dying, I understand," he gritted out.

Jonas hadn't known he could feel at all, much less the cascade of feelings inside him then, each more acutely painful than the last.

Bethan's jaw actually dropped. Her eyes got wet, though no tears spilled over. She shifted forward, reaching out and grabbing his hands. Then holding them tightly.

Fiercely.

"I didn't think I loved you because I knew I was dying, Jonas." She held his gaze, and each word she said was deliberate. As if she knew she was speaking to parts of him he'd never let out before. Parts he didn't know himself. "I've loved you for years, and I never intended to tell you, because it never occurred to me you were willing to hear it. That's the only thing knowing I was about to die changed. But not my heart, Jonas. Never my heart. That's been yours for years."

Her hands in his were a miracle. He remembered walking through Midtown Manhattan, their fingers laced together. He had thought they were both doomed, and still, he'd been happy. Happier than he'd ever been before.

"You make me want to live," he told her, as if this were an altar and these were his vows. "You make me want to grow things, not only destroy them. You make me happy.

You make me believe in things I thought were lies when I was a kid, things I dismissed a lifetime ago. You make my heart beat when I thought it was dead. You make me imagine that somewhere inside, I'm a regular man."

Her eyes were so bright then. Her voice was so thick. "I love you, too," she whispered.

"You make me want to be human." And Jonas didn't have it in him to be horrified by the sound of his own voice cracking. Not with Bethan. "You make me imagine it's possible. For you. Only for you."

"Jonas," she said, coming even closer so she could take his face between her hands. "You always have been human. Always."

And then she showed him.

She leaned forward and she kissed him, as if she were turning him from stone into living flesh. She kissed him as if it were all a foregone conclusion, life and happiness. Bright and reckless and almost too beautiful to bear.

Bethan kissed him until the sweet of it shifted into that kick of familiar heat. And they were both *alive*. They had survived too many wars to name, SuperThrax, and Grand Central. They had more fights in front of them, because that was who they were.

And still she kissed him as if these were the kind of happy stories someone could tell while raising a glass under a wedding tent someday.

Jonas couldn't believe that something in him wanted that. Not the stories, maybe, but the rest of it. The whole wild pageant with Bethan front and center, smiling at him in a pretty white dress.

He needed to stop being so surprised at the things she brought out in him.

He pulled away, his eyes tracking over her face, trying to take in every detail. There was color in her cheeks again. That pallor that had terrified him in New York was gone.

She looked like his Bethan again. Those serious green eyes, those freckles, and that mouth he couldn't get enough of whether she was kissing him, fighting him, or smiling at him and making him real at last.

"I love you," she said again. And when she smiled this time, it was like summer. "It's okay. You don't have to say it. You don't ever have to say it. I know who you are."

And she did. His whole life, Jonas had assumed that all there was to know about him was what he could do. The wars he could wage. The fights he could win.

He'd been born an afterthought and fashioned into a crude weapon by careless hands. Then the military had gotten to him and made him sleeker. Meaner. Templeton and Isaac had tempered him some, but he'd still gone his own way to that cabin in the Alaskan interior to weigh his options. He'd always thought that someday, he'd end up there again.

But Bethan had never looked at him like he was broken. She never looked at him like she was trying to figure out how to use what he could do to her advantage.

She looked at him the way she always had, from the day they'd first met. As if he were nothing more and nothing less than a man.

Human straight through.

And if she believed it, he would try.

For her, there was nothing he wouldn't do.

"I love you," he said, because he did. "I've never loved anyone else. Not like this. And Bethan, I never will."

She grinned at him then, his sweet, soft soldier, made of steel. "You certainly won't. Or I'll kill you myself."

Then she took his hand again and pulled him down into the embrace of that couch.

Where together, they celebrated the fact that they'd survived.

More than just survived. They *lived*. Bright and hot, tough and tender, and marvelously alive.

And more often than Jonas had ever imagined possible, happy.

The first time Jonas saw Bethan cry was when he took her to his own cabin.

And maybe he'd known how she would react, because he could suddenly see this home of his through her eyes.

Stark. Empty.

Dark and cold, the way he'd always been.

"We will never stay here in this horrible crypt," she said roughly, brushing the moisture from her eyes. "You will never sleep here again."

And that was just the beginning.

Her pretty little pink cabin wasn't big enough for two, but neither one of them wanted to lose it. Together, they built it out. And over time, though it never became less pink, it became other things as well. More theirs than hers, and never a secret again.

Until Jonas could hardly remember a time when they hadn't lived together like that.

They'd visited her family later that summer, and Jonas had been forced to explain that while most of what he'd told them about himself was true, some of it had been a cover. He'd expected the general and Birdie to freeze him out, but they'd taken it well.

"Good thing," the general had said. "I never did trust a man who smiles that much. Good thing."

"I like thinking of you doing those dangerous things together," Birdie had said in apparent agreement. "It feels safer, doesn't it?"

Bethan had liked that her parents knew the real Jonas. But she'd been much more concerned, at first, that their teammates wouldn't like the fact that they had so obviously gotten together. A couple on missions? It wouldn't be a shock if their colleagues objected.

"What if it throws everything off?" she'd asked. "What if everything gets reduced to a sexual innuendo and I become nothing more than average after all?"

"If they treat you differently because you're sleeping with me," Jonas had said in that pitiless way he knew she liked best, "then they'd better treat me differently because I'm sleeping with you. I think that's unlikely."

She'd scowled at him. Of course. "I don't need you to fight my battles."

He'd kissed her, there in that cabin that at that point had still been her secret pink refuge. And the happiest place he knew. "It's not your battle. It's ours. And you could never be average."

But they'd underestimated their friends.

"About time," Isaac had said sometime after Jonas had moved in to Bethan's cabin. He'd grinned. "Guess I'll cancel that mediation session."

And that was all he said.

Templeton, meanwhile, merely laughed and laughed, then offered to help with the remodel.

And it wasn't for months, after too many missions to count, that Jonas and Bethan realized that nothing had changed as far as their teammates were concerned.

"Nothing's going to change," Bethan marveled one night while they were tucked up in their loft bed, just the two of them. Just the way they both liked it most. "I like that. But I'm forced to think it might have something to do with the fact that they all kind of thought we've been sleeping together for the past ten years."

"I wish," Jonas said.

And then he rolled her over and showed her how much he loved her all over again.

Of all the missions he'd ever had, he took that the most

seriously. And planned to keep on taking it seriously, forever.

Which as far as Jonas was concerned, would be a good start.

But not nearly enough.

A hundred forevers would never be enough, but he figured they'd try them all out anyway, just to see.

Acknowledgments

To everyone involved in the making of these books, my thanks are never enough—but you have them! I'm so grateful for all you do.

To my marvelous readers, I can't thank you enough for joining me on these Alaska Force adventures!

And most of all, to Jeff, for the world.

Don't miss

DELTA FORCE
DEFENDER

*Available now! Continue reading
for a special preview.*

Julia had already ignored her father's summons as many times as she could. It was time to go back home or face the consequences.

Or, knowing her father, both.

Twenty-two-year-olds about to graduate from college *should* assert their independence. Or, anyway, that was the excuse she planned to use when he lit into her about it, assuming he was in a mood to listen to excuses. Because he was going to be furious—there was no getting around that.

No one was suicidal enough to ignore Mickey Sheeran for too long.

Julia was one of the few people who dared pretend otherwise, and—filled with bravado while safely on campus and protected by university security—she'd decided to prove it.

She was already feeling sick with regret about that as she turned onto her parents' street in their unpretentious neighborhood outside of Boston proper, which was filled with the regular Joes her dad claimed he admired as true American heroes. Julia knew that what he really meant by that was that all their neighbors were as in awe of him as they were afraid of him. Just the way he liked it.

Most people were just plain old afraid of him, Julia included.

More so the closer she got to the house she'd grown up in and hadn't been able to leave fast enough. And never seemed to be able to put behind her, whether she lived there or not.

There wasn't a single part of her that wanted to go back. Ever. And particularly not when she'd deliberately provoked him.

Sure, all she'd actually done was ignore a couple of phone messages ordering her to leave her dormitory and come home. But she knew her father would view the delay between the messages he'd left and her appearance as nothing short of traitorous. She was expected to leap to obey him almost before he issued a command, as she well knew. He didn't care that she had exams. He probably didn't know she had exams.

But Julia knew it was foolish to imagine her father was dumb. He wasn't. It was far more likely that he knew full well it was her exam period and had waited until this, her final semester of college, to force her to take incompletes and fail to graduate. He was nothing if not a master at revenge served cold.

Mickey hadn't been on board with the college thing, something he made perfectly clear every time he sneered about Julia's "ambitions." He'd also refused to pay for it and had gone ballistic when Julia had found her own loans and a job in a restaurant to help with costs.

She still thought it was worth the bruises.

Her sister, Lindsay, was fifteen months younger and had

never made it out from under their father's thumb. She still lived at home, grimly obeying his every command in the respectful silence he demanded, because females were to be seen, never heard.

She'd even started dating one of Mickey's younger associates.

You know where that's going to lead, Julia had muttered under her breath when she'd been forced to put in an appearance on Easter Sunday. *Straight to an entire life exactly like Mom's. Is that really what you want?*

You're the only one who thinks there's another choice, Lindsay had snapped right back, her gaze dark and her mouth set in a mulish line. *There's not.*

Julia had looked across the crowded church, filled with the people who came to Mass one other time each year, and stared at the back of Lindsay's boyfriend's head. She wished her gaze could punch holes in him.

I don't accept that, she'd said quietly. *I refuse to accept that.*

Next to her, her sister had sighed, something weary and practical on her face. Julia had recognized the look. Their mother wore it often. Soon it would start to fade and crack around it turned into beaten-down resignation.

He's not a nice guy, but at least it gets me out of the house and away from Dad every now and again, she'd said. *That's not nothing.*

Their brother Jimmy, the meanest of their three older brothers, had turned around from the pew in front of them. He looked more and more like Dad by the day, and the nasty look he'd thrown the two of them had shut them both up. Instantly.

Sometimes Julia lay in her narrow cot in the dorm, squeezed her eyes shut so tight she expected all her blood vessels to pop, and *wished.* For something to save her. For some way out. For the limitless, oversized life her college friends had waiting for them, with no boundaries in sight. No rules. Nothing but their imagination to lead them wherever they wanted to go.

Maybe she'd always known that she wasn't going to get any of that.

And maybe her father had been right to oppose her going off to college, because all it was going to do was break her heart. Worse than if she'd been a good girl like Lindsay and done what was expected of her.

Hopelessness only hurt if you were dumb enough to hope for something different.

Julia couldn't remember, now, when she'd first realized that her father was . . . unusual. That he was the reason the other children kept their distance from the Sheeran family. But she could remember, distinctly, the first time she'd Googled her father's name and found a wealth of information about him. Just right there, online. For anyone to see.

She'd always known her father was a bad man.

Still, it was something else to find all those articles detailing the criminal acts he'd been accused of over the course of his long career. She thought sometimes that a good daughter would have been appalled, disbelieving.

But she'd looked at her father's mug shot in an article from the front page of the *Boston Globe*, and she'd believed. She'd known. He was exactly as bad as they claimed he was, and probably worse, and that likely meant she was bad, too. Deep in her blood and bones, no matter what she did.

Every year they failed to catch him in the act, the bolder and more vicious he became. And the more she accepted that his DNA lived in her, too.

Because if Julia were as brave as she pretended she was when she was across town on a pretty campus where she could squint her eyes and imagine she was someone else's daughter, she would have called the FBI herself.

But she wasn't brave. She didn't point the car in some other direction, drive for days, and disappear. Instead, she was obediently driving home to face her father's rage. And the back of his hand. And whatever other treats he had in store for her.

Her throat might be dry with fear and her heart might be pounding, but she was still doing what he wanted. In the end, she always did.

All things considered, maybe Lindsay's grim acceptance was the better path. Julia liked to put on a good show, but they were both going to end up in the same place.

Her stomach was killing her. Knots upon knots.

She eased her car to the curb and cut the headlights, then forced herself to get out into the cool night air. It was a force of habit to park a ways down the block. There were always flat-eyed men coming and going from the house, and it would go badly for her if she inconvenienced any of them. And Mickey was never satisfied with small displays of strength when bigger ones could cow more people and show off his cruelty to greater effect.

In his circles, the crueler he was—especially to his own family—the more people feared him. And fear was what made Mickey come alive.

She leaned against the closed car door and pulled her phone out of her pocket. It was cold enough that she wished she'd worn more than a T-shirt, but there was a part of her that liked the chill that ran along her arms. It would keep her awake. Aware.

You couldn't really dodge one of Mickey's blows, but there were ways of taking it, and falling, that lessened the damage.

She'd learned that lesson early.

She pulled up Lindsay's number and texted her, announcing that she'd parked and was about to walk in to face the music.

Don't come in, her sister texted back almost instantly. *It's weird in here.*

A different sort of prickle worked its way down the back

of Julia's neck and started winding down her spine. Her hair felt as if it were standing on end in the breeze, except there wasn't a breeze.

I'm coming out, Lindsay texted.

Julia found herself holding her breath, though she couldn't have said why. The night felt thick and dark, suddenly, though she could see the streetlights with her own eyes. Something about that caught at her, and she moved away from the nearest pool of light to the shade of a big tree. She stood there, keeping still. She put her back to the trunk, hoping that if anyone were looking, they wouldn't see her.

And she tried really hard to convince herself that she was just being paranoid.

But when her sister appeared out of nowhere and grabbed her arm, she bit her own tongue so hard to keep from screaming that she tasted copper.

"What are you doing?" she whispered fiercely at Lindsay. "You scared the—"

"You should go back to your dorm," Lindsay said, and this time, there was something stark in her gaze. Too much knowledge, maybe. Something unflinching that made the knots inside Julia's belly sharpen into spikes. "And stay there."

And all the things they never talked about directly seemed to swell in the cool spring night. The truths that no one spoke, for fear of what it might unleash. Not just because they were afraid of Mickey and his friends, whom he often called his brothers but treated with far more respect than he gave the members of his actual family, but because acknowledging a thing made it real.

It had never occurred to Julia before this very moment how deeply and desperately she'd clung to the tattered shreds of her denial.

She and her sister stared at each other in the inky black

shadows of the ominous night, and she couldn't tell anymore if it was the dark that threatened her, or if it was the truth.

Whatever was coming, there was no escaping it. Had she always known that? Whether it was this night or another night or twenty years down a road that ended up with her seeing her mother's tired, fearful face in the mirror, this life she'd been so determined to imagine as a path she could choose had only ever been a downward spiral. To one single destination.

Sooner or later, they were all going to hell. Or hell was coming for them. It didn't matter which. She was going to burn either way.

Julia wanted to throw up.

But at the same time, a heady sort of giddiness swept over her, and it took her a second to realize what it was. Freedom, of a sort. Or relief, which amounted to the same thing.

She reached out and laced her fingers through her sister's, the way she used to do when they were little. Back when it was easier to pretend.

"Come with me," she said fiercely.

And Lindsay looked as if she wanted to cry.

"It's too late," she replied. Her voice was soft. Painful. "He asked me to marry him."

"You don't have to say yes."

"I love that you think it matters what I say."

"All the more reason to come with me," Julia said stoutly. "We can figure it out. We can . . . do something."

Lindsay's smile pained Julia, like someone had prized her ribs apart.

"Julia," she began.

But when hell came, it came out of nowhere.

A bright, hot, terrible flash of horror.

They were both on the ground, dazed and stunned, and Julia lifted a hand to her temple, where she felt something sticky. But she couldn't find her way to caring about it much. Something was wrong with her ears, her head. Something was *wrong*.

Car alarms were going off up and down the street, there was a siren in the distance, and she couldn't remember how she'd gotten to the ground. She pulled herself to her hands and knees, grabbing for Lindsay as she went.

And they knelt there, hugging each other even though it hurt, and stared at the roaring fire where their childhood home had been.

Their mother. Their brothers. Even their father—

Julia couldn't take it in.

Lindsay made a shocked, low sort of sound, like a sob.

And somehow, that crystallized things, with a wrenching, vicious jolt inside of Julia. Half panic, half resolve.

She turned to her sister and took her shoulders in her hands, ignoring the stinging in her palms.

"This is the other choice, Lindsay," Julia said, her voice harsh and thick and not her own at all. But she would get used to it. She would grow into it. If she survived. And she had every intention of surviving. "But we have to choose it. Now."